Brothers, FOREVER!

Brothers, FOREVER!

Frits Forrer

Holland's Glory   PO Box 488, Gulf Breeze, FL 32562

This is a work of fiction. Names, characters, places, and incidents either are the product of the author's imagination or are used fictitiously. Any resemblance to actual events or persons, living or dead, is entirely coincidental.

Copyright © 2008 by Frits Forrer

All rights reserved. No part of this book may be reproduced or transmitted in any form or by any means, electronic or mechanical, including photocopying, recording, or by any information storage and retrieval system, without permission in writing from the author.

This edition was prepared for printing by
Ghost River Images
5350 East Fourth Street
Tucson, Arizona 85711
ghostriverimages.com

Cover illustration by Betty Shoopman
bcshoop@bellsouth.net

Contact the author at:
fforrer@bellsouth.net   or
www.fritsforrer.net
850-916-7566
Fax 850—916 1861

ISBN 0-9714490-9-0

Library of Congress Control Number: 2008921063

Printed in the United States of America

April, 2008

10 9 8 7 6 5 4 3 2 1

Contents

Morocco 1990 9
Peru 1990 15
Morocco 1991 20
Peru 1991 27
Morocco 1992 33
Peru 1992 40
Tampa, Florida 1992 46
The Shriners Hospital 52
Tampa, Florida, 1992 52
Young Love March of '92 64
Fort Walton Beach, Florida Oct '96 70
Gator Country 1998 74
Florida State University 1998 80
Daytona, Florida 1999 86
Para Training 92
From Daytona to Patrick and Back 98
9/11/2001 104
Patrick 9/11 111
Over The Atlantic 117
Canary Islands 124
Moving to the Promised Land 130
Cordoba 136
Spain, September 29, 2001 142
Madrid 148
Davis-Monthan Air Force Base 154
Road to Kabul 160
Vengeance 166
Falcon Down 172
Chopper Down 178
Taliban on the Move. 184
Fraternization? 190
Contact 195
Nuclear Waste? 201
The Onslaught. 207
HOG Down 213
To Waste or Not to Waste? 219
Para "Jolly Blue", Going In. 225
A Preview Of Hell 231
Blackhawk Up! Nuclear Delivery 238
The Burning Slopes 246
Sad Journey, Bagram to Qandahar. 252
It Could Get Worse. Not Much. 259

(continued)

It Did Get Worse	264
The Long Road home	270
Laysh ya Allah?	276
Central Command	282
News Break	288
Amazing Grace	294
Epilogue–Farewell!!!!!	299
About the Author	323

Other books by Frits Forrer

Five Years Under The Swastika
Growing up in Holland under German occupation.
ISBN 0-9714490-0-7

The Fun Of Flying
Jet fighter training during the Korean Affair
ISBN 0-9714490-3-1

Someone's Smiling Down On Us
A love story
ISBN 0-9714490-1-5

Tampa Justice, No Money, No Justice
Injustices in the Florida penal system
ISBN 0-9714490-5-8

Smack Between The Eyes
A suspenseful murder mystery
ISBN 0-9714490-6-6

To Judge or Not To Judge
Another fine mystery in the Forrer style
ISBN 0-9714490-7-4

The Golden Pig
Another fine mystery full of action and adventure
ISBN 0-9714490-8-2

www.fritsforrer.net

AUTHOR'S NOTE

This is a work of FICTION, pure and simple. Exciting, but simple.

Many thanks to my number one spelling genius, my Katy.

Also, thanks to the dedicated members of the West Florida Literary Federation that make up the *"Writers Anonymous"*, Joe Hefti, Jack Beverly, Andrea Walker, Dr. Joe and Marilyn Howard, Anne Gross and Jack Beach. My *English* improved daily under their watchful eyes.

The critique from my buddies in the *Belles & Beaux* was very helpful and inspiring. True buddies, Kay, Selma, Fred, true buddies indeed.

Special thanks to Admiral Jerry Unruh, Chaplain Larry Horne, CMSGT Tyler Foster and the staff of the Shriners Hospital for their technical advice.

Again, many thanks,

Frits.

Chapter One

Morocco

Chefchaouen 1990

At the foot of the Rif Mountains, the river Ras Maa provided the valley with clear, cool, potable water. It kept the grass on the soccer field green, solid and soft. Two dozen Berber boys raced across the field, playing football, the world's most popular sport.

It was a match between two rival villages, one team was decked out in red jerseys with white shorts and the other in white shirts and black shorts. Considering the time of year, it was cool at that altitude but there was no end to the excitement and energy of the youngsters. Like most of their ancestors, they were fairly dark skinned and all of them had coal black hair, some curly, some straight.

The local team was winning, three-zip and the red-shirts were keeping up the pressure to score at least one more goal before the final whistle, but in the end the score remained the same: 3-0.

The boys collected their schoolbags and started going their separate ways, some on bikes, but most of them on foot. A group of four meandered in the direction of the Kasbah in the center of town and their discussion was heated, as always after a match.

"You should have passed more! You should have made that header! Who would have been the real hero of the day, if that last goal hadn't been called back because of 'off-sides'?" Et cetera.

At the fountain, in front of the ancient fort, they stopped to drink and splash themselves with the refreshing water that flowed straight out of the Rif Mountains, the rugged western end of the Atlas ridge that crosses the northern portion of Africa.

The skinniest one of the four proclaimed loudly that his three assists made him comparable with *Franz Beckenbauer,* the star centerfielder of the German team, but his buddies egged him on by telling him to gain some weight before he could compare himself with the great *Kaiser Franz*.

With some good natured slaps on the back, they parted and disappeared into the narrow alleys and streets that make up the ancient Kasbah.

The thin one, only twelve years old but already five foot nine, was the oldest son of Ibrahim Addalin Bin Mohammed and named Yousef, after his grandfather. He hurried home because his father expected him on the fourth floor of the narrow building that housed his father's business and their living quarters. The family lived on the ground floor, the store and the showroom were on the second, the raw materials were on the third floor and the workshop was on the top, with a window to the east, so they'd have good light most of the day. In the afternoon, the sun had swung too far to the south, so that the eyes of the grandfather could not continue his tedious work on the loom. That's where young Yousef fit in. He worked until dark, weaving the intricate patterns and colors into the carpets that were sold to the tourists in the second floor showroom.

Every afternoon, the short, funny tour guide came in with his flock of tourists that arrived by bus from Tangier and were treated to a colorful display of hand woven tapestry. Ibrahim and his brother displayed the many items and in four different broken languages trying to sell their wares to the eager visitors. Sometimes business was good, especially in the summer when the hotels at the beach in Tangier were crowded and several tour companies sent their guests to Chefchaouen to visit the ancient city, founded by the Berbers, and expanded by the Spanish from Andalusia in the fifteenth century.

The Jewish population that left fifty years ago had painted the white walls of the inner city with a pale shade of blue, supposedly to ward off ghosts and demons. It made the city famous. Not the demons, but the beautiful blue houses. Most of the winding streets were so narrow, one could touch both walls by simply sticking out one's arms. The old Kasbah attracted many foreign tourists. Also a lot of vendors, including Grandfather Yousef had come down from the mountains, gave up the life of a Berber and started a weaving business. After many years of hard work, father and sons had managed to become owners of the skinny building that provided them with everything they needed: a place to live, a place to sell and a place to weave. All they had to do now was pay for it. That wasn't easy. Some days, during the slow season, they hardly took in enough money to eat. They sometimes sold a few beautiful pieces at a loss, just to have bread on the table. But they kept right on hustling. Ibrahim wasn't sure what he would do if his father passed away or became incapacitated, because he would be forced to hire help until young Yousef was old enough to quit school and work full time. The kid was good. He had the eye and the feel of an artist.

Just as Ibrahim was wrapping up a carpet for the last customer, Yousef ran in, waved at his dad: "We won!" and kept right on going. His grandfather had already quit for the day and instead of asking how the old man was feeling, the kid told him in excited Arabic what he had accomplished on the field and Yousef the elder just grinned from ear to ear at the enthusiastic boy, who started to weave, while talking a mile a minute. His smile disappeared as the boy told him that he was going to be a professional football player and expected to move to the big cities by the time he was fifteen in order to get in with the big-time teams. He fully expected to be playing for the national team by the time he was eighteen and he would bring home bundles of money, so his grandpa didn't have to work any more.

The patriarch sighed. He had dreams like that when he left the mountains, the goats and the mules, but all he had to show for it were calloused hands and arthritis. Plus, he started to grin again, a happy family. He excused himself, hurrying down to his quarters where his hash pipe would take away some of his aches and put him in dreamland together with the Prophet.

At supper, the young lad again boasted how all three goals had been scored off passes that he put in the goal mouth, but Dad wanted to know how much homework he had and how his French and Spanish were coming along. He tested his son with a few questions in each language and threw in a few questions in English. Yousef got the hint and retreated to the corner of the room with his books. He loved foreign languages and was pretty good at them. Singing foreign songs helped his vocabulary and American television taught him English without learning it in school. He was a happy camper.
Until…

Until?

On Thursdays, the day before the Muslim Holiday, Ibrahim would take the weekly receipts and wind his way through the narrow streets, down to the square to make a bank deposit and pay some bills. Then he'd stop for mint tea in a local café and chat with his old friends and neighbors.

This particular Thursday, young Yousef was early, no soccer, and was working away on the top floor. His father called upstairs for him to come down, and while his brother was still dealing with some German tourists, he instructed his son where and how to make the deposit and to hurry back.

Eager and ready, Yousef slung the bag over his shoulder and raced out of the house, first upwards in the alley in front of the house and then down to the intersection of four narrow streets that merged near the vegetable shop. He nearly tripped and staggered right into the arms of a group of teenagers, five of them.

"Ho, ho, ho there little fellow, don't you show no respect for your elders?"

"Let me go! I'm running late."

"Late for what? What do you have in that bag, boy? Let's see!"

"No, no, it's my Dad's money. I got to get to the bank, let me go!"

"Money? Did you hear that guys? Did he say money, now, let's see."

"No!" He held on to the bag with both hands and tried to wrestle loose, but five pairs of hands held him captive and one of them cut the strap of the bag and opened it. Money spilled out. All sorts of money. Marks, dollars, dirhams, francs and pesetas, lots of colorful bills.

"Wow!, look at that! Grab it boys!"

"No, you can't do that!" He put his teeth on the nearest thing he could reach and in desperation, nearly bit off one guys' ear. His victim screamed, turned and slugged Yousef smack in the face, blood spouting out of his nose in seconds. His face a bloody mess, he fought with hands and feet, kicking, scratching, biting while screaming bloody murder. He was no match for five bigger boys and they unceremoniously picked him up and threw him down the steps of the street that led to the square. His hip broke in three places and his lower left arm doubled up as if some giant hands snapped a twig. He passed out from the pain.

He woke up with a scream. Someone was trying to manipulate his hip back in place. Four hands held him down on his bed while four other hands tortured the lower part of his body. A wet rag was pushed in his face and the funny smell put him out again.

Five months went by. The pain was gone, but his body was twisted. He could barely walk. The inexperienced hands did a lousy job of setting the broken hip and it healed the way it was set: all wrong. He would never walk properly again. His parents and grandpa argued every night about the poor medical care because of the lack of money. They couldn't afford a doctor and they couldn't expect medical free care at the local hospital. In this little town in a backward section of an antiquated country, poor people simply suffered with whatever means were available to them. Grandpa would gladly have sold the building or borrowed money in order to help his grandson, but his sons feared they might never be able to recover from such actions.

So, Yousef sat on a pouf in the showroom, day by day, holding his end of the carpet his Dad was demonstrating and smiled at the customers while he cried inside. His language skills improved rapidly. Though he couldn't go to school, his sister carried his assignments back and forth and by kibitzing with the tourists, he really learned the art of negotiating fast. He already spoke his grandpa's native tongue, Derijah, and of course Moroccan Arabic and French. Now, Spanish and German were his next projects. He knew what he wanted. He was going to be a *football announcer*. He was going to work on radio and television and become a world famous announcer.

But playing? Never again! He couldn't even sit behind the loom upstairs and couldn't even work his way up the narrow stairs.

Many nights, he cried himself to sleep. But he could dream. He took on entire teams and beat them. In his dreams!

No soccer star named Yousef. Allah hadn't willed it that way.

Chapter Two

Peru

Huaycan February 1990

One of the world's largest slums is south of Lima, Peru. Literally thousands of cardboard dwellings are packed together against the horseshoe shaped mountains The northern slope features a huge sign, a thousand feet up: **CRISTO TE AMA.** (Christ loves you.)

That's good to know, because that's about the only positive element in the entire area. On three sides, the shelters ring a valley that's the common garbage dump for the whole community. Most dwellings have no electricity or sewers. For laundry, water is brought up in an old rattling truck to fill the cisterns that were constructed here and there along the dusty roads. Potable water is lugged up the mountain in large bottles on the shoulders of those who are strong enough to carry them.

In the valley, along the edges of the slopes, bouncy three-wheel taxis race back and forth trying to hustle a few pesetas from those who need a ride to a store or a bus stop.

The sun bears down brutally and there's not a cloud in sight, so no chance for rain. It's summer in the southern hemisphere and in one of the freak twists of nature, the air from the Pacific rises up and up, passing over the desert without releasing a drop. It then forms towering clouds over the Andes and sends torrents of rain down on its eastern slopes into the tributaries of the Amazon which don't need any more water at all.

Over the last number of years, the Rotary members in the United States, along with many church groups, in a concerted effort, have attempted to ease the plight of the poor descendants of Inca by installing outhouses on the slopes, and by building compost stations in the dump that's known as the valley.

Also in the planning are a park and sports fields as well as a school and a clinic for the many invalids. The intentions of those Missionaries are great, but the results are still minimal.

In the future park area, a volleyball net has been erected and a soccer field cleared of all the rocks and pebbles. The outline of the field is marked by all the hand picked stones and although there are no other markings, nor a goal, it provided a great practice ground where brown skinned kids played their hearts out in bare feet. Not a blade of grass anywhere in sight, but the kids had never known a grass field, so what the heck? They didn't care.

There were some teams of grownups, who played competition ball with the many other communities around and most of them had managed to find enough work, so they could afford balls, uniforms and shoes. The kids weren't that lucky. They played with whatever was round, tennis balls, volleyballs and an occasional worn out soccer ball, *un balón!*

Juan Pedro Cordero was one of the most enthusiastic of the young players and when he got home from working in the hardware store in the village, he headed out to the field after dropping off money to his mother. He was eleven years old and had already been working for two years and was the only breadwinner in the family. His father disappeared three years ago and nobody knew whether he went back in the mountains, was in jail or dead. He'd never been seen again. Juan's job was restocking and sometimes helping at the counter. It didn't pay much, but he was a loyal, hard working young person and the TV in the store was always tuned in to *futbol* programs, so he kept up with all the leagues in South and Central America. Juan Pedro knew all the players and all their statistics, but his favorite was Pelé. There was no doubt in his mind that when he'd grow up, he'd be like another Pelé, One more year and he might already get on one of the adult teams, but he had to grow a little more first.

His mama wanted him to study and learn a trade, but study what and where? If he'd attempt to get into a school somewhere, who would bring home money for bread and rice? He got paid every day, which had an advantage; there was some food all the time. It also had a disadvantage: he could lose his job any day. No job security whatsoever. His boss, a middle aged woman had never given any indication that he might be out one day, but the threat was always there. Sometimes, she'd have a boyfriend who came to work as well, but when she tired of him, he'd disappear and Juan would feel secure again for a while.

As usual, after work a match had been organized among the teenagers. The match had been exciting. There were only sixteen boys on the field, so the teams consisted of only eight players and they were easily identifiable. Juan's team wore shirts, the opposing team played in their bare chests. Juan had played three positions, goalie part of the time, midfielder for a while and forward for the remainder of the game. Since there were no goalposts and no net, they heaped their shirts and hats on each side of the field, about fourteen feet apart and those were the goals. No problem.

His sister Maria attended a Catholic school on the far side of the valley and although she was three years younger, she taught Juan Pedro what she had learned that day and that kind of appeased his mother. At least he was getting some kind of education. His handwriting was unbelievably bad, but his reading improved rapidly. All in all she was content that her three children were happy and healthy, although she was very lonely and missed her husband terribly.

Juan Pedro's *fútbol* skills had not gone unnoticed and on occasion the adult teams would ask him to play with them on Sunday as a substitute when they were a man short. That was great! He ended up owning two pair of old soccer shoes, several colorful shirts and even a pair of shin protectors. He felt he was in heaven. His dream of becoming a professional soccer star was starting to come true, little by little.

One day, it all came to a tragic end. On Wednesday, the counterman and Juan had to deliver boxes of nails to a construction site. A little three wheel taxi was engaged and the baggage rack behind the passenger compartment was loaded with boxes of nails. The little vehicle was like a motorized rickshaw. Thousands of those little machines roam the streets of Peru and they are relatively safe. They're actually motorcycles with a two wheel attachment that makes up the passenger compartment. It has a canvas cover of sorts and the driver straddles his motorcycle seat and steers the contraption like a motor bike. Their maximum speed is approximately 40 mph and they are narrow, so they can get into and out of just about every alley and every dirt path they may encounter.

Benjamin and Juan made themselves comfortable in the rickety machine and the driver kicked the engine into action. Juan loved those trips, because it got him out of the store and he frequently picked up a tip. Not that Wednesday!

The construction site was less then ten miles away and mostly over paved roads. When they made a right turn onto a dirt path, a truck bore down on them from the opposite direction and the taxi driver veered to the right and skidded into a ditch. He corrected well, but when he poured on the gas, the vehicle bucked like a bronco. The weight of the passengers and the nails behind them, made the front too light and the contraption started to roll. Juan was thrown out to the right and he would have been okay, if the vehicle hadn't slipped back into the ditch and landed on top of him.

The impact broke his leg in four places and part of his thighbone was crushed like a nut in a nutcracker. People could hear his screams for blocks, it ricocheted off the mountains

The nuns in the Catholic School and the Father of the church next door were very helpful, but they had very few medical skills. There was no money for an ambulance to take Juan to a hospital, so they did the best they could. In a makeshift cast, he healed little by little, but the crushed part of his thighbone left his lower leg paralyzed and not till five months later could he attempt to walk. His mother came by every day with her youngest daughter Amelia, but all she could bring was hope and prayers and thanks to God that the nuns were taking care of him. She had moved in with a man who had four children and she promised that there would be room for Juan when he could walk again. He was so depressed, he cried and cried.

He did not move in with his mother after all. The pastor, Father Dominic Cabrera let him sleep in the screened-in porch. Juan earned his keep by peeling potatoes, cleaning vegetables and washing dishes for the Sisters' and the pastor's household. With make shift crutches, he moved about and to his joy, he was allowed to watch TV when he wasn't working. The Sisters also took time to teach him, so his handwriting and Spanish grammar improved day by day. Much to his surprise, he gained weight and kept growing, but he wasn't particularly happy with that.

"That's what I needed when I could still play soccer," he'd moan, stifling the sobs in his throat.

The visits from his mother became more infrequent and when she showed up, obviously pregnant, Juan told her to never come back anymore. He was old and wise enough to know what caused it and he did not cherish the thought that his mother was sleeping with a man, other than his father. He was too young to understand the feelings of a lonely woman, whose husband deserted her years ago. When she did come by with a little baby boy, he forgot all about his resentment and made up his mind, he would coach the little rascal to become the best soccer player in the world. He'd be his coach and his manager. He perked up. He had dreams and goals again.

Chapter Three

**Morocco
One year later**

Tangier, 1991

"Honey, look, that must be the Rock of Gibraltar over there!" Tracy Dixon had opened the curtains and a brilliant morning sun brightened up the whole panorama in front of her. The beach, the harbor, the Mediterranean and the distant coast of Spain. From the ninth floor of the hotel, the view was spectacular.

They had arrived the night before on the ferry from Algeciras and crashed immediately without taking time to enjoy the scenery. Now at seven in the morning, they enjoyed their first glimpse of the beautiful northern coast of Morocco.

"I think the rock is further to the east, over there in the distance." He pointed off to his right, but Tracy stood her ground; "No, no, we came straight across and it must be right in front of us."

"Whatever. I don't like turning in my passport to the hotel. These sonsabitches may very well make copies overnight and use them to smuggle terrorists into the country."

"Oh honey, you can't be suspicious of everyone you meet here in Europe..."

"We're not in Europe. We're in Africa and we're smack dab in the middle of a Muslim country. You better believe that I'm suspicious of everyone."

"Come on! Let's get some breakfast and enjoy the culture. There's oodles of history here and I'm gonna love seeing the old towns and the markets and…"

"The markets? Yeah! You'll enjoy the markets. Just remember that we're only allowed seventy-five pounds of luggage each on the airplane back, or we'll be paying a big fine and that would ruin all the bargain prices that you've negotiated in those markets."

"Oh honey, do you have to be so grouchy? Look at the scenery. Look at the sky. It's gonna be a beautiful day and we're in a beautiful hotel and after you shave, you may even look beautiful. Now go wash up."

"Well, at least the bathroom is clean. How much is this costing us per night?"

"Go shave!"

Back in Dade City, Florida, George had finally sold his Insurance Agency to his younger partner and at Tracy's insistence, they were 'gonna spend the grandkids' inheritance'.

The Dixons were on their first trip out of the U.S. and were staying in a friend's timeshare in Malaga on the Costa del Sol in Spain. At least that was free, just a maintenance fee. George Dixon could live with that. There were certain things he couldn't live with, however. Driving was one. On the first day in Malaga, they had rented a car, an American car. A Chevy. There was no way that George was going to drive around in one of 'them little sardine cans'. Well, the Chevy didn't fit in any parking spaces, the streets were too narrow to pass anybody and by nighttime, they had given up and gone to a *flamenco* show in a taxi. In the morning, George turned in the car. "Them Spaniards are crazy, the way they drive." So, it was trains and buses from then on. A tour operator talked them into going on a two day trip to Tangier and although George objected, "I'm not going into any terrorist country." Tracy won the argument. They went.

"Breakfast is included, honey." Tracy called into the shower.

"Good, at least we won't have to go out and shop." George answered from inside the steamy tub.

The little Moroccan minivan held twelve passengers and a driver and left promptly at nine o'clock. "At least they're punctual." George grouched. Among the twelve passengers there was only one more who spoke respectable English, a nurse from Canada. All the others spoke English, but with different accents. To George's ears, it sounded like they spoke in at least ten different tongues. He resented it the same way he felt going to Miami and being surrounded by nothing but Spanish. Tracy kept bringing up the positives, George could only see the negatives. She read from her guide book, how Chefchaouen was built before America was discovered and how they would walk in buildings that were built long before Dade City was established.

"I hope they won't crumble while we're in them."

"These structures have withstood earthquakes and hurricanes and many wars, they'll keep standing while we're there, I'm sure."

"Why do people throw all their garbage along the roadside? Look at it."

"George, it's still a primitive country, you have to remember that."

"Someone could invent primitive garbage cans, I'm sure."

"I'm gonna stop talking to you."

"Good."

The cutest little man in a long camelhair caftan, with yellow pointed harem shoes and a red fez was going to be their tour guide. He was funny in ten different languages and even had George smiling when he discovered the Dixons were Americans by saying; "Semper Fi." Old Dixon could relate to that.

The narrow blue streets of the Kasbah were interesting. Apparently the Jewish community had painted the walls pale blue before being ordered out of Morocco and they added an unusual charm to the scene. George chuckled when he saw a donkey, loaded down with soda bottles, making deliveries to the little stores. "Beats the price of diesel." he laughed.

In a second floor showroom, two busloads of people were sitting around on soft deep pillows, admiring the many colorful tapestries that the salespeople displayed.

"They stole some of them designs from the Apaches," George commented, but Tracy wouldn't listen. She was fascinated by a young lad, sitting on a leather pouf, while holding up the ends of the carpets on display. He had a beautiful smile and seemed to understand most of the comments and questions of the tourists. His body was somewhat twisted, as if he had a birth defect. He stood only once and then only with the help of a cane.

"Poor kid." She thought. "Wonder what brought that on? Polio maybe?"

She bought one of the tapestries, green and white, her favorite colors.

"Where are we gonna put it? I hope you hang it somewhere. It's too expensive to walk on." Tracy wasn't even listening. She sat down next to the boy and asked: "What's your name? Mine is Tracy."

His dark eyes smiled and his perfect teeth just dazzled. "I'm Yousef, his son." He pointed to the man who had done most of the talking.

"You speak good English Joseph. Where did you learn that?'

"It's Yousef, not Joseph. We sing American songs and watch television. We learn."

"I hope you don't mind my asking you, but I noticed you can't walk very well. Did you have polio?"

Yousef angered. It was not any of her business, but he remained polite, "No, no polio. Accident."

"How terrible. Can't anything be done? "

"Be done? Like what?"

"Like corrective surgery or therapy?"

"Therapy? What's therapy?" He held up his hand to stop her from answering. "Besides, there's no money for that."

"How old are you Joseph?"

"Its Yousef. You...sef. I'm twelve."

"How long ago did this happen? Just a minute." The funny little man was urging everyone to leave in order to continue the tour and Tracy hollered at him; "I'll join you in a while."

"You'll get lost, but make sure you are at the fountain in the square at four. Bus leaves at four."

"Okay. George! Come over here a minute. George this is You.. sef. He had an accident. How long ago?"

The boy really didn't want to talk about it, but his father had joined the trio and asked, "Can I help with something?"

Tracy kept control of the conversation. "I was asking how long ago he had that accident?"

"Why you wanna know?" His eyes reflected his suspicion.

"Maybe we can help." She lifted her head. "Right George?"

"Oh. Tracy, don't get these peoples' hopes up, you know..."

She cut him off. "Yes I know, George and I also know what can be done and I'm gonna give this a shot." She turned to the shop owner; "What's your name, sir?"

"My name is Ibrahim, but why you ask?"

"Have you ever heard of Shriners? The Shriners Hospital?'

"Shriners? No. What is Shriners?"

"Shriners are men, all over the world, who dedicate their lives to helping crippled children like Joseph."

"Help? How?"

"With corrective surgery, with bone transplants, with artificial limbs, with every bit of modern technology that's available. We have several Shriners Hospitals in the United States and we live near one of them. I volunteer there regularly and I witness miracles every day. It's unbelievable what modern medicine can do in this day and age and..."

Ibrahim interrupted, "That's nice, but we're in Morocco, not in the States and we don't have money for that, so..."

"You don't understand..." She waved her hands in desperation. "It wouldn't cost you a cent. The Shriners pay for everything, the flight, the surgery, the hospitals, the therapy afterwards, everything."

"Why would anyone pay for my son? You don't even…"

"Because he's crippled, that's why. That's the whole purpose of Shrinedom.

They raise money to help crippled children, that's all they do. My husband is a Shriner, he goes around, wearing his *fez,* collecting money…"

"He wears a *fez?*"

"Yeah! As a matter of fact, his is taller than the one our guide is wearing and…"

"Tracy," George was getting annoyed. "You should not get these peoples' hopes up. There's no way we can guarantee these people that we'll get this boy in there. There's a lot of red tape and it takes forever…"

"I can guarantee you one thing; I'm gonna do my damnest to get him in there." She turned to Ibrahim and said, "Write down everything about your boy. His date of birth, the date of the accident, your correct mailing address, your phone number, everything. And like my husband said, we can't guarantee anything. All this is handled through a committee, but I know that your boy is as eligible as any kid I've ever seen in that hospital and I'll get right on it when I get home." She whipped out a little pad from her purse and handed it to the astonished father. "Do you have a pen?"

The middle aged Berber looked down at his son and raised his hand in a questioning motion. The boy reached for the pad, "I'll do it. I like going to America."

Tracy smiled from ear to ear. "Attaboy. You gotta stay positive. All we can do is try, right?"

"You try, I try." Yousef accepted a pen and started writing.

While the youngster was practicing his best penmanship, Tracy took Ibrahim aside and explained more about the Shriners and how Ibrahim or his wife would be flown over as well and how he or she could stay at the hospital at no expense, whatsoever.

Slowly, the doubts faded from his face and he even started to smile a little.

"I would have to hire help when Yousef's gone."

"We'll work on that too. George? Do you have a business card? These people don't even know who we are"

Card and paper were exchanged and Tracy got into hugging everybody and they were gone.

Yousef laid back on the pile of carpets on which he had been sitting and closed his eyes. "Maybe, I'll play football again."

Chapter Four

Peru
One year later

MiraFlores, February 1991

"…..and may our Heavenly Father guide us in all our undertakings. Amen."

The group of eleven men and women lifted their heads and repeated in unison: "Amen."

They were on the top floor of Hotel Betta in the city of MiraFlores, an affluent suburb of Lima, the capitol of Peru. Four were members of the Rotary of Greater Fort Walton, and seven were members of a nearby Gulf Breeze United Methodist Church. It was the first of their daily *devotionals* that would follow breakfast every morning during their weeklong stay in Peru. For many, it was a return mission trip to the area, for some it was a first.

Standing around the table, holding hands and heads bowed, the appeal to God for guidance and support was certainly sincere. They had come a long way and spent thousands of dollars each in an effort to make life a little more bearable for the many crippled children in the slums surrounding Lima. Hundreds of wheelchairs had been collected, stowed in a container and sent ahead of them. Their job today was to get the wheelchairs unloaded and assigned to the most deserving youngsters. Most of them would be children who received no assistance from any government agency and who now had to be matched with the best fitting vehicle for their size and situation. It wasn't going to be easy. There were three times as many crippled children as there were wheelchairs and they feared an avalanche of applicants.

Two of the volunteers, a lady doctor and a physical therapist were in charge of measuring and evaluating the patients and the rest of them would unload, assemble and adjust the chairs as needed. It was going to be a long day.

They gathered their lunch packets, (they wouldn't eat the local food in the slums) and packed their water bottles. It was summer in the desert and brutally hot.

For Emil Pagliari, one of the Rotarians, this was a first. He had never been on a mission like this before and he didn't pray much as a rule. He hadn't been near a church since his divorce twelve years ago and felt no need to ever go back to one. Yet, the sincerity and devotion of the other members of the group had an impact on him. He stood there, holding hands, eyes closed, and felt an unusual sensation of warmth and love flowing through the circle of missionaries as their leader prayed.

"Whaddayaknow?" He said to himself, "Am I getting sentimental in my old age?"

Emil, Emilio to his fellow workers. was a successful restaurant owner and had always done his share of supporting good causes, but this was the first time he had actively gotten involved in a mission where he would work "hands-on" with the recipients of his goodwill. It excited him. Thinking that this trip would not be all work and no play, he had brought his accordion and was encouraged to bring it along to the jobsite and entertain the locals when the waiting time became unbearable.

The jobsite was a walled-in area of approximately two acres, on which a structure had been built as a rehabilitation center. The first floor was completed in two seasons and now that more money had been collected, the second floor could get started. The rebars were sticking out of the roof around the building's edge like a giant porcupine and in due time would become part of a first-rate second floor addition that would house offices and therapy rooms.

A rickety bus transported the happy team from the affluent part of town through the more rundown section of Lima to the slum areas that surrounded the capitol. At every corner, at every traffic light, they were nearly ambushed by a flock of peddlers, selling everything from shoelaces to magazines, from chewing gum to bottled water, but at the advice of their Peruvian-born group leader, they kept the bus windows closed in spite of the oppressive heat. The bus had no air conditioning.

At the site, a gate opened and the bus edged its way through without hitting either side of the opening. One inch on each side seemed enough for the enthusiastic young driver.

Emil was astounded. Four ten-foot adobe walls enclosed an entourage of a hundred people on crutches, in wheelchairs and some with walking sticks. In the corner, a rock shelter, covered with blue tarp was the kitchen area and a tent-like structure of about 30' by 50' provided shelter for most of the invalids that crowded the area. For years he had read about, heard about and talked about poverty in the Latin American countries, but this was overwhelming.

The bus pulled to a halt next to some old wrecks of '40's model cars and the missionaries descended. Initially, there was a hush from the gathered crowd, but after the group leader, Panchico, made an introductory speech, there was a rousing round of applause for the *Gringos* from *Los Estados Unidos*.

Everyone seemed to know what to do and Emil's job was to unload and hold on to the wheelchairs as they emerged from the container that had been delivered the week before. Initially, there was a mad dash for the mobile units, but Panchico managed to stem the crowd and made them wait their turn.

By lunch time, Emil was sweating profusely and while he sat in the bus devouring his sandwich, he wished he had brought a cold beer. Water was not his favorite beverage.

The native kitchen had cooked up enough *arroz con pollo* (rice with chicken) to satisfy everybody present. It smelled great, but Emil had been advised not to eat anything in that camp and definitely not to drink their water. Not even brush his teeth with it, nor lick his lips in the shower. "Montezuma was still out for revenge," he'd been told.

One of the boys on crutches caught his attention. A good looking young fellow, who dragged one of his legs behind him as he limped around on a homemade set of sticks. He might have been ten, eleven, maybe twelve years old, but the crease in his forehead told Emil that he'd had too many worries at an early age already. The Rotary man climbed off the bus and addressed the boy, sticking out his hand, "Hi!, I'm Emilio and you?"

The boy took the extended hand and answered; "No. No Emilio… Juan Pedro."

Emil laughed, " No, I'm Emilio. Not you." He pointed at the boy's chest. "You are Juan, right? And I am Emilio. In America they call me Emil." He held on to the hand. "So, just call me Emil."

He could tell by the blank look on the boy's face that he didn't understand. He looked around and hollered at Marina, one of the church girls: "Come over here a minute. Come translate."

Marina was an American born Cuban girl who was fluent in both English and Spanish. Emil explained, "I introduced myself as Emilio, but he apparently thought I was calling him Emilio, so would you kindly do the proper introductions?"

"Be glad to." In rapid Spanish she did the introductions and translated the questions and answers of the two opposites of age brackets and hemispheres.

The old restaurateur was surprised to hear that Juan Pedro wasn't born that way, but that he was deformed as a result of a scooter accident.

"No, no! Not a scooter! One of those three wheel taxis."

"No kidding? Why is he dragging that leg?"

"Just a minute." Marina turned back to the youngster and listened patiently as he outlined the disastrous events.

"Good God!" Was all Emil could come up with after the story had been relayed, "Which ones are his parents?"

Another long discussion resulted between Marina and Juan and the answer Emil finally received was that Juan didn't know his father and his mother was living with an other man.

"Where does he live? I hope he doesn't live in this dump?"

Again a longwinded conversation in rapid-fire Spanish resulted in a surprising answer, "He lives and works over there at the Catholic Church." Marina pointed to the west where a pair of steeples indicated that there might be a church out there.

"He works? How old is he?"

"Just a moment." She swiveled toward Juan Pedro, "*Cuantos años tienes?*"

"*Doce.*"

"He's twelve."

"Doesn't he go to school?"

"Just a moment." She turned back to the boy with that question.

"The nuns teach him some when he has time and they have time."

"Good God." That was the second time he said that and it underscored his feelings. "What a mess. Is there a priest in charge over there?" He pointed to the church steeples. "Find out what his name is. I'm gonna talk with him."

Father Dominico Cabrero was a charming, greying, Franciscan Priest. He listened patiently to Emil's explanations of all the things that could be done for that boy in the United States, but he shook his wise head and countered, "Do you know what that would cost? And we are a very poor Parish. Very poor." he emphasized.

"Don't worry about the cost. I'm concerned about the legalities. Where's his father and how do I get hold of his mother? We need their permission to transport that boy to a Shrine Hospital and get him put back together like God intended him to be. How do I proceed?"

"Let me find out. How long will you be here? Five days? Where will you be tomorrow? In the Barrio?"

"In the what?'

"The Barrio. Where you're working. The neighborhood, you understand?"

"You mean where we are putting up the facility and delivering the wheelchairs?"

"Yes. I'll find you there tomorrow."

"Thanks Padre. Thanks."

Father Dominico did appear with some of the answers. The mother was ecstatic and would sign anything that would help her boy, even if she hadn't seen him in four months. The father was a problem. There was no death certificate, no jail record, no trace. Mother would have to be declared the legal guardian and the Padre could help execute all that. He and the nuns would do anything they could to facilitate matters as long as it didn't cost the church or the school any money.

At night, from the hotel, Emil called a friend in Pensacola, a Noble in the Hadji Shrine Temple. Of course. he had to listen to all the potential negatives and the possibility that the boy might not be accepted, but he shrugged that off. "That kid looks like my youngest son when he was twelve and I want him fixed."

Chapter Five

**Morocco
One more year.**

Tangier 1992

Yousef had never seen a real plane. On TV? Yes. Contrails way up in the sky? Yes, many times, but a real aircraft? Never! And here he was at Tangier International Airport, about to board an airplane. Not a big one. It was smaller than he had anticipated, but it was an airplane. On the side of the fuselage, in two types of script, Arabic and Roman, it read **Royal Air Maroc.** He felt like he was about to go flying with the king.

Of course, the king was not aboard and Yousef had a hard time making it up the steps. The adjustable crutches that Mrs. Dixon had brought from America really didn't help him going up. It took two pairs of strong hands, but once he was in, he could maneuver to his seat without a problem. He sat on the first row, so he could stretch his damaged leg out in front of him.

The plane as a whole was exciting. The smell, the looks, the hostess, the vibrations, once the engines started, and the racing propellers, (he could actually only see the one on the left) everything was a new revelation for him and he cherished every second of it.

Once the plane turned into the wind and the engines really started to roar, he felt a twang of panic. It was much louder than he had expected and for a while he wondered if the plane would really leave the ground. His knuckles turned white, grasping his armrests. Well, it did finally, and once it was up a few hundred meters, the engines roar became more of a hum. That was better. To his surprise, they headed out to sea. He hadn't expected that. He had been told that they would first fly to Casablanca and then change to a bigger plane, a jet, in order to cross the Atlantic. He knew enough about geography that he realized they were heading over the ocean, rather than the Mediterranean. From up high, it looked like a giant version of the maps he'd seen in school and he was anxiously plotting the course in his own mind. Five minutes into the flight, the pilot changed course and started to follow the coast to the south. That made more sense. Casablanca should be just an hour away in that direction. He relaxed. For months, he had pictured the trip in his mind and experienced many doubts about survival, crashes, thunderstorms and downdrafts that he had learned about on TV. Now everything seemed so simple.

Mr. Berman, who had come from America with Mrs. Dixon, was sitting next to him, while his Mom and the American lady sat behind them. The plane had a row of two seats on the left of the aisle and just one seat on the right. Most of the passengers were men and the few women aboard were dressed like his mother, covered from head to toe.

It had taken a lot of persuasion to convince his parents that the Americans really intended to fix up their boy, at no expense to them. Then suspicion arose whether he would be allowed to come back home. The old folks were afraid that the Americans would rehabilitate him and then keep him over there.

"As what?" Tracy Dixon had asked, "As a slave? That was abolished a hundred fifty years ago. No, once we're convinced that we can do nothing more for him, he'll come home. He may never be 100%, but even 80% is a lot better than what he is now."

The family had finally given in with the understanding that Mother Miriam would go with him for two weeks, as long as the

Americans paid all her expenses. They still couldn't quite believe that anyone would go to this length to help a crippled child, but they were going along. Of course, both mom and Yousef had to get passports, had to be inoculated and each time they had to go through a new procedure, they nearly chickened out, but Tracy remained insistent and talked them into proceeding, time and time again. Thank God or Allah for phones.

George, back in Dade City, Florida, didn't thank anybody when the bills came rolling in. He cursed under his breath every time he had to write a check. He didn't really believe that his wife would pull it off. It had taken fourteen months, but she met with all the committees and doctors, completed all the forms, made all the calls and flew back to Morocco with a specialist in order to get the final joint approval of the Shrine and the Moroccan parents.

Now, they were finally on their way and she gloated as she conversed with Miriam in the most awkward attempt to bridge the language barrier. Miriam literally spoke nothing but Arabic. She was never directly involved with the public aspect of the tapestry business and consequently had not learned to communicate with any of the foreign customers. To Tracy, that didn't mean much. She kept right on talking.

Casablanca looked captivating from the air. Endless beaches, crashing surf, whitewashed buildings and a massive minaret, rising hundreds of feet in the air, disappeared underneath their wings while the scene changed from blue to brown as the ocean disappeared and the desert took over en route into Mohammed V International Airport.

The landing surprised him. Mr. Berman taught him how to pop his ears and they were on the ground with just a little squeal of the tires and that was all. He didn't really know what he had expected, but it all seemed much simpler than he thought. Getting out of the plane was just like getting aboard. Two sets of strong hands put him on the tarmac and a huge, long bus took them to another part of the field. An Air France jet was waiting for them and this time the trio had to manipulate a long stairway in order to get him aboard. His seat was not up front, but on the right side of the plane, directly behind a partition.

"Business class in front." Mr. Berman explained, but Yousef couldn't imagine any business being conducted on the way over the ocean. This was indeed a big plane, a very big plane. Yousef counted; two seats on the right, five in the middle and two on the left. That was nine in a row.

"How many rows are there?"

"Let's see." Mr. Berman retrieved a card from the pocket against the divider in front of them and read off; "Airbus 340, forty three rows. That must add up to 300 passengers or more. That's a big bird, boy. Do you think it will get off the ground?"

"Oh, I'm sure. Maybe if I can't play soccer anymore, maybe I can be a pilot and fly these all around the world." His English improved daily and he was adopting a distinct American accent. "I think I would like that. See all of the world, all the big cities, all the oceans and all the mountains. Wouldn't that be great?"

"It sure would. Let's get you buckled in. We should be leaving in ten minutes."

Their seats were just in front of the wings and the engines started so noiselessly, that he was surprised when the plane started rolling. As a matter of fact, it rolled backward. His eager mind was absorbing all the action. The little vehicles scooting around below him, the men with their orange vests, the other planes with their exotic markings, he couldn't get enough of it. Finally, the plane started forward and that was really the first time that he could hear the engines. They were a lot less noisy than the propeller plane had been, but once the plane started its take-off roll, the engines roared so loudly that he was afraid they might explode in front of his eyes. They didn't of course, and after an endless race down the runway, the plane finally lifted up and then nosed up so sharply, that he gripped both his armrests. His heart heaved in his chest and he hoped the pilots knew what they were doing till they leveled some and Casablanca reappeared below them, this time much farther down. The ocean started to stretch in front of them and small, puffy clouds appeared below like sheep in a blue pasture. He was really flying this time! What a thrill!

The monitor in front of them switched from safety instructions in two languages to an aerial map of the northern hemisphere and showed a little white plane that pinpointed their position on the globe. In seconds it reduced, showing a close-up of their position and continuously changed given information about their altitude, their speed, the outside temperature and the time at the point of departure and destination.

"How do they do that?" he asked Mr. Berman, but he could only tell the boy what he knew himself and that was very little. "This is all done by GPS and computer…"

"What's GPS?"

"G.P.S.? Let me think… Global Positioning System, I think."

"Huh?"

"Anyway…, the way I understand it, there are many satellites in orbit around the earth and each one pinpoints the position of the plane and by using at least three different ones, they get three different beams that cross one another and that's where the plane is."

"Wow!"

"Your English is improving fast."

Throughout the flight, Mr. Berman tried to get Yousef to go to sleep, but the boy was too excited about everything that was going on around him and in front of him.

To his disappointment, the monitor changed from positioning to movies, but when he was given earphones, he enjoyed that as well. Mr. Berman dozed off from time to time, but the maps reappeared every so often and in nine hours they descended into the Atlanta area and landed at the airport that had so many planes at the various gates that he exclaimed: "Mr. Berman, all the planes in the world are here!"

"Not quite boy, not quite. Welcome to America! Let's get ready, but stay seated with your seatbelt on until the sign goes off."

Mohammed V airport had impressed him, but Atlanta International completely buffaloed him. By the time they had moved from the terminal in a golf cart and by subway to the exit, he believed that the airport was bigger than all of Casablanca. His eyes were wide with excitement.

A limousine was waiting for them and they rolled along a number of interstates and highways that had both Yousef and his Mom baffled. In spite of everything they had seen on TV back home, the real thing was unreal.

"A million cars!" He exclaimed. "Where are they all going?"

"Probably home to watch a football game." Tracy quipped.

"Football? I play football." He forgot for the moment that he couldn't play anything anymore.

"What you play, we call soccer. Football here is more like rugby. We have an egg-shaped ball that we throw around. You'll learn about the difference. Something else, tonight we're staying at the home of one of the Atlanta Nobles and you'll get a good night's sleep before we drive to Tampa in the morning. It's already two o'clock in the morning in Morocco and by the time we hit the sack, it'll be four or five your time, so we need to get some sleep. Would you kindly explain that to your mother?"

"Okay. What's a Noble?"

"You'll find out."

The Noble turned out to be somebody who talked like the men in the cowboy movies and Yousef didn't always understand him, but he was a big man with a big stomach and an even bigger smile. The house was very large too. It seemed more like a palace to the Moroccans and they had never seen so much luxury. They were assigned a huge bedroom and mom and son were going to sleep in the same bed, which was fine by them. Back home, quarters were so crammed that this seemed overly luxurious.

A great meal of unfamiliar food was prepared for them. At home they didn't eat corn, nor collard greens and okra, but most of it was very appetizing. The only surprise at the dinner table came when Miriam asked Yousef to make sure that the meat was not pork, because it looked so pale, but she was assured that it was turkey. Yousef didn't know the Arabic word for turkey.

They slept well. The bed was big and soft. Yousef dozed off the moment he lay down. So far America was well beyond their expectations.

Chapter Six

Peru
One more year

Huaycan 1992

The whole school was excited. All the students were out front watching Juan Pedro being helped into the back of a limousine. Emil distributed five dozen little American flags and the students waved them enthusiastically as Juan stuck his head out of the car window one last time.

"Vaya con Diós," Father Dominico whispered while he made the sign of the cross and swallowed hard to hide the tears that were welling up. "Will miracles never cease?" He said to himself. "How can people ever doubt God's work? Here goes a young boy from the slums of Peru to the United States to be re-created.! Well.... Recreated is maybe too strong a word. Re-assembled seems more like it. God be with you, son."

Meanwhile, Juan was having the ride of his life. He was dressed out in new clothes and his usually unruly hair was neatly trimmed and combed. In the back of the limo, he was sandwiched between Emil, (Señor Emilio to Juan) and a Mr. González, who had flown in from Tampa to handle the transportation and all the detailed paperwork.

For months, while all the formalities were being worked out, Juan had dreamed about the trip and his stay in the States, never quite comprehending why this was happening to him. There were so many other crippled children in Peru, why him?

His mother had made some token objections and cried that she would miss him so, but Juan doubted that very much. She had a new baby, a son, and four more kids by her live-in husband to take care of. No, he doubted if she had time to think about him at all. After all, she had rarely come to see him while he lived with Father Dominico and the Sisters.

The important thing was, he was on his way and would return as a completely healthy teenager. He had no doubt about that whatsoever. Señor Emilio had assured him that it would take time and many operations, but he would be totally rebuilt, just like the bionic man on TV. All this conversation between Juan and Emilio had taken place with the help of an interpreter, because, Juan couldn't speak a word of English yet. His intentions had been to really study hard and practice, practice, practice, but in reality, there was no one to teach him and nobody to practice with. Señor Emilio spoke a few words of Spanish, but not enough to hold a conversation. Mr. González, on the other hand, spoke it fluently, but to Juan's ears, in a strange accent. He explained that he was born in Cuba, but came over to the United States with his parents when he was only four and always spoke Spanish at home.

Well…, that helped. While driving away from the mountains, the slums and the desert where he grew up, Juan had a chance to learn more about Shriners, Masons, and their purpose in helping crippled children. He found it very hard to understand why anybody would do all that for perfect strangers, and, as a matter of fact, it was way over his head. He was just glad that he was one of the chosen ones.

The traffic around the airport was one big turmoil. Hundreds of old, rundown taxis mixed with many new shiny ones and an endless line of people trying to get into the building. Mr. González was expected by the Airline officials and the limo was met by a large golf cart that seated all three of them plus the luggage. They bypassed most of the shuffling line of people. Inside the building, the air-conditioning was not very effective with all the construction going on, but it was better than outside. The Shrine team seemed to have everything well under control.

They were hustled through a special gate and a pleasant security officer in a dazzling uniform came over to check their papers and within minutes they were on their way to the terminal. They were early enough to enjoy a hotdog and a coke, and Juan believed he was in the States already.

Through the huge display windows, Juan hungrily took in the scene of all the airplanes, coming and going and was amazed at all the beautiful colors and designs on the various aircraft.

Theirs was to be a Delta 747, the biggest airplane in the world. (At least that's what Mr. González said.) From the golf cart, he had been placed onto a wheelchair which was staying with him onto the plane. Everything was going well and he couldn't wait to get on and actually touch an aircraft for the first time in his life. His chance came within fifteen minutes when wheelchair-bound people and mothers with young children were boarded first. The long tunnel leading to the entrance surprised him. It was longer than the entire plane, he thought, but finally, he was helped out of his chair by some beautiful ladies and brought to his seat. Mr. González joined him, and Señor Emilio sat directly behind them. From his window seat he could watch the little cars and trolleys shuttling back and forth between the planes and sat with his mouth open when a truck pulled right up to the plane and the entire body raised up to the aircraft level which had to be at least ten meters off the ground.

Turning to González; "What's he doing?" In Spanish

"They're loading our food." Mr. González had to lean way over in order to see what the boy was talking about.

"Our food? We're gonna eat again?"

"At least twice before we land."

"You got enough money?"

"Hahaha, it's all paid for already boy. It's all paid for. You just sit and enjoy, okay?"

"How we fly?"

"What do you mean, how we fly?"

"I mean, we fly over Colombia, no? and…"

The Shriner understood the question. "No, I don't think so. Wait a minute. Let's get this magazine and there should be a map in here." He rifled through the pages of the flight magazine and stopped. "Here we are. This is Lima, Peru. We should fly in a straight line, nearly due north, from here…." His fingers traced the route, "over Panama, the Caymans, Cuba, Miami…"

"Cuba? They're gonna shoot us down?" The boy looked worried.

"No, no. We have permission to fly over through their airspace. No problem. From Miami, we continue on to Atlanta…"

"Atlanta? You said we go to Tampa and here is Tampa and we're flying right by it." He pointed at the digression on the map.

"You're right. This flight is non-stop to Atlanta. We'll stay there overnight and take a car to Tampa the next day. Getting a flight from here to Tampa with all the stops and transfers would have brought us into the middle of the night. This is easier and by the way… we're moving."

Juan's attention was again drawn to the window and he watched a man with an orange light walking right beneath the wingtip. He wondered how far the man would walk along, but just as he was about to ask his neighbor, the man stopped, turned off the light and started back toward the terminal. The plane also changed direction. It started going forward and before long, all the glitter of the other planes and the buildings was behind them and nothing but darkness lay ahead.

Earlier Juan had asked why they left in the evening because he hadn't considered that planes flew at night. Mr. González patiently explained how the plane left the U.S. during the day, arriving in Lima late at night. It then took several hours to clean the plane, fuel it, change crews and get ready for take-off again. In turn, once the plane was on the ground, the same procedure would take place in the States and the plane would take off for Peru again.

"Every day?"

"What do you mean, every day?"

"That plane flies back and forth every day? It never gets a day off?"

"No, no!" The Shriner chuckled. "The crew gets a day off, but the aircraft doesn't. That's how the airlines make money. Fly, fly, fly!"

"Don't the plane get tired?" Emil didn't understand that question, but Mr. González cleared that up by explaining regular maintenance and inspections, so in a way, the plane also gets some time off.

The plane taxied along quickly and before long, they stopped at the end of the runway and Juan wondered if they weren't going after all. Just when he turned to ask that question, the engine started roaring and they moved forward. Slowly at first, and then faster and faster. The little lights along the runway became a blur and suddenly they were off the ground. A heavy 'clunk' startled him, but his neighbor anticipated this and said, "The gear's up. We're sitting right over the wheel-well."

"Oh!"

Lima beneath them became a string of diamonds and rubies. The young lad had never in his wildest dreams expected a panorama like that. It was gorgeous. The Pacific gleamed in the moonlight but disappeared when the aircraft turned north and he couldn't see the coastline anymore. The view to the east was mostly black, with an occasional sparkle of light and he soon lost interest.

Food was served, two cokes and two meals. He asked for seconds and got it. At the urging of his companion, he tried to sleep and after some shifting of positions, he finally dozed off.

Morning arrived before they reached Cuba. The waters of the Caribbean were a combination of dazzling blue and teal and Cuba was virtually all green, with a few dots that must have been cities. It surprised him. He didn't know what he really expected, but all green wasn't it. Many clouds started to interfere with his view, but with the help of the map in the airline magazine, he could make out Miami and all the adjacent cities to the north. They were getting close.

Atlanta was mostly overcast, so he saw more clouds than land. The landing surprised him. First it seemed like a long time of flying low and then, all of a sudden, squealing tires and they were on the ground. To Juan it seemed that they taxied for two hours before the plane finally stopped and they disembarked.

One surprise after another... What a huge, magnificent, clean airport with art everywhere. Then, thousands of big, new automobiles and wide, wide roads. After that... fabulous houses and beautiful gardens... a grand three story home and a pleasant couple, awaiting him with open arms.

"Welcome to America, boy, welcome to America."

Chapter Seven

Tampa, Florida

Shriners Hospital 1992

Dr. Jonathan Olson shoved his reading glasses back onto his balding forehead and rubbed his eyes. The paperwork was always the most necessary, but also the most boring part of the job. He had started as an intern in the Houston Shriners Hospital, but after four years of orthopaedic residency was picked to assist in Tampa on a pediatric orthopaedic fellowship. Three years later, he was the Chief Surgeon. He loved it. Being part of what he called *"the miracle team,"* was what he had dreamed of all the way through Med-school. The most deformed and mangled children in the world were sent to him and his team. They were given more freedom of accepted surgical ingenuity as to how to repair those crippled bodies.

True, sometimes it seemed like experimentation, but how else were they going to learn if new techniques and implementations were going to work? Like other physicians in other hospitals they had to consult with parents and get their approvals, while worrying about malpractice suits, but he and his staff were allowed to use all their skills and all their imagination in order to make a near-normal human being out of the wrecked bodies that were entrusted to them.

He sighed, lowered his glasses again and reread his final paragraph. The young man who had lost both his legs in a train accident had just been released with a perfect set of prostheses and walked without cane or crutches. His walk was a bit stiff and he would never run again, but he would otherwise be able to live a normal life. The parents had been ecstatic. Tears welled up in his eyes as he remembered the emotional farewell with the grateful parents. "That's what it's all about," he said to himself. "That's what it's all about."

He looked at his new file. A boy from Morocco was going to arrive late that afternoon. "I'd better stay on and greet him." He really could leave and go home to enjoy a drink with his wife out on the back porch and meet the boy in the morning, but the report about the new boy intrigued him.

At thirty-nine, Jon Olson was in great physical shape, had a pleasant boyish face with a most infectious smile. Tennis kept him fit and creative work kept him young. His hairline was receding a bit, but his wife, Annette, told him it made him look more intelligent. "A little more mature," she had said, "after all, you are a bit young to be chief surgeon." At nearly six feet, with dark blue eyes and brownish hair, he belied his Danish ancestry. He could have been blond like his father, but he inherited his mother's darker hair. What was important; he was a happy man. Great wife, great job, good health and a very positive outlook on life and the future.

His handsome face changed into a frown as he read the history of his new case and reread the portion about the boy's accident. "Those bastards!" he murmured, "Those rotten bastards. "Probably terrorists in the making. Five teenagers against one little kid. The bums! I'm anxious to meet him."

He didn't have long to wait. When his intercom buzzed: "Mrs. Dixon with her protégé," Doc Olson jumped up and made for the door.

The boy was a delight. The darkest brown eyes Jon had ever seen, a beautiful young face, crowned with pitch black curly hair and the whitest teeth a person could possibly ask for.

"Hi! I'm Doctor Olson. I'm so glad to see you. You're Joseph, right?"

"I'm Yousef,.. You..." he pointed at the Doctor, "sef."

"Okay, You... sef." He imitated the boy's emphasis on the two vowels. "How are you and how was your trip? Do you understand English?"

"Pretty much, but I need to learn more. Much more."

"Great! Well hello Tracy." He gave her a hug, "and hello Brad."

He shook Mr. Berman's hand, turned to the lady with the headdress and a long gown. "You must be the boy's mother? Yes?"

Tracy answered for her. "This is Miriam and this is Doctor Olson."

Dr. Jon warmly shook her hand. "Happy to know you. Let's get you settled. Well, how was your trip?"

Yousef's eyes lit up as he answered. "I can't believe it. I know I'm here, but I still can't believe it. The plane was fantastic, the home in Atlanta, the food and the trip to Tampa. We even ate Kentucky Fried Chicken on the way over here. Everything is fabulous and this is a beautiful place."

"Well, thank you. This is going to be where you will spend some happy times. Let's roll him to the elevator. We're going down to *one*. Come on young man. You'll have to learn to run that chair all by yourself. Here we go."

The massive elevator moved them noiselessly to the lower floor, where Mrs. Dixon wheeled the Moroccan boy to room 104. The suite had two beds with a reading desk in the corner, TV across from the beds and a private bathroom with a huge door that opened and closed by pushing a knob on the wall.

"This will be your home away from home for a while and tomorrow you will get a roommate, a boy about your age. He's from Peru in South America. I don't know if he speaks any English and I'm sure he doesn't speak Arabic, but I hope you'll get alo..."

"But I speak Spanish." Yousef interrupted.

"You do? Well, that's just peachy, and you can save us a lot of trouble. You can be his interpreter. That's great. How come you speak all these languages? Did you learn them in school?" Dr. Olson was flabbergasted.

"No! Yes. Some! Most I learn working with the tourists in my father's shop where I met Mrs. Dixon."

"Beautiful. I hope you have thanked that lady for making all of this possible."

"Oh, I have and I do and I will. You better believe it."

"Good, the staff will take good care of you and I'll see you in the morning, okay?"

"Okay! What's your name, Doctor?"

"Doctor Olson. I'll see you tomorrow."

"Thank you Doctor, thank you." The team left and all of a sudden the boy burst into tears. It all had become too much. It was all really happening.

The morning provided more surprises. The night before, Yousef had met many other patients in the rec- room. Some on crutches, some in wheelchairs, one even on a stretcher. He had tried his hand at the game of *foosball*, twirling the handles and manipulating the ping-pong ball trying to score goals. Every two minutes brought another surprise. The expanse of the building, the amount of aides that seemed to be at his beck and call, the beautiful paintings and tapestries that lined the walls.

Now he found himself in the dining room, where he had a choice of many foods and drinks and he couldn't decide fast enough what to eat now, and what to try later.

Another surprise was the girls. There were several young ladies in the crowd and at least three of them in his age bracket. One with long blond hair and a very white skin intrigued him the most. His experience with the opposite sex was nil and all he could do was stare, without being too obvious. He didn't have the nerve to roll over to her table, but he positioned himself so that he could see her clearly across the room. He already liked everything about the hospital and about America, but this was beyond his wildest dreams.

At first he was perturbed that his mother was eating in the adult dining room, but once he spotted the girls, he was glad that his mother wasn't there. He felt more manly without her.

Breakfast passed without getting to meet any girls, but at least he knew they were there. He couldn't wait for lunch.

Dr. Olson and his staff interviewed him in a cozy conference room with big windows and an oval table of the shiniest wood Yousef had ever seen. He corrected them a half dozen times when they called him Joseph, but he finally gave up and by the time they had spent an hour getting acquainted and asking questions, his name was reduced to 'Joe' and he didn't mind it after all. 'Joe' meant he was now an American. That was alright by him.

By the end of the session, his schedule of examinations and x-rays was explained to him and he was glad to hear that the first operation would take place in two days. He was asked to be very patient and was assured that he would be nearly perfect by the time they were finished with him. He was content and anxious to go to lunch and look at his blond idol again.

The x-rays tested his endurance. He had to wait so long in different rooms and he had to change positions a dozen times while they x-rayed his lower body from every angle. The worst part was, it was cold in every room, especially the examination rooms and he started to sniffle. That only happened back home in the winters at the foot of the mountains. He survived.

At dinner, he sat at the table next to the blond girl's table and admired her face and her smile and wondered what had brought her to the same place. She walked with crutches. Not well, but independently. Interesting.

When he returned to his room, five other people were in there. Their attention revolved all around another boy in the bed near the window. When "Joe" rolled in, the attention shifted to him and Dr.

Olson announced, "This is Joe from Morocco. Joe meet Juan from Peru."

"Mucho gusto!" Joe's remark floored everybody, but Juan's face lit up like a lantern in spring. *"Cómo estás? Me llamo Juan Pedro, y tu?"* (How are you? My name is Juan Pedro.)

"Mi nombre es Yousef, pero los americanos me llaman Joe." (My name is Yousef, but the Americans call me Joe.)

"Bienvenido!" (Welcome.)

"Hey, you guys, you'll have to converse in English in order to be understood." The doctor grinned from ear to ear. "Well, come over and shake hands. You're going to be roomies for a while and I hope you can teach Juan some English fast. I'm gonna bring you some basic instruction materials. You like the idea of teaching English, Joe?"

"Sure, that way I can learn more myself."

"Good show, good show. Let me introduce these folks here; Mr. González, Señor Emilio and you met our head nurse, Miss Doris? Good. Leave us alone for about twenty minutes, would you, and then come back and show Juan around, once we've changed his clothes and he knows how to steer his machine. Okay? Twenty minutes, okay? Thanks."

Joe moved out, all excited. His roommate looked like a great guy. This was going to be great fun, if only he could get up the nerve to talk to the blond... "Oh, well. Let me find Mom and tell her about my roommate."

Chapter Eight

The Shriners Hospital

Tampa, Florida, 1992
9 AM

Doctor Olson and his staff were peering over x-rays, The lower limbs of patient Juan Pedro were examined, speculated about and analyzed as if they were discussing a long putt on the 18th green. Dozens of choices were opted, but the final choice narrowed down to a massive surgery of the lower left leg. A lot of nerve damage had been done and the chances of repairing them all were between fifty and seventy percent. A transplant or amputation, maybe? Organ transplants were a common occurrence, but finding a lower leg of a young boy? They would have to be patient and real lucky.
    Dr. Olson needed to confer with Emil and possibly Juan's mother back in Huaycan, Peru about their options. That wouldn't be an easy task

    Emil and his son flew in the following day in his '76 Beech Bonanza. It took them just four and a half hours from Fort Walton. From Vanderberg Airport to the hospital was just a twenty minute taxi ride and they went straight for Juan's room. They weren't alone. Mrs. Tracy Dixon was sitting alongside Yousef's bed and Juan was astride a chair in front of it. Introductions all around were most pleasant and the interpretations by Yousef were very helpful. Tracy beamed with pride and explained that the staff had decided to name them Joe and John and the boys laughingly agreed. Sean was new to all that. He had just come down from Michigan to start running his father's restaurant, and being recently divorced, it meant a welcome diversion. He had no idea what his father had up his sleeve, so he just shook hands and smiled a lot.

Tracy, at sixty-two was still a fine looking woman, who had preserved her shape very well and with a new hairdo and a few yellow streaks, she looked like she was fifty.

Emil, at sixty, appreciated a good looking woman and immediately asked if her husband was the Shriner who had sponsored Joe and when the answer was affirmative, he knew when to back off. All in all, it was a happy get-together when Dr. Olson walked in, shook hands all around and invited Emil and John to follow him to the office.

Addressing Emil first, after everyone was seated, "May I call you Emil?" A nod answered his question. "Emil, if I understand it right, you're not a Shriner, right?"

"That's correct."

"I'm working on some of the legalities here. Where do you fit in, in this picture and what authority, if any, do you have?"

"I found the boy and contacted my friend Frank Dammer, who is a Shriner at the Hadji Temple in Pensacola, and he agreed to sponsor the boy on my say-so. Then I made all the arrangements and have been given Power Of Attorney by the boy's mother, because his father is nowhere to be found and---."

"Shouldn't Mr. Dammer have been given Power Of Attorney?"

"Well, he wasn't there, but he received all the details from me and he presented it all to the Shrine Board and they approved it, because the boy is sitting right here. Right Juan?" He smilingly pointed to the boy in the wheelchair.

"Then who is Father Cabrera? Dominico Cabrera?" Dr. Olson tried to make sense of the whole situation.

"After Juan," Emil smiled, "I mean John got hurt, Father Dominico put him up in his parsonage and became his unofficial guardian and...."

"Unofficial?" The dear doctor frowned.

"Yes, you haven't been in Peru, have you? You wouldn't believe that country. Anyway, we've made it all legal. You see Doctor, many of the Rotarians in the U.S. as well as in Peru are lawyers and they helped us to make it all quite legal. I'm the legal guardian here instead of Frank. It's all under control. Why did you ask?" Emil beamed him one of his most disarming smiles.

"Why did I ask? Because, when we make certain decisions, we have to have the consent of the parents or the guardians, you understand, so in this case that would be you and his mother, right?"

"Wrong. His mother gave me total authority, so Doc, you deal directly with me and that should make things easy. You see, I'm going to approve everything that you put before me because I believe that you will do everything in your power to fix the boy as best as you can. So what's the next step?"

All this time, Juan looked from one to the other and he changed his expression from serious to smiling, depending on whether Emil smiled or not.

"Well, Emil, you will be asked to sign a number of documents and you'll see that we're going to look for suitable surgical corrections for his leg because the nerve damage is in bad need of repair. If I understood you right, you have full authority and that will immediately put us in position to start with the procedures, as soon as our lawyers confirm your status. That okay by you?" He stuck out his hand and Emil pressed it warmly. Turning to Juan, he also shook the boy's hand and said, smilingly; "You are a lucky cuss, you know? Very lucky."

The young Peruvian didn't understand a word, but felt the emotion that permeated the room. His eyes filled with tears.

Doc Olson ordered; "Bring the boy back to his room and come

back here, I'll get the papers ready. And by the way... thanks Emil."

In room 104, the attitude was very upbeat. Joe (the former Yousef) was in an animated conversation with Sean and Tracy while Miriam was watching and Sean remarked for the tenth time, "I can't believe how much English this kid speaks. And he has never before been in an English speaking country? That's unbelievable. We Americans are kinda backward in comparison. I'm lucky I can express myself in English and now that I've moved south, I've got to learn '*Y'all.*" He thought that was very funny.

The arrival of Juan and his sponsor interrupted the conversation and Emil spoke up the moment he walked in, "I've got to sign some papers. Tracy, are you staying a while yet? I wanna go and grab a bite. Can you hang on and join us?"

"I guess so. I'm not in a rush."

"Good, I'll be back in a bit." Emil disappeared again and Joe immediately asked John in rapid fire Spanish what was going on and all the young lad from Peru could say was, "I don't know. I don't understand anything, but it is good!"

When Joe translated, Sean and Tracy cracked up.

""Atta boy, John. Always positive! That's great!"

A late lunch in the nearby Ramada was delightful. Tracy thought that Emil was a prince of a fellow and that Sean was most charming. The men felt the same about Tracy and Miriam, although the Moroccan lady never uttered a word.

When Emil offered to take her flying, she flushed, "In a little plane? Your plane? That sounds like fun, but you're already on your second beer, so maybe we'd better not."

"Two beers? That's nothing."

"Pop, you better not!" Sean was adamant. "I know you can handle it, but we're not gonna take the chance, you hear. We'll stay here overnight. We'll make sure everything at the hospital is under control and we'll fly back early in the morning." Looking at Tracy, Sean continued. "You're right. Take a rain check. Dad's a real good experienced pilot, but there'll be many other opportunities. He'll be coming back here regularly to check on his protégé, I'm sure, so next time, make sure he takes you up before he has a beer, okay?"

"Sounds like a winner to me. I need to be heading home, gentlemen. Thanks for lunch and... do you have a card?"

"Oh sure, and how can we reach you, Tracy?"

"Wait, I'll write it on this napkin. Here you go. That's my cell. Do call when you're back down here. You guys are fun. Toodeloo!" And she was gone.

"Dad! What's with you? Are you trying to hit on a married woman now? What's with you?"

"Oh boy. You got a lot to learn. Married women can be very grateful!"

"Oh Dad!"

Back at the hospital, the team of doctors and assistants put on a presentation for Juan, Emil and Sean, complete with x-rays, pictures of previous operations and graphs, showing their percentages of success. It was impressive. To Juan, it was also very frightening. One of the nurses, who was fluent in Spanish translated his fears for the group and in turn explained that the pain involved would be minimal. The young boy related to her how much pain he had endured and in spite of his courageous façade, he was terrified. The end result was positive, though. They convinced him that he would be 70% normal, maybe even 85%, when it was all over and the meeting broke up with a lot of hugs and smiling faces.

Emil broke down and cried after the boy had been wheeled from the room.

"What's the matter Emil?" Doctor Olson came over to personally console him.

"I can't believe it. You people are unbelievable. This can't be happening."

"It's happening, Emil. It's happening. Come and let me buy you a drink."

"I wanna say goodbye to the boy."

"The boys are leaving for dinner. They'll be busy and happily entertained. Don't worry. Where are you staying? Come on, I'll drive. You're a good man, Emil. Come on!" He grabbed Emil under his arm and lifted him up. "Come on. My car's right out back. Come on!"

Chapter Nine

Dade City, Florida.

Fall of 1992

The first time they left the hospital, they made a trip to the Dixon home in the hospital van. They were able to roll in with their wheelchairs and although both of them protested that they didn't need them, the hydraulic lift brought them up to the car floor level and from there to the latches that kept their chairs in place.

The home of their hosts was not as elaborate as the one they had stayed in overnight in Atlanta, but compared to the dwellings back home, it appeared to be a mansion.

Both boys had undergone multiple operations and they were allowed to move around on crutches, but only for an hour a day. The pain had been minimal, the discomfort maximal. After each operation they were confined to the bed for a spell, as the therapists worked with them day by day. While one recuperated, the other entertained him. John's English improved daily and Joe's Spanish was near perfect. Not only had they become fast friends, they became brothers. There was no question in their minds that Allah and Christ meant it that way. Destiny determined them to be *brothers*.

Miriam had returned to Morocco after two weeks. She felt unneeded, now that her son was in good hands, and she was lonely for her family and her native tongue. She hadn't learned a word of English and nobody on the staff spoke Arabic. Yousef felt sad for just about one minute and after that he hastened out of his door, distracted by the pretty blond who happened to roll by. Miriam watched him go, sighed and whispered; "Allah Akbar." (It's God's will.)

Before lunch, the whole group, George included, drove to Zephyrhills to watch Emil come in for a landing in his neat little plane. After tying down, he shook hands with George Dixon for the first time and tried to talk everyone into going up for a ride.

"My plane holds six, so I can easily get four of you in there and one of you boys can help me fly the plane."

Tracy wouldn't hear of it. "These boys are going nowhere without the written consent of the doctors and that includes air travel." That settled that.

"Would you teach me to fly?" Juan wanted to know.

"Of course, of course. I was an instructor in the Navy for years and may I say, I was one of the best."

"I'm sure of that!" Tracy couldn't keep the skepticism out of her voice. "Right now, we're gonna look at horses. Neither of the boys has ever touched a horse or a cow and they're excited about it, so let's go. Do you wanna drive George?"

"Not me. You're doing fine. I'll sit in the back with the boys. By the way boys, you gotta stop growing. Pretty soon you won't fit in this van anymore."

George was right. Both boys had grown an inch or two and especially Yousef had gained at least fifteen pounds. He didn't look like a gangly skinny kid anymore and he had shaved for the first time in his life. He even considered a mustache.

Emil retrieved his accordion from the backseat of the aircraft and plunked down next to Tracy in the front.

"How's it going boys? About ready to play soccer?" He leaned across the seat in order to face the rear.

"Buckle your seatbelt. I'm a dangerous driver." Mrs. Dixon shouted orders while backing the van on the tarmac.

"Okay, okay! Are you boys latched in back there?"

"Yep. They're secure." George checked the floor couplings and the seatbelts.

"You gonna play, Mister Emilio?" Yousef regretted that he hadn't brought his *"tabala"*, his Moroccan bongo drum that his mom had sent him. Ever since the Egyptian Band from the Egypt Temple Shrine performed for the kids in the hospital, Joe was intrigued by drum music. The Egyptians in their colorful outfits and their curly-toed harem shoes fascinated him and the rhythm of their Oriental tunes was very native to him. He already knew all the lyrics to the song: *"I'm The Sheik Of Araby,"* and happily entertained anyone who wanted to listen. He felt that his drum and Mr. Emilio's accordion had a real future together.

"Probably. We'll check out what the horses will like to hear."

George wasn't too convinced. "The cows might stop givin' milk when they hear you."

"No, not really." Emil wasn't discouraged easily. "If we can get them to dance, they may give buttermilk instead." The whole bus cracked up.

The boys chose McDonalds for lunch and Emil complained that they didn't have the decency to serve beer in those places.

"Emil, are you flying back today or are you staying overnight?" Tracy wanted to know.

"I'm in no hurry. My son is running the restaurant and. . . "

"Sean's running it already?" Tracy seemed surprised. "Will you stay in Tampa or do you wanna stay at the house?"

"Oh, I don't wanna put you out or anything. . . "

"That's no problem." George chimed in from the backseat. "I'd like to get to know you better, you know..., so that way, we can share a few brews and talk. And we can get you back to your plane in the morning within a half hour, any time you wanna go."

"George is right. We need to talk about a lot of things, so we'll just head back after we drop the boys off this afternoon. They're expected back by four. So we'll beat the traffic, okay?"

"Okay by me, if it isn't any bother.'

"No bother." George seemed adamant.

"Fine." Tracy picked up the trays and started cleaning up. "Did you boys have enough?"

The way the boys exchanged glances, it seemed that the answer was 'no'. She smiled, "We're going home and you'll have ice cream with pecans and honey, so that'll hold you over. I can't believe how much you kids can eat. What'll happen when you get to work out and run again? You'll eat even more, right?"

The boys smirked and their eyes told it all. They were completely in tune with one another. They even thought alike, like twin brothers.

After they dropped off the boys at the Shriners Hospital, Doctor Olson and Emil conferred for quite a while and the result was that George, Tracy and Emil were stuck in the afternoon rush hour that was leaving Tampa every afternoon. George drove the Lincoln and didn't seem to mind because the two men were involved in an emotional conversation.

"George, you can't imagine what filth these people live in. I can't understand how that came about. At one time, they were proud Incas or Tetchuan Indians, who worked the fields and raised their llamas, and now they're just beggars and bums. For some reason, they leave the green mountains behind and move close to the city to live in cardboard boxes. It don't make no sense. I've gone out into the outlying country and they're not rich by any means, but they live in houses. Little adobe houses, but why would they give that up to go somewhere in the desert, without water, without electricity and no toilets? It makes no sense. And their government? They don't do a thing. Nothing! I can't let that boy go back there. He's got no father. His mother lives with some other guy and they have seven kids between them in a small shack. It's disgusting. Just plain disgusting. I can't let that boy go back there. Doctor Olson agrees with me, but he says the legalities are impossible to overcome. Let me tell you something George. I don't care what I've got to overcome. I'm gonna adopt that boy. I'm gonna keep him here. He's gonna get an education, I'm gonna teach him to fly, maybe he can become an airline pilot and make a good living for himself. You've seen him, George. He's a wonderful kid. Loads of personality and even though he has no education to speak of, you can tell that he's intelligent, right? You can spot that for yourself, right? I'm gonna keep him here. I won't even let him go back there to see his mother until he's eighteen and makes his own decisions. Right now, I'm making the decisions for him and my decision is, he's staying here. He'll be out of the hospital within a year and he's going home with me to Fort Walton and come hell or high water, that's what's gonna happen."

"How does your son feel about that?"

"My son? Sean? He's all for it. He would love to have a little brother. Teach him how to play ball and card tricks and teach him how to dance and get along with girls. Oh yeah! Eric's ready and I'm starting the paperwork tomorrow. I'm gonna send some money to that church in Y-can, or whatever the name of that town is and the priest there, Father Dominico will help me with all the paperwork in Spanish. Over here, González, have you met him?"

George shook his head.

"Well anyway, González will help from this end. The only obstacle may be his mother, but I betcha, that if I promise to send money regularly, she'll cooperate alright. I know George, I know. It don't sound right. It sounds like I'm buying the boy, right? But let me tell you something, George, money still opens a lot of doors and my concern is that boy and that's all. You should have seen how twisted he was when I first saw him in that dump in Peru. It's a friggin' shame that there's nobody in that country that seems to give a damn about these kids. It's a damn shame. I'm just sorry that I can't do more for some of the other kids, but George, I ain't dead yet. Who knows, I may go get me a few more. Right now, I'm fighting to keep this one here and I'm gonna win that fight. You'll see George. You'll see."

Over drinks on the porch, the story was repeated and Tracy and George had a chance to give their input as well. It was hard to shut up Emil, but they managed.

Tracy was the main spokesperson for the Dixon family.

"We agree with a lot that you were saying Emil, but we're in a different boat. His parents would never give up Joe, but we can probably convince them to let us educate the boy over here. That would be great. Do you know what's even greater about it? Our kids agree. We have one son and one daughter and they have four children, one and three, and they have met the boy in the hospital, they've seen the pictures of the Kasbah that he grew up in in Morocco and they don't mind that we would spend some of their inheritance on educating that boy. That thrills me so, I could cry. We really have great kids, don't we George?"

George had dozed off and Tracy didn't even notice. She continued, "Thank God, Joe's father speaks pretty good English and we can communicate. I think they're dying for that boy to come home, but they're also very thankful for what we're doing for him here and I'm sure they'd let him come back here to study. To get out of that rut that the family has been in for years. We're praying and we're getting good vibes. I think God is with us every step of the way."

"Amen to that Tracy. Amen to that."

Chapter Ten

**Young Love
One year later**

Tampa, March 1993

It was a great day and it was a sad day. It was great, because Virginia, the blond heartthrob was going home after fourteen long months, and it was sad for the same reason. Yousef had developed a real crush on her and he felt a serious pang in his heart knowing that she would be gone. Compared to Juan, Joe had rapidly grown into a teenager, while Juan was still at an age when girls were "just a pain".

It had taken an entire month before Joe and the blond girl finally talked and it was only after she took the initiative. She was only thirteen, but maturing rapidly, physically and mentally, and those Moroccan good looks and that infectious smile were having an impact. It might be only "puppy-love" as far as the rest of the world was concerned, but to Joe it was eternal devotion. They got together at every chance they could find and after four months, they finally held hands. They played *foosball*, he sang for her while he played his drum and she made beautiful sketches of him, some so good, he sent them home. The times that either of them was restricted to their bed, recuperating from another surgery, they'd visit each other and hold hands. The staff did not encourage that type of conduct, but as long as it was done with open doors or in the company of others, they let it slide.

Since Joe's room was shared by Juan (John), who could come in any time he wanted and when Virginia was laid up, her roommate, a little six year old, rolled in and out of her room constantly, the two young lovers were allowed very little privacy. That might have been a good thing. Joe was getting too emotional about his first big romance in life and he would lace into John, when he had the nerve to make fun of them.

It started when Virginia wore her hair in two braids one night at dinner and John was taught the new word: *'pigtails'*. When the meaning was explained to him, he burst out laughing because he visualized two tails on a pig, *dos rabitos de cochino*. At first it was good for a laugh, but when Juan kept teasing Yousef with the Spanish expression or when he insisted on calling her *Piggy* or *Miss Piggy,* Joe threatened to slug him and for a while, their friendship suffered considerably.

Little by little however, when they referred to Virginia in private, they both got in the habit of calling her *Miss Piggy,* but never to her face. It became their private little joke.

On that lovely morning in March, Virginia pushed Joe around on the beautiful grounds of the hospital. She walked nearly normally now, but when she released the handles of the wheelchair and walked unassisted, she appeared stiff and a bit hesitant, but she wasn't despondent because she'd been told, with constant therapy and great exercise on her behalf, she should be normal in a year. She was jubilant, but it was hard to wait.

They had exchanged addresses and phone numbers and both pledged to write nearly every day and visit each other very often. He would come to Washington, North Carolina, and she would get her parents to take her to Morocco to visit him there. Of course, there was also a good chance that Joe might come to live in Florida with the Dixons and get his schooling in America. That was still uncertain, but they were very optimistic about it coming true.

Virginia's parents had driven down the night before and were due to pick her up at ten, for there was a little farewell party in the rec-room for her. She had become a popular sight around the hospital, but finally, after fourteen months, it was time for her to move on.

Under the tall oak trees, she sat on a bench and held his hand against her cheek and cried. To others it might have been puppy love, but to them it was real. Joe couldn't control his tears either, so she stood up and pressed his curly head against her chest and just held him. Held him tight. That's how her parents found her. When they drove up and saw the young pair, pretty blond and handsomely dark, they sat silently in the car for a few minutes, not knowing what to think. They had met the boy before on different visits, but their girl... their little girl..., she was still so young, so frightfully young!

It all went against their grain, but there it was... a young couple in love.

Finally, the father honked the horn and the pair looked up, but didn't break their embrace. They had nothing to hide or be ashamed of. After the second honk, Virginia straightened up and rolled Joe in their direction. It was the beginning of the end for them. And they understood that.

As the months went by, the trips to Dade City became more frequent and both boys got to ride in the front seat of the plane with Emil and learned the very basics of flight and flight control. Both were ecstatic. If soccer was not in their future anymore, then flying would be. No question about it. Emil had gotten them the most elementary flight instruction manuals and they eagerly absorbed them. In their room, they tried to outscore each other on their test exams and, with the okay of Dr. Olson, they got to play *FLIGHT* on the computer and both felt sure they would solo an airplane on their fifteenth birthday.

The letters from Virginia were not as frequent as she had promised and Joe was guilty of the same thing, but both had their excuses, a new school and new friends up in Washington and flight training down in Tampa. Even so, their love was still in full bloom when Joe went back to Chefchaouen.

Mrs. Dixon flew back with him, but Juan had one more operation to go and wouldn't be able to leave for another three months. The goodbyes with Emil and Juan were as emotional as Virginia's departure had been. The boys had really grown to be brothers and it seemed cruel to separate them, but both counted on a speedy return to Florida for Joe, and Juan was definitely staying with Emil upon his release.

Morocco and the mountains were a welcome sight. "Florida is too flat." Joe observed from the old taxi that took them on the two hour trip to the Kasbah. "But I love it. I'll be back soon, Mrs. Dixon." He steadfastly refused to call her "Tracy". He squeezed her hand and she kissed him lightly. "I know, I know."

The welcome in the old homestead couldn't have been more timely. The store was filled with about twenty tourists and young Yousef had to tell his story about America and his recovery in about five different languages. The result was, the customers stayed longer, asked dozens of questions and bought more rugs than usual.

Of course, there was no end to the hugs, the tears and the exclamations, "You've grown so tall. You're a man now, no more boy!" It was good to be home.

Grandfather insisted on celebrating in a local restaurant because their quarters were too small and Miriam was too overwhelmed to cook for everybody. It became a feast, a typical Arabian feast. All the lamb, chicken and goat, prepared according to age old Arabic and Berber tradition, were a joy to behold and to taste.

Yousef alternately hugged his mother, his sister and Tracy, he was just overwhelmed. Unfortunately for Tracy, most of the people present didn't understand English, so she didn't get to say much, but Yousef made up for it by telling in glowing terms all about his operations, the American people, his glorious roommate and his new found love. That brought on a lot of cheers from the men and scowls from the women. A blond? Not just blond, VERY blond. Beautifully blond. The more he bragged, the more his mother frowned.

It all ended with a friendly shouting match. Tracy wanted to pay, Grandpa Yousef wanted to pay but it was all settled by the owner who insisted, "There is no bill!"

It felt good to be back home.

Tracy slept at the hotel in the square, because there was no space in the family quarters and now that young boy had become a man, it was nearly impossible to bed down everybody. Yousef ended up sleeping on the fourth floor with the looms, but on top of some of the most beautiful wool carpets his Grandfather ever created. For two more days, Mrs. Dixon stayed and talked with the boy's folks. They generally agreed that it would be best for Yousef's future if he received an American education. That he wanted to become a pilot was not so well received. Couldn't he become a doctor? An accountant? A merchant like his father? Some sort of a safe, steady job?

"Steady? What do you mean? Steady? A pilot's job is steady and I want to become a military pilot, a fighter pilot."

That turned out to be the dumbest thing he could have said. If a moment ago the mood was 80% in favor of American schooling, it dropped quickly to 10%.

"A fighter pilot? Why do you want to kill yourself?" That was his mother.

"A fighter pilot? For the Americans or for Morocco? You don't want to give up your Moroccan citizenship, do you? Become an American? Give up Islam?" That was his dad.

Grandfather seemed to be the least emotional one. "Will you ever be able to pass a physical exam with all your operations? Fighter pilots have to be in exceptional shape, no?"

"That's my only worry. But commercial pilots make a lot of money. I would make more in one year than all of you together in twenty years."

"Is money that important?" Mother again.

"Isn't money all you work for, all the time? Very little money. Imagine having a house instead of living here in the Kasbah in a crowded apartment. Grandpa wouldn't have to work any more. You could hire a maid. Mama and Papa could have a big store in town and make millions, hahaha!" He had to laugh at his own enthusiasm.

"Maybe you want to marry the blond, no?" His uncle interjected.

"That's not a bad idea either, hahahaha." Everyone chimed in. The anxiety was broken, the spirit became relaxed. Grandfather was the most adamant that education should be first and foremost and that there was no future for Yousef here in the tapestry business. The following day a decision would be made, and father and son walked Mrs. Dixon back to her hotel. That would be her last night before flying back.

It took a while before she finally got connected to Dade City, but when she got her husband on the phone, she was nearly jubilant, "George, we have no commitment for sure, but we're on the right track. They'll make a decision tomorrow and I'm confident the boy will be back with us shortly and we'll look into high school for him. Isn't that wonderful, George?"

"Yes, Tracy, it really is. It really is." He hung up the phone while wiping a tear from his eyes.

Chapter Eleven

**Fort Walton Beach, Florida
Four years later**

Saint Mary's Catholic High School
October 1996

John Cordero, (nee Juan Pedro), had finally adjusted to school life in America. At first he had to have tutors and sat through endless extra classes during the summer, but as a sophomore, he was right up there with the rest of the class. He had risen to President of the Spanish club and as a result he ended up tutoring other students after school. That was the fun part. Many of his club mates were female and consequently, many of his pupils were some of the prettiest girls in Fort Walton Beach.

Because his Dad (he started addressing Emil as Dad even before the adoption was final) worked long hours at the restaurant, John had a lot of leeway. In the morning, he would leave the house before Emil got up and many nights, the boy was already sound asleep when his new dad got in, sometimes staggering a little bit. The restaurant closed officially at nine at night, but when some of the regulars hung around a little longer, Emil would gladly have a drink with them and before he knew it, he wasn't out the door till after eleven.

In the beginning, right after the adoption, Sean was home a lot as well, but when he got a chance to buy a little place in Perdido Key, he only came around on Sunday mornings. That was the only day that he didn't serve breakfast in his new place and therefore he had the morning to himself. Some weekends, John would board a bus on Fridays and spend Saturday and Sunday with Sean, who had fast become his best friend. It started as a brother/brother relationship, but it had grown to be some sort of a father/son feeling between them. Sean loved the boy like the son he never had. He was strict with him, yet spoiled him, and for his sixteenth birthday, Juan Pedro was going to get a car. The little pick-up was being worked on in a local shop, so that it would be in tip-top condition. New tires, new brakes, engine tune-up and a new paint job. Bright red! It was an '89 Dodge, but it would look like new.

At first, John had struggled with the language, with an unforgiving therapist Elena, and the fact that soccer was permanently out of the question for him. When the therapy was finally completed after one year, he had to admit that he was 100% better than when he left the hospital and they threw Elena a great farewell party.

At school, the kids started calling him "J.P." because when he explained that his name was really Juan Pedro, one of the boys said, "That's too complicated. Why don't we just call you J.P.?"

"Well, .. it has a nice ring to it." and soon the name stuck. From there on in he was addressed as J.P.

A bike got him wherever he wanted to go and life was better than he could possibly have hoped for. Emil had taken him flying many times and even hired a flight instructor at the Regional Airport, but Juan never took to it like Joe did in Central Florida. The instructor finally advised Emil, "Let it go. Don't push it. If he wants to start again, fine, but don't push him. In my opinion, he has a bomber pilot attitude, not a fighter attitude like you had and maybe still have. He's plenty safe, but he's no eager beaver, so let it rest. I hate to lose a student, but I also know when I shouldn't push someone against his will."

The adoption had taken three years to become effective, but it didn't matter much. John came straight from the hospital to Emil's house and never left again. He didn't even want to go back to Peru to see his mom and Father Dominico. He had found his niche, America.

By hanging around the soccer practices, he had endeared himself to the coaches and was appointed assistant to the assistant coach. He helped with boy's as well as girl's soccer and that suited him just fine. He was a busy, happy boy. When Joe had left a few years ago, he didn't understand the infatuation between Joe and 'Miss Piggy', but now that he was pushing sixteen, he knew all about it. He couldn't wait to get his truck, because getting dates on a bike had never seemed to work too well. Just three more weeks.

JP and Joe had maintained regular contact through mail and phone calls and twice, Emil had flown him to Dade City for Joe's birthday. They were still the closest of brothers and bosom friends; but school, girls and all the other activities cut into their communication. Besides that, Joe pursued flying with a vengeance and got involved in Civil Air Patrol and was convinced that he would enter Air Force R.O.T.C. in Gainesville immediately upon graduating from High School.

John felt the same way about college and a career in the military, but he would eventually go in a different direction. He loved spy movies and TV mystery programs. When asked to do an essay in his freshman year, he received an A- for a 2,000 word suspense story. Intelligence was what he was going to pursue. Working undercover in Russia and taking on the KGB were some of his dreams. All he had to do was get good grades and he knew he would. Making his dad proud of him was the only way he could ever repay him for all Emil had done for him. John would make sure that both of them would be proud, Emil and Sean.

His mother? He hardly gave her a thought.

November 1997

ACT tests were taken and applications filled out, controversy started up between J.P and his dad. John wanted to go to the University of Florida because that's where Joe was going, but both Sean and Emil wanted to keep him closer, by either going to the University of West Florida, right near town, or to Florida State in Tallahassee.

F.S.U. won out for different reasons. It offered the courses that John wanted and Florida turned him down anyway. So that settled that. "It's only a three hour ride from Tallahassee and I can handle that."

"Great! You graduate with honors and I'll even buy you a new car!"

"Oh, Dad! That won't be necessary and besides, I like my little truck!"

"Well, you haven't graduated with honors yet either, so don't fret it, boy. Keep plugging. You're doing fine!"

During a school sponsored *Career Day,* he talked at length with an Air Force recruiter and told him about his friend in Dade City and his desire to become a fighter pilot. When the Airman asked about John's ambitions, he explained his interest in spy stories and intrigue and as a result he received a number of pamphlets about the U.S. Air Force Special Operations Command and pay grades from Airman to General. John was hooked. FSU did have an Air Force ROTC program, so that could all be worked out and it would only take Emil's consent and John would be inducted.

"Air Force? What's wrong with the Navy? I spent twenty glorious years there and they're right here in Pensacola."

"Oh, Dad! Hurlburt Field is also right around the corner and I wouldn't be at sea for six months or so. Besides that, I'll be involved with planes too."

"Yeah! Jumping out of them."

"Oh, Dad!"

Chapter Twelve

**Gator Country
Five years later**

Gainesville, Florida
October 1998

"Colonel Wright... meet Lieutenant-Colonel Bongers."
The two colonels shook hands. Col. Wright was the Air Force R.O.T.C. commander at the University of Florida and Lt. Col. Bongers was the detachment head of Army Intelligence at Fort Bragg, North Carolina.
"What gives us the honor of your visit, Colonel Bongers?"
"Bruce, just Bruce will do."
"Okay Bruce. I'm Jerry and again, what gives us the pleasure of your company?"
"As always..., searching for talent. Trying to steal some of your finest cadets." Bongers smiled broadly as he said that, but Wright knew it was true. The Army, the FBI, the CIA, U.S. Customs and the U.S. Marshals were always fishing for young talent among the college kids and especially among the ones that had already pledged their allegiance to their country by their solemn oath as ROTC cadets.
"Let's grab some coffee and sit down." He led the way.

In his office, decorated with pictures of planes, airmen and officials, the two sat back, loosened their ties and were joined by a sergeant-major in a short-sleeved blue shirt. "Colonel, this is Sergeant-Major Dunkins, my staff manager and right hand man."

Getting up, the colonel shook the airman's hand and said, "Hey, nice to meet you." He sat back down and continued. "As you know, we don't want to shortchange the Air Force, but there's always the chance that a good man or woman might not want to finish your program and might be a great candidate for intelligence work. We have to keep looking. Our agenda is a lot like yours…," he hesitated and sipped his coffee, "always recruiting. How's your year going?"

"We're having a banner year, thank God and it's mostly because Junior ROTC's throughout the state have been doing a great job and Civil Air Patrol Cadets have more than doubled over the past few years. All that makes us look good." Wright grinned from ear to ear. "After the Gulf War, we had a cutback on pilot training and that hurt our enrollment, but it perked up lately and we have a lot of youngsters with *pilot-slots*. Boys and girls alike. As a matter of fact, for the first time, we have more than 25% female pilot applicants. They all wanna fly fighters. Interesting trend!"

"Of course, you don't want to donate," Bruce smiled, "any of those to us."

"You're right about that. Sergeant-Major, what may we have that we can spare or share, as the case may be?" Col. Wright turned toward the NCO.

"Well sir, one prospect comes to mind, because just this morning he came in and wanted to know how he could get out of ROTC and into a flight program at Embry-Riddle in Daytona."

"Why?" Bongers wanted to know.

"Excuse me, why what?"

"Why does he want to go commercial instead of Air Force?"

"Oh, that's right. You wouldn't know. This young man lost his pilot slot last week and…"

"What happened?"

"Oh, as you may know, the cadets have to go to MacDill Air Force Base for the altitude pressure test and the kid came out screaming when the pressure altitude exceeded 30,000 feet."

"Really? How come?"

"Well Colonel, he had several operations on his left leg and apparently the pressure inside his leg wouldn't equalize and caused him excruciating pain. That automatically kicked him out of the pilot program. He cried when he had to turn in his little silver wing. I felt like crying along with him. He's such a good kid and such a dedicated cadet, it broke my heart."

"What does he expect to do in civil aviation?" Bongers was puzzled.

"Well, sir, civil airplanes are all pressurized to a maximum of 5,000 feet, so that wouldn't bother him at all."

"What's the boy's name and background?" The Army colonel took out a little notepad.

"His name is Joe Mohammed, actually Yousef, but he goes by…"

"Mohammed? Where's he from?"

The Non-Commissioned Officers opened his briefcase, fingered through some files and answered; "His address is Dade City, Florida, but he was born in Morocco."

"Morocco?" The colonel's tone of voice reflected his surprise. "How'd he get here?"

"I can copy his entire file for you if you wish, but briefly, the Shriners brought him over and fixed him up. That's it in a nutshell."

"Wow! Okay, I'd like to meet him. Who else may you have?"

After another hour of deliberations, it was obvious that the Air Force wasn't particularly anxious to give up or volunteer any of its cadets and Bongers arranged for an appointment to meet this Yousef.

The Army Colonel, six feet four with an athletic build and blond curly hair, stood up and stretched luxuriously after the sergeant-major left and smiled at his Air Force counterpart, "Where do we grab a good steak for lunch? I could eat a horse."

Wright laughed, "No horsemeat here in Florida, but I can get you some fine gator tail."

"That'll do." And they walked out.

Same day. 4 P.M. The ROTC General Hap Arnold Building.

"Hello Joe, I'm Lieutenant Colonel Bongers. How are you?"

The young man saluted, even though he was not in uniform and shook the extended hand.

"Do you go by Joe or Yousef?" Apparently Bongers pronounced it correctly.

"Here in the U.S. I go by Joe. Back home I'm Yousef." He accepted a seat as he talked, but sat very upright.

"Relax! Tell me about yourself. What brought you here and what are your plans?" The Army Intelligence man did not produce a piece of paper or a pencil and smiled at the good looking young Moroccan with the dark curly hair. The boy visibly relaxed. Within five minutes he had related his entire life story without going into too many details. They could come later if needed.

"As far as my plans?" He frowned. "They were shot down last week. I had my mind set on becoming a fighter pilot, but my past injuries kicked me off the candidate list and now I hope to get into commercial aviation, but I don't know where I would get the money, once I'm out of ROTC."

"How about the Army?"

"The Army? You're kidding, no?"

"No. I'm dead serious. Army Intelligence, specifically. We don't fly much above 20,000."

"Really? You're not kidding?" He leaned forward, his eyes sparkling.

"No. Again…, I'm not kidding. I'm here to recruit intelligence people if I can and you might very well make the mark. Now, not all intelligence people fly. I'm one of them, but we certainly can use some that do." The officer leaned closer. "In your case, I might have some special interest in mind. How many languages do you speak?"

"Me? About six."

"Six? Now it's my turn, are you kidding me?"

The boy laughed uproariously, displaying all his even white teeth. "No, seriously. Obviously, I speak English and of course my native tongue is Arabic, plus I speak the Berber dialect of my grandfather's tribe. I'm nearly fluent in Spanish, but I could stand to take some grammar and spelling. Same with French and German. I speak them well enough and I can read a newspaper, but I couldn't write an essay in either of those languages."

"How'd you learn all those?"

"By dealing with the public in my father's business and in the Shrine Hospital I had a Peruvian roommate who spoke no English at all, so I picked up Spanish fluently. Comes in handy sometimes."

"You bet. Joe, I heard you wanted to go to Embry-Riddle and get your commercial rating, but..."

"That sounds like a good alternative, no?"

"True, but the cost might be prohibitive, you realize that?"

"I know, I know. I can't ask my parents or my sponsors. My parents could never afford that and I don't want to ask my sponsors in Dade City, because they have children and grandchildren that need them too, so...?"

"I'll tell you what Joe. This is just preliminary, you understand? But I can nearly guarantee you that we'll, the Army that is, cover the cost of your training with one understanding; after commissioning and flight training, you serve a four year stint in the Army Intelligence Corps. Can you do that?"

"Would I then be a U.S. citizen?"

"Sure! What do you have now? A student visa?"

"Yes, but I want to get a regular visa, so my time will count toward my citizenship."

The colonel grinned. "No problem. I'll work out the details. How about your parents? And your sponsors? How would they feel about all this?"

"My sponsors will do anything to keep me here. They think of me as their son. My parents is a different story. They would like me home or at least closer to home. They'll cooperate though, I'm sure. They love America and what Americans have done for me, so they'll be anxious, but they'll support me in my decisions. Besides that, I'd like to someday help my parents and grandfather retire. They scrape by on a meager but honest existence and especially my Grandpa, he needs to stop working that loom."

"Loom?"

"Yeah!" He sighed, " He still makes tapestry and he can't even see well anymore."

"Good grief. How old is he?"

"Eighty-nine, I think. Maybe eighty-eight. Anyway, he's old. He can barely make it up four flights of stairs any more."

"Wow! I see your point." The concern on Bongers' face was genuine. "Here's what we'll do. I'll draw up the papers. We get you transferred to Embry-Riddle. You start taking flying lessons as soon as possible. Your new curriculum may include some additional languages and some intelligence courses. During summer breaks we'll have you over at Fort Bragg and we'll make an officer and a citizen out of you. If everything works right, you'll be privy to some top secret information and you'll be working on my team. You may not fly as much as you've hoped to, but you'll have an exciting career lined up for you. What do you think?"

"I don't know what to say. An hour ago I was down in the dumps and now I'm on cloud nine. I don't know what to say."

"Can you say yes?"

"Yes! Of course. YES!" He stood up and saluted. "Yes Sir! Yes!"

"Great! Let's get rolling!"

Chapter Thirteen

Florida State University

ROTC office, 1998

Young Juan Pedro Cordero-Pagliari (J.P.) was standing at attention.

"These sit-ups are killing me, Colonel. I just can't do them the way the other kids can. The one girl is fabulous. She did 105, can you believe that?"

"Pagliari, you can do anything you wanna do if you put your mind to it, including sit-ups. For crying out loud, all we are trying to do is to get you in condition to be an officer, a leader of men..."

"Yes Sir, I understand, but I physically can't do that."

"And why not?"

"I've had seven operations on my hip and legs and..."

"You what? Sit down, Pagliari, sit down."

J.P. found a seat. He favored one leg a little as he took the three steps to get to the chair.

"Is your leg bothering you now? You limped as you sat down. Why did you have all these operations and how come you passed your physical?"

John had been put on report by an upperclassman for not completing his calisthenics and was now facing Colonel Davis, the ROTC commander.

He relayed the whole story about his accident and all the operations that made him nearly perfectly healed.

Colonel Davis shook his head. "Yet, you passed the physical. That's odd. I'll tell you what Pagliari, I'm gonna excuse you from P.T. for the time being and schedule you for another exam. You have a fine record so far and we want you to complete the program, but we have to be sure that we don't do you any physical harm, understand?"

"Yes, Sir!"

'Keep attending all classes and meetings, stay at the top of your class and I'll schedule a physical for you and then we'll talk again, okay?"

"Yes. Sir."

"Dismissed."

After a trip to the clinic at Eglin Air Force Base and an additional journey back to the Shriners' Hospital, it was concluded that it would take years before his muscles would reach normal strength, but in time they would. He would even be able to jump out of planes without the worry of breaking anything.

"Your breaks have healed beautifully and the junctures of the bones where we operated are actually stronger now than the rest of your bones. You'll be okay. It will just take a little longer and the Air Force will be pleased to keep you, but not in the R.O.T.C. program."

"Whew! Not in ROTC? Then what?"

"You could finish your degree and apply for O.T.S (Officer Training School) after graduation. You could join the Guard or the Reserve and start picking a career."

J.P changed his mind. He joined the Air Force Reserve and it involved ten weeks of boot camp training at Lackland Air Force Base in San Antonio Texas before the Para Rescue would start. Emil was furious.

"I don't want you to go through life as a Non-Com. I want you to be an Officer. Believe me, son, there's one hell of a difference in lifestyles, whether you're a Sergeant or a Captain in the Air Force. And what is wrong with the Navy? I had a great career and you could too, but in any case it would involve getting a College degree first and that's why I don't want you to quit school now. Finish college first and then select what branch of the service you want..."

"But Dad, I already signed up."

"You what? You signed up without telling me first? What am I? Chopped liver? I got nothing to say anymore? I'm just the dude who went through all the trouble adopting you and making you an American Citizen? Don't I count for nothing, no more?"

"But Dad..."

"Don't you 'but Dad' me. I should definitely have some say in your decisions and your future, shouldn't I?"

"Yes, Dad, but this is what I wanna do. I wanna become a Para Rescue man, like the guys at Hurlburt Field. They do great work. They rescue people, serve in all parts of the world..."

"But why now? Can't it wait till you have finished school? I'm sure they'll still be there three years from now and they'll still be needing people. Why the hurry? Why the mad rush?"

"Well, I was so mad that I got kicked out of R.O.T.C that I figured I'd join the Reserve and..."

"You got kicked out? Why? Whacha do?"

"I didn't do anything. I just didn't pass the physical and..."

"You didn't pass the physical? So what makes you thinks you'll pass the physical for Para Rescue? That also requires a *Flight Three physical...*"

"Yeah, but the doctor at Eglin and Colonel Davis were confident that I'll pass it..."

"Then why did you get kicked out of the R.O.T.C. program? I'm gonna call that Colonel and find out what's going on."

"Please Dad! Don't! I've made up my mind and I signed up already. I'll be leaving for Lackland in four weeks."

"Well, I'll be damned. You know something son, you'll be saving me a lot of money by dropping out of college. Maybe now I can afford to buy a better airplane."

He shook his head and tears welled in his eyes. "Come here, Son. Give me a hug. I've always wanted what was best for you and whatever makes you happy should be best for you." He pulled the boy close and shook with emotion.

"You know boy, I really don't give a damn about a new plane. I was just saying that. I do give a damn about you, kid. You know that."

"I just want to serve my country…"

"I did the same thing in '52 during the Korean War, so go with God, Son. Go with God."

The boot camp training at Lackland, Texas, nearly broke him and yet it helped him immensely. It was all very basic military training, a lot of running, marching and calisthenics. At first he was always the last man on the team and he ended up more exhausted than the other guys, but the predictions of the doctors became true. His leg muscles grew stronger with every exercise. Apparently, the bones had grown together well and endured all the operations. The muscles responded as expected. He graduated Lackland as an Airman.

Winter survival training in Washington State was the toughest thing he had ever undertaken. At Fairchild Air Force Base, he had to go through what every pilot and Para Jumper had to endure.

The snow and cold were bad enough, but the trek from one hill to another, with nothing but survival gear and instructions on how to snare rabbits was nearly suicidal. He and his traveling buddy religiously added pills to their drinking water, so they wouldn't get sick as they looked for all the plants that the book prescribed, but none were available during the winter. He nearly died of starvation. At least he thought he might. The days were so short and the nights so cold, that they just kept moving all the time. He was afraid if he fell asleep he'd never wake up and would certainly freeze to death.

It turned out that the trek wasn't even the worst. He was interrogated by what he called *the Viet Cong* and while his hands were tied behind his back, they questioned him endlessly. The pain of the leather straps that held his hands together was excruciating, but he could handle that. He could handle pain. *The Viet Cong* got nothing of value out of him. Just his name, rank and social security number. He held fast, for hours on end. He didn't give an inch.

Without food he was locked in a pit that was so small, he had to bend over in order for them to lock the bamboo cover in place above his head. It wasn't cold, so at first it didn't bother him all that much, but after an hour, his back started to hurt and after a few hours, he screamed in agony. The bamboo door lifted. "You ready to talk?"

"No!"

Slam!

He passed out after four hours, actually fell asleep. The sleepless night in the mountains simply caught up with him and knocked him out.

He didn't even wake up when they pulled him out and he remained in a bent over position as if he was frozen. He nearly was. After ten minutes in the warm interrogation hut, he thawed out and screamed at the top of his lungs when he tried to straighten up.

"Water! Water! Please! Some water!"

Nobody budged, nobody gave him water and the questions started over again. He told them nothing. He passed out again.

When he awoke, his hands were untied and he was lying on a cot with all his clothes on. A glass of milk was handed him and a bowl of soup. He nearly fell asleep again.

Back with the "Cong", they played back the tapes of the interrogations and that became the worst experience of the whole exercise. They had spliced the tape in such a way, that his answers seemed like admissions instead of denials. When he was asked if he operated out of Hurlburt Field and he had answered; "NO", they had spliced in a "YES" from another section when he was asked if he was cold. The whole tape was reconstructed in such a way that it came out as an admission of guilt. An admission of having infiltrated their country illegally and that he knew he was a murderer.

"I didn't say that!" He screamed. "I didn't say any such thing! You crummy bastards! I can't believe you're from the same country. That stinks! You're making me look like a traitor! You bastards!"

The *Viet Cong officers* simply left the room. Juan felt destroyed. How could they do that to him? If they turned over the tape to his commanding officer, it would mean the end of his career. He collapsed with his head on the table in front of him and broke down.

"Get up soldier!" An Air Force Officer in full uniform walked in and said, "Good show, Pagliari. You did good!"

J.P. was flabbergasted. "I what?" He straightened up some more. "I what? I did good?"

"You did better than most."

"Yeah, but did you hear that tape?"

"Oh, yes. I put it together."

"You did? Why? Why?"

"To teach you that you never say more than, "Name, Rank and Social Security number. No 'yes', no 'no', no comments whatsoever, but I must tell you one thing, you endured pain better than any human being we've had in here so far. Man, you're good. Now rest up, shave, change clothes and get ready for your return trip. I'm confident that you would survive if you were caught in the wilderness. Dismissed!"

The young Peruvian walked out in a daze. He couldn't believe what had just happened to him.

In the summer, they ended up in Yuma, Arizona at a Marine Corps Air Station for desert survival. The main difference from winter survival was, he learned how to get moisture out of different cacti and how to snatch lizards and eat them heartily. The heat didn't bother him too much. Peru was hot as hell every winter and to him this was like a walk in the park. This time, he wasn't tortured as much, and he didn't let out a sound but, "Name, Rank and Social." He was okay!

Chapter Fourteen

Daytona, Florida

March, 21, 1999

"Colonel Bongers, please!"
"Who can I say is calling?"
"Joe at Daytona."
"Joe who?"
"He'll know. Just tell him, Joe from Daytona."
"Just a moment."
Joe fiddled with his cell phone. This was something new to him and he wasn't a hundred percent sure if he was doing things right.
"He's in a meeting and he'll call you back."
"Ask him to call on this number, 704-883-8834, okay? How long will he be?"
"I don't know, but I'll make sure he gets the message."
"Thanks." Joe had gone through the great expense of buying a cell phone because he didn't want to call from his dormitory. Too many ears. Since he wasn't involved in the busy schedule of the ROTC program anymore, he had time to work and found a job in a fast food sandwich shop and worked the seven to twelve shifts, four days a week. It was a good job, he had constant food available

and he received a fair amount of tips, especially from the late drinking crowd. All of a sudden he had more money than he ever had before, but he was very frugal with it. The cell phone was a luxury that he should really do without, but phone privacy was becoming important. Very important.

His bike was next to him against the bench near the lake and he could see an occasional gator pop up along the shore among the weeds. He was very much on edge and he wished that Bongers would hurry and call back. He should have brought some study materials so he could make his time more useful, but he simply hadn't thought that the colonel would put him on hold. After twenty minutes he called back. He received the same answer, but this time he added, "Tell him it's urgent." It worked.

""Colonel Bongers."

"Colonel, I'm talking on a cell phone and it's important. I think there is a bad movement out here. I've been asked to join a suicide gang and…"

"What are you saying?"

"I need to talk to you fast, but not here. Not in Daytona, because…"

"When do you go home to Dade City and how do you get there?" Bongers was all ears.

"My stepmother picks me up this Friday afternoon and I'll be there by five."

"I'll meet you there." Click.

MacDill AFB, Tampa, Friday 7:30PM

In one of the private offices of *Central Command*, the International Headquarters, Lieutenant General O'Doull, Colonel Bongers, (Bird Colonel by now), Captain George Holswood and Joe sat around a conference table while a recorder turned silently.

"Joe tell us now, what you told me earlier. Start from the beginning."

"Okay. I started going to a Friday service in Daytona Beach in

December. We're not the most devout Muslims at home, but I feel good about saying thanks to Allah on occasion..."

"We understand." The general commented.

"I met some fellow flight students and of course, we started off swapping tall tales and we ended up in a restaurant at the beach and when I ordered a beer, they frowned at me, so I switched to tea, like the rest of them. There were four of them and they were way ahead of me in flight training, so it was good to hear what they experienced. I could learn from those guys. They all had money coming out of their ears and I had to explain about my poverty situation and how the Army paid for my schooling. You can't imagine the looks I got. I might as well have told them that the devil himself supported me. Mind you, all this conversation is taking place in Arabic and they asked if they could be of any help with anything, money, studies, transportation, anything,,,,,,? I said, No thanks, except for a ride back to the dorm."

He reached for the water bottle in front of him and took a long swig from it. "After the next service, the week thereafter, by the way, they picked me up at my dorm this time, we went to someone's house in the suburbs, nice house and they tried to convince me that I was all wrong, joining the Army and having the Army pay for my flying and I told them, I was also getting my degree and a commission when I was finished and that I would be proud to serve for the country that had done so much for me." Another pause, another swig. Nobody interrupted.

"Three weeks later, same thing. They picked me up, great service, a new Imam, great speaker and again to someone's home for tea and we were introduced to a new member. Mohammed already had his pilot's license and he..."

"Mohammad who?" The general wanted to know.

"I don't know, he..."

"What did he look like?"

Joe hesitated. "Look like? He was short. Very short. Maybe five four, maybe less, short clipped hair, no mustache and..."

"About how old?"

"Old? I would say about thirty five… maybe forty… narrow face…"

"Atta?"

"Huh?"

Bongers spoke up, "Was his last name Atta?"

"I don't know. They just called him Mohammed."

"What did he say?"

"Well, that's the scary part. He talked about the great Islamic Cause and how we have to kill as many infidels as possible and how we would earn our place at the right hand of Allah and all the benefits of the "hereafter." It was scary, but everyone besides me seemed enthusiastic about the whole deal. I have no beef with Christians or Jews, as a matter of fact I love'em. They've been good to me and my folks and…"

"Did this Mohammed say anything about his background?"

"I believe he said he was Egyptian and he was in an Israeli jail for…"

"Atta!"

"Huh?"

"That's got to be Atta." The general took over. "How the hell did he get back in this country? George," he addressed the captain, "as soon as we get out of here, contact the CIA. I wanna know how a clown like that gets back in here. It's bad enough that the U.S. put the heat on Israel to let him and his murdering bunch out of jail, where they should have kept him for life, but then he's got the balls to come right back in here under our noses and challenges us. That criminal bastard." He turned to the Moroccan again. "Excuse me Joe, but what you're telling us is invaluable. You are going to be of great importance to us and probably will help save a lot of lives. The Colonel will brief you about what to do and we count on you being strong and vigilant. Good God, I'm glad we have you on our side. Now if you'll excuse me," He shook hands and left the room.

Joe sat back through that brief discourse and his head was spinning. He didn't know what to think.

"Let's go to the club and get something to eat. Then we'll talk some more. George, are you joining us?"

"I wish I could."

Bongers and the young flyboy got into an Air Force vehicle, headed for the O' Club, where a great buffet and a dance band welcomed the hungry Army men, one young one and one middle aged.

"Joe, you may be much more important to us than I had ever dreamed. The biggest question is: could you ever kill innocent women and children because their beliefs are different from yours?"

Joe jumped up; "Never!"

"Sit Joe! Sit. I know you're not the type, but the problem is, the other guys in that group may have felt the same way as you do right now, but they've been brainwashed, the same way these young kids in the Middle East become suicide bombers and believe that they're doing the right thing. It's frightening what these fanatics can do to the human mind. Joe, we have to be able to rely on you to stay steadfast in your present beliefs. The Quran and the Prophet don't condone that type of violence. It's just a hardcore of idiots who blindly follow a few strong willed terrorists. Joe, you gotta remain on our side, even though you're not a citizen yet. Okay? Joe? Okay?"

"Of course, Colonel, of course!" He jumped up again.

"Sit, Joe. I trust in you. All the way." He reached across the table and took Joe's hand, who squeezed it firmly.

"When you get back, keep going to any meeting that they invite you to. Keep me updated on your cell. We'll pay for the cost of it." He raised his hand as Joe started to protest. "We'll pay for it. Call often. Keep your ears open. You may hear the name '*Osama Bin Laden.*' Without being obvious, find out who he is, where he is, but make sure your interest must seem casual. Don't make them suspicious."

"Who? Osama who?'

"Bin Laden, maybe Ben Laden. He maybe in Iraq, Iran or Afghanistan. Anyway, he's dangerous and probably their leader. We don't know enough about him. He's an Arab with lots of money with more money coming in and he seems dedicated to spending all his money on killing 'infidels', especially Jews and Americans. We don't know exactly what his beef is, but we know he hates us. Too bad. Look around…. Aren't these nice folks?"

They both scanned the diners and dancers and indeed, they seemed like the nicest people on earth.

"That's what I wanna be, an American like them. That's what I'm gonna be. Colonel, for sure. That's what I'm gonna be."

Chapter Fifteen

Para Training

Summer 2000

Jump school in Fort Benning was a challenge and a half. Juan Pedro had to prove to the doctors that he could handle the impact of the landings and he had to clear the obstacle course the same way as any other paratrooper. He made it through the program and on the first jump on the static line he was nervous, but confident. Truthfully, it startled the hell out of him when he first stepped out of the plane into the void called 'air'. He hollered. "Wow!" more from fright than from enthusiasm, but once he floated down, he felt like singing. What an experience. Free as a bird, soft wind in his hair, he was so enthralled, he nearly forgot his instructions, "Turn into the wind!"

The other jumpers around him were drifting away from him (or vice versa) and he realized what was causing it. He understood that the forward motion of the chute was 5 mph, so if the wind was 10 mph, he would land with a forward speed of 15, but if he turned into the wind, his landing speed would only be 5 mph. He turned swiftly and that was a good thing, because thirty seconds later he hit the ground, rolled like he had practiced a hundred times and got up to gather up his chute.

"Wow!" This time it was a shout of jubilation. "What a ride! What a ride!"

He felt he could do that all day long, every day of the week. "What a ride!"

As the doctors had predicted, his leg muscles gained strength day after day and he passed every test, on paper and in the field with flying colors. He was making Dad and Sean proud and it held him in great esteem with some of the girls too. Twice he had gone kind of steady. Kind of, three months or so, but he hadn't really been in love and that was okay. He was not in a hurry. His training came first and so far, he was right on track.

Kirtland Air Force Base, New Mexico.
10 AM. Local time, 8 AM in Fort Walton Beach.

"Hey Dad? You wide awake?"
"Who's this?"
"Who's this? How many people call you Dad?"
"Oh shit. Wait a minute." There was a thirty second pause and Emil's voice came back on. "Sorry, Son, I just gargled a bit with Scope and I swallowed half of that stuff. Damn. Don't ever drink that stuff, it's terrible."
"Dad?" J.P. sounded concerned. "Are you okay?"
"I'll tell you in about an hour."
"What's happening out there? What are you doing?"
Emil grunted, "Doing? Nothing. We had a late emergency flight, an E.L.T. (Emergency Locater Transmitter) went off and we went up tracking it, thinking it was a downed plane or a downed pilot. Turned out it was set off by accident by a guy who lives on his sailboat and then when we got back, we stopped at the bar across from the airport and talked 'til two in the morning and then we went to my house and talked some more and..."
"And you talked so much you didn't have time to drink, right?"

"Whadaya mean? Of course we drank. That's the damn trouble, I think I drank a quart of Scotch, but it was all in the line of duty, all for a good cause. Hahahaha, hick..."

"I'll call back later. Get some sleep."

"No you don't. Why did you call? You having problems?"

"No Dad, I was gonna tell you I'm taking some courses at the University of New Mexico..."

"What the hell are you doing out there?"

"That's part of the training, Dad. We are stationed at Kirtland Air Force Base and part of the training is handled by NMU. It's great. The country is a bit like Peru, lots of hills and deserts and cactus and the air is great. You oughta come out and visit some time... Dad? Dad?" J.P. hollered into the phone a few more times and finally hung up. "I guess he fell asleep again. I'll call him later at the office. That old man really knows how to tie one on, but he's having a great time and that's what counts."

To J.P. it seemed that all he ever did was study and train, train and study.

From Albuquerque, Kirtland and the University, they proceeded to Yuma, Arizona again, this time to practice free-fall.

Freefalling had a great advantage. They got there faster. To the ground that is. From 20,000 feet, the human body needs to pass through thin air and temperatures of minus 30 degrees Fahrenheit in one hell of a hurry or not survive.

Passing through 10,000 feet, he learned to pull the ripcord and open his chute that deployed with a jerk and nearly cut his legs off, right at the crotch. From that altitude, J.P. could steer his floating canopy to a landing point and touch down within a foot of his pre-determined target.

The thrills just didn't end. He was having so much fun and was kept at the pinnacle of his endurance to the extent that he was on a continuous high. As far as Juan Pedro was concerned, he lived the ultimate life.

It would take three full years before he would be qualified as

Para Jumper and before he would jump into a war zone and see real action. But…, time flew by so fast, that it seemed to him like all that would take place tomorrow. Next week. Next month maybe. Anyway, sometime soon.

When someone in the upper echelon noticed that he was bi-lingual, J.P. went through a special course, back in Albuquerque at the University of New Mexico. The possibility of jumping into enemy territory where the bad guys spoke Spanish seemed remote, but whispers went around the class that jumping into the coke fields of Colombia might be a possibility. The young Peruvian American couldn't care less. As long as he could be in the middle of the action.

Here's where he met what he thought was, 'the love of his life', Marguerita Lopez, known as Margie. She attended one of his Spanish classes and they shared a lunch table in the cafeteria. The girl was born in Columbus, New Mexico, right along the Mexican border where both of her parents held steady jobs and didn't move all over the country as many of the farm workers did. Her papa was an auto mechanic and her mother worked at the local hotel, first as a cleaning woman, then as supervisor and after twenty two years as assistant hotel manager. It had provided Margie with a stable background and a firm Catholic upbringing.

After a few lunch dates on campus, J.P. got up the nerve to ask her out and she obliged by picking him up in her little Chevy sedan. She knew the town, where to eat good Mexican food and where to find a club with some good Latin rhythms. He wasn't much of a dancer, but he was a quick learner and they had a ball. Too bad, both of them had early classes so the evening was cut short. The goodbye kiss in the car held a lot of promise. Margie hadn't dated much, but she really liked this boy.

Of course, the military intervened again and after completing the course at NMU. J.P. was ordered to Patrick Air Force Base in Florida. That would become his permanent assignment for now. *For now* meant he might be there for three years if there were no major catastrophes anywhere in the world.

For Margie it was a real bummer. She had taken J.P. home to her family and they were welcomed with open arms. Her parents had worried about their beautiful daughter because she never seemed to have time for dates or boyfriends. This was her real first crush in life. They liked the young man with the Italian name and the Peruvian accent. J.P. was equally impressed with the Mexican family, their neat little home in Columbus and their devotion to their Catholic religion. He felt right at home.

Their dating became more regular and before long they spent all their time together. J.P. moved in with his Latin beauty and soon, they did everything together. Studying was the hardest part, because when they were sitting at opposite sides of the table, they still could play footsies under the table and that would lead to giggling, kissing and invariably they were in bed together and studies had to be resumed in the middle of the night. For both of them, it was the time of their lives.

When J.P. had to return to Yuma before departing for Patrick, Margie drove him all the way to the Marine base in Arizona and they spent one last night together in a little motel room and they cried more than they slept.

"Juan, as soon as I finish my courses, I'm coming to you in Florida, I promise."

"Yeah, you can continue your schooling at one of the nearby colleges. I'll find out what school offers the best courses and that way your parents will know that you're not quitting. You'll just be getting your degree from a different state, that's all. They gotta appreciate that, right?" He hugged her tightly. "Then we'll find a nice place to live. I'll make Sergeant and there is some nice base housing right along the Atlantic Ocean and I'm sure I'll be eligible for that. And my dad can fly in and get to meet you too. You'll love him, I'm sure."

She responded by kissing his forehead, his eyes, his nose and finally his lips until they collapsed on the bed again.

At the gate, at 5 AM, they clung to each other one last time and he was gone. A proud airman marching onto a Marine compound. She stared until he was out of sight and started the lonesome trip back through endless deserts in Arizona and New Mexico.

J.P walked in a daze. He had never been so deeply in love before and even though he knew that it was only a temporary separation, he was absolutely broken hearted. But... duty came first. He understood that.

Chapter Sixteen

From Daytona to Patrick and Back

Summer of 2001

Patrick Air Force Base, Florida.

"Yousef, mi amigo, mi hermano, cómo estás?" J.P. gave his old buddy a bear hug and grabbed his hand to lead him into his apartment. It was part of an attractive little duplex between highway A1A and the Atlantic Ocean. The two *brothers* hadn't seen one another for a year, but the affection and love between them hadn't diminished for a second.

"You're lookin' good, man." Yousef switched to English and smiled from ear to ear when he realized that his buddy had matured considerably and that his body had really developed. The T-Shirt read **PARA + RESCUE,** his biceps and his chest were very muscular and his neck had expanded by at least two inches. "You must have been really workin' out, man. How much do you weigh now?"

"A hundred seventy and all muscles, boy. The Air Force will do that to ya. We work out and jog five miles every day. They keep us in tiptop shape. What'll you have? I have Corona and Bud. Take your pick."

"I'll have the Corona, I'm not driving back today."

"Good man, good man. You're looking older, but that'll attract more mature women, right?" J.P. opened a couple of Coronas and forced a piece of lime down each neck.

"Yeah, but at my school, there are a lot more men than women, so the competition is greater, but I'm okay. I have a couple of girls I date on occasion, but I'm too involved in my studies and flying, so when I don't show up for a couple of weeks they find themselves other boyfriends. I don't care, I got plenty of time."

"Let's sit in the sun on my porch. Don't you love it here?"

They took their cool ones outside where a twelve foot square concrete slab was enclosed on two sides by a palisade fence. J.P. had installed several planters with tropical flowers and several cacti, so it gave the scene a very distinct Florida atmosphere. When they were stretched out comfortably in their chaise-lounges, J.P. picked up the thread of their conversation again.

"Thinking of girls, do you still hear from Miss Piggy?"

"Hahaha, Miss Piggy?" Yousef thought it was funny. " No, she got married a couple of years ago, right out of high school. I think she was pregnant already."

"Madre mia! How old was she? Seventeen?"

"Yeah, barely. Couldn't wait for sex, I guess."

"Did you ever see her again?"

"No, we talked about it all the time, but she never came down to Dade City and I never went up to North Carolina. I guess her parents had something to do with that. They didn't like Miss Piggy hanging out with foreigners, especially not Muslims. That's okay. I got over it, although when I was fourteen, I was so madly in love, I could hardly sleep." He took a long swig of beer and asked, "How about you? Anyone special in your life?"

"You won't believe this." J.P. stopped and leaned closer. "I'm thinking about getting married."

Yousef shot upright. "You're kidding! Married? Why and to whom?"

"To a girl, of course, hahahaha. A real girl. Let me tell you, she's a real woman."

"Wow!" Yousef was flabbergasted. "Who is she and where did you meet her"

"Her name is Marguerita, but she goes by Margie and I met her at the University of New Mexico in an advanced Spanish class."

"Spanish? You already know Spanish, so what...?"

"The Air Force wanted me to perfect my grammar and diction, so I'll be able to converse with people other than the uneducated of the mountains of Peru."

"Well, what about the girl, what's she like? Do you have any picture?"

"Sure." J.P. jumped up and disappeared inside the house. He appeared a minute later with a big photo album.

For the next hour and two more beers, Yousef listened to J.P. jubilantly explaining each picture. Margie in many different poses, including a bikini shot and several pictures of the neat little adobe house in Columbus, New Mexico.

"So when are you getting married and where?" The Moroccan brother shared in the glow that J.P. radiated.

"When? I don't know yet. I haven't asked her yet."

"You haven't asked her yet? How do you know she'll say yes?"

"Oh, she will. She will. We're very much in love and I wanna talk to her parents first, because they will probably want her to finish college first. She's gonna be a Spanish teacher, but she can finish her degree right here after we're married and she's gonna come anyway after the semester and I think her parents would rather see her married than living with someone, what do you think?"

"I think you may be right and I'm so happy for you. When do I meet her?" Yousef smiled from ear to ear at the enthusiasm of his brother.

"She's flying in after her final exams for the semester and she may just stay and start school here. That's the plan anyway."

"Wow! Wow again! My little brother Juan Pedro is gonna be a married man. Whadaya know?"

"Ain't it great. I'll let you talk to her in a little while. There's a two hour time difference, so I always call at six our time after I get off from work and by four, her time, she's always back from class. It's a good thing I have unlimited long distance calling. I would go broke otherwise."

"Thinking about broke. Are you gonna be able to support a wife and family when…?"

J.P. interrupted, "I just made Sergeant. I get housing allowance and I get extra pay for being a Para Jumper, so we won't be rich, but we'll hack it. I still drive the same little pick-up truck that Sean gave me for my sixteenth birthday and I keep it in good shape. Every so often, Sean sends me money to buy tires or do some repair. But you saw it out front. It still looks grand, doesn't it?"

"Sure does. Did you say Sean sends you money? Not Emil?"

"No, Dad always offers to send me more money, but I always tell him I don't need it. He set up a checking account for me when I started FSU, and he could easily deposit more in it, but I keep telling him, 'I'm fine Dad' and that's true. I watch my pennies very carefully."

"Does he know about your wedding plans?"

"No, not yet, but he's flying in Sunday after next. He's flying into Merritt Island and after I have told him and calmed him down, we'll meet up with you somewhere and we'll party."

"That sounds great. I'm ready and I'm anxious to see how he'll react."

"You just wait till he meets Margie and her family. He'll go crazy over her. I know it. I know it. He'll love her at first sight, just like I did. You'll see, Joe, you'll see. We'll probably fly out all the way to New Mexico in his plane. He's got a new plane by the way. Not new, really, but another one. A Beech Bonanza. Real neat and real fast. I think he can cruise two hundred plus."

"Jeez, he must be doing all right."

"Oh yeah, the restaurant and the marina are doing great, business-wise and he got involved in a dredging company as well. He's doing okay. That man is a workaholic but takes time to party and live a little at the same time. Great guy." He leaned over and put his hand on Yousef's arm. "I'm a lucky bastard, having him for a Dad." His eyes clouded over a little. "As a matter of fact, we're both lucky bastards, aren't we?"

"We sure are. You know, we sure are."

The phone rang and after a half hour phone conversation, during which Yousef got to talk to Margie for two minutes, J.P, said, "Let's go eat. We'll eat at the club and I'll show you around the base. It's a beautiful facility. We'll take my truck. Come on."

"Let me hit the potty first. I have a gallon of beer to get rid of."

"Okay!"

Yousef was duly impressed with the field. Patrick Air Force Base is located on one of Florida's prime stretches of Real Estate, right on the Atlantic Ocean. Because of the proximity to the Kennedy Space Center, the base was intimately involved with all the rocket launches, ready for support and rescue within seconds. The young flight student had never seen so many different planes together on one field. Transports, bombers and fighters lined the field for miles and support buildings and hangars appeared to be the size of a small city. He felt a pang in his heart when he realized, he might never fly one of those supersonic fighters, but he knew he'd fly some of the sleek corporate jets one day. Just another year and he would transition to the Army and they had a multitude of aircraft available as well. He couldn't wait.

Dinner in the mess hall was outstanding and he was surprised to see that officers and NCO's shared the same dining facility. J.P couldn't tell him when the change came in, but he knew that he could use the dining room from the moment he made sergeant. It sure made him feel good.

The food was great and both boys ate like wolves. From the mess hall, they drove to the N.C.O. Club and again Yousef was surprised at the fancy layout of the place. It was more impressive than any nightclub he'd been in.

"Don't lay eyes on any of the girls in here," J.P. warned. "they all belong to guys that are present, so there's no one here that's available. Just keep your eyeballs caged."

His brother obeyed reluctantly, although there were several attractive women in the place, they were all out-of-bounds.

Just two beers and some handshaking with other airmen and they were off.

"Tomorrow we get out early and I'm gonna teach you how to surf. Okay?"

"Okay, boy. Okay!"

Chapter Seventeen

9/11/2001

CIA Headquarters Washington, D.C.

"Mister Director!!!!! Sir!!!! Mister Director... Turn on your TV! A plane hit the Twin Towers... Oh, my God!!! Another one... Oh, my God... We're under attack... We may be next... I'm hitting the basement...."

Mary Ellis, the director's personal secretary was in complete hysterics. With a swift dash, she was out of the office, heading for the stairs, remembering not to use the elevators in case of fire or emergency... "Oh, my God! Oh, dear God!"

The director was beside himself. "Those bastards... Those lousy bastards..." He picked up the phone again... "Mary... MARY!!!! Damn...," He pushed another button while watching the repeated sequences on his big screen TV. "Kenneth? You there? Are you watching New York? Those bastards!!!! Where's the President?... Where?... Get him up in the air... Fast!"

The fifty-four year old Taylor pushed another button while running his fingers across his greying skull. "Gavin? Who's this?... Where's Gavin? In the bathroom?... Get his ass in here. I want every goddamn Muslim who's taking flying lessons arrested. Now! You hear?... Now!!" He slammed down the phone.

Fort Bragg. Army Intelligence Headquarters.

"Georgia? This is Bongers... Are you watching TV?... Turn it on... any channel, any news channel... You better believe it. I'm about twenty minutes out. Get Joe Mohammad on the phone. He's at Embry-Riddle... Yeah... and have him call me immediately on my cell... Yes, yes! This number... Now."

The colonel was about fifteen miles from the base and stepped on the gas, while putting his red flashing light on top of his car.

"Those bastards... They pulled it off..." He listened to his radio while speeding down the road. "Another one? The pentagon? Great Scott... what's next?" He was talking to himself as he expertly raced by other automobiles on the four lane highway.

His phone rang. The intelligence officer pushed the overhead button, "Bongers... Yeah Joe... Have you watched TV?... You slept?... Listen... Do you still have your Vespa? It's not a Vespa? I don't care what the hell it is... it's a scooter, right? Get on it immediately and head for Dade City... Now! don't speed... don't get arrested... get to Dade City right now and hide out. I'll be there later. I'll fly into Zephyrhills within a few hours and pick you up... Just do it before the Feds arrest you. I have different plans for you. Do it now! NOW!" He shouted the last word as he disconnected.

While driving like a maniac, he pushed another button, "Georgia... I know, it's terrible, I know... Quit sobbing... Have an airplane ready for me in ten minutes... I'm driving directly to the tower... No prop plane... The fastest we've got. Ten minutes.!"

He'd had a pleasant breakfast meeting with an FBI officer who tried to convince him that he should join their force when he retired. "I love the Army," he had told the Fed, "but after twenty-five years, I could stand being home more often, so I'll keep it under advisement." Not now, obviously. It seemed his country was at war and he was going to be in the midst of the action.

The soldier at the gate had stopped all traffic and Bongers turned on his siren while bypassing everyone on the grassy shoulder. For a minute, it appeared that nobody was allowed on the base, including the Intelligence Chief. He wasted two minutes, arguing with the Military Policeman and his immediate superior, a First Lieutenant with paratrooper's wings.

The base was in chaos. While trying to reach the airport, he was slowed down by trucks and troops, tanks and cars, military and civilian, criss-crossing all over the place, in seemingly the most unorganized fashion. A Grumman Gulfstream was warming up on the tarmac in front of the tower and with screeching tires, the Intel Chief slammed to a halt in front of the left wing.

"Park it!" he screamed at a mechanic as he took the steps two at the time.

"Destination, Sir?" The co-pilot asked as he hauled up the door that doubled as the stairs.

"Zephyrhills! Get the clearance as we taxi. Orders from Army Intelligence."

The swift little jet started rolling immediately as the pilot worked the radio while the co-pilot and Bruce strapped in. His phone rang the moment he sat down.

"Yes, Georgia, yes. I'm in it now. Thanks. Good work. Has D.C. called yet? Good. If they call, don't tell them where I am. Just say that you'll try to reach me. Get Captain George Holswood, General O'Doull's assistant to call me. Yes... MacDill. Thanks. Also have Major Van Trump call me in about thirty minutes... Yes... thirty... not before."

The speedy white jet had lined up on runway **1-2** and started its takeoff roll with roaring engines. Bongers always wondered if he should have gone into flying instead of intelligence whenever he felt the push against the backseat when a jet accelerated. It pumped his adrenaline every time.

Once they were at 25,000 feet, heading south, he called back. "What are you saying, Georgia? One hit the Pentagon and one is down in Pennsylvania somewhere? Wow!... No other plane hijackings so far? Where's the President?... Aloft?... That's good... They said that on the news, so now everybody knows, including the terrorists?... Are our fighters up?... We better report our position to MacDill and Tyndall before some supersonic jet gets on our tail. Can you find Mrs. Tracy Dixon's phone number in Dade City for me? Call me back."

The tall Army man undid his seatbelt and walked forward. The Captain at the controls looked over his shoulder with a question on his face. "Sir?"

"Are the defense fighters aware of our presence?"

"Yes Sir. We had a Navy F-18 sitting on our perch right there," he pointed over his left shoulder, "checking our destination and clearances. We're okay. We may see Air Force One in the distance."

"You're kidding?"

"No sir! Took off from Florida on his way to the Midwest."

"Well, at least he's safe. What a mess. Wonder what that plane... 'scuse me. My phone." He opened his cell. "Bongers," was all he said. "Yes Captain. Thanks for getting back to me so soon. Yes, yes... I'm a step ahead of you. Do you have a tanker leaving MacDill soon?... How soon?... about noon?... Reserve me two seats... urgent... I'll clear it with O'Doull. Thanks."

He had strolled back to his seat as he talked and just as he sat down, his phone rang again. "Mrs. Dixon's number... do you have a pen?"

"Just a sec. Go ahead... Thanks. Anyone call from CIA or FBI yet? Not yet? Good. Maybe they're blaming themselves for once. They'll start laying guilt later, I'm sure... Huh?... Nothing... Thanks."

"Mrs. Dixon? Colonel Bongers here... No, no..., I'm not in danger and neither is Joe, but I don't want you to worry. He's on his way to you on his scooter and when he gets there, would you please take him to Zephyrhills Airport...? To the FBO building... just ask for FBO at the gate. Tell them you're meeting a white Grumman Army Passenger jet and drop off Joe at the plane. I'll be there waiting. We need him... What's he done? Done?... Nothing, I need him and his linguistic skills, that's all. He may be of real help in this mess. Yes... Very fast... Thank you."

He got back up and walked to the cockpit again. This time he addressed the co-pilot. "Is there a way of making coffee on this thing without a stewardess?"

"I'll do it sir. We're on autopilot anyway and besides, the Captain knows the way. We should be there in an hour." He unbuckled and got up. He was surprisingly short and with his crew cut, he looked like he was seventeen years old, in spite of the first lieutenant bars on the collar of his flight suit.

With coffee at his side, Bongers relaxed a moment and went over all of his decisions in his mind. From the moment the radio program in his car had been interrupted by the first crash into the Twin Towers, his brain had been on fully automatic. He functioned well that way. The more pressure, the cooler he became. That had always been his strength. He had joined the Army in his father's footsteps while still in college and like his father he had gone into intelligence.

His dad had gotten started in Occupied Holland during World War Two, when he escaped from a labor camp as a teenager and hooked up with the underground. In late '44, during the GARDEN-MARKET (A Bridge Too Far) debacle, when the Allies were to take all the major bridges in Holland and that way, clear the way to Berlin, he had linked up with the American forces and received a field commission a year later while working in Germany as an interpreter with the Intelligence command, charged with the rounding up of Nazi criminals, especially SS officers. Being fluent in Dutch, German and English was a definite asset in that trade. In '47, he married his high school sweetheart and was transferred to the U.S., where his new wife joined him four months later.

Bruce was the first born of five kids and like his dad was totally dedicated to his country and his job. Totally! Four boys over a fourteen year period had him wavering though. He needed to be home with them more often because his wife had her hands full. Too full, sometimes.

His reverie was interrupted by his phone. "Bongers... Yeah,

yeah... didn't see it. I was on the road, but heard about it on the radio. Is the total still four?... No other planes missing or unaccounted for?... Well, maybe this is it... You're right,,, it's certainly enough. George, the reason for the tanker, I'm landing in Zephyrhills, picking up our young Moroccan and I got to get him out of the country fast... What?... Yeah, fast... If the CIA grabs him, they'll stall us for months... You know they will. Anyway, I'll land next at MacDill, can you have O'Doull meet me at the tower? I want to get his clearance and input. I wanna take this boy to Spain and lose him within the al-Qaeda organization and smuggle him into Afghanistan. We gotta pinpoint where Bin Laden is operating, because I'm sure he's behind all this. I need the general's approval, though. I know he's busy, but this is of the utmost urgency. I should be there at eleven, maybe eleven fifteen. I'll call you George, I'll call from downwind." He disconnected.

At Zephyrhills, they had to wait ten minutes for Mrs. Dixon who was not allowed to clear the gate. The Army Reserve had taken over guard duty at the field and they weren't about to let anybody on the airport. Colonel Bongers had to personally bum a ride to the gate to retrieve his pupil and it had taken at least three minutes to reassure Tracy Dixon, that Joe was going to be alright.

Minutes later they were winging their way south to the Air Force Base and they could already see it from twenty miles out. The tower made them circle the field while they verified the identities of the occupants with Fort Bragg. Clearance was obtained, although they did not know of the existence of a young Moroccan aboard.

After landing, two armed security officers came aboard, searched the plane, checked picture I.D.'s and allowed General O'Doull to come aboard. This was not what Bruce had in mind. He wanted to talk to his chief out of earshot of Joe Mohammad and the pilots.

"Follow me." The General waived Bongers off the plane and as they strolled slowly toward the tower, Bruce explained, "General, as I see it, we have to locate Bin Laden fast. This is our chance. Spain has a network of al-Qaeda militants, they've already made one attempt on the palace, but it didn't go well. One of their own was blown up and two were arrested. I'm going to propose to Spanish Security that they spring the two Iraqis they're holding and then with Joe's help, they'll escape to Iraq and on to Afghanistan. They'll trust him to be on their side because, because his Arabic is flawless. I had him study Farsi so he'll be believable. We gotta get him into Afghanistan and when he pinpoints Osama's location, our rockets can take the bastard out and we'll retrieve our boy. Sound good?"

"Is he willing to…?"

"I haven't discussed it with him yet, but by the time we reach Spain, I'll have him convinced. He feels he's a staunch American and I'm sure he'll do it. I'll be mentally with him every step of the way and he trusts me implicitly."

"I can't give you anything in writing at this point, but I'll get orders drawn later. Right now, everyone is so screwed up that they won't have time to think about you or your protégé, so go for it. A C-135 is waiting for you at hanger C. They have to file a flight plan yet, so get going. And… Bruce… good luck!'

"Oh sir, one thing… Please call my wife about 2PM and tell her I'm wrapped up in this thing and I'll call in a day or two. Can you?"

"Will do and again," shaking hands, "I hope you pull it off."

"Thank you, Sir, we will." While turning away he murmured to himself, "I sure as hell hope we will."

Chapter Eighteen

Patrick 9/11

Patrick Air Force Base. Space Coast, Florida
9:15 AM.

"Dad, Dad! Can you hear me? Turn on the TV." J.P. was screaming into the mouthpiece. "Any channel, any channel.... You got it?" Apparently, Emilio was still a little groggy.

"I got it. Oh my God! Good heavens! What's going on John? Where are you?"

"I'm in my room. Another one clobbered into the Pentagon. Yeah, Yeah! What's happening Dad? Are we at war?"

"We might as well be. I'll call Civil Air Patrol and get my plane ready. I may fly up and come and get you, but I may have to go on patrol."

"Don't count on it, Dad. I doubt if you'll get clearance to get off the ground. I'm sure by now they've scrambled fighters all over the country and you'd get shot down before you reach altitude."

"You may be right, son. I'll call CAP and I'll call you right back. Stay by your phone."

"I'm calling my unit, I may as well get in my uniform. We may get mobilized."

"Okay, but stand by for my call."

11:30 AM

After the country settled down somewhat and the apparent suicide missions totaled four and no other suspected planes were reported anywhere, John contacted Emil again. "Dad, we're in uniform and we're being flown to Hurlburt. I'll call you from there. It looks like we're going to draw arms and will be added to their security forces. It'll be at least a three hour trip and I have no choice. No personal vehicles, so my car stays here. At least I'll be close to home."

J.P. was proven correct. All commercial flights in North America were cancelled and all existing flights were terminated. Planes landed all over the globe and no new take-offs were allowed. Air traffic in North America came to a standstill. With the exception of fighters. F-14's, F-15's, F-16's and F-18's raced around the skies with permission to bring down any *suspect* airliners. The country seemed at war. At war with an unseen enemy. At least until a tape was played by the media, portraying a jubilant Osama Bin Laden.

Not knowing when or if another attack might be imminent, the entire security and military structures were in a '*High Alert*', near-panic mode. The tension could be felt on the C-130 as Colonel Milo Johnston spoke to the Reservists while the Air Force plane flew westward over the Gulf of Mexico..

"This is not a first. We've been attacked before and we've always come out victorious. We will this time as well. Unfortunately, we're not dealing with a visible foe and we're not sure how the Air Force is going to react. You may be sworn into the regular service immediately and receive a Non-Com rank and Non-Com pay. At this point, we just don't know. This whole tragedy may also be just a one time affair, but I doubt it. It was all too well orchestrated and executed. It must have been years in the planning and when people plan something that long and that thoroughly, it usually is just the first opening salvo. We can expect more. I may be inducted into the regular service again and that would change a lot of things for me, but I'm ready and I hope you are too."

He paused and turned forward to look at the cockpit. The pilots concentrated on their instruments and seemed oblivious to the proceedings behind them. The colonel was a trim good-looking man of about fifty-five and his cropped graying hair and the deep lines along his mouth gave him a sound military appearance. He had been a fighter pilot in Vietnam and had survived an F-4 crash and three weeks behind enemy lines. His injuries grounded him forever and that was his number one regret in life, not being able to fly fighters anymore.

Apparently satisfied with their progress, he turned back to his crew and looked at each one of them. "I see no fear in any of your faces and that is good, because you all remember the old saying; ' We have nothing to fear, but fear itself.' Who said that?"

Several hands went up, but someone in the back already shouted; "President Roosevelt."

"Which one?"

"F.D.R."

"Very good. Let's look at this as a great adventure and let's learn all we can."

Hurlburt Field, Florida Panhandle

"Attention!"

The Reservists snapped to attention in unison and stood stiff as boards until Brigadier-General Wilding reached the podium and ordered, "At ease. Sit."

The youngsters, their faces eager with anticipation sat down and faced the general. He looked quite young, maybe forty or forty-two. Dressed in desert camouflage, he was an imposing figure. Six-two, broad shoulders, handsome suntan and dark crew cut, his presence demanded respect. The reservists had been fed in the NCO Mess and were comfortable and duly impressed. Their adrenaline was pumping.

"Welcome to Special Ops." His voice boomed. He didn't need a microphone.

"You'll be our guests for a few days. You'll be armed, trained and be pressed into guard and security details. You will also be evaluated and assigned different duties, based on your qualifications. You're going to help us where you will do the most good. When I say 'US', I mean the country. We are in a very peculiar position. We have lost thousands of lives and we haven't fought anybody yet. In Normandy, we lost thousands within the first hour, but those were soldiers. In Pearl Harbor we lost thousands, but they were sailors. In this case we lost thousands, but they were civilians, innocent men and women. This is not our kind of war. This is a different type of enemy. These are cowards. They hide in caves. We can't see these animals. Yet we have to rout them out and destroy them before they destroy more of us. We need your help." He shouted at the top of lungs: "ARE YOU READY?"

"YES! YES!" They young airmen shouted in unison.

"When?"

"NOW! NOW!"

"Let's do it!"

J.P. was issued a desert outfit, boots and helmet, a 45 automatic, socks and underwear.

They were taken to an apartment building on base that was to be their home for the following weeks. There were four bunks to a room and after making beds and loading their footlockers, they were called into meetings again, but this time in smaller groups.

A Master Sergeant was in charge and he sat down on the edge of the table in front of the room.

"Men, we have no official orders about anything yet. I think the high command is still in disarray because this is a most unique situation, something we've never experienced before. We are taking action based upon what we anticipate and we'll be ready when the orders come. What we are preparing for is an invasion into Afghanistan. It may not be full fledged war and we may not do this alone. We may again have a NATO alliance as in Kosovo, but one way or the other we'll be ready. Our part of the mission will be Para-Rescue, getting downed pilots out of the war zone behind enemy lines and sometimes within our lines. One way or the other, we'll get them out. We have a great, experienced group of men and women ready for action, but we need more." He stopped and looked around the room. "You all finished your P.J. training, right?"

Everybody boomed. "Yes, sir!'

"We hope some of you will enlist in our permanent ranks right now and join our efforts. Some of you may be eligible for a Direct Commission. It's like a Field Commission. The Reserves use it more frequently than the Air Force, but these are unusual circumstances. You'd receive your regular pay to start, but because you already have three years of military training behind you, promotions will be coming fast. As of now, we have no official orders to do any of this, but when the orders come, Special Command will be prepared. Tomorrow you'll be receiving your shots, but most of you may want to call and inform your folks and we will honor and respect their decisions as well."

He stood up and added, "Chow will be served at 17:00, phones are available in your rooms and in the offices down here. Complete your calls as soon as possible and after chow, we'll narrow our ranks somewhat and lay down our plans. Any questions?"

The troops were mum.

"Dismissed."

When J.P. finally got through to Emil, his reaction was typical. He took charge.

"I'll be there within fifteen minutes."

"Dad, security is unbelievable. You may not even get on the base..."

"I'll be there." Click

It did take forty minutes, but because Emil had a base pass and knew many of the senior officers personally, he did get on.

"First I wanna listen to you son, what you gotta say and then I wanna hear from the brass, and then we'll talk about what's best for you…"

"But Dad, I don't want what's best for me. I wanna do what's best for the country! You gotta understand, Dad….."

"Hold it. Hold it." Emil raised his hand. "Let's slow down. Tell me what you're thinking."

"I'm thinking. I wanna be there when the shooting starts and when the airmen come down and need to be rescued. I wanna be there Dad. It's my job. It's my duty…" He broke into tears and grabbed his dad by the shoulders. "Dad, I gotta go, don't you understand?"

"Son, when I was your age, I volunteered for Naval Flight Training during the Korean conflict. I understand." He hugged him tight. "I understand, but I hate to see you go. Do you understand?"

Chapter Nineteen

Over The Atlantic

Aboard a USAF KC-135 tanker.
Nine/Eleven, 2001

    Colonel Bongers and young Yousef Mohammed made themselves as comfortable as one could be on a tanker and buckled in. It was the only military plane available, that would get the two of them over the Atlantic to Africa or Spain.
    "Sit back Joe and relax as best you can. It's going to be a long flight. How long, I don't know. We may be diverted a few times to fill up some other thirsty aircraft, but you probably will enjoy that part. You'll be able to sit in with the boom operator as he refuels the other planes. It's a sight to behold boy! Way up in the sky, six miles high, at a groundspeed of 600 miles per hour over this huge expanse of water, two dots on a radar screen will find one another and transfer thousands of pounds of fuel. It'll blow your mind when you see it."
    The colonel reached into his briefcase and said, "Now, into the more serious matter of this trip." He turned sideways and looked into the young man's deep dark eyes. "Joe, after I lay out the plans, give me an answer. You can back out and everything will return to normal. You go back to flight school, finish your degree, get your

commission and work directly with me in intelligence. You'll get checked out on a number of planes and live an exciting life. The only change there'll be is your name. Nobody, privately or the feds, is going to let you live in peace with the name Mohammed. We don't have confirmation yet, but I'm betting my pension on the fact that Mohammed Atta either flew one of the jetliners or organized the whole deal. Or both." He hesitated a moment.

"Joe, I've worked with the Secret Service, CIA and FBI before and I know how they think. If you were in Daytona right now, you might already have been arrested on suspicion…"

"But Sir, I didn't do anything…'

"Joe, I know that and you know that, but the first thing they do is round up suspects, guilty or not. You might be in the can for months, maybe years before you'd be cleared. Trust me. Like I said, I know their thinking. The second thing they do is lay the blame on someone or some other agency. Heads will roll. I wouldn't doubt it if they scream for impeachment of the President, even though the whole operation was organized during the previous administration. You bet that right now, my office is being bombarded with calls; 'Where the hell is Bongers?' Before the night is over someone will probably have found me guilty of mismanagement and dereliction of duty because they'll find that I've been working with you and General O'Doull's office about this very problem…" He raised his hand to keep the young Moroccan from interrupting. "Of course, we know and they know that all our intelligence was immediately turned over or shared with the other authorities, but for a while they'll conveniently overlook that. Like I said, I know how they work and how they think." Bongers summoned a young female Airman and asked, "Is there coffee available yet?"

"Sir, we're leveling off in five more minutes. How do you drink it?… Black with sugar?"… and turning to Joe with a broad smile, "And you Sir?"

"Do you have tea? Thanks… with sugar… thanks."

" I'd forgotten that it takes these things forever before they get to altitude when they're fully loaded. Back to my speech…Do you know Joe, in retrospect this whole affair with the planes may turn out to be a good thing"

"Sir? A good thing?"

"Yes, we have let our enemies infiltrate us as if America was a sieve. Just think about your own group. They were trying to recruit you for their terrorist acts on our own soil. This must have been going on for decades. How many Mid-Easterners with loads of money have walked into flight schools, plunked down hard cash and learned to fly without the immigration people or the CIA checking them out? You should see the stacks of reports, I've sent them. Thank God, I have copies, but my hands were tied. 'Bongers, your job is Army Intelligence, ours is civil. We'll handle this.' Can you believe that? It'll change now. How many innocent people had to die before they learned this lesson. Here comes the tea and coffee."

He stopped talking long enough to accept the refreshments and say thanks to the woman soldier, who smiled longer at Joe than protocol called for. The young man didn't mind at all and showed her all his pearly whites while his eyes sparkled.

Bruce drank carefully of the steaming brew and continued, "That's what irks me the most. Their willingness to sacrifice innocent women and children. It makes me sick. I probably inherited that from my father. After World War Two he pursued Nazi criminals with a vengeance. He knew that from Holland alone, 92,000 Jews were deported and killed, without any justification whatsoever. Finding the SSers and other Nazis, their Sicherheits Dienst and all those other lousy bastards that took pleasure in killing women and children. That was his goal and greatest satisfaction, catching them and bringing them to justice."

He took another sip. "Joe, that takes me to your mission. I don't know if you recall the hearings with Ollie North?"

"Who?"

"Lieutenant Colonel Oliver North, U.S. Marines?"

"No, I never..."

"That's right, that may have been before your time or you didn't pay much attention to that type of news. Anyway. Congress was trying to burn his ass for building a huge fence around his private property at government expense and he answered that he was trying to protect his family from Mid-Eastern Terrorists, especially one called Osama Bin-Laden who, according to Ollie, was out to destroy Israel and the United States. The panel nearly laughed him off the floor, including Senator Al Gore, because they had never heard that name and thought Ollie was making that up. Well, they're eating crow today, I'm sure. Bin-Laden has struck and maybe by now has already appeared on international television, bragging about his accomplishments. Joe... that man has to go. Period! He is part of an Arabian oil family and is reported to receive twelve million dollars a month from their business and he's willing to spend it all on destroying us. Most of that income comes from us, Americans, who keep sucking up their oil" He finished his coffee.

"He's gotta go, Joe, he's gotta go." Bruce finished talking and looked at his notes. "The problem is; that much money buys a lot of protection and a lot of weapons.

Worse... we don't know where he is. I've been on his trail for years and all I know is that he's surrounded by the Taliban in the Afghan Mountains. The freedom fighters, who received all their weapons from us when they were fighting Russia are now using our weapons against us to protect their 'God', their 'Prophet'. I'm not kidding. I'm not insulting Allah or Mohammed. They treat Bin-Laden as if he were the new Prophet and they're willing to die for him on demand. It's a situation like we've never experienced before. We're at war with an enemy that we can't see. It's most frustrating." He stopped again and looked Joe in the eyes from real close up. "Joe, here's where we need you. If I didn't have blond hair and blue eyes, I would go out there myself, but obviously, I wouldn't get very far. I love this country enough to go out there and put my life on the line, but I don't fit the picture. You do."

He grabbed the young man's hand. "Joe, again... you don't have to do this, but I hope you will and..."

"Colonel, I owe so much to the United States and its people, that I'll do anything you ask, even if it will cost me my life."

Bongers couldn't speak for a few moments and swallowed hard. Joe thought he even saw him wipe away a tear. The Intelligence Officer coughed a few times and continued; "Joe, you're going to grow a beard. Don't laugh…. A big, black, bushy beard." He had to laugh when he watched the young man rub his cheeks with a serious frown on his face. "You'll get a different name. You will first work in Spain and then you'll be recruited into al-Qaeda, a terrorist group and…"

"Al what?"

"Al-Qaeda. Do you know what that stands for?"

"It means *'base'*. That's it. What kind of base?"

"I don't know for sure either. Anyway, they bonded with the Taliban in Afghanistan. You'll be introduced to a few new languages and dialects. You are not to let on that you know any other language than Arabic and Spanish. It's going to be difficult sometimes when you understand what's being said, but you can't react to it. You gotta play dumb. Believe me boy, that's not easy. I'm not kidding." He turned the hand loose and grinned. "You'll end up in Afghanistan by means of North Africa, Turkey and Syria. You'll be taught the use of many different weapons and they'll expect you to be ready to kill many infidels." He raised his hand again. "That's going to be the most difficult part. You may end up in situations where you're facing Allied, possibly American forces and be asked to shoot. Follow orders, just don't hit anyone without being too obvious. You gotta gain their confidence. You've gotta gain their trust. It's imperative if you're ever going to locate Bin-Laden. Now, it won't be up to you to kill him. You just pinpoint his position, get us the coordinates and we'll have a missile take him out. If at all possible, him and his whole rotten band. Are you still with us?"

"All the way!"

"Attaboy!"

"Don't say that around me!"

"Say what?"

"Atta … boy!"

"Hahahahaha! I see what you mean. Anyway, tonight we're going to spend the night in the Canary Islands and you'll meet a beautiful young woman. She's our operative. We'll do a lot of briefing and you'll leave with her for Spain in the morning. I have ways of contacting her, so pass on all information to her. You may not hear from me directly, maybe not for months, but I'll be with you every inch of the way, okay?'

"Okay, but Colonel, do you know what is the worst part about this whole affair?"

"No, tell me."

"I won't be flying for a long time."

"True, but for now, let's see if we can get invited to the cockpit and to the rear, so you can watch some of this action."

"Alright!"

Watching a formation of four little jetfighters fly up behind the tanker at 32,000 feet and one after another fly up to the *boom*, get connected and pull away after a few minutes, was the most exciting precision flying he had ever seen. The *boom* was a long pipe, about 20 feet, with little wings attached. The boom operator, lying flat on his belly, with earphones in his helmet and a microphone in front of his mouth, controlled the boom with a joystick, like a computer game. The plane would fly into position, below and behind the tanker and a little door popped open behind the cockpit. The separation between the planes was no more than ten feet and Joe held his breath each time one came up *"for a drink"*, hoping they wouldn't collide. Of course they didn't and after every one of them had quenched their thirst, they wiggled their wings, waving "goodbye".

He watched it three times on the way over and he would've done it a hundred times if it had worked out that way. During the lulls in the action, the boom operator let Joe lie in his position and *"fly"* the boom. He was literally on cloud nine, (or fifteen, or twenty)

And full of questions.

"How fast are they going? How fast are we going? How much fuel do they take? Will they be back? How long do these guys stay up there? Where can they land? Are they intercepting other planes?

Brothers, FOREVER!

Have they shot down any? What kinda missiles were they carrying?" His questions were endless and the young sergeant who operated the boom was the most patient teacher anyone could have asked for.

When he joined Bongers, back 'up top', he asked, "Sir, have you ever done that? No? Have you ever seen that?" His enthusiasm was endless.

Chapter Twenty

Canary Islands

Tenerife
Hotel De Comta
23:00 hrs. 9/11/01

"Joe, your room has been scanned for bugs and we haven't found any, so we're going to talk in here. Rina should join us shortly."
"Who?"

They had finished a late dinner in the hotel restaurant below after Bongers had obtained some civilian clothes. He hadn't even brought a change of underwear and being six-four made it difficult at that hour to find something that would fit him. The Air Force officer who had met them at the plane understood that the colonel couldn't appear in public in his uniform, because paparazzi were everywhere, and Bruce surely didn't want to be confronted by any of them, asking about the Twin Tower bombing.

Their late arrival didn't coincide with passenger planes coming in, so no reporters were hanging around the airport, but they were certainly visible in the hotel bar.

The pants were too big, but an oversized Hawaiian shirt covered them up pretty well. "It's a good thing our guys are picking me up again tomorrow," he grinned, knowing he'd leave again on a U.S. Air Force plane.

"Who? Rina of course. Sorry, I've only referred to her as the beautiful woman, but you'll know her as Rina. Spelled; 'R I N A'. She's in the hotel, but she's making sure she's keeping a low profile. She flew in earlier from Malaga with a companion, whom you'll meet later, but Rina is going to be your instructor, your fellow terrorist, your watchdog and your friend in Spain for the next couple of months. Don't look so startled. It may be just a few weeks, but it might well be three or four months."

"Who's gonna inform my folks and the Dixons?" Joe's voice quivered a little bit as he asked that question.

"I'll cover that part. Your parents must be very worried by now, because I'm sure the word has gone out all around the world and they may even worry that you were in on the nine/eleven plot. When they call your dorm, they'll learn nothing, but when they check with the Dixons, they'll know that you're alright. I'll follow through on all that. I can't call from here, but I'll call tomorrow from the Embassy in Las Palmas on the next island because their lines are secure." There was a quick rap, 'Tatata'. Bruce stopped and raised his hand.

"Here she is now. I'll get the door." He got up and answered her knock.

Without a greeting, he opened and closed the door and stepped aside in order to let a dark haired beauty slide by him. Slide was the word that came to mind when Joe watched her, because she moved with the grace of a ballerina dancer. She halted, waited for Bruce to latch the entrance and then embraced with three kisses on his cheeks.

"How are you Bruce?" She made it sound like 'bruise'.

"I'm fine, Rina, I'm fine. How are you? Come and meet Yousef."

Joe had risen from his chair and extended his hand. *"Mucho gusto, señora."*

"*Ah, muy bién, hablas español?*" ("Ah, great, you speak Spanish?")

"*Si, bastante.*" (Enough.)

"Very good you two," Bongers interrupted. "grab a seat. I can only offer you soft drinks or water, but..."

"But I brought *Filipe Segundo*. I don't know how well it mixes with sodas. What have you got?"

"You brought what?" Joe wasn't sure he understood her.

"Here!" She whipped out a square bottle from her canvas shoulder bag and showed him the label.

"What is it?"

"Some of Spain's best inexpensive Brandy. It goes well with coke. It's almost like a Cuba Libre, but do you touch alcohol at all?"

"I've had beer and wine, but I don't think I've ever had anything Cuban."

"Good. This will be a good start."

Bongers interrupted, "Rina, wait a minute. We aren't here to celebrate something, we're here to talk business, serious business."

"I know, I know, but at this hour your brain functions better with a little stimulation." She turned back to Joe, "Do you want to sip some straight to check the taste or shall I fix you a cocktail?"

"I'll try the cocktail."

She disappeared into the bathroom to find glasses and Joe's eyes followed her every inch of the way. She was indeed a beauty. About five foot five, olive skin, beautiful shiny black hair and an hourglass figure. She might be about thirty, but with a pair of white toreador pants and leather slippers, white silk blouse and a red bandana around her head, she looked like a teenager.

The colonel interrupted his thoughts, "Joe, I don't know why she wants this to appear like a continuous party, but these Spanish women have their own way of doing things and..."

Rina reappeared with plastic cups. "I'm not Spanish."

"You're not?"

"No, I was born in Spain, but my mother was Iranian and my father was Armenian. Hence my name."

"Rina is Armenian?" Bruce was surprised.

"Sure is. My full name is Virginia Esterina Shobabian, but I go by my middle name Esterina, or Rina."

"Okay, okay. Let's settle down, get focused and..."

"First a toast!"

"I wonder how many she's had already?" Joe asked himself. She seemed unusually bubbly.

She raised her glass and the men followed, "Here's to a successful mission."

"Here! Here!" Bongers sipped and Joe followed as he murmured, "I sure hope so."

She was absolutely sober, it turned out. For every question Bruce came up with, she had an answer without referring to a single note. She had to have a mind like a steel trap.

In fast order, the following was established: Joe was to fly to Malaga in the morning, tickets were provided.

"Quick work," The young Moroccan whispered..

From there he was to take the train to Cordoba, where he would report for work at a carpet warehouse. There he would receive his new identity and lodging instructions.

Rina took charge. "Ask for Señor Des Vasquez. He'll call you Juanito. Don't feel insulted. It's a good cover. It'll sound like an endearing abbreviation for Yousef. You'll work there for at least ten days and you'll be contacted by a young bearded man named Juan El Barbo and he'll invite you to a party or a meeting. Make sure that you refuse all alcoholic drinks. Absolutely refuse. Insist that it's against your religion, no matter who tempts you, including good looking women. They'll be testing you. Don't let on that you understand anything but Arabic and Spanish. By then, I'll have been in contact with you and we'll take it from there. The important thing is that you gain their confidence. If everything works right, you'll be inducted into a group at an out of town location by the name of *Los Conquistadores*. The man in charge is a real creep. An unscrupulous man, known as *El Condor*. He'll watch you like a hawk, he'll have you trailed and will check out your background. Make sure that you come across as a devout Moslem. Pray five times a day, even when no one is watching, attend all the services you can and grow your beard." She paused and sipped her Cuba Libre.

"Your excuse for having been in Spain is that you have a warrant outstanding in Tangier for attempted murder, because you slugged a man, who tried to rob you, but was really a Moroccan intelligence officer. You cracked his jaw and he broke his neck when he fell. He lives, but you're still wanted. How does that sound?"

"I better take boxing lessons. I don't know if I could convince anybody that I could pull this off." Joe had a very serious look on his face.

"Just don't talk too much. Talk *futbol*, soccer. Read the papers, remember scores and the names of stars. Choose a favorite team and learn all about them. All their past statistics and heroes. Act like that's your only interest in life. You'll be watched and once you're committed to their cause, you'll be tested. They'll assign you a lousy assignment, something that will definitely go against your grain and it might include killing innocent people. Don't look like that!" She held up her hand.

"We'll make sure that the attempt won't succeed. We'll have the authorities intervene before you pull a trigger, but make it look convincing. You may even be imprisoned. Don't worry, we'll spring you and that will bring you even higher up in their criminal circles. Quit looking so worried." Joe's face was all wrinkles.

"Bongers interrupted. "Joe, do you feel you're getting in over your head?"

The young Moroccan shook his head slowly... "Boy, oh boy..."

"Sleep on it, Joe. Tomorrow morning at seven, we'll go over this once more and if you're not 100% convinced that's what you wanna do, we'll call it off, okay?"

"Boy, oh boy..., this morning I was a happy flight student and now I'm a potential terrorist."

"No, no Joe. Now you're a potential undercover agent, poised to put a stop to terrorism at the highest level. Right now, you have the opportunity to perform the most important humanitarian job in the history of the world. Thousands of lives depend on you." He paused, took a deep breath and continued with emphasis, "Innocent lives, Joe. Women and children. Just think what some bastards did to you when you were eleven. Just…"

"I don't have to think till morning, Colonel. I told you I would do it. You can count on me."

"Okay, we'll meet at seven and decide. Let's turn in. Are you safe, Rina?"

She stood up, took off her red bandana and whipped a wide colorful scarf out of her bag and wrapped it around her waist. It was long enough that it hid her toreador pants and she looked like a different woman.

"I'll be fine. I always am, right Bruce?"

"See ya at seven."

"Buenas noches!"

Chapter Twenty-One

Moving to the Promised Land.

Hurlburt Field, Florida
Sept. 20, 2001

J.P. couldn't be more excited. They were really going to get into action. Everybody was packed and ready to go and then things changed. "Get into your civvies."

"Civvies? For what?"

"You're flying commercial. Change clothes, be packed and ready at 1600."

Sgt. J.P. Pagliari was astonished. Was the Air Force short of planes? Did they have to be flown into Afghanistan as tourists? Was this whole war scenario a big secret?

Might the United Nations object to military intervention by the U.S.? Whatever the reason, his unit was ready to travel at 1,600 and instead of a snappy looking squad of soldiers, they looked like tourists going on a pleasure cruise.

From Fort Walton Regional, the carrier took them to Baltimore-Washington-International, where they transferred to a British Airways 767 and lifted off for places unknown. They knew their final destination, but had no clue where the the next stopover would be. The plane was chock-full of young soldiers, but there were no outward signs what branch of the service they belonged to. The only thing that stood out was their very short haircut of what had to be marines. Some tried to sleep, but most of them were too wound up to even close their eyes.

J.P. relived his last phone conversation with Margie. She had cancelled her lease on her apartment and had not enrolled in fall classes at UNM. The young Latin beauty was all geared up to drive to Florida by herself or with J.P. if he could fly into Albuquerque to ride back with her. Nine-Eleven changed all that and both had cried their hearts out on the phone, especially after he told her he planned to marry her before the end of the year. She was inconsolable.

"I don't know when I'll be back. Probably three months. They'll rotate us every three or six months and…"

"So now you're saying six months!" She sobbed into the phone.

"No, honey, no! I don't know. This whole affair may only last a few weeks or a few years, we don't know. All we know is that the Air Force rotates their crews, so nobody stays away from home for too long a time at a stretch. I'll be back soon, I promise."

"Oh, J.P., I wish I could be there to hold your hand before you leave. I wish…, I wish…" she broke into tears again. It was heartbreaking.

Emil's goodbye was quite different. They sat at the bar at J.D. Rockers, the restaurant on the base and Dad and son spent thirty minutes talking, arguing and hugging.

"You mean to say, you planned to get married and never even told me about…"

"Dad, I was gonna have you meet her first and I know you would love her and you'd be more than enthused to give me your blessing, I…"

"If you're so sure about that, I want her address and the address of her parents, because I'm going over there to see for myself what you…"

"Great Dad. Would you really do that? That would be fantastic, so her parents can also find out what kind of a guy you are and..."

"You really want them to know that? Hahahaha! They may be in for a surprise."

"They'll love you Dad, I know they will."

"Well, if you love'em as much as you say you do, then I'm sure I'll love'em too. I'll look after them, son. I will. I just wish you had told me sooner. You're not to keep secrets from me like that. Is she pregnant?"

"Dad, how can you say that?" He jumped up and shouted.

"Come here son. Give me a hug. Stay safe. Vaya con Diós, son. May God be with you."

The young sergeant did sleep after all. He woke up when they were letting down into Lajes Air Facility on a Portuguese island in the Azores. A new crew came aboard, including some oriental looking stewardesses. There was very little time for some R & R, some walking, shopping, but before long they were back in their seats, winging their way farther eastward. Eight hours later, on the Isle of Crete, they were given an opportunity to shower, stretch their legs and walk around some. The flight crew was changed again. Apparently they were not allowed to fly more than eight hours.

Well, eight hours didn't do it because ten hours later the 767 descended onto the Ali Al Salem Air Base in Kuwait. From the air they could still see the many places where the Iraqis set fire to the oil wells during the Gulf War. The whole scene gave J.P. an eerie feeling. "We're going to be dealing with a weird kind of people. I hope I'm ready."

The base in Kuwait was a huge tent city and after being marched to their new quarters, the first thing they did, was get into their desert camouflage suits.

The temperature was still hot, but not unbearable.

"Enjoy the heat while you can." First Lieutenant George Grau told his squad. They were sitting in a sort of a briefing room, much like a grade school classroom.

"Pretty soon we'll be in the mountains of Afgha and you'll be shivering." He smiled as he looked at his team. They were all eager young men, ranging in age from twenty-one to thirty five. At twenty-six himself, he knew that some of the older Jumpers had more experience than he did and that maybe they should be in the lead of his squad, rather than himself. But..., that's the way the system works, he thought.

"We'll be here for three days and we'll receive our winter gear and supplies and be briefed on the situation up there with the bad guys. So far, it seems very confusing. During the Russian occupation, we supplied the Taliban with weapons and the CIA provided a lot of the training for their covert operations. Now, the roles seemed reversed. Now they're against us and all other *infidels* in the world. It's going to be difficult to identify the enemy sometimes, because they wear no uniform. They all look alike. A farmer with a plow may have an AK-47 under his robe. A truckload of workers may be armed with hand-held rockets. Most times we'll have to rely on satellite imagery and aerial photography. Anyway, we'll figure it out. The aircraft activity is not too heavy as yet, but they're arriving on the scene on a daily basis." He looked at each man, walked forward a few steps and continued. "Whatever..., we'll be in place in a few days and we'll be ready to rescue anyone or anything that goes down. Right?"

"You bet, Lieutenant!"

The grandson of a World War II bomber pilot of the same name smiled confidently. He had been with these guys for over a year and he knew what they could do. Like his grandfather, he had wanted to be a pilot, but he couldn't pass the physical because of his eyes, so he did the next best thing. He didn't fly the planes, he jumped out of them. Tall, at six foot two and blond like his ancestors, he was a good looking young man, who radiated confidence. Smart enough to know that some of his men knew more than he did, he had learned to use their expertise by putting them in command of certain operations and the results were always pleasing. Well, nearly always. On a rare occasion, actions would have to be repeated, but all in all, he felt he had one of the best teams in the force.

A C-130, filled to the brim with soldiers, lifted off three days later on their last leg to Bagram. The luxuries of the previous airline trip were soon forgotten, because there weren't any. Just canvas seats lining the sides of the aircraft.

From the air they had a preview of the rugged mountainous region they'd be working in. It didn't look too appealing and the farther they moved to the north and the east, the more uninviting it became.

"Let's hope nobody ejects," J.P. told his neighbor, another brand new sergeant. "it's gonna be a bitch to get in there with a chopper."

"We'll manage buddy. We'll manage. We always do, don't we?"

The young Peruvian American sighed. "I guess you're right. We always do."

At their destination, they were welcomed by some huts, tents and some fairly decent housing with electricity. Most of the buildings had been built by the Russians and their presence was evident everywhere. Anti-aircraft gun emplacements still ringed the field, but the guns didn't look like they had been fired in years and were really dilapidated. On one side of the field, a civilian operation seemed apparent and on the other side it was all military. U.S. military. Fighters, transports and 'copters were lined up in irregular rows and a beehive kind of activity was ongoing between the hangars and the runway. One long runway seemed to be handling all the incoming and outgoing activity and the roar of the departing jets was continuous.

ABLE squadron was housed in units 21 and 22, Lieutenant Grau's squad bunkered in the rear of twenty-two. Not too bad. At least the wind was not howling through the cracks and electric heaters were already in place for the upcoming cold nights.

The chow hall was not bad either and the food was nearly excellent.

"The Navy must be in charge of the grub." J.P. quipped, while he cut into a juicy New York Strip steak. "Have to tell my Dad about this. He'd be proud."

The days were filled with exercises and reconnaissance of the area. They didn't jump at all, but went everywhere by helicopter. There were a few Blackhawks, Pave Lows and CH 47's and apparently, more were on their way. Because the terrain varied so much, they practiced arriving at a jump site, disembarking quickly, rescuing a dummy downed pilot and getting out in minutes. That was when the territory was flat and accessible. In the steeper mountains, they would get out by roping down and descend to a so-called victim or climb up to one along the vertical slopes. Slings and pulleys would retrieve the whole team and the next day they'd repeat the entire exercise in a different scenario.

The squad was getting ready and could barely contain their eagerness. They were now regarded as a *Tier One Team*. J.P. slept well from sheer exhaustion. Lieutenant Grau was pleased.

Chapter Twenty Two

Cordoba

Carpetas Y Alfombras
Carpets and Rugs

Life was strange for Yousef. He worked mostly in the warehouse of a carpet store, did some deliveries and learned about many different kinds of carpets and tapestries. Persian, Armenian, Spanish and Algerian. He felt he could use that knowledge if he ever ended up in the carpet store, back in Morocco. That was always a possibility.

The work was boring, it didn't pay much and he missed school, flying and the camaraderie of the college campus. He lived in a dreary two room apartment and grew a beard. He didn't like his own appearance and he was dying for some communication from Bruce or Rina.

Rina's communication arrived with a bang. Literally. After eating some *tapas* (Spanish hors d'oeuvres) and drinking tea in a little local pub, he climbed in bed with a good Egyptian book. The written Arabic was different from what he was used to back home, but the story was intriguing. He hadn't made any friends. He didn't want to hang out in some club in order to meet girls, because his image should be Islamic and pure, so he read books and newspapers. Two weeks had gone by and the only information he could gather was from the headlines about New York. Osama had been identified and even bragged about his achievements on a tape. "What an animal!" Joe thought.

He was midway through the book, dying for a beer, because there was no air-conditioning in the room, when a knock on the door jolted him upright. He grabbed his pants... *"Quién habla?"* He called it out as if he answered a phone.

"Una amiga!" The answer was a bare whisper.

Joe zipped his trousers and unlocked the door. There she was, in all her glory! Rina, looking gorgeous.

"Amigo! Cómo estás?" (Friend, how are you?) She hugged him as if they had known one another for a hundred years. It took his breath away. She kicked the door closed with her heel and stepped in. There was no place to sit but the bed and one chair that was loaded with clothes, clean and dirty. She chose the bed.

"We have to be very quiet. No-one knows I'm here. You have neighbors who can hear us, no?"

"No, the man downstairs works at night and I think he's gone already."

"Good. Then we can speak Spanish. Is easier for me." She grabbed his hand and pulled him next to her on the bed. "Tomorrow after work, you go and eat at the Gallo de Oro, you know where it is? No?" Yousef shook his head. "It's on Calle de Aleman. Middle of the block. Easy to find. You eat. When a man with a white beard and a white jacket over black pants joins you at the table, you make room for him but don't talk. He'll finish and walk out. Wait five minutes, walk out too. Go west, follow the sun, two blocks, turn right on Avenida de Virginia and you'll see a blue Toyota van. Get in the back seat. That's it."

"What do I tell Fernando, my boss?"

"Nothing. Just walk away. He works for the CIA. He'll know."

"Wow!"

"Don't say that. That's too American. Don't say 'wow'. Say, ayayay, okay?"

"Don't you say 'okay!' Okay?"

"Muy bién." She grinned. "We have to be very careful." She twisted her position and pulled her long tan legs under her and looked Joe deep in his dark eyes. "I need to sleep here tonight. Is there room for two?"

"In the bed?"

"Of course, you dummy. In the bed. Yes or no?"

"Yes, yes, of course, of course." He was so flustered, he nearly stuttered. He didn't know what was expected from him. She was at least ten years older than he was and he wasn't sure what she had in mind. He didn't have to wait long.

"I brought some *Felipe Segundo* and some coke. Can you handle that?"

"Boy, can I?"

She handled the rest of the details. All through the night. He had an education like he never had before.

El Gallo de Oro, Bodega.
5:55 PM Wednesday

The *tapas* would have tasted better if they had been accompanied by some hearty red wine, but he had an image to project. A bearded man in a white jacket moved toward his table with a plate and glass in his hands and Yousef moved over a bit. The man put his food down, and started eating without giving Joe a glance. On the other hand, the young Moroccan glanced over from the corner of his eyes and noticed that the man was impeccably dressed. Expensive shoes, black trousers, cut just right, a sparklingly white sports jacket over a blue shirt and a white tie. It was hard to determine if he were Arab or Spanish, because his beard covered just about his entire face. "Arab." Joe concluded, because he drank tea with his tapas, which a Spaniard would never do.

The man ate at his leisure and wiped his hands and mouth on the *servillette* that appeared out of a side pocket. One last wipe of his mustache and he walked off. As he walked away he made a near elegant impression. His perfectly groomed hair and beard, his broad shoulders in the immaculate jacket and his military posture indicated a man of authority and class.

Joe timed five minutes, (he had no watch) and followed the man out the door as he had been instructed. When he reached the van and got in, the vehicle took off immediately and he felt a gun poking in his ribs. "Sit still and listen." The words were spoken in Arabic by a deep voice and at the same time, a kerchief was tied around his head from behind, rendering him sightless.

"We have traced your background and we think you're an imposter. We don't think your name is Yousef Ibrahim and we don't think you're from Algiers. We think you have been planted in our organization in order to undermine our objectives…"

"What organization?"

"Quiet!" The voice boomed. "I'm speaking!" The barrel of the pistol poked harder against his chest. "You listen. Do you know how to handle rifles and rockets?"

"No."

"No? You said no? You have not trained in Algiers with the Wild Eagles group?"

"No. What group?"

"I ask the questions, you just answer. Why are you in Cordoba? Why did you come to Spain?"

"My father died, our business went down. I have to earn money for my mother and her father, he's eighty-ni…"

"You lie!" Another poke with the pistol.

"I want to go to Germany and work, make much money and…"

"You lie! Why you work in Cordoba?"

"I save for train fare. I already have…"

"Your clothes are not from Algiers, your clothes are from Spain.."

"No, I got them in Cuesta, in Morocco, when I came through there, before I got on the ferry…"

"Why you lie all the time? You came into Algeciras from Tangier, not Cuesta. Why you lie?"

Yousef was starting to tremble, he was afraid he might say the wrong things.

"I don't lie. I came to Spain, was refused entrance and was sent back to Morocco, but this time to Tangiers. I got clearance from the Consul..."

"Which consul?"

"The Spanish Consul, Señor Javier de Agusto Vasquez."

"You know him?"

"No, I never met him, but I talked on the phone from downstairs..."

"Downstairs? Where?"

"From the consulate. His office is upstairs, I was down..."

"And he gave you permission on the phone? Why? Are you special?"

"Special? The girl who helped me thought so. I had..."

"Enough, enough! We'll put you to the test."

They drove in silence and Yousef could only determine from the setting sun that they were heading North most of the time and North-East some of the time. For a while, they drove through city streets, then on a major highway for about forty minutes and when the sun set, they were on a narrow country road, he could tell from the traffic zooming by, and then onto a dirt track. Bouncing around for about five minutes, the ride ended inside a barn and his blindfold was removed. It was a barn alright. Old horse wagons and plows lined the walls and two more vehicles were parked behind one another in the moldy building.

The atmosphere changed dramatically. Mr. WhiteJacket slid out of the car after Joe and extended his hand. "I'm El Condor. Welcome. Address me as Condor, Bién?" He added the last word in Spanish.

"Muy bién!" The young man sighed a deep sigh of relief.

It turned out they were in a big farmhouse in the foothills of the mountains. The kitchen had a huge wooden table in the center, surrounded by a dozen hand carved chairs.

"Expensive stuff." Joe said to himself, but he didn't have time to linger on the subject, because El Condor raised his hands and bellowed; "Attention Señores. This is José. He's from Algiers and is joining our cause. Teach him all you can without saying too much or asking too much. He'll be on our next mission. Let's eat and then we'll plan."

"Next mission?" Yousef, now *José*, wondered what that would entail.

Chapter Twenty-Three

Spain, September 29, 2001

"Colonel Bongers, this is Georgia, an urgent call came in for you and I couldn't transfer…"

"Urgent? From whom?"

"I don't know, Sir, but it was from overseas and I have the number here, I think it's Spain. It's a woman and she said it was very urgent, she'll only be there for five minutes."

"Call her back. I can't call there from my cell. I'll get off the road and find a landline. What's the number? Wait, I'm writing on my wrist. Go ahead."

"34…"

"That's Spain alright. Go ahead…"

Bongers was speeding south on I-95 on his way back from Washington D.C. and turned off at the first exit he came to and swung into the lot of a Days Inn. Two phone booths were right there in the lobby and he dialed 0 for the operator. It seemed to take forever to get an operator to understand how to process an emergency call from Army Intelligence to a location overseas, but when he got through, he was immediately greeted with hysterics.

"Bruce? Bruce… he's gone, I don't know where he is…"

"Slow down Rina…"

"I can't. I've tied up this phone now for twenty minutes and people are waiting and they look like they're ready to keel me. Yousef is gone..."

"Where can I reach you in a half hour, where you can sit and talk?"

"Half an hour? No! One hour? Yes! Call me at my cousin's number. I take a taxi. Here's the number..."

"Wait..., Okay, I'm writing..."

Bruce had hoped to have reached his office within an hour, but couldn't quite make it and stopped at a local police station in Smithfield, North Carolina where they offered him a private office and a secure line.

"*Quién habla?*" A pleasant female voice answered, not Rina's.

"Bruce, Rina please."

"*Bruise? Momentito.*" ("Bruce? Just a moment...) Silence, as if she had hung up the phone

"Bruise? I had to send her out of the room. She understands too much English."

"What happened, Rina?"

"I instructed him according to plan. He followed it to a tee, but the blue van never arrived at the Monastery. They took him somewhere else and I'm afraid he's with the Basque resistance fighters and that they'll use him to blow up police stations and city halls and things like that. When he gets caught or killed, who cares? He's not Basque, I'm afraid they'll be willing to sacrifice him and I don't know how to reach him and how to rescue him, Bruce..."

"Rina, have you talked to Leopold?"

"No, I don't know where he is."

"Can you stay at this number for a few hours, so I can get back to you?"

"No, it's eleven o'clock here. Call me here nine hours from now. I'll come and have breakfast with my cousin at eight. Okay? Ciao!" She hung up.

As soon as the intelligence chief walked into his office at Fort

Bragg, he addressed Lucy, "Get me Taylor at CIA, if he's not in get me Andrews." He kept right on going, stopping at his desk and picking up the phone while he undid his tie. "George, get in here!"

Major George Van Trump appeared within minutes. He saluted the sitting colonel and received a simple order; "Sit."

Bongers pulled a file from a desk drawer and looked up at the young Major, "George, I hope to get interrupted momentarily by a call from D.C., so bear with me. What do you know about "El Condor" and what have you got on him?"

"Well, he is a wealthy Basque, with shipping and warehouse interests and he's a staunch supporter of the independence of the Basque people. He made a lot of money playing Jai-alai, including in the U.S., mainly in Tampa and Ocala. He was quite good in his day, but has gained considerable weight. He maintains a condo in Madrid and a villa in Cadona Laredo off the Bay of Biscay. He's on his third marriage..."

"By George, George, you're a walking encyclopedia. What's he up to now?"

"Let me get my..."

"Here's my call... Get his file." Bruce picked up the phone as the major walked out to retrieve his intelligence data.

"Andrews? How are you Jack? Thanks for getting back with me so quick. I may need a favor. Let me rephrase that. I do need a favor. I have an Army boy undercover in Spain and he's lost. What can you tell me about *'El Condor'* and what he's up to?"

"Let me call you back in five minutes, or better yet, I'll have Gus Quintero call you, because he was in Barcelona on nine-eleven and he was in the middle of things. He can help you better than I can. Give me five minutes." He was gone.

George walked back in with a zippered plastic folder, marked; *"Top Secret, El C."*

"Colonel, the last we heard about him, was when he was questioned and released about that botched attempt on the Spanish Coast Guard Boat. They held him for four days, but had to let him go, because, all they had was suspicion."

"The attempt in San Sebastian?"

"Yep. That's the one. You see, one of his freighters was docked next to the cruiser and pulled away just a half hour before the explosion, which turned out to be perfectly legit. The dingy with the explosives came from a local fisherman and nothing could tie El C. in with the plot. The terrorists, two of them, were identified as Basque, but they really botched the operation. They blew a big hole in the water and the seawall and blew themselves to bits, but the Coast Guard boat had very little damage."

"Where did the Condor go after that?"

"He was seen in Malaga, again on business and in Cordoba, where he buys olives and olive oil. He may have a stake in those groves, we don't know."

"Damn!"

"Sir?"

"Cordoba? That's where I put him."

"Sir?"

'Remember our Moroccan Boy at Embry-Riddle? He must be in Condor's hands. What I'm afraid of, is that they may use him to blow up something some place and that the boy may go right up with it. Do you know, George, if they have a training camp within a hundred miles from there? Somewhere in the mountains?"

"They have used the old Monastery in the past, near…"

"No, that's the point. He never showed there. Is there any other hidden spot that you know of…? Here goes the phone.. Bongers here." As he pressed the phone to his ear, his look of concern turned to one of fright.

"Damn. You sure? What do you think? A bigger plot this time? Where? That doesn't help much…. But that's all you got at this time? .. Thanks." He hung up. Turning back to the major, "They lost him out of sight at the same time we did. That's frightening. I hope they didn't get wise to our boy and are using him as a sacrificial lamb. Damn!" He banged the table in frustration. "CIA is checking with all their agents and Spanish security and I don't think that's wise. The Basque sympathizers have infiltrated that whole rotten system and I wouldn't trust any of them anymore. Our boy was supposed to be in the hands of the Taliban and being readied for war in Afghanistan. He may be in the hands of the wrong group and he doesn't know it."

Rancho La Vaca Blanca

"José" was totally unaware of the anxiety he caused around the globe. He was introduced to assault rifles, pistols, hand grenades and handheld rockets and was enjoying it. The other fellows were mostly Spanish and with just one other exception, they all drank wine and beer. Yousef had the hardest time staying with tea and sodas, but he felt very strongly that he was being tested. As a devout Muslim, he would never let a drop of alcohol pass his lips and that was the image he had to project. Climbing the mountains, heavy loads and heat didn't bother him much. He was in top notch condition.

He nearly flunked one night, when he was offered money to send home to his mother. When they gave him dollars, he said, "What can my mother do with that?" and when they handed him an envelope, he started to write down his mom's address in Chefchauoen. He caught himself just in time and asked for stamps.

"Don't worry, we'll mail it."

He was sure that the envelope would be opened, his note would be read and the money might never leave Spain. He didn't care. His "*mom*" in Algiers didn't exist anyway.

After eight days, five of the team were loaded in a truck and started a long trek across country and ended at the foot of the Pyrenees, north of Barcelona. Up in a loft, a map was produced. It detailed the inner city below and the Gaudi Cathedral *Sagrada Familia* which had been under construction for forty years and was to become the most beautiful structure of the sort in the whole world. That was their target. They were to blow it up. *El Condor*, dressed in Army fatigues was conducting the briefing.

Yousef gasped, "I don't want to kill women and children. I want to fight soldiers, not women."

"You ass. They're all infidels and they'll all rot in hell anyway, whether you kill them or not!" It was the other Muslim, who spit the words at him.

"No, no, wait. Wait!" The white haired Basque interrupted. "We're blowing it up at night, when there are no visitors. We want these damn Spaniards to understand that we mean business. That we demand our freedom. Viva La Basque!"

"Let's kill some infidels while we can." The Muslim again.

"We may leave you here. You may blow the whole operation with your temper."

He pointed back at the map and detailed where every person would deposit their explosive package with its timer. They would be back in the loft before the building would blow and they could watch the proceedings from up here. Before dawn, they would split. By truck, by bike, on foot, hide out and eventually get back to Cordoba.

"Any questions? Viva La Basque."

At midnight, they piled back into the truck and started to back out of the yard onto the dirt road when all hell broke loose; "Halt! Raise your hands!"

Shots rang out, tires exploded and spotlights lit up the back of the truck. The driver tried to gun the engine, but ten bullets snapped his head in two and the truck chucked into the ditch. Yousef hit the floor and rolled under the wooden bench on the left and covered his ears.

Chapter Twenty-Four

Madrid

American Embassy
October 3, 2001

"Yes Sir, it's very important. Ask for Colonel Bruce Bongers, please. It's very important."

The assistant to the Ambassador was not accustomed to making phone calls for strange women without identification or clearances, but the woman had worked herself through bureaucratic channels from the receptionist out front, past assistant after assistant until she nearly got to talk to the Ambassador himself. That's where the buck stopped. He ordered Jack Lowell, his assistant to handle the situation, because the woman knew the direct number for Army Intelligence so she had to be legit.

Rina sat in an empty conference room, assured that the phone was a secure one and that it might ring any time. It did. She snapped it up.

"Bruce?"

"Just a moment."

"Bruce? Rina."

"Holy Moses, this must be important. You're in the Embassy? Does anyone know you? How'd you get a line?"

"That's not important. Joe is in jail. We gotta get him out."

"Where and how?"

"El Condor sent a team to Barcelona to blow up the new Cathedral…"

"Gaudi?"

"Yes and.."

"Good God, did they succ…"

"Leesen, please leesen. They got caught. Joe was not hurt. They thought he was Basque, but his accent betrayed him and he's held by the Guardia Civil outside of Barcelona. They may torture heem. We gotta get heem out."

"Who do you know in Barcelona?"

"I have a team on Ibiza…"

"The island? How long will it take them to get to you?"

"They'll take the hovercraft and I'll drive. We can meet tonight…"

"Do it. Give me the Ambassador."

That took a lot longer than Bruce had anticipated and when he did get to talk with him directly, he ran into more objections and negatives than he normally dealt with in a week, but a final statement got everything cleared up. "Sir, I'll have the White House verify the details within the half hour."

"The White House?"

"Yes, within the half hour."

Rina and her team met in the basement of the old Tavern *El Cuento de la Cuenta.*

A young civilian, about thirty, met them with a schematic of the Guardia Civil barracks and re-emphasized; "No killing. It's not necessary. Tasers only! Free everybody, not just our men, or I should say El Condor's men, even though they are really our enemies. Free every prisoner. Have them scatter. Create as much confusion as you can. Do not come back here and don't travel together. Scatter. *Vamonos!*" (let's go!)

The morning paper headlined: "A blatant attack on the *Carcel de Guardia*. (Prison of the Civil Guard) Dozens escaped. No casualties. The Inspector General suspects an inside job."

Bongers read it on the internet and had it translated for him.

"Nice job. Hope Rina's got him."

Rina indeed had him. Not the way Joe would have liked; in bed, but she had him. She was sitting across the table from him in the back room of a stevedoring company on the waterfront.

"You have to memorize this. You can not write anything down, so repeat after me: My name is José Gaspar DiSantangelo."

"Wasn't José Gaspar a pirate?"

"Doesn't matter. Just remember. You were born in Tormolinos on the Costa del Sol. Your dad worked in the arena with the bulls. Your mother was Moroccan, she went back after your father left her."

"What for?"

"Huh?"

"What did he leave her for?"

"He didn't wanna get trampled by a bull, so he left for Germany to find better work Very unfortunate. You were only sixteen. Remember all that, okay?"

"Okay."

"Tomorrow, you will help load the cruise ship Norwegian Fjord. On one of the trips aboard you will meet *Djongo,* an Indonesian chap with a clipboard. On the third trip, he'll lead you to a cabin and you stay. Your passport will be ready in a half hour. We're making you look younger. Just a mustache."

"Will the passport say José Gaspar DiSantangelo?"

"Of course. What do you think we are? Amateurs? You will work and live with the crew. You learn a little English. Don't let on that you understand it all. Djongo is also Islamic, so watch your beer. He'll watch over you. You will stop in many harbors. If the crew can go ashore, you go too. In Istanbul, you walk away from the dock, at least ten blocks. Take a taxi to number 110 Babylon Street. Make sure nobody sees you get in a taxi. Report to the basement apartment and see Mustafah. That's Mustafah with an h. He'll direct you from there. You'll be in the hands of the Taliban from there on in."

"The who? "

"The Taliban, the rebels that defeated the Russians with American help and American weapons. They now harbor Bin Laden and you'll be sent out there to fight the NATO forces that are trying to capture him."

"Oohlala!"

"Don't say that. That's French. Say *Ojala!* That's Spanish of Arabian descent. Now let's rehash all that. You can't afford to make a mistake."

Djongo turned out to be a stocky brown skinned man, who corrected José fast. "Those skinny guys over there are Filipinos, I'm Indonesian, from Celebes. Don't call me Filipino anymore, understand?"

"Yes Sir, I meant no …"

"I know, I know. Come. After we sail, I come get you and you work okay?"

"Bueno."

After spending five hours in a dark cabin with a narrow bed, Djongo appeared with black slacks, white shirt and a white apron. Because Joe had no watch and slept on and off, he had no idea of time, but the movement of the boat told him he was at sea and very hungry. His stomach seemed to slosh back and forth.

In the kitchen, he did what he had done for years in the Deli in Daytona, he cleaned and sliced cucumbers and tomatoes, washed beans and potatoes and disposed of empty cans. Lots of empty cans. The evening went fast and he ate well. After spending an hour in a crew room with mostly kitchen workers, he was called back to help prepare for the midnight snacks on the upper deck. Finally at 2:00 AM, he fell asleep on a bunk along with twenty other guys in the same room.

On Corsica, where he admired the scenery from the deck, while the tourists roamed all over the Island, he ate his heart out. But... by the time they pulled into Naples, he had been approached by a young Finnish girl named Trish, who worked in the kitchen as a dietician. She spoke Norwegian, Swedish, Danish and English, but very little Spanish. Joe avoided her as best he could, but she interpreted that as shyness. She kept coming on to him and talked him into going ashore to see the sights. They were only allowed four hours, but she promised it would be worthwhile. It was. From the harbor they could see Vesuvius and Capri in the distance and they snacked on some great Italian ice. He refused wine and beer although the temptation was horrendous. She started holding his hand but Joe had such mixed emotions, that he reacted very cool to her advances. On the one hand he would have gladly skipped into an alley and let her rape him, on the other hand he felt that she would only spell trouble if he gave in.

Back on board, she found ample opportunities to corner him, kiss him and fondle him, but it was nearly impossible to consummate their illegitimate love. Too many people around at all times and no privacy. On Sicily, she went ashore without him. He had to work, but on Malta, they were barely off the boat before she rented a room along the harbor and they finally went at it. Tenderly at first, then more and more passionate but with a very tender ending. They walked back to the ship hand in hand.

Djongo turned out to be a very understanding manager. He slipped Trish a key to an empty cabin and from there on in they slept together every night and instead of going ashore, they spent their free time in the *lost cabin*. Joe had really wanted to see Athens, but the Finnish blonde wanted only sex and more sex. The young Moroccan was eager to oblige and he wondered who had started the rumor that Latin ladies are hot. The Finns had it over anybody.

Too soon they docked in Istanbul and he had to engage Djongo in a scheme to get ashore without Trish. He was sent off with a team to load supplies and he simply walked away, slipped into a store, came out on the other side in a different street and rounded a dozen more corners before he called a taxi.

In spite of his confidence, he shivered. He didn't feel good about the whole affair anymore. As the vehicle sped along, he closed his eyes and asked Allah for strength.

Chapter Twenty-Five

Davis-Monthan Air Force Base

Tucson, October 2001

Captain Susie Overton was all excited. She was scheduled to deploy to Kabul, Afghanistan with her entire squadron, in support of the troops. The international war on al-Qaeda and the Taliban was getting in high gear and that was part of the reason for her excitement. The "International" involvement that is.

During the action against Kosovo, she was not involved in the actual fighting. Her squadron was, very much so. Susie was not. She was brand new to the squadron and helped with much of the planning and the logistics on the ground, while her squadron mates flew seven and eight hour sorties, nearly every day. By the time she was fully qualified to get in the fray of the fighting, the conflict ended and she never fired the first round. This time it would be different. This time she would be in the midst of the action and she was looking forward to it.

Another reason for her excitement was the fact that she had learned that a contingent of the Royal Netherlands Air Force was to be stationed in Uzbekistan with two flights of F-16's. That in itself didn't mean much, but the fact that their commander would be Henk Ten Bruin, was plenty reason for exuberance.

When Henk was still a captain and Susie a first lieutenant stationed in Aviano, Italy, they had started a passionate love affair. The fact that Henk was married had not bothered either one of them, but when he returned to the Netherlands after the conflict, she was left with a serious pain in her heart. He went back to his family and she went back to an empty apartment in Tucson.

They had e-mailed on occasion, but otherwise had no contact whatsoever, especially not physical contact and in her imagination, she felt they might get back together, now that they would only be one country apart. By jet, maybe one hour.

They prepared for a long trip. Mid-air refueling would be cumbersome with 24 planes, but that was the way things were done nowadays. On the way to McGuire AFB, New Jersey, they'd land twice for refueling, then rest overnight in Jersey. The next morning, the squadron would cross the Atlantic, accompanied by a tanker to Lajes Air Base in the Azores. There they would spend two weeks in training and briefings before flying to Kuwait and finally, Kabul, Afghanistan. It would be winter by the time they'd land in that combat zone. She didn't cherish the thought of cold weather flying, but it was better than not flying at all.

At five foot three, blond and blue eyed, she was a real looker and it surprised many of her old friends that she was still single. With the looks and the sense of humor of a Goldie Hawn, she was thought to be the life of any party and the Belle of the Ball, but she didn't date much. 'They're all too young or married', was her excuse.

Her call-sign was *'Groper'* and she had earned that name in UPT, (pilot-training) when at an Officers Club Dance, she was spotted dancing rather close with one of the jocks, while both her hands were in the back pockets of her dance partner's jeans. The name stuck.

Her first choice in flight school had been "Fighters", but flying the A-10 Warthog was as close to fighter flying as she could get. True, she couldn't chase other fighters across the skies, she couldn't kick in the afterburner and go straight up like *a homesick angel,* but she could barrel down from 10,000 feet and put a tank out of business with her Gatling gun or her rockets. The "Hog" was a thrill a minute and she loved flying it with all her heart.

Within two weeks, the squadron would be off and within two months they'd be in the midst of the action. She couldn't wait.

The A-10 Warthog had been nicknamed the "Tank-killer", although the AC-130 claimed the same fame with it's 110 Howitzer sticking out of the side of the fuselage. In Desert Storm, the HOG had picked off many of Saddam's tanks by rolling in at twenty thousand feet, putting *the pip* on the target and pulling the trigger on the *Gatling gun*. The 30 millimeter bullets would tear right through the upper structure of the Russian built tanks and explode and they'd set the armored vehicle on fire within seconds. Coming in from that altitude at a high angle meant rolling the plane on it's back and pulling it down into a vertical dive onto the target. After firing a fast round, a six "G" pull-out bottomed out at ten thousand and within seconds the twin engines would push them back up to 20,000. By attacking that way, they presented a small and fast moving target for the *SAM* missiles that were eager to pick them out of the sky.

In Afghanistan the tactics would be different. For one, there were no *SAMS* reported. Second, the terrain was very mountainous. Third, the targets would be different, probably buildings, troop formations and small vehicles. Clouds in between the mountain peaks might also become a problem, so they might have to use entirely new tactics. All that had to be learned and practiced.

The squadron flew mission after training mission, bombing and strafing at the *Goldwater Range* near Yuma, Arizona. Susie was having a ball. There was fierce competition amongst the pilots and the males on the team weren't about to be out-shot by the only female in their group. It kept her on her toes.

Hours and hours at the controls of a single seat fighter was an exercise in endurance. Staying alert in formation for eight hours was a near super human effort. Yet, the pilots of the A-10 squadron had done it time and time again during the Kosovo conflict. Taking off from Italy, mid-air refueling over the Adriatic Sea, then combat over Kosovo and Serbia for two hours, again refueling over the water and back to base in Italy.

Although the hours in a cramped cockpit were grueling, the men loved their missions and the support they provided for the ground troops was immeasurable.

THREE WEEKS LATER.

After leaving the U.S., the overnight in the Azores was a welcome break and the two weeks gave them a chance to stretch their legs and get familiarized with the mission ahead.

On the next leg, they lucked out. There was a problem getting cleared into Kuwait, so they landed on Cypress and got two days to tour that exotic island. From there on in it was all downhill. Kuwait was a nice base, but very basic. No luxuries at all. Bagram was worse. It was a disaster area. Remnants of Russian planes and gun emplacements were all over the field and their quarters could barely be called, "huts". A truck shuttled them back and forth from the planes to their bunks and food was served in a tent that resembled a MASH operating room.

Flying immediately became a *winter* exercise. Snow had already fallen and the clouds covered the tops of the mountains most of the time. Actual combat missions were rare, because intelligence had a hard time determining who was what? *A cart with a few men?* Farmers or Taliban? *A load of timber in an old pick-up truck or cases of handheld rockets?* The orders were: "Don't shoot or bomb unless an enemy target has been definitely identified."

Most days, they flew without bombs, because if they didn't release them over a target, they'd have to bring them back and landing with live bombs could prove to be bad for their health. A hard landing might jar one loose and explode right under their wing. Every so often, the A-10's would send some rockets into a cave and sometimes they had the satisfaction of witnessing a huge explosion, indicating they hit an ammo dump.

It was frustrating to know that most of the weaponry they were trying to destroy was American made and supplied to the Taliban when they were fighting the Russians.

Although there were no known SAM sites, it was disheartening to know that the handheld rockets could easily pick them off while flying low or coming in for landing.

When the weather allowed, most of the missions would take them to the Bora-Bora region near Pakistan, where supposedly, the al-Qaeda training camps were located and where Osama Bin Laden was reported to be living in a cave. The mountain peaks to the north reached as high as 12,000 feet and most of the time they were hidden in the clouds, so the flying was done from one valley to the next.

Susie had pumped rockets into the many caves, but no one was sure what the effectiveness was or if they were merely wasting time with empty holes in the mountains.

Four pilots and their planes stood on readiness alert at all times, in case an Army unit called for help and then the planes could be up in five minutes, trying to get the ground troops out of a tight spot. It happened at least every other day and some with questionable result. The local press always accused the Allies of attacking innocent civilians and Army intelligence kept insisting that it wasn't true. It was very frustrating for the pilots, because invariably they had to report in detail what they observed and how they had reacted. Half the time, it seemed they were on trial and had to defend their actions and their judgment. It wasn't like fighting a regular war at all. The Taliban wore no specific uniforms and dressed just like the farmers or laborers and sometimes the pilots could report for sure that they were the bad guys, when the figures on the ground fired at them. Most of the time that was too damn close or even too late.

The hunt for Osama was the prime objective and American Intelligence reported sightings and locations dozens of times, but he kept evading capture and brazenly appeared on TV again, claiming the Americans to be fools. Sometimes they were made to feel that way. With all its might, all the helicopters, the planes, the rockets and the tanks, the Allies could not report any significant progress, but they did rebuild a lot of schools and hospitals and tried to make life more comfortable for the average citizen. For the pilots, comfort was a foreign word.

Susie's hopes of flying to Uzbekistan to meet Henk were just that; hopes and dreams. She could never get permission to depart on her own in a HOG and fly north for an hour to meet a lover. By the same token, if the Dutchman flew down in an F-16, where could they meet? Holding hands across a wooden table in the mess hall? There was no privacy anywhere. She concentrated on flying and learning the local language. They had a choice of four native tongues, plus Farzi and Arabic and she chose Arabic because that language would be more universal. The excitement she had felt when she first heard about the mission had changed into a mood of boredom and gloom. There were no great achievements and no victory in sight. She longed for Arizona and the sun.

Chapter Twenty-Six

Road to Kabul

Istanbul, Turkey
October 2001

"Your job is to protect the Sheik." The bearded man, named Mustafah, wiped his forehead. It was hot and his turban must have been cumbersome. "That's your main task. The infidels will try everything in their power to obliterate him and our entire organization, but Allah is on our side and we will be victorious!" He raised his hand in a mock victory salute. "You will be trucked through Turkey and into Iran, where you will receive additional training and from there you'll be moved into Afghanistan. The exact location of the Sheiks' fortress is unknown to everyone but a few and your job will be to defend it against all intruders. We are teaching the world a lesson. Any questions?" His black eyes circled the room.

"Emir, you refer to the Sheik. Is he a new Prophet?" Yousef was one of the twelve recruits in the meeting room below a furniture store and he was careful not to ask too much.

"The man we refer to as the Sheik is like a Prophet. He has unusual wisdom and has Allah's guidance and blessing. He's Arabian, well educated and a true student of the Quran. He will lead us to victory over Israel and the United States, We have already shown them that we can reach their shores, by attacking their embassies in Africa and destroying the twin towers in New York. His name is Osama Bin Laden, but when you meet him you'll address him as the Sheik. Any other questions?"

Many other questions were asked by the assembled mercenaries. They were a mixture of Arabs, Lebanese, one more Moroccan, Algerians, Egyptians and Iraqis. Yousef absorbed as much of the information as he could, but worried at the same time about how he would get it out to Bongers or Rina. He had no notion as to whom to contact and how, or if someone would contact him, like Rina did back in Cordoba.

Cordoba? It seemed to him that it was years ago that he was in Cordoba and just a week before that, he was happily learning to fly in Daytona. In reality it had only been five weeks. It boggled his mind to think about how much he had experienced and how many different places he had been in such a short time.

The bearded Emir spoke up again. He was a short chubby man, whose entire face seemed to consist of a big black beard. "Your families will receive much money. First of all on a monthly basis and in case of your death, they'll receive a large sum. You will have enough money in your pockets for all your needs, but you may not have time to spend it." Groans all around the room.

"Don't worry, Allah will reward you richly. You will travel as contract laborers and your outfits are in the next room. Check out all the clothes you need for a three week trip and be ready to depart at 5 o'clock."

So far, Yousef had been treated as an absolute equal, although one of the older Egyptians had the habit of imposing his age and authority on the others. Apparently, he had fought with the rebels against the Russians before they were known as Taliban, and he seemed to feel that it gave him the right to order people around. His pockmarked face and his graying beard made him the ugliest member of the team, but his voice and his flawless Arabic indicated a good educational background. Yousef felt instinctively that he would have to distance himself from that man as much as possible.

Ismael, the other Moroccan on the team was a short muscular teenager from Casablanca and he tried to befriend Yousef at every chance he got. It became annoying and dangerous. When he talked about his youth, growing up in the big city along the Atlantic, he'd ask Yousef if he had similar experiences and that made it very difficult for the young undercover man. There were too many gaps in his story. He couldn't relate to schools in Morocco, 'cause most of his schooling had been in the U.S. He couldn't talk about experiences with Muslim girls, because he had never dated one. To make it worse, his assumed identity did not resemble his life and his background even if he had spent his entire youth in Chefchauoen. Besides that, he was supposed to be born in Spain of Moroccan parents. Without being rude, he avoided Ismael as much as possible and when they talked, he tried to answer his questions with questions, but the boy was eager to keep talking. So far. Yousef wasn't sure how long that would last.

After evening prayer and a hearty meal of lamb and rice, they climbed in two Toyota mini-busses and started their long trek through Turkey. With rolled up coats and jackets that served as pillows, they managed to sleep through a good part of the night.

From Istanbul, they bypassed Ankara and by morning they traveled along the southern coast of the Black Sea through the ancient city of Samsung. Yousef would have loved to spend a few days exploring the old sights they passed, but other than for gas and bathroom stops, the little caravan kept right on chugging. It was surprising to him that the roads were much better than the ones in Morocco and that the gas stations and restaurants were much cleaner than he anticipated.

After they drove by the city of Erzurul, they turned south toward Van and west again to the Iranian border. All of them had to exit and walk to the border patrol gates. Leaving Turkey was simple, entering Iran was more complicated. It took more than a half hour and the main problem was Yousef. His papers didn't seem to match his story and the ugly Egyptian had to act as an interpreter between the armed guards and the young Moroccan. The grey bearded man spoke perfect Farzi and Yousef, who had studied that language for three years, could understand most of it, but couldn't let on that he did. The entries in his passport from Cuesta, Algeciras, Tangier and back to Algeciras had to be explained twice and his reason for leaving Morocco and living in Spain were questioned time and time again.

"Yousef, José, whatever you call yourself, why did you live in Spain."

"To earn enough money to travel to Germany to see if I could locate my father.'

"Where is your father in Germany and why?" The guard wanted to know.

"I don't know. He left twelve years ago and wrote to us once and then he sent no more money and we don't know what happened."

"Maybe he found a blond woman." The Egyptian thought he was funny.

"Maybe he did." Yousef acted agitated, but inside he was really worried that he might be held by the Iranians.

"Why did you travel to Spain and then back to Morocco and back again?"

"The first time they wouldn't let me enter and sent me back, but in Tangier I talked to the Spanish Consul and he approved my visa, so I tried again."

"What was the problem?" The guard was persistent.

The young man nearly blushed. "Please don't send me back. There's a warrant for my arrest and I really didn't do it."

"Do what?"

"I thought it was a hold-up. I thought I was being robbed, so I slugged the man and broke his jaw. He hit the ground hard and hurt his head and I was accused of attempted murder. You see, the man was an undercover detective, but I didn't know that and I…"

"Okay, okay. Pass on through. Next."

The little Toyota buses returned to Istanbul and the motley crew of *laborers* climbed aboard an old former Army truck and started bouncing their way through Iran. Their first stop was the town of Khvoy where Amwar, the Egyptian, took Yousef aside.

"You understand that the Iranians are real worried about American spies entering their country, especially ones with a background in Nuclear science. You're not a scientist, are you?"

In spite of the seriousness of the situation, the young man had to laugh. "I'm a bit too young for that, but if I were, I might go to work for them and really make some money."

They left it at that, mounted the truck again, but before they did, Yousef noted that the ugly one was huddled in a whispered conversation with Ismael, the other young Moroccan. He had a bad foreboding feeling about that.

Indeed, his fellow countryman made it a point to sit next to him on the wooden bench and involved him again in conversation about their home country. Thank Allah, the teenager from Casablanca was dumb enough to enjoy hearing his own mouth and Yousef had little problem answering questions with questions, so by the time the truck stopped outside of Tabriz, the younger man had not gotten any wiser.

The young undercover man from Daytona was on pins and needles though and he worried that the older Egyptian might get wise to him and upset the entire purpose of his mission. He had to get away from him, but how? Could he be eliminated? Hurt, maybe?

The only way into Afghanistan was to remain with the team, so running away was no option. He had to get rid of the *ugly one,* but he had no idea as to how.

Half an hour after leaving Tabriz, the truck turned north and the road quality got worse in a hurry. They twisted and turned in the foothills of the looming mountains and disappeared behind a tall fence, consisting of wood palisades and tall cactus. A compound, rustic and dirty appeared before them and the vehicle rolled to a stop in front of the main building. It looked like a three story hotel from an old Western Movie. Everyone, but the Egyptian stayed on their seat, and after ten minutes, he boarded again and they chugged and bounced for another five minutes, stopped and unloaded. They had arrived at their destination for the next two weeks. Here they would practice mountain fighting, hand to hand combat and handling all sorts of American, Russian and Chinese weaponry. It promised to be exiting.

As expected, the two young Moroccans were assigned to the same room and again, Yousef noticed the Egyptian and the Casablanca youth in a huddle, in a whispered conversation and chills ran up his spine.

Chapter Twenty-Seven

Vengeance

Boot camp, Taliban style.

The pace was unbelievable. From 4 o'clock in the morning till 9 o'clock at night, everything was done in double time. From their bunks to the latrine, from the barracks to the mess hall, from the compound to the range, every distance was covered by running. The only rest they got was when they were lying around, waiting for their turn to shoot or launch a grenade.

On the primitive firing line, there were only four targets and only two scorers, so learning to shoot became a slow process. Huge circles were painted on cardboard and then mounted against an earthen wall. In front of the targets was a seven foot deep ditch in which the scorers stood and pointed to the bullet holes with a long pole, headed with a red arrow. That way, the shooters immediately knew where their bullets had struck. With Ak-47's, they fired single shot and semi-automatic, concentrating on three round bursts. The recoil from the shots caused the rifle to buck upwards with every shot, so shooting more than three rounds simply caused the gun to fire a string of rounds, each one hitting three inches above the other, so firing ten rounds in rapid succession only resulted in three holes in the target and seven in the air above it. Three shot burst, re-aim, three more and again re-aim before pulling the trigger gave the best results. The teams alternated; two would score, the other ten fire and then two others would take over in the ditch. They learned fast and Yousef was excited. This was more fun than he had experienced in a long time.

Firing shoulder held grenades was exhilarating. Too bad they didn't have actual planes to fire at, but they learned to lead their target by aiming at a mock-up automobile that was pulled along a rail some two hundred yards in front of them. It was amazing how many of them missed the moving target most of the time, but it was also satisfying to see how a few of them really got the hang of it and blew up the mock vehicle time and time again. Yousef was one of them. He had a good eye and a great feel for hunting. Skeet shooting in Dade City with George Nixon had taught him a lot about leading a moving target.

Unfortunately, it made the Ugly Egyptian more suspicious than pleased.

"Very good, José! Where did you learn that skill? Your resumé doesn't show any military training. Where'd you learn this?"

"I used to shoot rabbits with a slingshot. I got to be pretty good at that." He surprised himself by coming up with snappy retort. He had to get pretty sharp at lying and thinking quickly. He wasn't sure he liked that about himself.

The ugly one seemed only half satisfied with the answer and at night confronted the young Moroccan in the barracks.

"The Emir in Istanbul informed me that the first payment to your mother was returned. No such known person. Are you telling us the whole truth? Where is your mother and how can we reach her?"

Again, Yousef had to think quickly. "Send it to a carpet store in Cordoba. The owner is a good friend and he'll know where my Mom may have moved to. She may have gone back to Morocco, I don't know. She still waits for my Father. Let me write down the address. Just a moment."

He returned with a sheet of scrap paper with a Spanish address and handed it with a smile. "Thank you Amwar. Thank you for doing this for me." He grabbed the man's hand, "And for my Mother. Thanks."

Inwardly, he gritted and his stomach churned. The man was becoming dangerous to his mission. By the same token, if money arrived at the carpet store, Rina and Bongers would learn about his situation and know that he was on track. In his bunk, he tossed and turned, thinking about the Egyptian and how to get rid of him. He could accidentally fire a round at the target just as the ugly one crawled out of the ditch after completing his tour as a spotter. Or..., maybe a rocket might misfire and hit the older man in the gut? He reviewed and retried his options in his mind until sleep overcame him and he had nightmares about being shot and wounded himself.

His chance came the following day. They were introduced to remote-control explosives. Each one learned to attach a bomb to a tree or a car, run for safety and detonate the device by pushing a button on a remote control. In a flash, Yousef switched controls with Amwar and watched as the older man ran down field and tied his bomb to the rear wheel of an old truck and Yousef quickly pressed the button. Nobody noticed his thumb on the control, but everyone did see the Egyptian explode into a dozen fragments of human flesh. Screams of agony roared from a dozen mouths as they ran toward the victim and Yousef ran right with them, dropping the remote in the dirt.

All bombs were inspected and reset, making sure that there would not be any more accidental deaths. Training was suspended for the rest of the day and a proper funeral was arranged for the bits and pieces that had once been the Ugly Egyptian.

In bed, the young undercover man tried to feel remorse or any other emotion over the fact that he had killed a human being, but all he felt was satisfaction that he had done it so cleverly and aroused no suspicion. Everyone felt that it was the grey bearded Egyptian's own fault or maybe defective equipment. Joe slept like a baby. No nightmares.

The two weeks went by fast and before they realized it, the training was over and they were back in a truck on their way to Teheran, where they slept in a small hotel on real beds with clean sheets. It was an unknown luxury.

Two days later they enjoyed similar pleasures in the City of Meshed. "Mashhad" the natives called it. In the hotel, they were issued papers that identified them as laborers for a German Construction company on their way to Qandahar for work on the runways and infrastructure. Crossing the border would become the trickiest part of the whole journey, because they feared that Americans would be working together with the Afghan Security and they might scrutinize everyone's passports and papers.

At five in the morning, they arrived at the crossing where the rivers *Atrek* and *Hari* meet. To everyone's surprise and relief, the guards looked at the papers the driver handed them and waved them through. They were in Afghanistan!

Yousef's heart pounded in his chest as he realized, 'here's where my mission really begins.' In his mind he played a dozen different scenarios of what an encounter with the Sheik would be like and how he would get that information out to the U.S. He really had no clue, but heartened by his success with his Egyptian nemesis, he figured, he'd come up with something.

The road was narrow, but well paved and it followed the river Hari up and up to the center of Afghanistan. The *Paropamasus Range* appeared on their left and snow already capped some of its peaks. In the town of *Daulat Yar,* they dismounted the truck for the last time and were put up for the night in the remains of an old cloister or military fortress. It was hard to tell what it had been once, because there was hardly a wall still standing in its original form. It was a scene like the many they had witnessed all along the road, devastation from years and years of combat, maybe hundreds of years. It was rare to see a house or a building that wasn't pockmarked by gunfire or bomb blasts.

After a hearty meal of goat and rice in the *'dining room'* of the old ruins, they were led in prayer by an impressive Mullah, whose robes and turban indicated a rich origin. He was a tall dark haired individual with a deep voice and a long, long beard. His gold rimmed glasses reflected the lights around the room and it was impossible to see his eyes, but everyone in the room felt that he was looking directly at him.

After the men got up from their prayer rugs or the cardboard they had knelt on, he addressed the group that now consisted of twenty-two men.

"Brethren," He spoke Arabic with a strange accent. Yousef assumed it was Pakistani. "We have all gathered here for an important task. Allah has chosen to send us a Prophet, who will lead us toward world dominance of Islam. The hours of the infidels are ticking away. We have made great strides in Europe, Africa and America. Mosques are being built everywhere. Islam is the fastest growing religion in the world. Only the Jews and the Americans are trying to destroy us, but they will not succeed." He raised his voice that started to sound like thunder. **" WE WILL DESTROY THEM!"**

He lowered his voice to a whisper. It sent shivers up Yousef's spine. "But first and foremost, we must protect our Prophet. The Americans and their heathen brothers have declared war on Islam and our leader and they will be here in great force to destroy him, but like the Russians, they will not succeed." He paused and looked around the room and seemed to stare at each individual for an eternal second. The young Moroccan felt naked and exposed, but the Mullah went on. "Your function is to protect the Prophet with your lives. You will be transported to his hideaway and stationed in the mountains surrounding his compound. Equipped with radios and rockets, you'll be able to report any advancing enemies and take them out. Their souls will burn in hell. They'll come in with jetfighters and helicopters. They'll bomb and strafe your positions. They'll drop paratroopers all around you, but you will prevail. You will kill many of them and Allah will reward you for every one of the infidels." Again he looked around the room with his reflective glasses.

"This is not, I repeat, this is NOT a suicide mission. You're of value to the Prophet only if you're alive and killing the enemy. So, use extreme caution. Use all you've learned. Train yourself to endure the harsh winter environment in which you'll live. Food and warm clothing will be provided on a near daily basis, so stay healthy, stay tough and above all, stay alert. We're dealing with the devil. Tomorrow, you'll be divided in four groups. Each group will have an experienced local scout, who will lead you to your positions. Get to know your group leader and obey him without question. Remember, Allah is with you, all the way."

Someone went up to him and led him away. He was blind.

Yousef shook inside. Fear mixed with excitement. "These people are fanatics," he said to himself, "but, we'll have radios. We'll be able to raise our troops."

He went to sleep, ready for the unknown.

Chapter Twenty Eight

Falcon Down

Bagram Air Base.
Para Rescue Squadron.
11 A.M. local time.

"F-16 down. F-16 down. East of Baghlan. Amber flight, you're on. Report to OPS for coordinates and details."

The loudspeaker in the crew room startled everybody and six men darted out the door.

"Where the hell is Baghlan?" The remaining airmen ran to the huge map on the east wall of the room.

"Just about due north of here. About a hundred, maybe a hundred and ten miles. To the east are the mountains, so he may be right near Baghlan in the valley, he may be in the foothills or on the mountain slope. Could make a lot of difference where he dropped.

Let's see what we can learn." The major who had done the talking turned away from the map and raised the volume on the radio.

Sergeant J.P. Pagliari felt his adrenaline pumping. This could have been his first actual mission, but they called "Amber" first. Maybe "Blue" would be next as a back-up.

The men sat down again at the wooden table of the crew room and the conversation got hot and heavy.

"What's up there? Do we have any troops up there?" One wanted to know.

Lieutenant Grau answered, "We're not looking for Bin Laden up there, but the 10th Mountain Brigade is doing some mop-up work in that area. The Russians left an entire unmanned airfield behind and that may provide the bad guys with some attractive housing and a base of operation. The F-16 may have been called in to take out some heavy opposition and got winged in the process. We'll know a little more in a few minutes. Colonel Wainwright will be in to brief us so that we'll be prepared in case they call on us for back-up."

Before anyone else could ask a question, the colonel walked in with two assistants, carrying a projector and a laptop. Everyone in the room snapped to attention.

"At ease, men." The troops sat back down. The colonel moved to the wall with the big map. "First some good news: The pilot ejected safely and was seen floating to the west toward the river, so he may land in the foothills or even the valley, if he floats long enough." He pointed to a spot halfway between the City of Baghlan and the mountains to the east. "The bad news, our troops don't have that part secured yet, so our chopper may be the only one that may reach the pilot before the Hadjis do. Right now, three F-16's are still overhead acting as *Sandys* but they'll have to leave soon because of fuel. *Hogs* are being scrambled right now and should be overhead within fifteen minutes. We gotta get this guy back and get him back fast. Let me give you the details."

A-10 squadron, crew room.
11:00 A.M.

"F-16 down, F-16 down. Sabre Flight, Groper, report to OPS on the double. Gasman, stand by."

Susie sprinted around the corner to the OPS desk, followed by her three wingmen.

Her heart pounded in her chest. "F-16 down? American?" She nearly shouted.

"Yes! What else? Here are the co-ordinates, get to your planes for immediate take-off. Here's his ISOPPREP card. Your call signs are *Sandy twelve, thirteen, fourteen and fifteen*. You'll have 1,000 rounds and two *Hellfire missiles*. I'll give you more details as you're rolling. Go!"

With the card in hand that held info that only the downed pilot could know the foursome sprinted out of the building. Their parachutes were already in the planes and the crew chiefs were standing by to strap them in. A quick preflight and they climbed rapidly up their ladders and into their cockpits. The crew followed them quickly and helped them into their straps, removing the stairs the minute the pilots were seated.

Groper made a circular move with her right hand and all eight engines roared into life within seconds. The team was good. All of the training and all of the practices had made them like one solid unit, rather than four individual ones. A quick oxygen, instrument and radio check and Susie pushed the button. "Bagram Ground, Sandy Flight for taxi and take-off, over."

"Sandy Flight, taxi runway Three-One, you're number one for take-off."

"Roger, Sandy for Three-One

The tower had already cleared all other ground traffic out of the way of the speeding *HOGS*. Susie and her team had formed up in a two-by-two formation and when they rounded the last turn onto the North-South runway, Susie switched to the tower frequency and calmly asked: "Bagram Tower, Sandy Flight for take-off, over." Her heart was pounding, but her voice was icy cold.

"Sandy, you're cleared for take-off."

"Sandy, rolling."

In less than a minute they were pulling up their gear and started a right turn to the north.

"Sandy, channel F." Her voice was crisp and within a few seconds she heard;

"Sandy Thirteen."
"Sandy Fourteen."
"Sandy Fifteen."

"Roger Sandy." She smiled. Her team was on the ball. On the squadron frequency, she announced, " Sandy flight climbing on a heading of 3-6-0, over."

"Roger Groper. Three F-16's are leaving the area within minutes. No enemy has been sighted near the pilot yet. His name is Dave Browning, call sign Buster Brown, code Victor 21. We may have an EC-130 up within minutes, to act as the Airborne Mission Coordinator, but that is not confirmed yet. Because of cloud cover we have no satellite visual, but his beacon is accurate. He is not hurt seriously, just an ankle sprain. A *Pave Low* is on its way and will be overhead at about twelve hundred hours. We have no tanker up at this time, so it's up to us to pull him out and protect him. Go get'em Groper."

"Wilco and out." Sandy Flight leveled off at 10,000 feet, just below the solid cloud cover. The flight leader, Susie, ordered armament checks and all three wingmen complied. Her team was ready for battle. They were carrying two missiles each and 1,000 rounds of 30 caliber ammo for their Gatlin gun. The missiles were heat-seeking, very accurate guided projectiles, nick-named; *Hellfire*..

Groper contacted the F-16's on her UHF radio. "Victor Flight, this is Sandy Twelve, what's your position?"

"We're at Bingo at Angels five, climbing out. Victor 2-1 is at 68-20-03 and 36-11-44. The Hadjis that got him were at the mountain top, 25 miles to the east. The 10th Mountain Division is out there battling them. Good luck, and thanks. Out."

From 10,000 feet, Susie could not see the departing F-16's for they had to scram because they were at *Bingo*, nearly empty. It was now up to her team to cover the downed pilot and scare away anyone who might approach him, other than their own helicopter.

The MH-53J Pave Low should cover the distance from the base to the downed pilot in just under an hour, so that allowed the team plenty of time to familiarize themselves with the terrain and the circumstances. She started a slow descent and made sure that she stayed as far from the mountain range to her right as she could, without losing her objective. From the caves along the tops, the Taliban fighters might have a clear view of the valley with the incoming planes and that was probably how the F-16 was picked off with a hand held *Stinger* missile. Groper was not going to take those kind of chances. She rocked her wings, signaling low-level battle formation. Number three and four, *Sandy's Fourteen and Fifteen,* moved out to her right about a half mile, while her wingman, *Sandy Thirteen,* slipped back and to her left, about three airplane lengths out.

It had only taken fifteen minutes and they already had their man in sight. With his ISOPREP information, she could verify if he was indeed the right man, but that wasn't needed this time. She could clearly see him and he was all alone.

"Victor 2-1, this is Sandy One-Two, do you read?"

"Five by five, One-Two."

"Chopper should be here in forty. Turn off your radio and your beacon till then. We're staying with you."

"Roger." His beacon went dead.

The flight set up a well rehearsed drill. Fourteen and Fifteen set up an oval above and around Victor 2-1 at 5,000 feet, while Groper and her wingman flew an oval pattern to the east of the pilot's location, losing him out of sight every five minutes for about four minutes, but spotting him again as they passed within a hundred yards of him on the western leg of their circuit.

For about thirty minutes all went well, until *Sandy Fourteen* called out, "Trucks barreling down at your 10 o'clock. Twenty miles out."

Susie swung to her left and saw the dust plume before she saw the actual trucks. There was no way to tell if those were armed enemies or some workers on their way to a job. Their speed was a worrisome indication. Workers would not drive that fast, she reasoned. Better scare them a little. She pointed her nose down to the incoming vehicles and from about ten miles out, she fired one of her *Hellfire* missiles. She purposely aimed about a hundred yards in front of the lead vehicle and the result was astonishing. They slammed to a halt in a cloud of dust and about a dozen men spilled out of each truck. Most of them dove into a ditch along the road, but two of them defiantly aimed their missiles at her, but she screamed so low over their heads that they didn't have time to get a good aim and only one of them actually was fired, but missed her by half a mile. She was clocking 450 miles an hour by then and didn't even see the stinger behind her.

"Sandy Flight, bad boys indeed. We'll keep'em pinned."

They continued their oval patterns, keeping their eyes peeled for other possible intruders. Susie could easily have taken out both trucks with her Gatlin gun, but they were at least twenty miles out and she might need her ammo later. The game was not over by a long shot.

"Sandy Flight, this is Jolly Amber, over."

"Amber, this is Sandy, go ahead."

"Amber is twelve minutes out, are the coordinates correct?"

"Roger, terrain is good. You can touch down within thirty yards. I'll advise him to turn on his radio and beacon again. Area is secure. Should be a piece of cake."

Famous last words.

Chapter Twenty-Nine

Chopper Down

Forty-two miles east of Baghlan

"Jolly Amber, do you have the target in sight?" Susie had pulled up to 3,000 feet, her wingman still off her left wing. From there she could see the chopper coming in, the downed pilot standing in the open and the two trucks off to the east, about twenty miles out.

"Negative. Have his beacon. Should be five minutes."

"Roger, Amber, you're right on course. Sandy Twelve."

"Roger Twelve. Got him now. Three minutes and we'll be gone."

Sandy tightened her circle around the downed pilot and noticed how the chopper created a funnel of dust as it touched down while the downed F-16 pilot ran toward the open door on the side of the helo.

"Great going," she said to herself. Not for long though.

"Incoming missile, Incoming!" The shout came from Sandy Fourteen, high above the action at 5,000 feet.

Sandy swung sharply to her left, watching helplessly as a smoking missile raced from the foothills to the chopper.

"Incoming!" She screamed, but just as the Pave Low lifted off, the missile struck the rear rotor and the craft spun briefly to the right and crashed on its right side. No explosion yet.

Inside the chopper, the pilot turned off switches as fast as his hands could move, while hollering on the intercom, "Out! Everybody out!"

That wasn't really necessary, because the airmen were already clambering out the side door, which was now on top of the fuselage. Pieces of the rotors were flying through the air like bullets, but most of the men were out and running within seconds without getting hit. The copter pilot, the last man to climb over the top, was struck by part of the top rotor blade and tumbled to the ground, unconscious.

"Captain down! Let's get him." The team sergeant and three others ran back toward the downed craft, hoping that it wouldn't explode in their faces before they rescued their leader. It only took a few heart-stopping seconds before they picked up the wounded man and raced away from the craft. Blood ran down his neck from the back of his head, but he was breathing. Behind a rock, a makeshift shelter was erected and first aid administered. Thank God, they were all trained medics. The captain would survive.

Meanwhile, Groper screamed into her radio: "Chopper down, same co-ordinates, standing by." She pushed another button, "Sandy One Four, take out those trucks."

An overwhelming feeling of guilt enveloped her. She should have taken out those guys immediately and the chopper would have been safe.

"Damn!" She scolded herself. "Don't fire unless fired upon." She again cursed under her breath. "Should have taken them out. I knew it, I knew it."

Bagram Air Base.
Para Rescue Crewroom.

"Blue to OPS. Chopper down."
J.P. jumped up so fast that he knocked his chair down but didn't

stop to erect it gain. He beat Lieutenant Grau to the desk and heard Colonel Wainwright holler, "You've been briefed. Here's his ISO-PREP, incase you need it. Go get'em guys."

Blue team raced to the waiting helicopter that was already warming up on the ramp. The young sergeant was shivering with excitement. This is what they had trained for, for three years. This is what his calling was all about. Saving the lives of young aviators. His lieutenant noted the flush on the boys face and the excitement in his eyes.

"Stay calm. Pagliari, stay calm. Keep thinking about all the details of the briefing, the coordinates, the terrain, the pilot, all the little details."

"But sir, it's not just one pilot anymore. It's about a whole crew of the chopper plus the F-16 pilot. It got a lot more complicated fast."

"True, Sergeant, true. Makes it more exciting, doesn't it?"

"Sure does. Sure does. We'll get'em out, though. We'll get them, unless we get shot down too."

"Don't worry about that. They'll send more F-16's up and more *Hogs* to protect us, so don't worry about that. We're gonna do it. Right?" He raised his right hand, as in a 'high five' and J.P. slapped it enthusiastically.

The chopper lifted off and headed north, as fast as it could fly.

Groper had watched Sandy Fourteen and Fifteen make a pass at the trucks, blowing them to smithereens. From her angle, she could see a bunch of Hadjis crawling through the ditch along the road and without hesitation she followed the pair of A-10's and raked the trench with her exploding 30 caliber guns wreaking havoc amongst the Taliban fighters. Just as she pulled up, her UHF sounded in her ear. "Sandy Flight, return to base. F-16's coming in at level eight. Call sign, Sandy Red."

She looked above her, trying to spot the fighters beneath the cloud cover, but she didn't find them. "Sandy Flight, join up at *angels five* over the target. Over."

"Roger, Sandy Fourteen, joining at five."

Groper flew a wide circle to her left, looking down at the assembled crew behind tall rocks and the element of two A-10's that appeared below her and slid underneath her to settle on her right wing. The flight leveled off on a southern heading and again Susie transmitted on UHF, "Sandy Flight leaving target area. All personnel survived. Sandy out"

The downed helicopter had not burned or exploded. Main reasons were the quick actions of the pilot, who cut all switches in a hurry and the fact that the missile hit the rear of the chopper and cut no fuel lines. The wounded captain was well tended to and resting comfortably.

The Para Rescue team commander sent two men back to the wreck.

"Check for leaking fuel. If everything seems safe, one of you climb aboard and retrieve a stretcher. We'll have the captain strapped on and ready to go when the next craft arrives, so we can expedite the departure. Don't take chances, though. If it looks like she might blow, retreat immediately. Questions? No? Go!"

Groper sat down while four officers seated themselves opposite her at the table. The coffee cup in her hand didn't shake, although underneath her façade, she was trembling. Not from fear, but from anger.

"Groper, you understand this is recorded?" She nodded. "Fine, start from the beginning."

The speaker was a balding Army major in a uniform, not a flight suit like the others. "Intelligence," she thought, but she answered. "Everything was A-OK, until Fourteen called in, 'trucks at high speed from the east.' We couldn't tell whether they were bad guys or good guys, so I decided to just stop them, not harm them. I blew a Hellfire in front of them, maybe a hundred, hundred fifty yards and they slammed to a stop and about two dozen men spilled out and hit the ditch. I came over the top of then at nearly 500, but I thought

I spotted guns and missiles. When I was back at three thousand, I made a pass and they stayed pretty much hidden, but I could still make out that they had weapons. My first thought was, take'em out, but I remember the rule. 'DO NOT FIRE UNLESS FIRED UPON, so I left them alone until after the chopper was taken down. Then I sent my number three and four element to take out the bad guys and after my team pulled off, I went back over there and obliterated them, which I should have done in the first place. I could have saved some equipment and some lives, but the Goddamn rules…"

"Easy, Captain, easy.!" The colonel in the flight suit patted her arm from across the table. "You did good, Groper. You did good. Go get some chow."

Pave Low Jolly Blue was speeding along at 110 knots and fast approaching the crash site. The lead pilot of Sandy Red was overhead familiarizing himself with the terrain, the location of the battered trucks and the condition of the troops on the ground. Except for a stretcher, everyone seemed to be mobile and that would help with the recovery. Blue was certainly going to have a hell of a load, he mused. The flight crew and the Para Jumpers that they had aboard, plus a similar group to be picked up. And the F-16 pilot, he added in his mind. He wondered how many persons that chopper could carry. He called back to base operations and was assured that the MH-53J was up to the task.

"We'll see, we'll see. They should be here soon." He pushed his radio button. "Rescue Jolly Blue, this is Sandy Red."

"Sandy Red, this is Jolly Blue, about thirty minutes from target. What's the status?"

"All peaceful here. We have four Falcons overhead serving as your Sandys. We're keeping an eye out. Call five minutes out."

"Wilco, Blue."

P.J. had relaxed considerably. He sat next to the door. He would be the first man out and his job was not to provide emergency medical care, no, this time he would jump out with an automatic in hand, ready to take down any approaching enemies. As far as he was concerned, the helo just didn't fly fast enough, but he understood that there was only one casualty and generally, everything was under control.

Sandy Red leader made a few more passes over the truck wreckage and made sure that the Taliban fighters were out of sight. That didn't especially put him at ease, because, these guys could be hiding behind a tall rock or a bush and still manage to get off a *Stinger* at the incoming chopper. He ordered his number 3 and 4 men to stay close and fire at anything that moved while he flew a higher circle so he could watch over any incoming traffic from the valley to the west. Fortunately, the crash site was nowhere near a passable road and it would be hard for anyone or anything to get close without being detected. The only danger was from the hills and mountains to the east, so they kept a close vigil.

"Sandy Red, this is Jolly Blue, five out. Over."
"Roger Blue, got you in sight. Proceed on course."

The troops on the ground heard the thump-thump-thump of the rotors coming in and while grabbing the stretcher, they moved to the clearing on the other side of the wreck and within minutes, the chopper touched down, men jumped out, others climbed in, the stretcher was secured and the last Paras, P.J. included, clambered aboard and the Pave Low climbed out.
It had been on the ground for twenty nine seconds.
"Sandy Red, this is Blue, mission accomplished."
"Roger, We'll guide you home. Out."

Chapter Thirty

Taliban on the Move.

November in the mountains.

"You'll be issued two SA-7's each. Theoretically, you'll be able to take down an enemy aircraft at 10,000 feet. Don't believe it. You'd have to have magical powers to do that. Nobody is that good. On the average, you try to take out a truck, a tank or an airplane within a thousand feet or 400 meters. The rockets are very efficient. You hit your target and it will disintegrate. Guaranteed."

The skinny Mullah who had led the morning prayer, kept instructing the young activists, Yousef included. They had traveled further east into the mountains on the back of a few horse drawn wagons and were inside a cave that looked like a converted condo. The young Moroccan had seen pictures of Montezuma's castle in Arizona and that's what it reminded him of.

"Each of you will also receive an AK-47 with 200 rounds. You're familiar with that weapon, I believe?" Heads nodded all around the room. "Also a *TOKAREV* pistol with five clips, giving you a total of forty rounds. A very good pistol, comparable to the *GLOCK* that a lot of Americans use. The Russians were nice enough to leave us more than ten thousand of these." He chuckled. "May they kill a lot of non-believers."

The Mullah bent over and picked up a box with little books. "This is a little helpful guide. Study it as much as you can. Most people you'll encounter will understand some Arabic, but the majority is more fluent in Farzi. Where you're going you'll find a lot of peasants that speak either Tajik, Dari or Pashtu. You may need to dig out this jewel and translate. Don't lose it. You will be split into two groups. Each group will have an experienced guide and let me introduce them now. This is Aram Bin Erod. He'll lead group one. This is Omar Kimbardi. Follow and obey them as if the were the Prophet himself." Both men stood up and if it weren't for the difference in noses, they could have been twins. Aram had a long pointed nose and full lips, whereas Omar had a more pudgy nose and no visible lips. Everything was hidden behind a beard and a mustache. Their size, build and clothes were identical. Both wore the peculiar caps that looked like a cross between English caps and Greek fisherman's hats. They bowed politely and sat down again.

"Be especially aware of snakes and scorpions. The scorpions are not deadly, but can cause great pain and nausea, but the snakes are *Cobras* and different members of the *Viper* family and their bite can be deadly. You'll be carrying antidotes for the bites, but it's better not to get bitten, hahaha!" He thought he was funny. "Your target is the canyon southeast of Kabul. It's a steep valley and ingress or egress from both ends is difficult. We will protect each end. The exact location of the Sheik will be unknown to you, but you just make sure that no one enters the canyon. The Americans have bombarded the caves with rockets and guided bombs, but they don't have Allah on their side, so they have been pitifully unsuccessful. The Great One, Osama, has been conducting his operations without interruptions and will continue to do so with Allah's help." The Mullah bowed in silence for a moment and nobody interrupted. "Your trip will be arduous and it will take you through some rough terrain. The biggest problem is, the Americans can detect your movements from their planes and their satellites, so you'll travel a lot in dusk and darkness. Keep your weapons hidden. I know that's not easy, but we'll have mules to carry them, so you'll look like farmers. You should be in position in three days."

Again he bowed his head as in prayer. "Your leader has a radio. Learn to operate it in case he gets killed." He looked down at the two guides and said, "Sorry, gents." Looking back at his class of eager killers, " Study the maps. Know your co-ordinates at all times. Memorize them. In case of capture, just kill yourself. Don't surrender. Allah will reward you." He looked at each of his eager young fighters. "Any questions?"

One of them raised his hand. "Will we meet the Prophet?"

"You may, you may not. Any other questions? No? Allah Akbar!"

Omar, Yousef and four others descended down the slope and followed a winding path that rose and fell every few hundred yards. The young Moroccan was the only one who had ridden a mule before and he handled it with ease. Attached to his makeshift saddle was a ten foot rope that in turn was hooked to the headgear of a pack mule.

Yousef grinned to himself, "This could be a scene from an old Western where a bunch of gold diggers cross the Rockies." Indeed, the only difference was their clothing. Their robes and headgear made them look like local farmers, not miners of the Old West.

Their main concern was airplanes. Their little caravan did not in any way look like a bunch of farm boys going to work. It appeared precisely what it was, a small mule train of Taliban fighters. Every time the sound of an airplane came across the mountains, they hid behind boulders, under shrubs and small caves along their path. The most important thing was their spacing: far apart, so they looked more like individuals than a caravan.

Yousef had a lot of time to think. He was pondering how he would pull it off if they did come upon Bin Laden's hideout Before he could use the radio in order to call an air strike, he would have to kill or disable the rest of his team. That might not be too difficult, he had plenty of firepower. He envisioned sitting under a huge boulder watching missiles strike the opening of Osama's cave and directing the fire. Then it would be time to call for a chopper to come and rescue him and he would be on his way home, a hero if there ever was one.

Killing his teammates didn't particularly faze him. He didn't know any of them very well and as far as he was concerned, they were all killers of women and children and he abhorred them. The longer he thought about it, the more convinced he was that he could pull it off without remorse or guilt.

Their target was a cave at 6,000 feet at the southern end of *Nuristan Canyon*. The other team would guard the northern end. Water was available from a little creek that meandered in and out of the rocks and was known to be potable. Food would be delivered on a weekly basis, but no fires were to be built and no smoke could be observed. It was going to be an interesting diet. The freedom fighters had extended the cave and its entrances during the Russian occupation and it had never been discovered. A long radio antenna was cleverly hidden in a tall shrub, with it's tip sticking up just one foot above the tallest branch. All they had to do was connect the wires and they would be in business. Other than a test, they were not to use the radio for anything but emergency broadcasts. The rest of the time, they would listen on a UHF band every three hours, just for five minutes at a time, in order to conserve their batteries,

On the fifth day the cave came in sight and soon their quarters were divided and a watch schedule announced. Watch was a two hour shift and the position was under a protruding rock shelf that provided beautiful shelter, yet allowed them to scan in all directions, except upward. That was fine, because there was no way anyone could approach from above.

Omar had brought his *surnai,* a sort of a clarinet and he posted a guard at each entrance to check if his music could be heard outside the cave. Both guards said it was minimal and Omar was pleased to the point that he played his wailing music six, seven hours a day. It didn't bother anybody and Yousef found it soothing. When he was not on watch, he busied himself with the language studies and his Farzi improved immensely. Omar proved helpful with the other complicated dialects and languages and the young undercover man could not find any logical connections to some of them. The Tower of Babylon really did its work in this region.

In his scribbles, he hid a diary with unidentifiable marks that only he could understand. He had no watch and wasn't sure of the date. He thought it was November 15, 2001, but none of the others were sure either. He figured, 'one or two days off, what's the difference?'

While on watch, he scanned the whole valley with his powerful German binoculars that might be a war prize from the Russian days. He tried to memorize every peak, every cave and every creek. In his mind a picture formed of the terrain, the distances and the heights, plus the possible obstacles and easy access trails that he might have to use in the future. In spite of the desolate setting and the empty cave, Yousef wasn't bored for a minute. The cold air at night forced them to bundle up tightly, but that was no problem. They came prepared. A light snowfall had dusted the slopes and the peaks, creating a very peaceful scene. It resembled a painting of a Colorado Christmas card.

Two of his teammates wanted to talk all the time, but Joe shut them out by concentrating on his language studies. Whenever he was approached by either one, he'd interrupt them with a question about one dialect or the other and that always seemed to turn them off. It worked well.

Every so often, a pair of planes would skim the canyon, but usually at a higher altitude than the cave's 6,000 feet and a rare helicopter made an appearance once. 'Probably a photo mission' Joe mused, while he tried to identify the model and number of the craft. Generally nothing happened and the days went by quietly. Omar initiated an hour long calisthenics program in the morning to keep the young muscles in shape. They might need them one day.

Little by little, grumbling started among the team. One man especially felt he should be able to get some R. & R. and find his way to the nearest village. The answer was an emphatic 'NO!'

One morning, at the change of his watch, he was gone. Omar sent out a two man patrol to find him and shoot him.

"One hour! No more. Kill him or come back or both. If you kill, bury him and take his weapons. One hour, no more. Be back here in two hours. Make sure you can find your way back."

Yousef jumped at the opportunity to explore outside the cave and really get to know the landscape. They took only rifles and pistols and descended to the east. After 45 minutes they decided to go back up, which should take at least a half an hour longer than going down. They didn't see a thing, not even a scorpion or a snake.

Omar was furious. "Allah will destroy him."

Yousef figured, 'One less problem to deal with when the time comes.'

Chapter Thirty-One

Fraternization?

Bagram Air Base

The base mess tent was overflowing. Officers mingled with Non-Coms as if they were brothers, which in essence they were. When on a mission, they relied on one another with their lives and each one of them realized that.

Sergeant Pagliari was in an animated conversation with Captain Overton and Colonel Bongers was getting an earful from Lieutenant Grau,

Everyone was patting the Blue team on the back for hauling out the downed airmen while the helicopter pilots and the Para Jumpers beamed with pride.

Groper was leading the conversation. "You see Sergeant, we were already called off before you fellows were even close. What happened, four F-16's were scrambled from Qandahar to take over from us as *Sandys* and that relieved us from overhead duty. The whole thing was different from what is the norm. In due time, there will be a tanker overhead, so we can pretty much stay on station and normally an AWAC or some other plane would be coordinating everything as *mission control*, but there was a solid overcast at ten thousand, the AWAC had to come in all the way from Kuwait, so you can imagine, nothing was routine. It worked though. You guys got the job done and we only have one casualty plus the loss of one Pave Low. I still regret that I didn't eliminate that bunch of murdering bastards when I had the chance." She drained her soda.

"Was this your first actual mission, Sarge?"

"Sure was!"

"Good going. They may get worse. You better believe it. When someone goes down in some of these rugged mountains, it won't be as easy as today. By the way, where are you from? Your name is Italian isn't it?'

"Yes, but that's my adopted name. Originally it was Cordero."

"Adopted? You're adopted?"

"Yes Captain, my Father found me in Peru and brought me to the States when I was only twelve and I became a Citizen four years ago."

"Interesting. Where is home?"

"Fort Walton Beach and you, Ma'am?"

"I'm from Idaho, but I consider Arizona home." She looked around, "I need to find another soda. I wish we had beer."

"I'll get it for you." And he was gone. When he got back with another cold one, Groper was in a huddle with three other pilots and J.P. just handed over the soda bottle and strolled on.

"So, when you got there, the situation was already under control?" Bongers wanted to know.

"Yes, Sir, the A-10's had already shot up the trucks and the Hadjis and the F-16's were overhead, keeping everybody's head down, so we slipped in, loaded and slipped out in thirty seconds." Lieutenant Grau had every reason to be gloating. His team had performed like well oiled machinery.

"Do you know for sure where the missile came from? From the trucks or from higher up on the mountain?"

"I don't know. I wasn't there. I believe Sandy Fourteen, the element leader, called in the incoming, but he might not have seen where it was fired from. I'll find him for you. He's here, I know."

George Grau turned away and tried to locate the first lieutenant who had been Sandy Fourteen.

Bongers had flown in with an Army Intelligence team to help find out where Bin Laden was hiding and how his protégée Yousef was making out. He spotted Wainwright and meandered over. "Harry, great party. First recoup of the action, right?"

"Damn right. The bad news is, it won't be the last. We'll have more of these, but I hope all will have the same positive result."

"I'm flying with one of your boys tomorrow…"

"My boys?" Wainwright's eyebrows knotted together. "I don't think so. We don't own a single two-seater unless you're going by helicopter."

"Right on. Major Foster made all the arrangements already. I want to look at the area called, *Bora-Bora,* along the Pakistani border. Rumors keep persisting that Osama is out there somewhere and I have some great satellite pictures, but I wanna see for myself what the terrain is like. Did you know by the way, that the CIA put a bounty of twenty five million dollars on Bin Laden's head?"

"You're kiddin'. I may go with you. I might want a piece of that pie. Have they scheduled cover for you as well?"

"Do I need that?"

"Bruce, this war is even stranger than Vietnam. You never know when and where the Stingers will come after you and they are deadly. We found out today, didn't we?"

"I guess so, what do suggest Harry?"

"I'll have a pair cover you. I'll send then to that same area on a photo-recci mission. What time is your flight?"

"O-eight hundred."

"Call me to make sure."

"Okay, thanks."

Groper had joined the F-16 pilots who were going easy on their soda pop because they still had to make it back to Qandahar. "Any news from the Dutch Air Force? Do they have F-16's in the theater yet?"

An attractive major with thick black hair and the name DOG-FACE on his badge, answered, "They're due in Uzbekistan shortly, but they have a problem with logistics. There's nothing there. No water, no fuel, not even wood. Everything has to come in by ship to the Black Sea then trucked overland. Personally, I don't know how they're gonna handle it. That place is worse than this and that is pretty bad. I don't know the details, but their government doesn't want them here, but they'll be able to fight here just the same." He acknowledged the look on her face. "I know, I know. It doesn't make much sense, but is there anything about this asinine war that makes any sense?"

Susie nodded. "You're right. Not much makes sense. Have a good flight. Hope we meet again."

"I'm gonna look you up, Groper."

"I'll be here Dogface."

Susie felt better than she had in weeks. All of a sudden she had been involved in an exercise that seemed worthwhile. Something with a purpose. Saving another pilot's life. She wasn't sure whether it was the euphoria of the mission or the attraction of Dogface. He might have something to do with it as she walked to the bar for another cold one. She bumped into J.P. again who was in line ahead of her.

"Oh, hi Sarge! You're hanging in as well, I see."

"Yes Ma'am, this mission has me going gaga. This is what we trained for all this time and I'm loving it. Tell you the truth, I'm flying high."

"Good for you boy, good for you. Where did you say you were from?"

"Fort Walton Beach, Florida. Right near..."

"I know where it's at. Used to fly in and out of Hurlburt and was stationed..."

"That's where our unit is from, even though I'm now..."

"Besides that, I was stationed for a while at Eglin," She was obviously very tired, she started slurring her words just a little, "and I used to hang out in Fort Walton a lot. There was the neatest nightclub that was shaped like a boat. Great dance place."

"It's still there. Pandora's.."

"Right on! Pandora's. That was it. Here we are." They had arrived at the bar. "What's your poison, Sarge?

"I'd like a Heineken, but that'll have to wait till we get back home. So I'll have coke instead, please."

"Same here, same here! I like everything Dutch. You're Italian though, aren't you? That's okay., but I like the Dutch."

"Okay by me Ma'am." Juan Pedro drifted away. He was puzzled. "Is this Captain making a pass at me, an enlisted man? No way, buddy, no way."

He moseyed back to his buddies and soon the Non-Coms filtered out of the tent and back to their quarters. It had been an exciting day, but the sun would rise again too darn soon and they had to be ready to go at it again.

As luck would have it, the computer was available and J.P. took advantage of it and fired off a long letter to Margie in New Mexico. The discussion and the proximity to the good looking female pilot made him ache for his love back home. His words didn't quite express the passion and the longing he felt, but he knew that Margie would sense his emotions exactly as he telegraphed them to her. A deep sigh emerged from his chest as he hit *"send."*

Colonel Bongers was still talking strategy with his Exec and they agreed that it might be better if they went up in two separate choppers and approached the area from different directions and different altitudes.

"Let's get with Wainwright and see what he has available. It's strange to be at an Air Force base and having to ask for things, while on an Army base, we just order what we want."

Major Foster agreed whole heartedly. "Yep. It's a bitch when you're in a strange hen house. I wish I could find a scotch, so I'd fall asleep when I hit the sack. It's been a long day."

"I'm with you, brother."

Chapter Thirty-Two

Contact

Way up in the Nuristan Canyon

A few things were keeping Yousef from going insane. One was the insistence of Omar to bow toward Mecca five times a day and say their prayers. It gave the young Moroccan more insight into the Islam Religion than he had ever known before. It puzzled him endlessly how Omar could contort the writings of the Qu'ran into something so hateful and spiteful that it justified killing anybody who was a so-called 'infidel', including innocent women, elderly and children. The more he listened to his leader, the more convinced he became, that he was going to kill him before this whole affair was over.

The other part that kept him from going bonkers was his ongoing studies of the languages and dialects of the region. Foreign tongues had always held his fascination and he was quite fluent in a number of them, but the many languages that divided this small country were baffling to him. Omar proved to be a good listener and a good teacher.

Their job of protecting the 'Sheik' was dull and unnerving. Nothing ever happened on the deserted ridge where they hid out and the diet of cold foods became aggravating. Their first week passed without any replenishment and Omar decided to use the radio for once. Yousef was anxious to learn all about the operation of the equipment and Omar was eager to teach him.

"Afghan Base, Afghan Base." The older man spoke into the mike in Farzi.

"Afghan Base, Afghan Base, this is the Lone Eagle, please answer."

Besides some crackling sound, there was no reply whatsoever.

"We'll try again in one hour." He picked up the portable radio and moved outside of the cave. "Maybe we get better reception here."

Yousef thought that was stupid, because the location of the antenna determined possible reception, not the location of the radio itself. Commercial flight training at Embry-Riddle at least had taught him something.

Of course the results on the ledge were the same as the lack of contact inside the cave. "We'll operate each hour on the hour when there are no enemy aircraft overhead that could pick up our signal. So, Yousef, when you're on duty tonight, you try and try again. When you get contact, wake me immediately. Understood?"

"Oh yes. Oh yes." They carried the radio back inside.

The young undercover man tingled all over. Here was his chance to reach an American aircraft and get a message out. For all he knew, the Army intelligence had no notion as to his whereabouts or his condition, so this might be his genuine first opportunity. He shivered at the thought. So far, he was not displeased with his accomplishments, but he was nowhere near his goal of locating Bin Laden. All he knew, he was protecting his southern flank.

The following night he got his chance. He stood, or sat, guard under the stars with the radio by his side. On the hour, he attempted to reach the Afghan forces, but in between time he listened for planes overhead. He wasn't entirely sure what frequency the Americans would operate on, but he had enough aeronautical training to feel confident that he would manage.

The night dragged by and his shift ended without any results whatsoever.

Sleep didn't come easy, because he couldn't escape the feeling that he had failed somehow. In spite of the cold and the lousy dried lamb strips, he eventually slipped into a deep nightmare filled dream.

At three-thirty the following afternoon, Omar and the other two Muslims were in a deep discussion, alternating with songs, so Yousef took a chance. A pair of jets were somewhere overhead and he turned to a UHF channel, that he felt might be a military channel, used in the war zone.

"Allied aircraft, allied aircraft, this is Number One Son, how do you read." He realized that Bongers had never established a call sign for him, so he made up his own.

No reaction at all. The Engine noise faded and he had to talk to himself in order to re encourage him. When he heard airplanes again, he tried four different channels with the same message until finally,

"Number One, this Fancier Flight Lead, how you do read?"

The young American nearly jumped, but he controlled himself. He had only a few seconds. "Fancier Lead. Inform Colonel Bongers at Army Intel…"

"One, repeat. Colonel who?"

"Colonel Bongers at Army Intelligence. Inform him of the following. Target is in the Nuristan Canyon. Repeat, target is in the Nuristan Canyon. Over and out." He quickly turned off the radio, afraid someone inside the cave might have heard him.

His concerns were unfounded, because the threesome inside was still busy singing to the tune of the native clarinet. All he could do was wait and repeat his performance on the next daytime watch. He had a hard time controlling his heartbeat and his adrenaline as he feigned deep interest in his language studies.

Food ran out the next day. No contact had been made with home base and no-one had shown up with food or water.

Water was no problem yet, as long as the little creek dribbled on down the edge of the cave. Food was something different.

"We'll have to hunt. There are some mountain goats around here. Also, there are some hare and snakes are good too. The problem is, we don't want to fire our weapons and take a chance at being detected by the Infidels, but it's better than starving, don't you think?"

The other three agreed. It was decided they would travel in pairs and never go further than thirty minutes from their shelter. Omar and Ali, a young Palestinian went first.

An hour passed and then another one. Nobody showed up. Finally, Omar returned with a pair of birds. Small birds. Smaller than a dove.

"What are these?" Yousef wanted to know.

"I don't know, but they're edible I'm sure. All animals are."

"How are we gonna eat them? We can't start a fire, right?"

"Eat them raw. They won't kill you."

"What are you gonna eat? Aren't you hungry?"

"No, I just can't eat."

"Where's Ali?"

"That's why I can't eat. Ali fell down a cliff. I couldn't get down there. He's dead, I'm sure!" He rubbed his forehead. "I'm sure. *Allah Akbar!*"

"I can't eat this thing. Not raw." Yousef felt repulsed.

"Well, starve. One way or the other we have to survive. If you know a better way, let me know." Omar seemed to be as hardnosed as anyone the Moroccan-American had ever encountered, so he didn't pursue it any further. So he just sat and stared at the dumb little bird. They considered slaughtering the two mules, that were starving anyway and that wasn't as bad an alternative as Yousef had considered. He had eaten mule meat before, but that was only after it had been cooked. Definitively not raw.

"My turn for watch. We'll have to start three hour shifts since Ali is gone, so relieve me in three hours."

"I don't have a watch."

"When it gets dark."

Hunger gnawed at his stomach, but sleep overcame him anyway. At dusk, he found Omar, sound asleep next to the radio and he nudged him gently. "Go inside and get some rest. You might freeze to death out here."

Indeed, the temperatures at night were approaching the freezing point and at the higher levels, snow was already decorating the taller peaks. On the hour, he did his thing with the radio, but right thereafter he started scanning the other frequencies. Not many aircraft were up at that hour, so he was surprised to hear: "Number One Son, this Geronimo, how do you read? Number One, this is Geronimo, how do you read?"

"Read you five by five. Over."

"Number One, what's your position?"

"Negative. Message for Colonel Bongers, Army Intel, over." There was no way he would tell anyone his position, although he knew they would trace him rapidly if he talked long enough. He wasn't about to do that.

"Colonel Bongers, target in Nuristan Canyon, out." He turned off the radio. The equipment in those modern planes could detect him in seconds, if he kept transmitting. He didn't need detection. He didn't need to be rescued. He needed to guide them to the fanatic Muslim with the long nose and the full lips.

His heart pounded inside his chest. They had found his original message and had sent up a plane to find him and communicate with him. He had done it! He had gotten through. No idea to what extent, or if Bongers had even gotten the message. After all, the intelligence chief might still be in Fort Bragg or Tampa. But his contact was important enough to send a plane overhead to get back to him. He was so excited, he forgot his hunger pains.

Should he open the channel again and see what they had to say? Check on the others, he said to himself. With the radio he walked back into the shelter and found both of them asleep. He was going to take a chance.

Back outside, he calculated how many hours would pass before he would be on duty again and then figured out what time of day or night that would be.

Since he had no watch, he guessed that it was about seven at night, so if he went off at nine and the other two would three hours each, he could expect to be back on duty by three in the morning. No good. No planes would be flying that late at night, so another nine hours would put him at noon sharp. Good thinking.

The radio warmed up again nicely and as if they had been waiting for him, the response was immediate. "Geronimo, this is Number one, over."

"One, Geronimo."

"Have Bongers contact me on this frequency at noon, sharp. Out."

It never happened.

Chapter Thirty-Three

Nuclear Waste?

Qandahar Air Base.
Wing Commander's office.

"Colonel, Captain Wilcox and Lieutenant Pate are here to see you and they said it was urgent." Sergeant Chapin stood at attention as he delivered the message.

"Urgent?" The graying pilot looked annoyed. "Let me just finish this last report. Tell'em five minutes, okay?" He saluted the aide without looking at him.

"Somehow I never get finished." He muttered to himself, but after four minutes, he hit the intercom and said, "Tell'em to come in."

Two young Air Force officers in desert camouflage walked in and saluted crisply.

"Captain Wilcox!"

"Lieutenant Pate, sir."

Colonel Springsteen returned their salute without getting up. "At ease, gentlemen. Sit. Grab the couch." He pointed to his left where a brown leather couch decorated the room somewhat, because everything else was sparse, makeshift even.

The visitors headed for the sofa, but before they even settled down, the Wing Commander asked, "What's so urgent?"

The captain answered him. "You see, sir, we're with the demolition team and we are in the process of clearing the base of…"

"I know, I know. But what's so urgent?"

"As you know, we're clearing the field of old Russian mines Sir, and while doing that, we ran into something unusual. While clearing out the wreckage of a damaged Tupolov, we came upon a sizable crate…"

"Alright already, but what's so urgent?"

"Sir," the lieutenant blurted out. "It's radioactive."

"It's what?" The colonel jumped up. "How do you know?"

"Well sir, we always test any area we work on for radiation of any kind before we submit workmen to the area and we rarely find anything to be alarmed by, but this time, all sorts of bells and whistles went off and we retreated immediately."

"Good God." Springsteen sat down again. "What do you do in a case like that?"

"We close off the area and call in the experts. In the U.S., we get the DOE and Nuclear Waste Removal guys involved and they handle it from there, but we don't have any of them here. So that's why this is urgent. What do we do? We have no way of knowing what's in there, how dangerous it is or how to dispose of it, so…"

"So now you're asking me to give you advice? I don't have a clue."

"No sir, we are not looking for your advice," The captain was still doing the talking. "We're looking for your permission to handle the situation."

"Before I give permission, I wanna know how? What are you proposing?" He rubbed his forehead and rested his elbows on the table.

The captain, a young man of about twenty-eight with a Marine type of a crew cut, leaned forward. "Sir, the nearest nuclear experts are aboard the closest carrier. If you would request their presence here on the double, they'll be able to analyze what we've got and advise us what to do with it."

"Good thinking, good thinking." He pushed the intercom button,

"Sergeant, get me Major Brosky in here."

Before he could complete his next question to the twosome, the intercom buzzed; "Sir, Major Brosky is flying."

"Damn. Get Major Geron." We'll get you guys going in a hurry on this project. How much danger are we in, or is anyone in?"

The lieutenant spoke up, "From what we can tell with the instruments we have, there is no great danger to anyone as long as we keep our distance. We don't know if it has been radioactive all this time…"

"What do you mean; 'all this time'?"

"I mean since the plane crashed and that is probably twelve years ago. Meanwhile, the Hadjis have been crawling all over these wrecks and some may have been exposed and don't know it."

"Enter!" the colonel interrupted him as a balding pilot in his flight suit came in.

"John, grab a chair. This is what I want you to do. Get these men in touch with one of our carriers in the Gulf. They need to talk to nuclear men. Get with the captain of the ship and arrange for these experts to be flown in here toute suite. Have the captain call Central Command in Tampa to get clearances. Also John, get with intell and find out what kinda nuclear devices, if any, a Tupolov would have carried during the Russian invasion here. Interrupt me if any problems arise, okay? Thanks gentlemen." He saluted and went back to his papers.

"Well," Major John Geron sighed as they seated themselves around the desk in his narrow office, "We might as well begin at the beginning. What carriers do we have in the Gulf. Let's ask OPS." He picked up a phone and dialed. Within minutes the two guests heard him ask, "Do you have a number for them? An e-mail too? Good show. Can we hear them by radio from here?" He waited and twiddled his pencil. "Good, give it a try. Get me at this extension."

Turning to his visitors, "Have you dealt with this kinda stuff before or is this as new to you as it is to me?"

"We've never dealt with it, as you put it. We've come upon it before and then we simply turn it over to 'Waste' and we back off. But we never ran into it before in a foreign country, where we have little or no authority to do anything. It's gonna be interesting to see how they're gonna handle this."

The intercom buzzed. "I have Commander Aldrige on the phone from the ENTERPRISE. Why don't you grab it, Captain?"

He handed the phone to Wilcox, who explained the situation as he knew it. The conversation went well until he raised his voice somewhat. "Commander, our wing commander wants you nuclear geniuses over here on the double and we're clearing it with Tampa and your skipper. I'm just passing the word. Can you connect me with your skipper, please?" He listened for a few seconds and said, "I'm holding."

With his hand covering the mouthpiece, he told his audience, "He's not too anxious to leave the comforts of his ship for the confines of a plane and the dust of a desert air base. We'll see. We may have to get Col. Springsteen in on this conversation."

Again he listened and after a while they heard him say, "Very well, we'll have Colonel Springsteen speak directly to Admiral Booth. I'll get back with you Commander in order to work out the details."

Hanging up the phone, he addressed his audience. "Let's grab some chow while we can. They're getting experts from Stateside involved. While we're eating we may find out from some of our brains what a Tupolov would do with nuclear material."

As they passed out the door, Geron told his assistant, a young airman, "We're at chow. Get me the moment they call me back."

"Who, sir?"

The major didn't even hear him.

A Navy C-2, a twin-engine carrier based jet, landed at Qandahar five hours later, with three Naval Officers in their khaki uniforms, followed by two sailors in dungarees. Air Force guards ushered them into the briefing room, where Springsteen, Geron, Wilcox, Pate and another half dozen airmen filled the front rows. Introductions were made all around, while water bottles and coffee were being offered to the attending group.

"Gentlemen," The wing commander started off. "I'll let our experts do all the explaining, while we laymen try to understand it." He aroused a few chuckles. "Captain Wilcox, come up here with your Lieutenant and give us your description of what you found."

The two had little to say except, that during a routine check of a piece of wreckage before demolition, they encountered radioactivity and immediately closed off the whole area.

The commander, the naval expert, had little to say. "We can't offer any kind of intelligent opinion until we go out there and run our tests. Inasmuch as there still is daylight available, let's do that now and reconvene here, let's say in an hour, maybe an hour and a half, okay? Let's do it gentlemen." He was addressing his team as they followed him out the door.

The two sailors in the dungarees donned suits and helmets that resembled space suits from a NASA team.

"Lead protection." Captain Wilcox whispered in Major Geron's ear. "They're not taking any chances."

The two spacemen proceeded toward the rumpled fuselage of the old Russian transport and stopped from time to time to direct their probes and read their instruments. One of them stepped briefly inside the old plane, but reappeared immediately. Apparently, they had seen enough.

All the while, jet-fighters and transports kept roaring down the runway, taking off and landing as if a real war was being fought somewhere. No artillery or explosions were heard on the base, but the hustle and bustle of the planes was evidence enough that they were indeed in a war zone.

The whole procession of officials and spectators returned to the briefing room, where Major Geron had the unpleasant duty of refusing entrance to anyone who he felt had no 'right to know' at this point.

Commander Aldrige took the stage immediately.

"Gentlemen, I was very skeptical when I came here, but I am no longer. We have, or should I say, *you* have, a real problem. I don't know what a bomber like that would do over here with an atomic bomb aboard and besides that, the Russians would have removed if it was, so let's rule that out. Come to think of it, an ordinary nuclear bomb would not radiate, unless ignited, so it's not a bomb. That's the good news."

He paused and looked around the room.

"Our man took some pictures of the so-called 'crate' and even though we haven't analyzed all of it yet, I would judge by the size, that it's a disposal unit. It is probably a lead container, encased in steel and then hidden in a wooden crate. It probably is a means of disposing of nuclear waste."

A murmur of comments ran through the audience.

Aldridge waited for it to stop and continued. "This is an opinion, strictly an unofficial opinion. The Russians may have used some remote area of Afghanistan for their nuclear waste disposal and when this plane crashed on landing, the ground crew didn't know or understand it's content and simply drug it to the trash heap."

Again, multiple whispers from the stunned audience stopped him and the commander seemed to enjoy the impact that his words were having.

"Gentlemen. This is what you have and the question now becomes, how do you get rid of it? We'll fly back to the carrier right now. Not that we don't like your company or your food," He grinned from ear to ear. "Nor is it the accommodations you might offer us," again he grinned at his audience, "but aboard we have better and direct lines of communications with the mainland and we'll be able to resolve this faster from the ENTERPRISE. So if you folks will excuse us. It is of the utmost importance that this is handled quickly." He saluted the crowd that sprang to attention and filed out the door.

"Well, whaddaya know?" was all Major Geron had to add.

Chapter Thirty-Four

The Onslaught

Bagram Air Base, o-eight-hundred,

"They woke me up with this news at four in the morning. It's hard to believe, but they relayed the message…"

Colonel Wainwright interrupted Colonel Bruce Bongers in mid-sentence.

"Who relayed what message?"

"The pilots of the AWAC, that recorded the conversation. Anyway, the tower at Qandahar got the word at seven o'clock last night and contacted Fort Bragg, which seemed like the proper thing to do. Fort Bragg was still asleep at that time, even though they should be on full alert since 9/11, so no-one passed on the message until my secretary walked in and contacted me here at the base."

"What was the message?" Wainwright was impatient. His crew had already been at work for three hours preparing for a mission, but he wasn't notified until seven about all the activity that was going on in his wing.

"All it said was, 'This is Number One Son. Inform Colonel Bongers that the target is the Nuristan Canyon' and it came from the southern end of that canyon. So…"

"Who is this Number One Son.?" Wainwright remained agitated.

"Although we did not assign him this call sign, I'm confident that it is my undercover man from the U.S...."

"How the hell did he get out there?"

"He grew a beard, speaks Arab and Farzi and is on a team of the Taliban that's assigned to protect Bin Laden. He..."

"How'd you fix that?"

"Well Harry, that's what intelligence guys do, infiltrate the enemy forces."

"I'll be a monkey's uncle."

"He is telling us that the 'Sheik' is further south than we had figured. We were looking at Bora-Bora, but this Nuristan Canyon is a deep chasm that reminds you of the days of Cowboys and Indians, where the Army is lured into a steep gorge and is pounded to hell by the Indians on the slopes and in the caves."

"Show me on the map."

The group rose and walked over to the big chart on the east wall, where Bongers indicated the location of the target with a pen-light, He picked up the thread again.

"What we don't know is, where in the canyon is the bastard? All we know is that Number One Son is at the southern end, so what we've been doing here, with the help of your staff, is plotting the locations of the biggest and best hidden caves, how to attack them and what kind of ammo to use. Any suggestions?"

"Wow! I would suggest that we hit every cave and crevice with all the varied types of weapons we have and obliterate the place. Are there any known villages or settlements out there that we have to avoid? If so, plan around them. Let's get an EC-130 up there to coordinate the affair and Lance...." He turned to a Lieutenant Colonel in the group. "get with Qandahar and set it up so we have around the clock action in that hell hole, so that no-one escapes our fury, alright?"

The young Squadron Exec jumped up. "Yes, Sir," and was gone.

"Let's get at it." Wainwright got up and the group divided into teams, each with its own agenda, everyone knowing what was expected from them.

Para Jumpers Blue was being briefed for potential action by Lieutenant Grau.

"We'll be up before the *HOGS*. The mountains to the north are quite high, some as high as 12,000 feet, so we've been assigned an area on the southern end of the canyon, where we'll be hovering or setting down at about 5,000. If we can find a good spot from where we can observe the action, we'll simply sit and watch with the rotors turning."

He stopped and looked at the eager faces of his men and he felt a surge of pride running through his veins.

"Let's hope we won't be needed, but we'll be ready to spring into action on a moment's notice. We'll have parachutes on board as well, because the terrain may not allow us to get into those rocky peaks with a sling. Some of that area looks like the *Bad Lands* in South Dakota. Very inhospitable. Let's find out which chopper we're assigned to and be ready for take off," he looked at his watch. "at o-8-45. Okay? Let's go."

Juan Pedro was the first one out the door.

"Not knowing the exact terrain very well, we'll go on our first mission with a variety of weapons. Parrot Blue flight will carry LGB's, (Laser Guided Bombs, 1,000 lbs), Purple will carry CBU's, (Cluster Bombs), Green will have Mk-82's, (500 lbs air-bursts) and Yellow will have LGB's. The helis will be off at 8:45, we're scheduled for take off at 9:30. Over the target we'll divide into four zones, mark your charts with the info from the poop sheet I just handed out. We'll separate the zones by ten miles, so we won't have any mid-air collisions."

Lt. Col. Higgins hesitated long enough to down the last of his coffee. He was a thin, athletic looking young man with deep blue eyes and a crew cut that started to show specks of grey here and there.

"As soon as we're off, the F-16's will bomb the gaps between our zones and when they're done, we should be overhead again with maybe a different selection of fireworks, depending on the results we've observed and the pictures that the observation planes have taken and whatever satellite images we'll have by then. The weather is great, so we should have a ball. Any questions?"

"What are we after, Colonel?" Groper wanted to know.

"Good question. We may be after a phantom, who knows? Unofficially, Osama the Butcher is supposed to be holed out in that canyon and we're gonna kill him or make the place uninhabitable for the next two centuries. Any other questions?"

"Will our pattern altitude be same or will each team go in from a different altitude?" A young red-headed pilot had raised his hand.

"Good point, Hamster, good point. Let's look at our charts for a minute. Since there are two sides to that canyon and consequently, possible caves on each side, let's set up an alternating pattern. Blue will be furthest to the north and with the sun behind them, attack the west side first. Purple will attack the east wall first, Green the west and Yellow the east. Two passes at each wall and we're gone. The terrain may be such, that we'll come back disgruntled about our results, because we might not be able to come down low enough to do an accurate job with bombs. If that's the case, we'll be back in an hour with Hellfire Missiles and send them deep into those shafts. Any other questions? No? Let's go do it."

Groper was Yellow Leader. A quick, but efficient walk around inspection assured her that the aircraft was in good shape and all the safety pins had been removed. She dashed up the ladder to her cockpit, followed by her crew chief, who helped with the parachute and the straps. Her checklist was next and when all the switches and gauges were in the proper positions and conditions, she began her start-up procedure.

Oh, how she loved that part of her job. Being in control of a powerful war machine and in charge of three similar sources of destruction gave her a feeling of being *Helen of Troy*. A woman in charge of her world.

When Higgins gave the start-up signal, she started her left and then her right engine, checked all the gauges and was ready to turn out of the parking spot and follow the three flights in front of her.

The sight was phenomenal. In front of her were twelve A-10s, two by two, taxi-ing in close formation. This was known as the *HOGWALK*. It thrilled her every time she saw it. "What a view, what a view." Just a look at that formation should shake Osama right out of his boots, if only he could see it.

After getting word from the tower, Blue leader and his wingman lined up on the runway and started rolling, when they were halfway down the runway, his element leader, Blue Three followed his example and pair after pair of *HOGS* took off behind them. Soon sixteen twin engine bombers winged their way east and south in four perfect formations of four, their shark teeth on their noses grinning at the landscape.

Over the northern end of the gorge, Blue peeled off to the left and a few minutes later, Purple turned to the right. Another few minutes Green Flight began its left circuit and Groper started her right pattern at the southern end of the Canyon.

"This is Blue. Commence at will."

Those were the only words heard on the fighter frequency and Groper aimed down at the floor of the gulley and looked for an obvious cave. There weren't any. Not obvious, that is. She selected a crack in the mountain wall and released her first Mk-83, a 1,000 pounder. Before she could look at any results, she had to pull up sharply to keep from flying into the mountainside. Looking over her shoulder as she was standing on her tail, she saw Yellow Two pulling up and Three going in. Four was ready to go into his dive when she arrived back on the *perch,* the level from which they started their attack. From up there she could clearly see the explosions of the other pilot's bombs, but there were no secondary explosions that would indicate that they hit any ammunition dump or supply. For her second target, Groper selected a huge crevice, further to the north. Again she put her *pip* on the bottom of the slit and pressed the button. With all her might she pulled back on the stick, so her G-suit inflated causing great pressure on her stomach and leg muscles, but keeping the blood where it belonged, up in her brain.

When all four planes were joined together at five thousand feet, the flight commenced a turn to the left and Yellow one streaked down again, this time, going for the western slope. Just like the opposite slope, there were no obvious gaping caves or cracks in the mountain wall, so again she selected what looked like a deep shadow and punched her bomb in it. Up again, full power, maximum G's and she observed Two Three and Four deliver their goods down on the canyon floor.

"Last pass," She said to herself as she rolled in to her left and dove steeply toward the shadowed bottom of the canyon. At 400 MPH, *pip* right on her target, she felt a tremendous jolt and her plane rolled sharply to her right.

"Lead, your right engine is gone. Bail out! Bail out!" That was number Two, who saw his leader's engine explode right in front of him as he was rolling in.

"Lead, get out!"

His last warning wasn't necessary because he saw Groper's ejection seat blow out of the cockpit and the chute billowing within seconds there after.

Yellow Two hit the UHF button. "HOG down, HOG down!"

It was heard over half of Afghanistan including in the cockpit of the Para Jumpers Jolly Blue team.

Chapter Thirty-Five

HOG Down

Nuristan cave.

Yousef awoke to the sound of nearby thunder, one thunderclap after the other. With a start, he realized the sounds were from bomb explosions. He jumped up and raced to the entrance of the cave, but Omar's voice stopped him.

"Stay inside! Stay hidden." The group leader was shouting at the top his lungs while the sound of jets roaring down intermingled with the sound of explosions.

"Americans!" Yousef thought jubilantly. "My message got across!"

He dove beneath a scraggy bush and peered between the leafless branches.

"A-10's! Halleluia!" His heart jumped a mile. He could make out the silvery aircraft as they pulled out of the valley and formed a circle high above him. They changed direction to the right and the first one started its dive again. This time in his direction. While the *HOG* thundered down, he could hear additional explosions further north in the canyon and he realized this was a coordinated attack all along the valley.

The flight leader disappeared from his view, but the second one rolled in and he prepared himself for additional bomb bursts, but closer this time. Instead he heard a softer blast and seconds later an enormous jolt. He realized the jet had hit the slope and exploded on impact. The second jet pulled out of his dive, right in front of his eyes and the other A-10's behind the number two plane followed him up instead of making their bombing runs.

"The plane crashed." He shouted as he ran toward Omar's hiding place behind a pointy rock.

"I got him, I got him!" Omar stood behind his boulder, waving an empty *Stinger* launcher. "I got him! Allah will burn his soul."

With a shock, Yousef realized that Omar had downed the plane and his first reaction was to shoot him.

"The pilot ejected. I saw him for a second. He's down there, right below us. I saw him. The chute opened and he was gone, but he may be alive. We gotta get him. We gotta bring him to the Sheik. It'll be our trophy, but the Master may want to question him. We gotta get him alive. Get your rockets and your gun. Tell whatshisname to stay here with the radio. We're going down to get him. Get going!"

The young Moroccan hurried inside, his mind twirling with contradictory emotions. 'The Americans are here, which is what I worked for, but one of the Americans is down and I gotta make sure that he doesn't fall in the hands of the Taliban. Besides, I gotta eliminate Omar, before he does more damage.'

His Stingers were slung over his shoulders in seconds and with his AK-47 in hand, he rushed back out to join Omar who was already climbing down. He moved from rock to rock, from bush to bush and Yousef followed him as fast as he could.

The pilot had to have landed at least a thousand feet down from their cave, maybe even more. There was no trail, just rugged boulders jutting out of the valley walls. It was treacherous going.

After about twenty minutes of rapid descent, an A-10 zoomed down at them and both of them dove for cover in wilderness of overhanging rocks and little crevices. Above them, a large bomb exploded and it dawned on them that the planes had figured out where the missile came from and were now determined to eliminate whoever was up there.

Before they recovered from the concussion, an avalanche of rocks, brush and debris came rolling over them. When all seemed quiet and Yousef got up to continue his trek, a second *HOG* came bearing down and he dove for cover once more. Two more minutes and a third plane came roaring in, repeating the blast, the concussion and the waterfall of rock and sand cascading down the mountain slope.

Finally, Omar's voice penetrated Yousef's covered ears. "Come on boy. Let's go. I think they're out of bombs."

Half sliding, half crawling, they made good progress for about ten minutes when the Taliban Leader raised his hand to signal a stop. He waved Yousef closer.

"I see the parachute. Over there on the left. Nobody's moving. Maybe he's dead. Let's go."

Moving more slowly and cautiously, they approached the American, while down the canyon, bomb blasts were continuing. "They must be guessing where Osama is hidden." The young Army man said to himself. "They're probably blasting every hole in the whole valley."

Omar silently slid from rock to rock, boulder to boulder, his rifle in front of him, ready to fire. He didn't want to kill the pilot, but he was sure American airmen carried a sidearm in their planes and he had no intentions to get shot and killed right here and now, just when he was to reap a peach of a price for Allah and the Sheik.

The closer he got to the chute, the slower he approached. When he had a good view of the silk sheet that was partially draped over a small bush and some boulders, he realized that the pilot had purposely spread that out so it would be clearly visible from the sky. That meant, he was in good health and on the ball. One more reason to be extra careful.

Ten more yards he hesitated again and looked back at Yousef, who was twenty paces behind him. With his left hand, he made a circling motion and pointed to the left, indicating that his partner should move over and go after the downed man from another angle, forty-five degrees over. When he saw the young man move in a northerly direction, he moved on until he was within thirty feet from the white chute. He hesitated again. "He's in hiding." he told himself, "But where?" Like the rest of the canyon, the jagged peaks offered great hiding places, so the man had plenty of choices. Hide above or below the chute. "Or move to an open area where a chopper can get to you?" Omar thought as he scanned the area. "No open spaces in sight, except further down. He's got to be up here."

He eased in front of a rock and "PANG", a shot to his shoulder knocked him down.

"Allah il Allah!" He screamed. "Damn them to hell!" He dropped his armament and reached for his shoulder. The pain was excruciating. It felt like that bullet had broken or shattered his left shoulder blade. He could hardly move, but he had to do something to keep from bleeding to death. "Where's Yousef? Didn't he hear the shot? He should come over to help me." But he didn't.

Yousef heard the shot and dropped to his knees. The shot was fired from about fifty feet in front of him, but it obviously was not fired at him, 'cause he would have heard the bullet whizzing by. Slowly, he raised up again and was grateful for the dirty brownish turban he was wearing. Like the rest of his clothes, they blended in well with the mountain brown and black that surrounded him. Inch by inch he moved lower in the direction of the shot, hoping the shooter would remain in place, rather than move around to other cover.

For what seemed like an eternity, there was no sound. Only the jet noise of high flying planes overhead. Every branch he stepped on startled him, every pebble that started rolling made him freeze, but there was no other reaction from downhill. Not from the pilot, nor from Omar. He wasn't sure who had fired the shot. Omar wanted the man alive, so it had to be the pilot who shot the Afghan. Now he wished he had learned to interpret the sound of the different caliber guns, but it was too late to start worrying about it.

Ten more paces at a crouch and he saw movement. It looked like blond hair. A head turning from left to right and up to the sky.

"A woman? A woman pilot?" He was astonished at the thought, but "Why not?"

A few more quiet steps and he was ten feet behind the lady. "Raise your hands" he shouted. "Raise your hands. This is a friend, but drop your gun." He didn't want to be shot by a startled female. He couldn't see if she dropped the gun, but he heard a soft *clunk,* which might have been the falling pistol.

"Turn around slowly. Very slowly."

She did. He was stunned. There stood a beautiful All-American girl in the middle of that desolate landscape. He couldn't believe it.

"Sorry, Ma'am, but I have to be careful. My name is Joe and I work for Army Intelligence. Lower your arms."

"You don't look American." Was all she could utter. The surprise was complete.

"I know." Yousef stroked his beard with his left hand. "I know. Comes with the job. Get down." He took a few more steps toward her and they both hunkered down.

She took his hand. "You scared the hell out of me. Who was the other guy that I shot at. Is he dead? Was he another American?"

"No, he's Taliban and I don't know if he's dead. How well did you hit him?"

"I aimed for his head. I rested my arm on that rock," she pointed behind her, "so I was very steady and he went down like a rock. I guess I killed him. By the way my name is Susie Overton. Captain Overton."

"Oh, hi, Captain. I better check out what happened to Omar because he could be trouble if he isn't dead."

"Don't leave, a chopper is due here in five minutes and the Paras will take him out, I'm sure."

"Are you in touch with them?"

"My beacon is on and I've talked to them. We'll see them in a minute."

"You better warn them that there is still at least one bad guy around."

"Was there just the two of you?"

"Well, there was another guy up in the cave, but I'm sure your boys took care of him. Nothing could have lived through those three bomb blasts."

"Just three of you up there? Then who brought me down?"

"That was Omar, the guy you shot. He was outside with his *Stinger*. I was inside and it never dawned on me, that he could get you with this handheld thing, he patted one of the missiles hanging off his shoulder. "You must have come real close."

"I did. Wait. Here's the chopper." The chuck-chuck-chuck sound of a rotor could be heard in the distance. She put her helmet back on, reached for her radio; "Jolly Blue, hear you coming in. You'll spot my chute. No place to land. Have to scroll down. Have another American with me."

Chapter Thirty-Six

To Waste or Not to Waste?

Qandahar Air Base
Briefing room 18.00

"Can you believe that? The implication is that the Russians needed to get rid of their nuclear waste and decided to unload it in a foreign country like Afghanistan. Maybe that was what the whole stinking war was all about. They had created so many nuclear subs and power stations, that they had more waste than they had counted on and decided to dump it here in some mountain hole."

Colonel Springsteen snickered as a new thought occurred to him. "Can you picture Osama bin Laden finding shelter in a gigantic cave and settling in with all his wives and cronies and slowly getting eaten up by radiation? Hahahaha. Wouldn't that be the joke of the year?"

Everyone laughed spontaneously or politely, depending on their rank.

The wing commander continued, "What's not so funny is that that stuff ate through the protective covering of its container and started to leak. If it hadn't been for that, we might not have discovered this for weeks or months and all of us may have become victims of that crap." He shivered at the thought. "First thing in the morning we're gonna have you guys," he looked at Pate and Wilcox, "go around the whole base with your gadgets and make sure we don't have a few more of these around. Could be hazardous to my health, hahaha." He laughed again and went on, "and yours. All of you."

Getting up, he added, "Wish I could offer you guys a drink and I could stand one myself, but that'll have to wait till we get off this shit pile called Afgha. Sleep well, gents."

The Navy men were back the following day.
"That was quick." The base commander remarked.
"That goes to show you how serious this is." Aldridge answered. "Let's get back to the briefing room. Gather all your pertinent people there, please. Let's start at fourteen hundred hours." Springsteen felt like he was being ordered around, but didn't say anything, just passed the word.

Promptly at 2 PM, the Navy Commander took the stage.
"This is the damnedest mission you'll ever be involved in. Assuming that our analysis is right and that we have a crateful of nuclear waste on our hand, we've got to dispose of it. Handling it like we do in the United States is out of the question. There's no way we're going to load that on a C-5 and expose people to that radiation, not here while loading, not while they're flying or when they're handling it back home. No way. Too many lives at stake. So, we'll have to dispose of it here."

A rumble went through the crowd like the soft roar of a distant thunder. Aldridge had expected that and politely waited for everyone to settle down again. "There will be no exposure for any of you to worry about, because of the way we're going to handle it."

A softer rumble this time.
"Within days, a giant thermal blanket will be flown in here complete with the technicians to install it. I call it thermal, because it serves the same purpose. It'll keep the heat in, the radiation. Once the crate is wrapped, there's no more danger." He stopped, took a sip from the water bottle on the podium and looked around the room.

"Now comes the tricky part. Our Government doesn't want it to remain here. Our Government would like to disavow all knowledge of the whole affair, since at this stage of the game they don't want to ruffle any Russian feathers, because we need their backing on too many issues, including our presence here. So.....," he looked around the room again, "*we* have to dispose of it and quietly."

Questions started popping up all over and hands were being raised, but he silenced them all by raising his own arm, well above his head.

"We obviously have not yet discovered a deep cave or cavern where nuclear waste has been deposited, so we have to find somewhere else to dump it. Somewhere where no innocent farmer and his family can come upon it and get killed by their curiosity. We can't drop it from a plane, so it'll have to be lowered from a helicopter."

This time, the murmurs and the comments were louder and continued longer. The commander kept his cool.

"We're not asking for volunteers…" he hesitated… "yet! We would hate to order someone on a mission like this, but it could happen. The one thing we can do is, study the map. Find a place, where men nor mountain goats would ever go and at an altitude that our helicopter can reach. After that, we plan to load it, fly it over and release it from here to eternity without blowing anyone of the crew to kingdom come. So, while waiting for our blanket, we'll study and plan. This time I'm staying here to enjoy your great food and hospitality. Thanks."

"Let's hear it for our brave Commander!" Springfield couldn't resist the pun.

Because of the altitude limitations of most of the heaviest helicopters, the tallest mountains near the Pakistan border were not considered. There was no way that a Mohawk could climb to 12,000 feet. Just not enough air. Populated areas were ruled out for obvious reasons, so it seemed that the ridge along the west side of Nuristan Canyon was probably their only choice. At 9,000 feet, the altitude was workable, the terrain was extremely rugged, absolutely inaccessible and far from any human habitat.

The coordinates were plotted and satellite pictures were scanned in order to pick the exact spot for disposal.

What they couldn't figure as yet was the size and the weight of the sensitive package. No one knew how thick the 'thermal' blanket would be and how many times the nuclear technicians would wrap the crate. One thing was for sure, getting it out of the wreck was going to be a chore and a half. Either the entire plane would have to be lifted up, so they could get out of the loading door in the rear of the plane or the fuselage would have to be cut in half, so each part could be pulled away, exposing the culprit. The latter seemed the most advantageous.

A crew was selected from the many volunteers among the pilots and mechanics of the copter squadron. All they had to do now was, wait for the 'blanket' to arrive, so they could go to work on the retrieval and disposal of the problem.

Four days later a giant C-17 landed with a team of twelve officers and enlisted men, plus a large wooden box with the mysterious 'blanket'.

The area had been roped off as a danger zone and all the bystanders could do was watch from a safe distance and guess what was going on. Four men in *'space suits'*, entered the battered plane and reappeared after about ten minutes. Seemingly satisfied with what they had observed, the box with the blanket was opened, a large cloth like a huge aluminum foil was extracted and the foursome disappeared inside the Tupolov fuselage again. Another twenty minutes and one spaceman reappeared, took off his helmet and signaled; *"ALL CLEAR"*.

Twelve Air Force mechanics descended on the old Russian craft with torches and cutters and within a half hour a tractor, attached to the cockpit, pulled half of the plane forward for about forty feet. Now, all the bystanders could see the silver wrapped item, peacefully sitting in the remaining rear half of the plane. It looked innocent enough.

Officers with gadgets and instruments approached the remaining wreckage and seemed satisfied that all was well, because they started packing their gear and returning it to the huge rear door of the waiting C-17 transport.

In the briefing room, thirty minutes later, Navy Commander Aldridge controlled the briefing.

"Ladies and gentlemen," (two female officers were present) "this is of the utmost importance. This whole affair, from beginning to end is classified. Top secret. Let me repeat; *TOP SECRET!*" He nearly shouted. "Of course, that's a near improbability, because everyone on the base must know by now what has been going on and that's where it has to stop. Every officer, every NCO must make it a point to instruct his subordinates that not a word, not a whisper about this leaves the base, especially when it comes to the press. If this leaks out to the press, the Russians will be thoroughly embarrassed and the diplomatic consequences would be devastating. The U.S. Government does not know about this disastrous discovery and does NOT want to know about it." He stopped a moment and a grin appeared on his face. "Does this sound reminiscent of *AIR AMERICA* in Vietnam and Laos?" The Navy man grinned at the assembled airmen and continued, "Anyway, you get the picture. Tomorrow, we fly the crate out of here and life continues like before, fighting a lopsided war with no clear enemies, while losing personnel on a regular basis. Remember: instruct all your men and women, that this is top secret. No ifs, ands, or buts about it. Any questions?"

A man in a flight suit raised his hand and spoke up. "Sir, is there any danger when the package is dropped or if the chopper crashes?"

"I like your terminology; 'package'. If the drop or crash is such that it would split or break the package, and the blanket is damaged as well, radiation could escape and the danger could be deadly. If that happens, get the hell out of there and call us back in. Just load it gently in the helo and put it down gently on the mountain top and fly away and forget that you ever saw it or were involved in this operation. It's simple enough, just set up a solid plan and then execute it properly and there shouldn't be any problems."

He looked around again. "Any other questions? No? Col. Springsteen, it's all yours."

"You heard the man! Mum's the word. Let's go eat."

After chow, a team was selected, take-off time decided and coordination between the ground crew and the aviators was established. The 'package' would be taken out by forklift, transported to the flight line, attached with heavy lines to a Blackhawk helicopter and secured. Cables would be attached to the overhead pulley, so while the chopper hovered over the final disposal spot, the crew would gently lower it to the ground.

Piece of cake.

Chapter Thirty-Seven

Para "Jolly Blue", Going In.

Over the Canyon.

Parrot Yellow Three rolled in for his second pass at the west wall of the valley when he saw his leader twist and turn in her dive and saw the plane explode on the floor of the canyon a few seconds later. He pulled up out of his dive, laid the plane on its side, so he could see the crash scene below and pushed his radio button.

"HOG DOWN! South end of Nuristan Canyon. Jolly Blue. Do you read?"

Before he got an answer he switched to the tower frequency and repeated. "Bagram tower, This is Yellow Three. Hog down! Hog down! South end of Nuristan Canyon. Over."

"Roger Yellow Three. Understand an A-10 down in the Nuristan Canyon, over."

"Affirmative. Calling Jolly Blue." He switched channels again.

"Jolly Blue, this is Yellow Three, how do you read?"

"Yellow Three, hear you loud and clear, go ahead."

Three kept circling, calling out to his team, "Yellow, fall in loose trail." And to the rescue helicopter; "Jolly Blue, Hog down in the southern part of the canyon. What's your twenty?"

"Yellow, we're at a hundred feet above the terrain, twenty miles out. Coming in."

"Blue, climb up. The bad guys have *Stingers*. We'll be covering you."

"Yellow, have you spotted the pilot?"

"Roger, we have the chute, half way up the western slope. Can't see the pilot but we hear her beep."

"We're on our way."

Yellow Three with Two and Four behind him in trail formation, kept circling overhead until he called out, "Going in. A cave at 5000 where the missile came from."

He dove in and aimed at the spot from where he had seen the smoky trail of the Stinger originate on the way to Groper's aircraft. Angling diagonally along the slope, he put his pip on the cavity in the south-western end of the ridge, pushing his bomb release button and pulling up sharply while shoving his throttles to wide open in order not to hit the ridge of the canyon wall.

Yellow Two followed the element leader and homed in on the explosion from his Number Three's 1,000 pounder. A light touch on the button and he soared over the rocky edge of the mountain range as his bomb continued it's trajectory down into the mountain side. Yellow Four followed the others down and by the time he had done his work, the cave, containing the last of the Taliban team, had become one big gaping hole. There was no way a human or a mouse could have survived that ordeal.

Satisfied that there wouldn't be any more incoming missiles from that location, Yellow Three concentrated on contacting his flight leader.

He could hear the beep-beep of her beacon and switched to Groper's emergency frequency. "Yellow, do you read?"

"Five by five."

"Have your chute in sight, Para Rescue on the way."

"Roger. Have two Americans down here."

"Two?"

"Roger. Two."

"Roger Yellow, we'll stay overhead. We're good." He meant, he had plenty of fuel as yet."

"Thanks. Out." She switched off the radio in order to preserve the battery and turned back to Yousef. "How the hell did you get into a fix like this?"

"It's a long story. I'll tell you when we get back. Let's concentrate on the rescue."

The F-16 squadron from Qandahar was on their way with 16 aircraft in order to continue the onslaught in the canyon that had been started by the A-10's when the call came through, "HOG down."

Lieutenant Colonel Smolders, *'Smokey'*, immediately followed through.

"Fancier Flight, continue as briefed, with the exception of Fancier Grey. Grey, take over the 'Sandy' duties from the A-10's circling over the southern end of the Nuristan Canyon. Cover the rescue operation of Jolly Blue coming in. Maintain altitude. The bad guys have *Stingers* and know how to use them. Do you read, Grey?"

"Roger, Grey. Taking over Sandy duty when over target."

Bagram OPS offices.

"HOG down, HOG down."

The crew room sprung into activity. "Para Jumpers Delta and Foxtrot, prepare for flight. Backup Jolly Blue." Two dozen men rushed out.

Colonel Wainwright jumped when his phone interrupted his conversation with Bruce Bongers. "What? Where? South end? That's Yellow? Who? The lead? Groper? God forbid!" He slammed the phone down.

Bruce had jumped up as well, "What's what?"

"A-10 down. The lady pilot. Let's get to OPS." He was already heading for the door.

"What have we got?" was his first question at the Exec, who was at the big map on the wall, plotting the coordinates of the downed pilot.

"Sir, we don't have a satellite picture yet, but it looks as if she is halfway up the western slope of the canyon, about five miles from the southern end. Lousy terrain. No landing spots. They'll have to hover and rappel down. No problem sir. That's what they do. The only worry is; are there more bad guys with handheld missiles that can take out a chopper. The one that brought down Groper came out of nowhere while she was on a bomb run. Based on previous pictures, there are no human beings on those slopes, but obviously they hide well, as Groper will attest to."

"Are the other ones of her flight up there acting as Sandys?"

"Affirmative. F-16's are on their way to take over and Jolly Blue should be within fifteen minutes from pick-up."

"Great." The wing commander sounded relieved.

"One thing, though, sir." The Exec again, "Yellow Three relayed a message that there were two Americans to be picked up."

"Two? Where the hell did the other American come from?"

"I don't know sir and I don't understand. There sure as the devil are no two-seater Hogs around."

"Damn right, there aren't."

"Excuse me," Army Colonel Bongers cut in. "Any information on the other American down there?"

The Exec shook his head, "No sir. Just that Groper said, 'pick up two Americans'."

"Why do you ask?" Col. Wainwright wanted to know as he turned to Bongers.

"It could be pure coincidence, but I have an undercover man down there who radioed the other day of Bin Laden's presence in the canyon and he may very well have caught up to the pilot."

"You mean, he first shot her down and now he's cozying up to her?" Wainwright was getting hot under the collar.

"No, no. I hope not. He is in there as part of a team, trying to locate and protect Osama and one of the other team members must have fired the rocket. My man would never shoot down an American plane. He's solidly American and…"

"If he is, how did he get in on this Taliban deal? Is he a Hadji himself or is he really American?"

"Harry, excuse me, I can not disclose the details here, but I hope it's my man down there with your pilot. In a way, I would be pleased to see that he is well, on the other hand, his job is to locate Bin Laden, and he may not have accomplished that as yet. If I can find out, I may choose to leave him down there to complete his mission. After we're through throwing all that destruction down there I would like a frontline witness who can verify if we got the miserable S.O.B. or not." He turned to the assembled airmen,

"Thanks folks, is there a way I can get through to the rescue helicopter directly?" He turned to the Air Force Colonel, "That's with your permission, of course."

"Of course, Bruce, of course. As long as it does not hamper or interfere with our mission.

"Yellow Flight, this is Fancier Grey. Have you insight. Where's the downed pilot?"

"Grey, she's down at your 10 o'clock low. Half way up the slope. You'll see the chute."

"Don't have her yet. Any other baddies on the ground?"

"Haven't seen any movement anywhere. May have been an isolated watch post."

"Roger. See her now. We're in position. Thanks, Yellow."

"Yellow out. Going home."

"Down pilot, this is Fancier Grey, how do you read?"

"Grey, read you fine. Jolly Blue is fifteen minutes out. I shot one Taliban. Don't know his stats. Another American with me. Pick-up should be simple, except, no landing zone nearby. We'll have to climb the rope, I'm afraid."

"That's not too bad. We'll keep an eye on any movements. Any action down below?"

"All quiet on the western slope."
"Hahaha, atta girl. Out."

"Jolly Blue, this is Fancier Grey, over."
"Grey, this Blue, go ahead."
"Blue do you have the coordinates for the downed Hog?"
"Negative. We're climbing and circumnavigating the western wall of the canyon. Should be ten minutes out from the mouth of the canyon. How far in is the pilot?"
"How far? About three miles from the southern rim."
"Roger. Do you have us in sight?"
"Negative."

Yellow Three, on his way back to the base. "Gray, this is Yellow Three. Blue is at your four o'clock, about ten miles out."

"Roger, I'm turning in that direction. Got him. Got him now! Jolly Blue, continue present course for three more miles, then turn sharply to your left to a heading of zero-one-zero degrees and you'll spot the chute at your eleven o'clock."

"Roger, Blue, one more minute, then zero-one–zero."
"Right."

Chapter Thirty-Eight

A Preview Of Hell.

Omar had lost a lot of blood, but was conscious. After watching the Warthogs coming in above and behind him, blowing apart what had been his hiding place for twenty days, he laid against a boulder that supported him at a slant. The blood had discolored the top part of his coat, but that helped him blend in even better with his surroundings. His clothing was drab, grey, brown and black, just like the rocks and the soil around him. He couldn't have invented a better camouflage if he'd been asked to do so.

The circling planes had left and it became deadly quiet in the huge crevice, called Nuristan. He could make out voices, one male and one female. That puzzled him. He couldn't understand them, but it did sound like English to him. Were there two pilots in that plane? One man and one woman? And where was Yousef? He had gone around in order to surprise the pilot from behind, but he hadn't heard any shots. He listened more intently and straightened up a little more. It sounded like Yousef's voice, speaking a foreign language. Was it possible that the young Moroccan had captured the pilot and was conversing with him? Then where did the woman's voice come in?

Should he raise his voice and ask Yousef for help? He could certainly use some first aid. Don't pilots have survival gear when they bail out? He was about to shout when he heard planes overhead again. Way up. Different sound. He scanned the sky and spotted them. Four of them, coming in fast, starting to circle around him. Inadvertently, he slid down a little farther.

"That must be the protectors." he thought. "The rescue helicopter must be on its way."

The wounded Taliban slipped to the rocky floor and crawled underneath a leafless bush. He could see out through the bare branches and was confident that no-one could see him. Omar was undecided. He still had one Stinger and his AK-47. In his mind, there were three choices. Wait for the chopper to come in low and take it out with his automatic rifle. 20 rounds could do it. That way, Yousef and the pilot would be at his disposal to treat him and get him out of there.

He could watch as the pilot was hauled into the hovering craft and than blow it up with his stinger or wait and see if maybe the helicopter would bring up Yousef as well and then blow it up.

"Could the pilot have captured his young team mate? Possibly!"

The jet fighters above him were getting lower and louder. They might have spotted him. Not likely though. If they had, they weren't doing a thing about it. Two stayed in a left hand turn above the two other ones who were circling to the right. In the distance a soft *thump-thump-thump* told him the chopper was getting closer. A look around convinced him that his position was very favorable for what he had in mind. Even if the heli would descend to twenty feet above him, his clothes would make him blend in so well with his immediate environment that he could feel undetectable.

"Bring on the infidels."

Surrendering to them never entered his mind.

Bagram OPS.

"Are you saying there's no way I can communicate directly with my agent on the ground?" Colonel Bongers was utterly frustrated.

"Once he's up in the chopper and above the ridge, we should be able to raise him, but right now the best thing we can accomplish is relay a message to the Sandys above him and hope for some reply from the emergency radio that Groper has on her. That's all."

"Well, maybe it's for the best after all. I don't know their status, how much food and water they have, if any, and how long he could survive down there by himself. I'm assuming that the rest of his team are all dead. I'll have to figure a way to insert him back in there later on if we need to. Of course, if we did get Bin Laden in this assault, his mission is accomplished anyway." Bruce consoled himself somewhat. "Oh, well. Thanks."

"Jolly Blue? Do you have the target?"

"Roger, going in."

The rescue chopper was aiming directly for the white silk draped over the rocks and bushes on the slope. The Major flying the left seat pushed the button on his intercom.

"Pilot to Lieutenant Grau. Will hover at fifty feet. Drop your men above the target on the slope and we'll move overhead when all is secured."

"Roger, Grau. Will send two men down. Signal when ready."

Nuristan Canyon
Southern entrance.

"Jolly Rescue Blue, ready to extract."

The pilot of the Pave Low made a 180 degree turn in order to put his hoist on the lee side of the slope. From his position in the left side of the cockpit, he could follow the proceedings of the para-rescue men behind him as they rappelled down to the ground and back up.

Lieutenant George Grau pushed the intercom, "Good position, Captain. Can you put me through to the pilot below, sir?"

"Wilco. Go ahead."

"Yellow Lead, this is Jolly Blue, how do you read? Over."

Groper had put her helmet back on. "Loud and clear."

"Rog, are there any bad guys down there?"

"I shot one, don't know his condition. May have been fatal. Hasn't shown his face, over."

"Roger Yellow, we have our guns out for cover. Man with sling is coming down. Can you step into the clear, please? Move under the chopper, directly under the chopper. Good, see you now. Move up twenty more paces, forward and to the right."

"Moving." As Groper followed her instructions, Yousef moved forward as well, exposing his AK-47 in his hands and two *Stingers* on his back.

"TALIBAN!" J.P., in the open door of the copter shouted as he fired a quick burst at the drab-clad figure below.

"No! No!" Groper shouted into her radio. He's American!" It came too late. Yousef received two slugs through his chest and fell forward. "No, No!" The Hog pilot screamed again as she ran back to the fallen figure.

"He's breathing. Help. Hurry."

J.P. Pagliari was already descending on the sling, letting him down and he hit the ground running. A stretcher was being lowered at the same time and two more Para-Rescue men followed suit.

J.P. had his pistol in his hand as he ran to protect the downed pilot, not knowing what had transpired, because he couldn't hear the radio conversations, only the *chuck-chuck-chuck* of the rotor above him and a series of shots he fired himself from the chopper.

"Are you okay, Ma'am? Are you okay?"

"I'm okay, but some stupid ass up there shot him." She was leaning over the so-called Taliban, desperately trying to stop some of the bleeding with her handkerchief.

"Who is he? He's a bad guy, no?" J.P. was hesitant to holster his pistol.

"No, he's Army Intelligence. Undercover. Help stop the bleeding before he dies."

"Good God. Guys, get the pilot aboard. Step aside please, Ma'am. Go! Get aboard. I got to cut his clothing, step aside." One of the rescue men guided Groper to the sling that was dangling down from the helicopter.

J.P. quickly slid open the overcoat of the prostrate man and carefully cut away his underwear. The Taliban smelled like he hadn't had a bath in weeks. Two more Paras rushed up, positioning a stretcher close to the victim. Fifteen handy and fast fingers quickly bandaged the man's back and carefully rolled him over to repeat the whole procedure from the front. Juan Pedro had his first look at the face of the bleeding man, but not until he opened his eyes did he notice something familiar about his features. Couldn't place him though. Before attempting to strap him to the litter, J.P. administered a shot of morphine, so the pain would be bearable when he fully came to.

The results were startling. Yousef shook and opened his eyes wide. *"Juan! Mi hermano."* (Juan, my brother.)

"Yousef! Eres tu?" (Is it you?") The headpiece and the beard made the Moroccan nearly unrecognizable.

"Si! Recuerdas a Miss Piggy?" (Do you remember Miss Piggy?)

"Madre mia!" Looking up at the other Paras, he hollered. "It's my brother! For real. That's my brother. Good God, let's get him aboard. We gotta save him. Let's go,"

Stunned as they were, the other two didn't hesitate, but eased the body onto the stretcher and started their perilous climb up the rugged slope. The sixty degree incline with all it's jagged rocks and loose boulders was giving them fits and several times they nearly lost their balance as they slip- slided their way up. It wasn't but twenty paces forward and fifteen feet upward, but it took a good five minutes before they could attach the lines to the litter for the trip up.

Groper had safely gotten aboard and laced into Grau, "Lieutenant, why did you shoot him? I told you he was American. I...'

"But he was carrying a rifle and he could've...."

"You could have asked. I was on the radio with you."

"But our gunner over there didn't know that and his job, like mine, is to protect you in the first place and ourselves next."

"Bullshit! The bum is just trigger happy. You knew you were going to extract two Americans and…"

"There they come. They got him on a strech, so he must be alright. Make room please. We gotta get him aboard and into a hospital fast. Let's go guys."

Ropes were lowered in order to bring up the stretcher with Yousef tightly strapped down, plus the other rescuers. The pilot in front was anxious to give it the throttle and head home. He didn't like the spot he was in. His rotor blades were constantly whipping only twelve feet from the nearest rock pile and he was ready to increase that distance.

Omar had passed out from blood loss, but was roused by the dust and the noise of the chopper overhead. For a moment, he thought they had spotted his brown and black clothing and were coming after him. He was very groggy, and slipped in and out of consciousness, but realized after a while that all the action was about sixty feet from him and that the target of the overhanging helicopter was to retrieve the pilot who had shot him and maybe Yousef as well.

"Can't let that happen. That boy knows too much. If they interrogate him, he may reveal all about our operation. Can't let that happen. I'll shoot him when I see him go up." He groped around for his rifle, but the effort was too much and he passed out again.

The sound of a quick burst of gunfire, *tatatat,* snapped him back to consciousness.

He couldn't figure where the shots had come from or who was shooting at whom, but in his groggy condition he felt he had to help. His AK-47 was not within reach, but his last *Stinger* was right behind him. Omar groaned as he rolled over, but the pain was so excruciating that he near blacked out again. He breathed deeply, and while lying on his back, the terrorist managed to pull the rocket launcher onto his chest and leaning it against one of the overhead branches, he had a direct line of fire at the chopper.

"*Allah Akbar.*" He whispered as he pulled the trigger.

A puff of smoke raced to the copter, just a hundred feet above him and with the loudest bang he had ever heard in his life, the craft exploded into a huge fireball, spilling burning fuel down the mountain slope.

The flames reached him in seconds and the skin was seared from his hands and face while his clothes started to burn like torches.

He screamed in agony. *HE WAS IN HELL BEFORE HE WAS DEAD!*

Chapter Thirty-Nine

Blackhawk Up! Nuclear Delivery

Qandahar A.B.

The weather cooperated. Cloud base was about 8,000 feet, but the visibility was fair. Eight to ten miles. The forecast was for light snow in the afternoon, so the mission had to proceed without interruptions. The F-16's had been roaring aloft for the last half hour already, while the crane neatly extracted the 'package' from the fuselage and put it out in the open where the Blackhawk could pick it up.

The technicians kept running around with their instruments, checking continuously for possible radiation leaks, but everything seemed to be well under control.

The big helicopter moved overhead and while the rotors blew up enough dust that it hindered the crew below, attaching of the ropes went without a hitch. Slowly, ever so slowly, the pilot increased power and started to tighten the cables. Nothing snapped, thank God. The ground crew had run for cover and the spectators remained at a respectable distance, keeping their fingers crossed. With an audible groan, the big box, lovingly known as 'the package,' started to lift off the tarmac and commenced swaying gently, underneath the huge chopper.

"Qandahar Ground, this is Blackhawk One, ready for taxi and take-off, over."

"Blackhawk One, cleared for northern departure. Avoid all buildings and towns, over."

"Roger, Blackhawk. Churning away."

The five man crew had volunteered for the mission. They felt strongly about their goal of getting the dangerous box away from all living creatures, if at all possible. Based on what they had learned to believe, if undisturbed, the box would not exude radiation for a thousand years. By then, they hoped, technology would be such that they could cope with it, one way or the other.

All went well. The big chopper, with the bundle swinging underneath, resembled a water supplier on its way to a brushfire. The trip should only take an hour one way.

After studying satellite and reconnaissance photos, they had selected a spot on the western ridge of the embattled canyon, 7,000 feet up and away from the fighters on their bombing runs. All they would have to do, was, set it down gently, release the cables and head home. Seemed simple enough.

The briefing officer had joked, "Just remember Tibbits, drop the bomb, turn sharply and dive and get the hell away from there."

"What's a Tibbits?" One of the crew wanted to know.

"Tibbits? Are you kiddin'? You dummy. He was the man who dropped the first atomic bomb over Hiroshima."

It had gotten a hearty laugh from the assembled military men, Navy and Air Force alike.

"Qandahar tower, this is Blackhawk One, I'm receiving some garbled transmissions about a HOG down. What's the call sign of the Sandy overhead?"

"Blackhawk One, Sandy Grey is on the way, have no further details. Can you be of assistance?"

"Negative. Still thirty miles out, carrying hazardous cargo."

"Understand. Proceed with mission. Qandahar out."

"What's going on Captain?" The look on the pilot's face told his crew that something wasn't quite Kosher.

"The Hogs and the 16's are banging the shit out of the canyon and it sounds like the baddies got at least one A-10. We can't help though. Got to lose our cargo first. We're twenty-five minutes from deposit. After that, we'll see if we're needed. We'll see. Relax. We're right on schedule."

As they came closer to the drop-zone, radio reception improved and he could listen in to the communication between the F-16 leader and Jolly Blue as they were closing in on the downed pilot. The A-10's that had been bombing the canyon had pulled off, so that was one group of planes they didn't have to scan the skies for. What they didn't need was a mid-air collision with a fighter-bomber on a gunnery pass. So far, so good. The pilot sighed a sigh of relief, but remained tense and alert. Just twenty more minutes.

The transmissions from Jolly Blue were getting clearer fast, indicating that both the helicopters were heading for the same spot on the map. The Blackhawk pilot kept his eyes peeled, but stayed off the radio, knowing that radio-clutter could radically undermine a mission.

The western ridge of the mountain range that edged the canyon came into view, but just barely. Visibility at their altitude was receding to maybe five miles. He slowed the craft a little, checking his GPS and all the other instruments.

"Five minutes out." He called on the intercom. "Stand by."

The whole crew got into a 'readiness' position. The pilot and co-pilots got ready to hover over the exact deposition point, the airmen in the back set up their equipment for a quick release, once they were over the exact spot where the 'package' was to be dropped.

"Two minutes out. Get set." The pilot relayed to the men in the rear. Everybody was in position. Everyone knew what to do and the whole team was aware of the importance of synchronizing their movements.

"Sixty seconds," The pilot's voice was calm and confident.

Brothers, FOREVER!

But then... "*Copter down*," came in over the radio. For just a second, the pilot thought that *his* helicopter was referred to and he jerked up sharply, while his technicians behind him hit the release buttons, disengaging the cables that held the contaminated box in place. The 'package' tumbled down for about fifty feet, hit a sharp rock, tore apart and rolled into the canyon below.

"Sandy Gray, this is Blackhawk One, Who's down?" The pilot swerved left and right, trying to determine if he was being targeted. One of his men, who detached a rope connection was thrown out of the open door and plummeted to his death on the jagged rocks below.

"Jolly Blue is down. Exploded, probably no survivors." F-16 leader reported.

"Location, please, this is Blackhawk One."

"About forty miles from the south end of the canyon, on the west slope. Big fireball, repeat, probably no survivors. What's your position, One?"

"Over the entrance to the canyon, at 8,000 feet. Descending to 5. Give me a fix, over."

"Blackhawk, head zero-one-zero degrees. Stay clear of canyon wall. You'll spot the fire within minutes."

"Roger, zero-one-zero, going in."

The pilot pushed his intercom button, "Loadmaster, what's your status?"

"Sir, Airman Bowman went overboard and package split open at about 6,000 feet."

"Damn. Is Bowman near the package?"

"Can't see him, must be close."

"Damn, nothing we can do?"

"Affirmative. Package is hot. May kill us all."

"Understand. We're going after a downed Pave Low, fifteen minutes ahead. Watch for rockets. There's already two down. May be crawling with baddies."

"Roger, manning the guns." On both sides of the helicopter,

gunners got into place, although only the slope on the left side threatened any danger. They prepared to pepper the Taliban fighters that weren't there.

Bagram Air Base,
OPS.

The speaker blared: "Jolly Blue down! Para Blue down!"
Col. Wainwright dropped his pen and dashed out the door to the briefing room. Several airmen were already facing the wall chart.
"Is Jolly Delta up?' He shouted at the Exec the moment he rushed into the room.
"Yes, sir. They took off forty minutes ago, they should be halfway there,"
"Get the Sandy on the speaker. Who's over there? Yellow?"
"Negative sir, Yellow pulled off, heading home now. F-16's from Qandahar are circling. Sandy Grey is their call sign."
"Get the leader on the horn. How can this happen when there are fighters overhead to prevent this. This very thing. Are they blind or something?"
"Because the canyon is very narrow, they practically have to stay above it and it would be very hard to make out just one or two persons on the ground when they're traveling 300 knots."
"Horseshit. I flew Sandy missions in Vietnam in 105's and F-4's and we never... Yes... Yes???? Put him through." The Wing Commander was interrupted by a voice on the speaker.
"Bagram OPS? This is Sandy Grey over the downed chopper."
"This is Colonel Wainwright. What's the status down there?"
"Jolly Blue is destroyed. No survivors. Blackhawk from Qandahar is five minutes out, will send jumpers down. Gonna be tricky, still burning furiously at two locations."
"Two locations? Explain."
"The craft exploded into a huge fireball and part of it went up and over into the canyon and a small part fell on the slope where they were extracting the pilot."

"Was the downed pilot aboard already as well as the jumpers?"

"We have no way of knowing that for sure. It seemed like they had one down on a stretcher and were hoisting him up when the rocket hit."

"Oh, shit. Did you see where the projectile came from? Are there other baddies out there?"

"No to the first question. Shooter must have been real close in. We never saw smoke. Don't know to the second. There's no movement down there at all, but there wasn't any before either and then: *poof*!"

"Any chance that anyone is alive?"

"Not likely, sir. Not likely."

"How's your fuel? Sandy?"

"One hour till Bingo."

"Roger, Thanks."

Turning to his exec, "Have a flight of Hogs over there within the hour, when the 16's have to leave."

Turning to Bongers, " Bruce, that's not the kind of news you wanted, is it?"

"Can't believe it." The Army Intelligence Officer was shaking his head. "He'd come so far. Can you imagine what this kid must have gone through in order to get in with the Taliban on a mission to protect Bin Laden?" He kept shaking his head. "I'm gonna sit down a moment and start writing. I'll have a lot of explaining to do."

Wainwright patted him on the back. "'s Not easy, 's not easy. Hang in there, brother."

Qandahar Air Base.
Operations office.

"Find Colonel Springsteen on the double." Major Geron had just finished listening to the conversation between Blackhawk One and Sandy Grey. "Get him to the briefing room. The Navy men too."

The C-17 was all set to go, just awaiting permission to leave and the Navy A-3 was being prepared for take-off as well. All they waited for was the word from the Blackhawk that everything had gone according to plan and the nuclear specialists would depart with satisfied smugs on their faces.

It was not to be.

Confusion reigned. No one knew exactly what happened and radio contact with Blackhawk had been lost the moment the chopper descended into the gorge and put the western ridge between Qandahar and themselves. Their only line of communication was with the Sandys overhead and whatever they could relay to and from Blackhawk One.

Springsteen was furious. "Do I understand, they abandoned their mission, dropped the package and went to play rescuers for a downed Para crew?"

"That's the gist of it, sir." Major Geron nearly sounded apologetic.

"Any word on the condition of the package?" Springsteen had a sad foreboding feeling about it. "Did the Sandy know?"

"I'll get on the radio and have Sandy relay the question. I'll be right back." Geron hurried out the door.

The tension in the meeting room was unbearable. Everyone had questions and opinions, but no one knew the facts. That is, not till John Geron came back in and took to the podium.

"Hold on to your hats. It couldn't be any worse. Blackhawk was about to deposit the package exactly as planned but just seconds before the planting, Sandy called 'Chopper down' and the pilot of the Blackhawk must have reacted instinctively, thinking the warning was for him, probably expected a missile coming in. He must have jerked the plane up and in doing so, one airman went over board and one of the ropes detached from the chopper, dropping the package into the canyon. Supposedly, it rolled down quite a ways and split open and..."

The noise in the briefing room was like an explosion. Everybody shouted at the same time until Springsteen jumped to the podium, knocked a few times without results and finally shouted,

"ATTENTION!" That quieted things down.

"At ease. The Major was right, IT COULD NOT BE ANY WORSE!" He shouted at the top of his lungs. "We now have created a nuclear disaster. Thank God, nobody lives near there. This was all to be hush-hush and our Government and our Military would disavow all knowledge of the package and now, the Russians and the Chinese will pick-up immediately on the escaping radiation and we'll be in a real pickle."

"Can't we act like the package was there all along and one of our bombs must have hit it. That way the Russians will get the blame." The Navy Commander grinned at the brilliance of his thought.

"Yes, and when they send an international team in there, they'll find that it was Russian alright, but wrapped in an American blanket. That'll clear us, right? My ass!"

"But sir," the same Navy Officer again. "The blanket was made in China."

The whole room burst out laughing, Colonel Springsteen included.

"Brilliant. Absolutely brilliant. Gentlemen, we'll immediately start reporting dangerous fall-out. Your instruments will verify that within the hour. Figure out, how low we have to fly over it to get a reading without endangering ourselves. Inform CENTCOM of the problem, let them involve the media and this way, we can lay the blame where it belongs and we'll watch the Russians worm themselves out of this dilemma. Let's get going on it. Now!"

Chapter Forty

The Burning Slopes.

Nuristan Canyon.
Pave Low explosion.

Sergeant Juan Pedro Cordero Pagliari was intently involved in tying down Yousef's injured body to the stretcher, before giving the signal to hoist when the copter exploded into a huge ball of fire. Part of the wreckage was ejected right over him into the valley and part was blown to his left, so instinctively he fell on top of his brother to protect him.

Heat waves scourged the exposed skin on his hands and his neck and he yelped like a puppy that had been kicked viciously, but he held on. His brother had passed out again and that was probably the best thing for him, J.P. thought. That way he didn't know what was going on around him.

The burning fuel that raced down the mountain trying to catch up to the flying debris, passed within ten feet of him, covered Omar. but didn't touch or engulf the two brothers. Just the same, J.P. stayed on top of Yousef's body to shield him from flames and flying copter parts. He passed out as well. Momentarily, the surrounding air was devoid of any oxygen and the young Para Jumper nearly suffocated.

Yousef was the first to regain consciousness, but he was so groggy, he had no idea where he was or what he was doing. He felt no pain. The morphine was doing its job. All he felt was a heavy, heavy weight on top of him. So heavy, he could hardly breathe. With all the strength he could muster, he rolled to his right and the weight slipped off him, creating more breathing room. What he didn't realize was that his efforts started the bleeding all over again, but he could breathe. That was most important. For several moments, he had no idea where he was, who he was and what he was doing there. Slowly, the acrid smell of burning flesh permeated his nostrils and he felt like sneezing, but couldn't. Fire was still raging to his left and burning rubber gave off a terrible stench. One more push and the weight on top of him was totally shifted to his right. Sitting up, the Army-Taliban man finally got a grasp of the situation. Obviously the chopper had been hit. "Omar". flashed through his mind. Then he remembered Juan Pedro.

"Juan!" He called out and sank down, totally exhausted. Darkness enveloped him again.

"Yousef! Joe! Wake up, wake up." J.P. had come to and was leaning over his wounded brother, looking for any sign of life. All around him there was stark devastation, caused by hundreds of gallons of burning high octane gas. There was no sign of the helicopter he had come in and all he could see that seemed worthwhile was his buddy, passed out next to him.

Down below, there was still the sound of fire, burning bushes or airplane fuel. Up where he was, it was deadly quiet except for some jets way up above him. "Joe! Joe!" He gently slapped his face. "Joe, wake up." He had no medical supplies on him, other than gauze and morphine and neither of them would be of any help at this point.

The cold air revived his memory quickly and he sat up, hoping to see somebody who could help. No such luck. Above him, where the helicopter had been, were just small brushfires, indicating where the burning wreck had hit the canyon wall and below him, fire and smoke roared out of control. With a shock, it dawned on him that nobody aboard the chopper could possibly have survived that inferno, so the survival of the two was wholly on his shoulders.

He could hear the circling jets overhead, but he had no way of arousing their attention. No flares, no radio, no mirror, no nothing!

"Madre de Diós," he prayed, *"ayudame, por favor."* (Mother of God, help me, please.) "Help my brother." J.P. checked Yousef's pulse. Weak, but okay, 63 per minute. The bleeding had stopped where the bullets had entered in the front, so he undid the straps on the stretcher and started to roll the unconscious man on his belly to check the exit wounds. The burns on his neck were hurting terribly, but he gritted his tongue and continued his work. "Save Joe first," was his determination. The turban, that was singed but still in fair shape, served as a pillow as the prostrate body slowly rolled on its side and then onto his belly. Making sure that his brother had room to breath, J.P. examined the bandages on his back and realized that both bullets had traveled through the lungs without touching any other vital organs.

He was grateful for small miracles. *"Madre de Diós, gracias."*

Unexpectedly, he thought he heard the familiar sound of a helicopter rotor and stood up to identify the sound for sure. It wasn't a Pave Low, he knew that sound too well. Did the Taliban have choppers, he wondered. Couldn't be! What other whirlybird could possibly be in the vicinity? Truly, he convinced himself, it didn't matter as long as they could help Joe get out of there and into the hands of a doctor.

Looking down, it seemed his brother was resting comfortably, so he started to concentrate at flagging down the chopper if it continued in his direction. The fire below was still roaring and that was as good a signal as he could hope for, so he took off his jacket, turned it inside out, showing the white of the sheepskin lining and got ready to start swinging it over his head in order to flag the rescuers.

Fortunately, the sound of the aircraft was getting closer fast and within another five minutes he could see it coming in.

"Blackhawk!" he screamed, forgetting that there was no way anyone aboard could possibly hear him. "Blackhawk? Where the hell did you come from?" The young sergeant started to swing his jacket frantically above him and it seemed like they spotted him, because the pilot made about a ten degree correction away from the fire.

"Over here! Over here!" As an experienced Para Jumper he should have known that he was wasting his breath, but in his enthusiasm, he wasn't thinking right. "Over here!"

Aboard Blackhawk One.

"Pilot to co-pilot. We have a man waiving a white flag at eleven. Do you see any sign of life near the burn?"

"Negative. The only live one is the swinger."

"Roger, get the crew ready. Send one man down. Cover both sides for potential Hadjis. The place may be crawling with them."

"Roger, hold overhead."

The chopper slowed and stopped directly above the twosome on the slope. A rope came down nearly instantly and an airman rappelled down in quick fashion. J.P. grabbed the rope and welcomed the incoming man with open arms.

"Come help. My brother is out and wounded badly." He rushed back to the stretcher and with the help of the amazed airman, rolled Yousef on his back and started to strap him in again.

"Who the hell is this?" The young airman couldn't believe his eyes.

"That's my brother." J.P. checked the straps. "Pick him up."

Four steps up the slope brought them underneath the cable and with a few snaps, the litter was attached and on his way up. While the two on the ground watched the stretcher disappear into the hold of the copter, the young fellow asked J.P.. as they were waiting for the rope to return; "Are you shittin' me? Your Brother? That's a damn Taliban. What are you trying to pull, Sergeant?"

"That's my brother alright. He's Army. Undercover."

While he grabbed the sling when it came down, he handed it to J.P. "After you Sarge… Brother??? My ass!"

Aboard the Blackhawk

"Sir, Captain, sir, I'm Sergeant Pagliari, Para Jumper. How fast can we get him to Bagram or any hospital that is nearer?"

The pilot ignored the question. "Is there anyone else alive down there?"

"Oh, I don't know. The explosion was unbelievable and the fire even worse. I doubt if there's anyone alive down there."

"Sorry, pal, I'm gonna look anyway. How did you survive?"

"I don't know sir. The blast knocked me out, it burned my neck and my hands but it must just have rolled over me. I don't know."

"Lieutenant, treat this guy. He's burned pretty badly." The pilot spoke into his mike and an officer appeared from the rear and took J.P. under his wing. Whatever he did, it was extremely soothing. The young Peruvian-American sank down on a canvas seat and collapsed.

"Strap him in! Tight!" The lieutenant ordered and bent over toward the open door to see if there was any other living being near the fire of the wrecked helicopter.

Five pairs of eyes couldn't even detect the charred remains of the bodies that had to be down there, in or out of the wreck.

The pilot punched a button. "Sandy Grey, Blackhawk One, picked up two survivors. Is a Pave Low on its way?"

"Roger, One, thirty minutes out. Any other survivors?"

"Not visible. Fire is too intense. Please vector me to nearest medical facility. Have wounded aboard."

"Qandahar is your best bet. Travel south, one-eight-zero for twenty minutes, turn to two-four-zero and contact the tower."

"Roger, Gray. One out."

With two wounded people aboard and a failed mission behind him, the pilot pointed the nose down slightly to gain more speed and wondered if his head would be on the chopping block by the time he got back to base.

"Look out for signs of broken 'package,'" he ordered over the intercom. He was hoping that at least he could give an accurate report about the location of the nuclear mess.

"God help me. My whole career may be on the line."

Chapter Forty-One

Sad Journey, Bagram to Qandahar.

Bagram Air Base.

Colonel Bruce Bongers kept pacing back and forth across the briefing room. He felt so helpless, he could scream. He was used to being in control, issuing orders and jumping into the action, wherever it occurred. Here, on the Air Force Base, he couldn't do any of it. He was totally dependent on the orders issued by the guys in blue and subjected to patiently waiting for results. He felt he should be up there with Jolly Blue, looking for his protégée, but all he could do here was, wait for radio messages being relayed between different aircraft.

He cursed under his breath and thought about all the questions he had to ask his undercover man Joe, because he didn't have the faintest idea what had transpired between Barcelona and Nuristan Canyon. He was sure that the young Moroccan had quite a tale to tell and much of that might help him in his fight against the Taliban. Most of all, he wanted the boy to be safe. Not only safe, but healthy, both physically and mentally. One of his worries was that Yousef had been exposed to so much indoctrination, so much fanaticism that he might have swayed toward the ultra extremist Muslim doctrine and be ready to become a terrorist himself.

Bongers stopped pacing. "I should kick myself in the mental ass for even thinking things like that. I believe in him 100%." He resumed pacing.

"Colonel, Colonel, news in OPS." An airman interrupted his revere. "OPS , sir!"

The Army intelligence man didn't really have to hear that twice, before he dashed out the door for the operations office.

"What's up?" He asked as he stormed in, breathing hard. "What's up?"

"Sir, the F-16's reported that Jolly Blue exploded, very few survivors..."

"Good God!"

"Then we had a message that a Blackhawk picked up two men and are heading for Qandahar. Heavily wounded, sir."

"Blackhawk? Where did he come in? The Army isn't operating in that area, are they? Were we aware of that?"

"No sir, we had no reports of any other activity in the area, but another team of Jumpers is only twenty minutes out and maybe we'll learn more."

Colonel Wainwright joined the fray and thundered: "Now a copter down? What are the Sandys doing? Picking their noses? They're supposed to suppress enemy fire so our guys can get in and out, what are they doing, for cripes sake?"

"Sir, the best we can reconstruct down here, the Sandys haven't seen any enemy movement down below at all..."

"They haven't? Then who fired those rockets that brought down our planes? Santa Claus? Or a bunch of ghosts?" He raised his hands in frustration. "What's going on out there? We figured we'd go in and clobber Bin Laden and instead, we're being clobbered ourselves." He turned around and faced Bruce Bongers. "Mr. Army Intelligence, what is happening? Do you know what's going on? Answer me. What's going on? For Pete's sake."

Bongers had a hard time containing himself. He was plenty upset without the Air Force Wing Commander getting on his case.

"Sir, I wish I knew. I had requested to ride along, and I would have had first hand knowledge of the proceedings in that canyon, but instead my request was denied and I've been hanging around this compound like an expectant father, not knowing how his pregnant wife and his future child are faring. So in brief, I don't know any more than you do and maybe even less, so now I'd like clearance to proceed to Qandahar and meet with the returning survivors and get some firsthand input about what has been going on, so with your permission sir, I'm gonna find out what's been happening." He turned on his heels and left a speechless Wainwright in his wake.

The Air Force Colonel recovered quickly. "Who's on the scene or on the way? What's the count? Did Groper survive? Why weren't the Hadjis taken out before they could bring our aircraft down? I need answers. I need answers more than I need more bad news, so hit it! Get me answers. Now!" He stormed from the room.

Col. Bongers had come in on a small Falcon passenger jet and at least that gave him the authority to command that craft at his beck and call and fifteen minutes later his team was loaded and ready for taxi and take-off. He loved the Air Force, but there was no way that he could command or control anything around him and it left him utterly frustrated.

"Army Four-twenty–two, this is Bagram Tower, you're cleared for taxi to runway One-Three, over."

"Twenty-two, for One-Three, rolling."

The ride to Qandahar would only be thirty minutes and Bruce couldn't stand the suspense. After unbuckling himself, he walked forward approaching the pilot and asked,

"Are you picking up any transmission between the Blackhawk and the Sandys or the tower?"

"Not since we left, sir. Based on what we know, the Blackhawk is fifteen miles out."

"Can you raise him? Ask him who he's got on deck."

"Try, sir." The pilot switched channels and called, "Blackhawk, this is Army 4-2-2, do you read?"

"Army two-two, go ahead."

"Blackhawk, you have survivors aboard, can you identify them?"

"Negative."

"Negative? Army Intelligence wants to know."

"Army Intelligence will have to report to Qandahar for details. Out."

"Oops. Sorry, sir. Classified, you understand?"

"Damn right, I understand. They're doing their job and they're doing it right, but I'd rather have had some of my answers."

"We'll be down in five minutes, sir and the chopper should be right behind us."

"Oh, well." The sigh came all the way from his midriff.

When the Blackhawk came in, the Army men were waiting on the tarmac, along with half a dozen medics and an ambulance. The moment the wheels touched, two nurses and a doctor ran up to the open door, not waiting for the rotor to stop. It was a like a scene from M.A.S.H.. Bongers was waved aside when he tried to run toward the craft and had to wait till the medics carried a stretcher from the innards of the chopper, covered with a blanket. Totally covered.

"Who's under there?" the Army Colonel wanted to know.

""Don't know, sir. Some Hadji."

"May I see?"

The stretcher was put down and the face of the dead man exposed.

"Good God! It's Joe!"

"You know him, sir?" The doctor wanted to know.

"Yes, I do. He worked for me. How did he die?"

"Two bullet wounds, but he died on the ride home. Too much blood loss."

"Holy hell! Who shot him?" Bongers could hardly control his tears.

"I did, sir." An Air Force Jumper with partially burned clothes stood behind the litter and cried.

"Who are you?" The colonel was baffled.

"I'm his brother, Sergeant Pagliari, sir."
"Sergeant, follow me."

They were directed to a small office, where Bongers and Major Geron offered J.P. a seat and some coffee. Geron got busy, scribbling on a legal pad.

"Now, son, tell me slowly what transpired out there. Slowly. Don't leave anything out."

"Well, I was in the gunner's position on the portside of the chopper facing the western slope, looking for any movement. When we came overhead the pilot, we turned 180 degrees, so now I faced the valley. Our pilot and Lieutenant Grau had been in contact with the pilot below, but I wasn't privy to that communication, I wasn't issued a headset." He raised his hands in a helpless gesture and went on. "I could clearly see the chute and about twenty paces in front of it, I mean between us and the chute, the lady pilot stepped out, holding a radio and her helmet. Our guys were already swinging down and I had to go next and then… and then… and…" Tears rolled down his cheeks and he completely choked up. The major handed him a napkin, whispering, "Easy boy, easy."

Bongers waited patiently for the young jumper to regain his composure, although inside, his emotions were reaching the boiling point.

J.P. blew his nose and continued. "She walked up to the sling and just as I was about to put my gun down, out stepped this Hadji with an AK in his hands and Stingers on his shoulders. I didn't hesitate one second, pulled the trigger, tatata, and took him out. I thought he was gonna shoot the pilot and us all at the same time. Well, he never got the chance. I blew him over in just a sec." He blew his nose again. "I didn't know he was one of ours. Why didn't he put his weapons down and raise his hands or something? What would you do Colonel if some bad guy came at you with a gun at ready? I was trained to take him out. Hot damn! Why didn't anybody say something?"

"What do you mean, nobody said something?"

"Well, after I shot him, the Lieutenant shouted: 'He's one of ours', but by then, it was too late. I had shot my own brother!" This time he totally broke down. He collapsed with his head on the desktop in front of him.

Bongers looked at Geron, "Water?" The major got up and disappeared.

A cold glass of water did the trick. The young sergeant calmed down.

"What happened then?"

"I'm not sure. All I know was what I did…"

"That's okay. Tell us what you did."

"Well, I rappelled down and they sent a litter after me and the first thing I did, I cut open his clothes, he was lying on his face and I stopped the bleeding as best I could, then we rolled him over, did the same with the front. Two bullets had gone right through his lungs, but not his heart, he wasn't bleeding too bad. That's when he came to and he recognized me and he spoke to me in Spanish. You could've knocked me over with a feather. You see, with his headgear and his beard, I couldn't see a thing I could recognize, only those beautiful black eyes of his…" He broke down again and again Major Geron urged him to drink some more. He swallowed hard.

"And then?"

"And then?" J.P. closed his eyes. "And then? …Oh, we, this other Para and me, got him on the stretcher, on his back, and we were gonna pick him up, when the copter exploded and I just fell on top of Joe to protect him. Man, it was so hot, the skin on my neck and hands burned instantly, look at them." He stuck out both hands, wrapped in gauze, so there was really nothing to see. "But the burning wreck either blew right over me or off to the side, because it ended up below, burning like hell. Nobody could have survived that. Nobody."

"So you didn't see any other Taliban, who fired at the chopper?"

"No, I was bending over Joe, taking care of his wounds."

"Holy hell. Major, drive the Sergeant to the clinic. I'm sure those bandages need to be replaced by now. I'll talk to you in a while Pagliari, " and standing up he took the young man by the shoulders and said, "I'm so sorry, my boy, like you lost a brother, I feel like I lost a son. I'm so sorry." He turned away quickly. So no one would see the tears welling up in his eyes.

Chapter Forty-Two

It Could Get Worse. Not Much.

Qandahar Air Base.
Briefing room..

"So where's Bowman?" Colonel Springsteen walked into the meeting room, having missed the first five minutes of the de-briefing.

"In the canyon somewhere…" An Air Force Intelligence officer spoke up, but was interrupted immediately.

"In the canyon somewhere? What kind of an asinine statement is that? Where's the pilot? The Blackhawk pilot, who loses cargo, but picks up wounded? There you are." The Wing Commander turned around to face the embarrassed pilot, seated ahead of the crowd in the first row. "Tell me, where is Airman Bowman in relation to the 'package'?" He nearly spit out the word 'package'. "Is he too close to attempt retrieval?"

"I'm afraid so, sir. He went overboard at the same time that the box went. He may be right on top of it."

"Damn." Springsteen turned around again, stepped onto the stage and said, "There's no way we're going to lose one more man over this lousy Russian contraption. I'll write his parents and explain why we won't be shipping him home for burial. We're sticking by our story. Our experts detected radiation in Nuristan Canyon and we are asking the international community to investigate that problem. When a team of nuclear specialist swarms down on the project and discovers Bowman as well, we'll all say, 'Oh. that's where he went! He must have been overcome with the radiation of that Russian contraption'." He looked up and down the rows of military men in the room, including the Navy personnel that had expected to leave hours ago,

"The story remains the same. We detected radiation, sent for Navy experts who determined that the Russians dumped waste in Afghanistan, how much we don't know, but they better clean it up. Headquarters in Tampa will release the news, we won't. Over here and on the carrier, 'mum's' the word. Everything we know is classified. Is that understood?"

A murmur ran through the crowd.

"Is that understood?"

An occasional; "Yes sir." But not enough to appease the colonel.

He hollered; "IS THAT UNDERSTOOD?"

"YES,SIR!" This time he was satisfied.

"Don't forget it."

Springsteen and Bongers had not met before. Their paths had simply never crossed. At that forsaken place called Qandahar, they sat across from one another at a wooden table, each with a cup of coffee in front of them. The Air Force man was in control.

"I know what brought me here, but what in the world are you doing here, Colonel?

"Call me Bruce. It's a long, long story, but briefly, I had one of our boys infiltrate the Taliban in order to locate Bin Laden."

"How did you do that?" Springsteen was amazed at the tale.

"That's another long story and maybe one day I'll write a book about it, but for right now, let it suffice, that I had my boy with a group of Hadjis in the canyon, where they knew Bin Laden was hiding. I don't think my boy ever got to meet the Sheik, as they called him, but he was getting close. As I understand it, his team was protecting one end of the gorge and another team was on the other side, guarding the northern approach."

"How many were on his team?"

"I don't know. I received an indirect message that told me that Osama was in that canyon and we decided to bomb the shit out of it and look for remains and pieces later on. That's still the plan. We bombed the hell out of it, but I have no way of knowing if we got the bastard or not. He's slick. He's been evading us for years."

"For years?" That surprised the Air Force man. "For years? How come I didn't hear about that?"

"Do you remember Ollie North's testimony to the congress as to why he wanted a huge fence around his property?"

"Yeah, I remember something like that, but what…?"

"Ollie said because he wanted to protect his family from Osama Bin Laden and Gore and the other Senators laughed in his face."

"Really? I didn't have time to watch the entire debates, but that's how long we've known about that bastard? That's unbelievable. In other words, we could have prevented the entire nine/eleven catastrophe?"

"We could have. But the CIA thinks we Army pukes are a bunch of amateurs and they disregard anything we feed them. The FBI distrusts everything the CIA and Military Intelligence comes up with, so we all end up in a blind alley, shooting ourselves in the foot."

"That's unbelievable. That's the second time I said that. So what do you do?" The veteran Air Force Officer was intrigued with the entire dialogue.

Bongers grinned. "I listen to all their junk, disregard nothing and draw my own conclusions with permission from my boss, General O'Doull in Tampa. He gives me a lot of leeway, a lot of rope you may say. Sometimes so much rope that I could hang myself, like right now. I had a beautiful, intelligent insurgent about to make contact and now all I have is a body to bring home and no positive results to show for his sacrifice. Damn."

"Don't be so hard on yourself Bruce. This is war. This happens.

It'll happen a thousand more times. Don't let it get to you."

"Yeah, but you don't know the details and my personal involvements. Like I told you, it's a long story. Right now, I need to know, whom to contact on your team, to prep that body for the long flight home."

"You're personally gonna take him back?"

"I'm afraid I'll have to. Right now I don't know if we're going to bury him in Morocco or in the States. I'll have to take that up with his parents and general O'Doull. One way or the other, he has to be preserved for a relatively long time, cause I don't know if I'll cross the Atlantic with him once or twice. It may be a month before he's ever interred." He took a long swig from his coffee, stared into the cup for a while and continued, "What a mess. What an unbelievable mess."

Major Geron interrupted the conversation by entering without knocking, "Oh, there you are Colonel Bongers. You better come quick. Sergeant Pagliari shot himself."

"WHAT?" Both colonels shouted the same word as they jumped to their feet.

"Where? Where is he?"

"Follow me," Geron turned on his heels and ran across the hall to the exit door that led to the tarmac. A golf cart was waiting with an airman behind the wheel. All three jumped on, clinging to the framework while the young driver attempted to lay rubber. Past four of the buildings, they careened left and halted suddenly in front of a double door that was wide open, but blocked by an armed guard. He snapped to attention as the three senior officers raced by him and screeched to a halt in front of a medic, who held up his hand.

"Quiet, gentlemen. The doctor is rendering emergency service in there, while we're preparing him for transportation to the base hospital. It'll be just a second."

"Is he conscious? How bad is he? How did he shoot himself? Was it an accident or was it deliberate? Where is the wound? Did he hit any vital organs? Did he say why?"

The two colonels fired questions simultaneously, but the medic just shook his head and raised his hand again.

"I don't know. I haven't been in there yet. We'll know in a moment. Here they come now."

The door behind him opened and he stepped to his left, waving the three spectators aside as well.

The stretcher rolled noiselessly into the hall, exposing a young face with a huge gauze bandage around his head.

A tall doctor, clad in white with blood smudges on his coat and a stethoscope around his neck, followed the medical team and was halted by the officers waiting in the hall.

"How bad is he doc? Was he shot in the head? Was he..."

"Gentlemen, there's a bullet lodged in his head. Please step aside. If we rush, we may save him. So, please?"

Base Hospital,
Waiting room.

"You have a lot of things to do, so go ahead. I'll wait here and I'll inform you as soon as I hear something." Bongers didn't want the wing commander to spend anymore time in the hospital, waiting for surgery results.

"Okay, I'll be in my office." The Air Force Pilot got up and Bruce started pacing back and forth again. He had informed Springsteen of the relationship between Yousef and Juan Pedro based on what little he knew, while he emphasized the fact, that they really regarded one another as brothers. Real brothers, brought together by God's will and Allah's will.

"What a world!" He said to himself. "Gods of love bring them together and then allow hate and prejudice to separate them and tear them apart. What a world!"

The doctors had worked on J.P. already for forty minutes and yet, not a sound came through to the waiting area and nobody made an appearance to explain the situation.

"Would he live?" Colonel Bruce Bongers kept pacing.

Chapter Forty-Three

It Did Get Worse

Qandahar Air Base
11 PM, Local Time, 9:30 AM Tampa

"General O'Doull, please, Colonel Bongers speaking."
"Just a moment, sir."
"Thank you." Bruce leaned his chin on his left hand and nearly dozed off, he was so exhausted. After about a minute and a half...
"The General will be right with you, sir."
"Oops! Oh, thank you." He nearly dropped the phone. "Yes sir. Sir?" he said to a dead instrument. "General?" It dawned on him that the female voice had said. "Will be right with you." He had to grin in spite of himself. He couldn't remember when he had been so exhausted.
"Yes, Bruce, O'Doull here."
"Good evening General, sorry... it's going on midnight over here. I'm a little groggy and it's not because of some scotch, because there isn't any down here."
"I understand, go ahead."
"May I assume you received my e-mail?"
"Major Holswood read it and wrote a little synopsis, so I know the content, go ahead"

"We had gotten so close after all these months and then it had to all come to this tragic end."

"Go ahead, Bruce, what's your question?"

"I'm bringing the body home, but I feel we should ask the parents in Morocco if they want him buried over there." He stopped talking and rubbed his brow.

"That's a possibility and I suppose that can be arranged. How will we find out?"

"That's the point of my call. I'd like to get your permission to go there personally and…"

"You want to fly to Morocco on your way here? Is that what you're asking?"

"Yes, sir. That's what I'm asking."

"We'll have to have a pack of clearances for a military plane to go in there, but I'm sure it can be arranged. What's the time frame you're working with?"

"Two days from today. Your time. That'll give your troops two full days and me one. That should work."

"Okay. Anything else?"

"Well… yes. The airman who shot him was his adopted brother, or blood brother and…"

"Good God, Bruce, you're kidding?"

"I wish I were, but it's true. They were roommates in the Shrine Hospital in Tampa some ten years ago and they formed a brotherhood of sorts. Anyway, a very strong bond. True love, apparently."

"Why did he shoot him?"

"In my e-mail, you'll find the details, but all he saw was some Taliban with rifle in hand behind the downed pilot, so he fired. That was what he was trained to do."

"Where's he now? "

"That's the other reason for my call. He attempted suicide this morning…"

"Attempted?"

"Yes, he didn't quite succeed, they took a bullet out of his skull and he's still in a coma in intensive care. He may not make it and if he does, he'll have permanent brain damage."

"Wow! No wonder you're groggy. It's worse than being in a battle zone. At least there you expect dead and wounded. And Bruce, you're in the middle of it. What if he doesn't make it? Would you be bringing him back also, or are you leaving that to the Air Force?"

"That was my question. I'd like to handle that as well, although I never thought I would be functioning as a funeral director. But yes, I would wanna do that."

"Do it man! Do it. I'll confirm by e-mail."

"Thanks, General..." but he was already talking to a dead phone.

The Army Intelligence officer started to search for his bed. He had been assigned a room, but couldn't remember where.

AM, Afghanistan time.

After a long deep sleep, filled with horrible nightmares, Col. Bongers felt as tired as when he went to bed. Normally, seven hours of sleep would suffice him, but this morning after eight hours, he knew he could have slept for four more.

First thing, before he even shaved and showered, he called the hospital and was informed, "His vitals are weak, but he's resting. He has not regained consciousness"

Breakfast and coffee in the company of Major Geron brought Bruce back to normal, or at least to 90%.

"John, have we gotten any analysis of the damage we have done in that canyon? Or should I ask, what good we have done?"

"Well, Colonel, the good news is, we didn't lose any more aircraft, partially due to the fact that we changed to all guided bombs and rockets from higher altitudes where the Hadjis couldn't reach us so easily. The bad news is, we have no verification of any collateral damage, other than one huge explosion on the eastern wall, where our boys must have hit an ammunition dump. Of course that means we blew up a lot of original American ammo, but the hope is of course, that Bin Laden was in that same cave and is now in hell in a hundred thousand little bitty pieces. Unfortunately, we can't confirm that."

"John, have they been able to retrieve the bodies of the Para Jumpers and the A-10 pilot? The female?"

"They're in there right now, with gun ships to protect the rescuers and we have F-16's overhead with laser-guided missiles to prevent a catastrophe like two days ago. We expect to have their remains up in Bagram by noon today. There may not have been much left to look for after that fireball the guys described."

"It's turning into a nasty little war, isn't it John?"

"No sir. It started as a nasty war when they hit the Twin Towers on nine/eleven."

"Uh-huh, you're right, but somehow, this conflict is hitting closer to my home than any other, even though I'm half a world away. Maybe I'm getting old and sentimental. How long have you been at this game and how much longer are you gonna stay with it?"

"I'm in my twentieth year and I may hang up my spurs after this tour."

"Are you still flying?"

"That's the whole point. I fly my desk most of the time. I don't get in a cockpit at the controls, but once a month, maybe. That's not the life of a pilot as I have dreamed it. How about you, Colonel?"

"I've had a most interesting career. This spy business, all this undercover work, is the most intriguing job I could possibly imagine, but the days away from home and my four boys is taking its toll on the family, my wife especially. I've been doing this for twenty-five years and loved every minute of it, but this affair with my young protégé got under my skin. I got to love that boy like my own son. That's not healthy in this business of war and killing. Right now, I am shook up like I have never been before in my life. I must be getting old."

"I know how you feel. During Vietnam, we could hardly afford to become close friends with anyone in our unit, because it would only tear you apart if something happened to them. Oh, " He interrupted himself, "someone's waving at us, excuse me a moment."

The major got up and returned a few minutes later.

"Bring your coffee. Pagliari is regaining consciousness."

Bongers had just about finished his bacon and eggs, so he shoved his plate away and grabbed the remainder of his coffee.

Like the day before, a little golf cart took them across the field to the base hospital, where they were met by the tall doctor, but this time in a sparkling white coat without any stains.

"Colonel, John, " he greeted them, "He's not lucid and I don't think you can question him yet, but let's just go in and watch him and see what transpires." He turned and led the way.

In the small ICU, with freshly painted white walls and clean white linens, the dark face of the young Peruvian made quite a contrast on the pillow. His dark eyes were open but they appeared glazed. The doctor bent over him while the two soldiers watched intently.

"John?" He whispered. :"John?"

"They call him J.P., Doc. His full name is Juan Pedro." Geron clued him in

"Thanks." The surgeon leaned over him again and this time said softly, "Juan Pedro?" The dark eyes flickered momentarily as if there was recognition. "Juan? Can you hear me?" The results were nil.

"Follow me, gentlemen." The doctor led the two officers to his office and pointed to two folding chairs in front of his desk.

"Sit, please, gentlemen, sit." He seated himself behind his desk, tapped with a pencil on the pad in front of him a few times and addressed his guests, "Gentlemen, what you just witnessed is probably the most reaction we may ever expect from this young man."

Bongers got up and walked out of the door. He was too choked up to continue listening. It took a full two minutes before he walked back in and sat down. "Sorry, Doc."

"That's alright. I understand. The boy apparently intended to kill himself, but did a poor job of it. What I want to know is, what made him do it?"

Bongers couldn't speak, so Geron answered, "He killed his brother. Accidentally."

"He did? How?"

Before John could say another word, the door flung open and a male nurse cried out, " Doctor, he's gone, he's gone. I…"

Three men stormed from the office to the ICU, but nothing could be done.

Major Geron grabbed Bongers' arm. "Sir, let's hope there is just one big heaven up there for everybody, because if there is, they'll be back together by now."

"Why, dear God? Why does this have to happen?" Bongers was deflated and sagged down into a chair.

Chapter Forty-Four

The Long Road Home.

Quandahar, Afghanistan
December 7, 2001

"It's hard to imagine that exactly sixty years ago, the 'War To End All Wars' had just started and here we are, six decades later and still fighting." Colonel Bongers hadn't felt that low in his entire life. Always the optimist, always positive, always uplifting other people, here he was, half a world away from home and thoroughly in the dumps.

He had called Mrs. Dixon in Dade City and she clued him in about the connection between J.P. and Yousef. Now he faced the horrendous task of informing the adoptive father in Fort Walton Beach of the tragic death of his son. He hated the prospect, but had very little choice. A chaplain at nearby Hurlburt Field had been notified and he volunteered to be the carrier of the bad news. Now Bruce had to wait for confirmation of the right phone number and the proper time to call.

"I hate to do these things on the phone. I'd rather go out and meet the folks in person, but I may not be in Florida for six more days and we can't leave those people in suspense for that long a period of time."

He was facing Major John Geron over lunch and was glad that he had a willing ear at his disposal, so he could air out his frustrations.

John had given Bruce a white civilian shirt, because the Army team had flown in with nothing but military uniforms and equipment and they wouldn't be able to wear those in Morocco. The other members of the team were scrounging around for civilian stuff to wear and then they would be able to take off.

The final clearance from Central Command in Tampa had not arrived yet and as it turned out, it wouldn't come.

"Phone call for Colonel Bongers," the loudspeaker in the mess hall announced.

"Watch my food. I'll be right back."

The phone call was not from the Panhandle of Florida, but from Tampa.

"Bruce, O'Doull here. Can't get you into Morocco, but that may not be too bad. You're expected by the British at the Rock of Gibraltar and from there you take the ferry from Algeciras to Tangier. Rent a car and... Do you know where you're going from there?"

"Chefchaouen."

"Chef...whatever! You know where to find it and how to get there? Good. Have a safe trip. Call me with results or if you have any complications. Good flight."

Back at his lunch, "Do you know something John? Things are working out better than I imagined. We'll land in Spain, we can buy the clothes we need and the fellows can go on the town, while I travel to Morocco by ferry. The only complications will be if Yousef's parents insist on him being buried in their home town, I've got to find a way to ship him over there."

"That shouldn't be too hard. I'm sure there are funeral homes right there that are used to shipping bodies across the Mediterranean. No, I wouldn't worry about that. Were you planning to bury the boys in the U.S.?"

"I'm not planning a damn thing. I'm just preparing for any and all possibilities I may encounter. I have to wait on what Pagliari's father has to say before I plan anything."

It didn't take much longer. The Catholic Chaplain at Hurlburt called and advised to call the following day. "It's past midnight here. The father is taking it hard and he's had a few drinks already. A few too many, I'm afraid, so this is not a good time to talk to him. Give it at least eight hours. He's at home till about nine and after that at his office. You have the numbers? Good. Remember this is Central Time out here. I wish I could add something more positive, but the boys are together with the Lord, I'm sure. They're in a better place. Goodnight Colonel."

"Okay, we're off. Colonel, John, I wish I could say, 'it's been a pleasure', but it was so tragic, that all I can do is thank you both for all you've done for us. Thanks."
They shook hands, saluted and walked onto the ramp toward their plane.
"I'll call from Athens, when we refuel. It'll be morning over there by then." The Colonel told his exec as they lugged their belongings to the aircraft. The bodies had been loaded and therefore the plane was rather crowded, barely enough room to get the four man team plus the two pilots aboard.
As the plane roared down the runway, Bruce looked out and murmured, "Goodbye, you Godforsaken country. Hope I'll never see you again."

Athens

While the crew took a break and looked for dinner, the plane was being refueled. Bruce decided it was still too early to call Emil Pagliari in Florida and he put it off until arrival in the southern part of Spain, later that evening. His cell phone wouldn't work all the way from Europe and his little jet didn't have some of the sophisticated new equipment aboard that could put him through from the air. Besides that, he wasn't about to undertake a conversation with a grieving father within the confines of the plane, surrounded by his young troops. It would have to wait till Spain.

Gibraltar.

The southern coast of Spain looked like a long string of pearls, interspersed with a few diamonds and rubies, It was absolutely stunning. There wasn't a cloud in the sky and the crew was anxious to hit the town. They had been in 'Alcohol-Free' territory too long and were dying for a cold glass of beer and maybe some Latin music.

A van was waiting for them at the British Air Base and delivered them to a hotel, just twenty minutes later. Bongers had advised the troops that they were off for thirty-six hours and, "Don't get in trouble, you hear!"

He bought a six-pack of Heineken and a quart of Dewars and headed to his room.

After finding some ice, he fixed himself a drink and finally picked up the phone. "International operator, please." He didn't dare to attempt using his limited Spanish.

It took five minutes before he finally had a connection with Fort Walton Beach.

"I could have done this faster if I had dialed directly," he fussed at no-one in particular, but the phone system in the hotel was not quite up to speed.

Finally, "Mr. Pagliari, this is Colonel Bongers, Army Intelligence, how are you?"

"What do you expect? How should I be? I loved that boy more than my own son and now I'm told he met with a tragic accident. That's terrible. I'm an old Navy Pilot and I can understand, 'Killed In Action', but I can not accept 'a tragic accident'. Colonel, what's your name again?"

"Call me Bruce."

"Okay Bruce, I'm Emil. What happened? I need to know. I don't need the kinda bullshit the Preacher was trying to feed me yesterday. He's dead, so that won't change. I need to know the truth. I can handle it."

"Emil, are you sitting down? Are you sure you can handle it?"

"Shoot. I'm ready."

"I would rather sit face to face with you and tell you, rather than on the phone..."

"Cut the crap, Colonel, tell me."

"You know he shot his brother, don't you?"

"He shot Joe? What the hell was he doing there? He wasn't even in the service, so..."

"Are you gonna listen or are you just gonna give me some hot air, Emil?"

"Okay, okay. I'll shut up. You talk. What happened?" Bruce finished his scotch and wished he had refreshed it before he picked up the phone. He reached for a can of beer instead.

"Emil, Joe was on an Army scholarship at Embry-Riddle..."

"I didn't know that, I mean I knew he was at Embry..."

"Are you gonna listen or what?"

"Alright, alright, I'll shut up."

"On nine/eleven, I whisked him out of the country because the Feds were rounding up all Arabic-speaking flight students and Joe went undercover, grew a beard and migrated into Afghanistan with a team of Taliban in order to find Osama Bin Laden. When an A-10 pilot got shot down, Joe's team and a Jumper team went after the downed pilot and Joe got there first. When J.P.'s team arrived on the scene, your son was manning a gun in the open door..."

"And he shot Joe?"

"Emil... Emil... are you listening?"

"I'm sorry."

"The pilot came out of the brush and a few seconds later a Hadji with a full beard, a turban, two Stinger missiles and an AK-47 stepped up behind her and J.P. took him out with a short burst. Two bullets ripped through his chest. He died three hours later."

"Hot damn! By then John knew that he shot his brother, right?"

"He did his best to save him, but the loss of blood did him in."

"Couldn't they...?"

"Emil, I'm gonna sit down with you shortly and go into all the details. Right now, what you need to know is that P.J. was so despondent about it that he shot himself..."

"God, no!"

"Yes, and Emil, I need to know what you want to do. I'm here in Spain and tomorrow I'm gonna have to face Yousef's parents and find out what they want, where they want to have him buried and.."

"I want him here, right at Saint Mary's church." He was getting hysterical and started to shout, "I want him right here! You hear that Colonel? I want..."

"I heard you and I'll personally deliver him. Do you want full military honors?"

"I what? Do I want what?"

"Do you want him buried with full military honors?"

"Oh, I didn't think about that. Of course. of course. Full military, right here from Hurlburt. Right." A sob interrupted him and Bongers continued,

"If Joe's parents agree, should we bury them together?"

"Damn right!" The phone slammed down.

Bruce stared into his empty beer can for long minutes. Totally drained.

"Why, dear God, why?"

Chapter Forty-Five

Laysh ya Allah?

Algeciras, Spain

Bongers had planned to leave early, but it was colder in Spain than he anticipated and the TV in his room told him that Morocco wasn't particularly warm either. The hotel van driver who took him to the docks was kind enough to stop at a store, where he bought a few clothes, including a warm windbreaker. The driver promised to have his military duds returned to his room. The store owner hadn't flinched when Bruce slipped out of his camouflage pants in the middle of his store and into some civvies. After all, it was a very military town, he had probably seen it all.

At the ferry, he thanked his lucky stars that he had remembered to bring his passport that he hadn't used in months. From one military base to another and from an Air Force jet to an Army plane, it had never been requested.

The Custom Officer was very suspicious of the fact that he had no luggage and finally accepted the fact that he was only going over for one day. Like the night before, the weather was beautiful, about fifty-five degrees without a cloud in the sky. The wind made it too chilly to ride on deck, but he found a nice window seat at the very front of the passenger lounge. When the boat slowed, going into Tangier harbor, he climbed to the upper deck and took in the view. The old city, the Medina, to his right looked as mysterious and mystic as it had in the past when he visited here and hotel row directly in front of him had grown considerably. The modern town, brilliantly white, rose up on the hillside behind the hotels and still dazzled in the sunlight as it had for hundreds of years.

He shuddered at the thought that Yousef would never see that sight again. He still couldn't believe it. It was still like a bad dream.

The Moroccan Custom and Immigration people didn't question his intentions very much at all. They simply took his passport and asked him when he would return.

"Before the last ferry back." seemed to satisfy them and they steered him to a taxi stand, that could take him to a rental car agency. That was not as simple. His driver's license and his credit card were okay, but they insisted that he should rent a car *with* a driver and when he protested, they suggested that he take a minivan along with other tourists to Chefchaouen and it would deliver him right to the center of that city.

"How about getting back?"

"You'll have four hours in the Kasbah and take the same minivan back."

"Okay!" He was on his way. As a matter of fact, there were only five tourists and a driver in a little Toyota bus that held eleven, so he had plenty of room and did not have to converse with the other two couples on the bus. He just sat back and enjoyed the scenery although there wasn't much to see. Small farms, narrow roads and trash all along the shoulders of the highway, if you could call it that. Just two lanes.

After passing through a few little villages, Chefchaouen came into view, built against the foothills of the Rif Mountains. It looked very picturesque, all white against the green slopes.

At the final stop, Bongers had to argue for five minutes with a little tour guide, that he didn't want the tour, but only directions or a guide to bring him to the Mohammed Tapestry Store. Finally he was issued a teenage boy, who would take him there for a dollar.

Actually, he wanted a Euro, but settled for a dollar.

Just ten minutes and they were there. On a street that was only four feet wide with all blue walls, there was an elaborately carved door, with no name or advertising whatsoever.

"Are you sure, this is it?"

"Just go in. Go in."

"You go in first."

"One more dollar."

"Okay, after I see the people and make sure it's the right place."

"Okeedokee." The teenager opened the door and walked in, but instead of turning behind a curtain to a room that smelled like a kitchen, he walked up the stairs and right into a rather large showroom. "Dollar please?" He held out his hand and turned to a clean shaven man, "*Salam Aleikum*. Meester Mohammed."

Bongers fished out another dollar and addressed the man who was obviously Yousef's father. 'Joe would have looked just like that in another twenty years,' he thought. Extending his hand, he said, "Mr. Mohammed, I am Colonel Bruce Bongers of the United States Army. Where can we sit for a few minutes?"

Mohammed took the hand, frowned and asked, "Why you come? What problem?"

"Can we sit somewhere?"

"Of course, of course, but I worry. Why you come here? That far? What is wrong? I worry."

"You have a perfect right to worry, Mr. Mohammed, because I bring bad news."

They sat down on one of the many benches that ringed the showroom floor.

"Let me explain. I'm the man, who recruited Joe, Yousef, for the Army and we paid for his schooling and flight lessons..."

"Good, okay, but what happen?"

"After nine/eleven, when the twin towers were targeted and brought down by two airplanes..."

""I know, I know, but where's Yousef?" Another man walked

in the room, this one dressed in a burnoose, a long flowing gown. Bongers stood up and extended his hand, "I'm Bruce Bongers."

"I'm the brother." Was all he said, while he lowered himself onto a nearby pouf.

"So where's Yousef? In jail in America or is he dead? Why Americans put everybody in…?" The father was panicking.

Bongers hesitated, he couldn't stall any longer. He whispered, "He's dead."

The Moroccan slapped both hands to his face, "*Allah Akbar!*" and collapsed on the bench. The brother jumped up and stepped right up to Bongers, shouting, "What you do? Why you keel heem?"

Father Mohammed recovered quickly and restrained his brother. "No, No. Thees man not keel heem. Thees man a friend, he come to tell us." A few words followed in quick Arabic and the brother ran up the stairs, while the father composed himself and took Bongers' arm. "I sorry. Tell me what happen."

Before Bruce could get started again, the brother came down the stairs, followed by an elderly man with a cane. He stopped, Bongers rose and the old man stepped forward and embraced Bruce in a minute long bear hug. A stream of foreign words kept rolling off his tongue and when he finally released the Army man and sat down. Mohammed explained, "He says, he knows who you are. Yousef write about you, all the time. You are the man who gave his grandson the money for school and flying and his grandson loves you so he, his namesake, also loves you for what you did for his grandson."

Bongers was flabbergasted and moved to tears. His big white handkerchief covered his face momentarily as he said, "Thank you, thank you very much."

"Before you tell all, I get my wife." Yousef's father got up and returned a few minutes later with the boy's mother, Miriam, on his arm. She was sobbing hysterically and didn't see the hand that Bruce extended.

"Now, tell us slowly, what happened to our son." Mohammed seemed to be under control, at least on the surface.

Bruce relayed briefly, how Yousef had volunteered to go underground and find Bin Laden. Every time that the father translated, Miriam would break down and at one point fell to the floor, banging on the carpet with her fists, while wailing in hysterics,

"Allah Akbar! Laysh ya takhud ibn na? Huwa ibn jayid jiddan. Laysh ya Allah? Laysh?"

Her husband tried to calm her down and unsuccessfully urged her to go downstairs, but she wouldn't leave.

"She's asking Allah, why? Why?" Mohammed explained. He insisted on hearing every last detail until they were interrupted by a tour guide with a string of tourists behind him. The brother quickly jumped up and hustled them back down the stairs. "We close." He said when he came back up.

The interruption made Bruce realize that time was flying and he had only one more hour to catch the van back to the docks of Tangier. He told his host, who understood after his American visitor explained that he and his passport were in danger, unless he got back that evening.

"Let's get to the business part. We want to bury him in the United States in a Military Cemetery with full honors and probably side by side with the boy who he considered his brother." He looked at all of them, one by one. "Of course that's with your permission. If not, we'll transport him here or anywhere you designate. If we do bury him in the States, we will fly you there to attend the ceremony and of course, we will pay all expenses."

"Where is he now?" To Ibrahim Mohammed that was a logical question.

"He and his brother are in Spain aboard an Army jet, awaiting your preferences."

A barrage of Arabic or dialects was the result and the only one who couldn't bring herself to participate in the conversation was the mother. Only when her husband asked her a direct question did she nod, shake or answer.

"When would the funeral be, Colonel?"

"It's now December eighth. I'm not familiar with your holidays when you can or can not travel, but how is a month from now. January 8, 2002?"

Again, the foreign word flow was such that Bruce wondered how they could possibly understand one another, but after about five minutes, the brother spoke up, "How about money?"

"Oh we'll arrange everything. I don't know at this point if we just send a plane for you or, if we issue you tickets on a commercial airline. I'll work all that out. Don't worry, I'll take care of all that."

"Yes, but how about money?" The brother again.

"Money? Travel money? That will…"

"No. Money because Yousef is dead."

"Oh, I'm sorry. I misunderstood. The insurance money will be directly paid to you, his father I mean, and he still has money coming for his months of service and for his undercover work. All that will come to you. If there's ever a question about that, you contact me directly, okay? Now can someone guide me back down through this labyrinth?"

"I take you." Ibrahim stood up. Grandpa Yousef again embraced the tall Army man, but the mother disappeared downstairs, still crying, so Bruce and the brother shook hands and grabbing his new jacket, they departed, the grieving father and the deflated Intelligence man.

At the fountain in the little square, Ibrahim surprised Bruce by asking, "The other father, the father of the brother, he knows?"

"Yes."

"How he?"

"Like you and me, devastated and heartbroken."

"Give my love. Salaam."

Chapter Forty-Six

Central Command

Tampa, December 10, 2001
O'Club, MacDill Air Force Base.

Emil had flown down to Vandenberg Airport, outside of Tampa, taken a taxi and met Bongers at the O'Club at six thirty.

"Emil, nice to meet you finally. I wish the circumstances were more pleasant."

"I do too. We're sitting down to dinner or did you just wanna talk over a drink?"

"I'm famished, let's find a table. General O'Doull is gonna join us in a bit and he may be hungry too. What you'll have?" A waitress had appeared out of nowhere.

"I'll have Dewars on the rocks."

"Make that two and wait about twenty minutes before you bring menus, okay?"

While waiting for drinks, Bruce asked, "Where are you staying, Emil?"

"Nowhere yet. I landed, caught a cab and came straight here."

"Stay put. I'll get you into the BOQ." He got up and disappeared into the hall. When he returned, the drinks had arrived and Bruce settled down. "You're booked in the general's quarters."

"Oh, finally some respect. It's about time." He sipped from his drink and smiled with satisfaction. "Good stuff. They don't scrounge on the booze here."

"Better than in your restaurant?" Bruce grinned back at him.

"'Bout the same. I hate it when I'm someplace and they serve weak drinks. What's this you wanna talk with me about anyway? Why did you have me fly all the way down here?"

Bruce kept grinning, "Because you love it, that's why. No, seriously, I have gone from the intelligence business into the undertaking business and I don't mind." He held his hand up, "I'm honored to do this, because, I owe these boys, you owe these boys and the whole damn country owes them, so that's why I wanna do this right."

Emil was taken aback a little by the sudden change in expression on Bongers' face. He went from smiling to very stern in just seconds.

"Oops! Where do I come in?"

"You're the father. You're the authority in J.P.'s case. We need your permission to execute this whole affair properly."

Emil chugalugged his drink. "What the hell do you want from me?" He waved at the waitress. "What can I do?"

"Emil, a dozen young men and women went down in that Godforsaken country in just a few days. For what? They achieved nothing. It's not like a front line where guys die, gaining a few feet of ground or pilots die, bombing strategic targets. They didn't achieve anything. This is not a war between two opposing forces. This is a war of religious hate. It's like Irish Protestants blowing up Catholic homes or vice versa, all in the name of God. This is a case of hatred for religious reason only and innocent people are dying because of a few fanatics that have others believing that God only wants certain people in the hereafter."

"I know all that. What's that gotta do with me?"

"With you?" Bongers calmed down a little. "With you Emil? I'd like you to change your mind about interring J.P. in Fort Walton."

"Why? What's wrong with that? What's the matter with you people?"

Bruce lifted his hand, trying to stop the onslaught of words that was about to be delivered, while shaking his head.

"There's nothing wrong with that Emil. Nothing at all and you're welcome to proceed with the arrangements... but... I hope to bestow greater glory on these fellows in recognition of the sacrifices they made."

"You what?"

"I want to bring national attention to the lives and contributions of the young people we've lost..."

"How?" Emil signaled for another drink.

"By having them all buried at the same time in different parts of the country and that way get all of America's attention focused on these kids. Maybe even international attention, because too many foreign countries still think of us as a meddling imperialistic nation that's only after property and wealth. I'd like to make this a sort of an international memorial day, emphasizing the hardships and the contributions of our young soldiers, working for, dying for, world peace."

"Wow! Where do I come in?" Emil was entranced.

"We need your permission to bury these two boys together and...?"

"Where?"

"In a Military Cemetery with full military honors."

"Arlington?"

"I don't know. I don't think so. General O'Doull has a lot more input than I. By the way, there he is." Bruce got up and walked into the bar, where the general was looking around for familiar faces.

"General," Bruce called out, "We're in the dining room."

O'Doull turned around, "Great, I'm starving."

After the proper introductions and once the food selections had been made, the General asked Emil, "I understand you're Navy. What did you do?"

"You might find this hard to believe, but I flew off carriers, went into the reserves, got called back, was part of Air America in Laos and survived it all, and I'm still flying."

"Wow, quite a career. Are you still in the reserves?"

"No, I quit after twenty four years and started a restaurant business, so now I only fly with the Civil Air Patrol and for fun. I have two little planes and I love it."

"Again, WOW! I heard all about you and the boy from Peru and I'm sorry we got to this cumbersome ending. That's so tragic and I'm so sorry…"

"Well, General, as you can well imagine, at first I was devastated, but now I'm changing my thinking. I've been walking into our church, Saint Mary's, right across the street and at first I was feeling sorry for myself, but by now I'm learning to be thankful for all the happiness that boy has brought into my life. I'm a better person because of it."

"Emil," O'Doul reached across the table and clasped his hand, "that's beautiful. That's real beautiful."

For a while they concentrated on eating. Scallops, steaks, home fries, baked zucchini, spaghetti with marinara sauce, it was American cooking at its best.

While waiting for desert, the conversation struck up again. The general wanted to know, "What exactly do you have in mind, Bruce?"

"Exactly? If I can arrange it," he stopped and smiled at his boss, "and if I can get your permission, I would like to arrange a 'burial day' for all the victims of that gruesome event in Nuristan Canyon. Let's suppose we pick January eighth as our target date, then in different parts of the country we would hold funerals for all of the airmen, the lady pilot and Yousef. We would have Yousef's parents here from Morocco to emphasize the international aspect of the war against terrorism and to show the whole world and all the peace mongers that this is not just a U.S. effort, but that it is an international problem and needs the support of the entire civilized world."

He added sugar and cream to his coffee and resumed his talk. "With the proper publicity, we would show the whole world the tremendous amount of needless suffering that has befallen the families of these youngsters. All the unnecessary grief that will be exposed on that day, will also show the determination and willingness of young Americans to go out and die for their country and for peace in the whole world."

"Good God, Bruce. That was quite a mouthful. What do you want me to do?" Emil was thoroughly impressed.

"Emil, I would like your cooperation in getting both these brothers buried together at a national cemetery with all the military honors we can muster and maybe the attendance of high level brass and Moroccan officials. Of course if you still want J.P. buried in Fort Walton, I'll respect your request and that's what we'll do."

"No, no, I see your point. After all they considered themselves brothers and they died for the same cause, I'm game. Let's do it your way and just tell me what I can do."

"I would want you to fly the **Missing Man** formation."

"You what?"

"Your last tribute to your boy would be that you fly over the grave site in a formation of four or five and exactly when the bugler plays 'TAPS', you pitch up as the missing man."

"Man..., I haven't flown formation in years, many years and where do I find the other guys to fly with?"

Bruce grinned at him, "Didn't you just ask me what you could do? Well, this is it. Round up a team of other present or past military pilots that have access to a plane and work it out. Shouldn't be too hard."

"What if I can't arrange that, you know..."

"Then I'll plead with the Air Force for a flyby of military jets. But I'd rather see you do it. It would give the whole process more meaning. In the case of the lady pilot, Susie Overton, I'm sure the A-10 squadron will provide the fly-over, but I'm not sure whether I can arrange that in every different location, because I don't know yet, where the other ones will be buried. They may be from all parts of the country and then again, the parents or spouses will have something to say about the locations of the services. I'm guessing, most will opt for national cemeteries, but as of this moment, I don't have a clue." He sipped his coffee and looked up at the general, "This is supposing that I have your and the staff's permission."

"You certainly have my consent. I'm just flabbergasted at your imagination, but that's a positive. I'll get it put through in the morning, Right now, I'd like to go see my wife and kids and get some rest." He stood up as he was speaking, shook hands with both men and departed.

"One last drink at the bar, Emil?"

"Just one?"

Chapter Forty-Seven

News Break

MacDill Air Force Base
Tampa, Florida.

Bongers grinned as he read the headlines of the USA TODAY, while enjoying a hearty breakfast. **AFGHANISTAN, RUSSIA'S GARBAGE DUMP?**

It continued in glowing terms how radiation had been detected in a canyon in eastern Afghanistan and how the military had determined that it was Russian nuclear waste. The newspaper speculated that it was probably one of the many dumping grounds for such disposals, but it didn't give a hint as to how the authorities had determined that it was Russian. Maybe they didn't know and were only guessing

Bruce had watched a small segment of the subject on *Good Morning America*, but it only reported the few facts that Central Command in Tampa had released. It raised more questions, instead of reporting substantiated details. Obviously, they didn't have any.

CNN really got carried away with it. **HAD RUSSIA INVADED AFGHANISTAN FOR THE SOLE PURPOSE OF DUMPING ITS NUCLEAR WASTE?**

Even though he wasn't at Qandahar when that whole scenario developed, he had been there at the tail-end when it was decided to go with an oversized cover up. He grinned again at the thought, and wondered what the international watchdog community was going to do about it. A special session by the U.N. Security Council had already been called for later that afternoon.

He grinned again at the thought. "Get the U.N. involved and that will really gum up the works." So far, so good.

The only problem was, there was no way that they could retrieve the body of Airman Spc. Bowman, because of the danger of exposure. So, he had to work out some sort of funeral service for Bowman, rather than a burial.

A staff car was due to pick him up at 7:45 and take him to Central Command, from where he could do all his planning and arranging. The bodies of the two young men were in the vault at Tampa's coroner's office, and the little jet had returned to Fort Bragg, so he could now devote his time to planning all the arrangements for January 8. 2002.

Just like the personal meeting with Emil, he wasn't going to discuss Joe on the phone with the Dixons. He was going to meet with them in person in Dade City after lunch. Mrs. Dixon had tried endlessly on the phone to get all sorts of information out of Bruce, but he insisted on coming over to discuss every detail in person, face to face.

'How did I ever get this job?' he asked himself, as he walked out with his briefcase in hand and the newspaper under his arm. He had changed out of his camouflage outfit into his regular uniform, and looked mighty impressive with all his ribbons on his chest and the gold braids on his hat. 'I haven't seen my family now for a month and I'm liable to miss Christmas as well. Maybe I should accept that job offer of the FBI when this is all over."

The blue Air Force sedan drove up and with a snappy salute, the driver opened the rear door and slammed it shut after the colonel settled in. The whole ride took but six minutes from the Club to the Central Command building. A small office with a bank of telephones had been set aside for him and after disposing of his jacket and hat, he was ready for coffee and work,

The addresses and phone numbers of all the victims of that fireball in the canyon were e-mailed to him already, and it took a dozen phone calls to get some semblance of a plan on paper. Thank God, all the relatives had already been informed by local chaplains and Air Force personnel, so he didn't get involved in too many emotional conversations, but there were a few. The most important details to work out were the logistics of getting family members to the National Cemeteries and back. Only a few wanted a private service. Most wanted a military Honor Guard, even if they demanded burial in a local plot. One of them had a family vault and wanted the body of the young man joined in the heirloom of many ages and generations.

By noon, Bongers walked over to O'Doull's office and after a five minute wait was ushered in.

"How's it coming?" was the immediate question before Bruce even sat down.

"Whew!" He made a motion as if he was wiping sweat from his brow. "Ninety percent finished. What's the news on Arlington?"

"Well, can be done! What is the possibility of getting them all together at the same time? The families, I mean."

"Mixed reactions. Some live near a military cemetery and prefer that over Arlington, but how do you feel, General, about exposure by having the services simultaneously at ten different parts of the country at the exact same time?"

"You may have something there. Are you going to be present at the service for the Moroccan boy, regardless of where it's held?"

"I intend to. I should be there, especially when you consider that his folks and maybe even his grandfather will be there."

"Sure, sure! Bruce you have complete freedom and authority to pull it off. I'm impressed by your plan and so is the General Staff in Washington. Of course there were some Nay-Sayers who wondered if all this was necessary, but generally they are impressed by the idea that this was not just an American Christian undertaking, but instead an International, Christian/Muslim effort. Good going. Do you have time for lunch?"

"I do now."
"Let's do it."

Over lunch, O'Doull pumped Bongers for more information about the *Nuclear Affair* in Afghanistan and how the Air Force came about discovering that in such a remote area. Bruce had been sworn to secrecy by Colonel Springsteen, so he pleaded ignorance of most of the facts. The media had really jumped on the case and the military had their hands full, keeping reporters from interviewing the troops overseas and denying all requests for flyovers. CNN wanted to know how many locals were exposed and how many had already been treated or even died. The more the day wore on the more massive the radiation story was blown out of proportion, to the point that neighboring Pakistan was protesting to the U.N. that the Americans had denied them direct access to the area, so they had no way of protecting their own country.

The Russians denied any and all knowledge or guilt. Putin himself made a surprise television appearance and the more he spoke of ignorance, the more the media accused him of lying.

It would be interesting to see what the Security Council would accomplish, if anything at all.

Meanwhile, it took away the attention from the ongoing war and the peace mongers in the U.S., who demanded immediate withdrawal from Afghanistan, while the Hawks advocated expanding the radiation to the point that it would kill all of the Taliban, including Bin Laden.

Bruce again had access to a government car and drove by himself to Dade City and was welcomed by the Dixons with mixed emotions. Partly hostile, because he had refused to give much information on the phone and partially with warmth and hospitality, because they felt he was a partner in their grief.

He refused beer or scotch, but did accept some excellent hot tea when they sat down on their screened-in porch.

"Love your yard. How many bananas do you harvest each year and how many oranges?"

"Too many," George answered. "They end up making more of a mess than we get to enjoy the fruits. Besides, these bananas are not like the ones you buy in the store. These are barely edible, you can fry them, of course and ..."

"George, let's not bore the Colonel with all that nonsense. I want to hear what he has to say and what we're gonna do about a decent funeral. Is he going to be buried here or in Morocco?"

"Mrs. Dixon,"

"Tracy."

"Okay, Tracy, if you call me Bruce. I spoke with his parents in Chefchaouen..."

"Did you go there?" When Bongers nodded, she went right on. "How are they taking it and..."

"Tracy, would you let the man talk?"

"Okay. What were you saying, Bruce?"

"I was saying, I went to see them and asked whether they wanted him buried over there according to their Muslim beliefs or if they would come to the U.S. and attend a military funeral. They're coming here."

"Oh, great! It would be so good to see them again and will Grandfather Yousef come with them? What's you gonna do? Are you gonna go get them with a military plane..."

"For God's sake Tracy, would you let the man talk?"

"Sorry, Bruce, but..."

"That's alright, but I do want to get to the point. You might want to bury him in your own local cemetery, but I would prefer to have a real great ceremony in Arlington Cemetery with all the military hoopla, because that's kinda what I promised the old folks in Morocco."

"Why Arlington? We would never get to visit his grave. Why not Bushnell?"

"Bushnell? What's Bushnell?" Bongers had never heard the word, other than a good Irish whiskey.

"Bushnell is right up the road here along I-75, Maybe a half hour from here."

"Tracy, it's at least an hour and…"

"Anyway, it's right near here, so…"

"Where would there be a Mosque nearby?"

"Why would you want a Mosque? We have a beautiful Methodist church in town and it's real…"

"We're going to provide a Muslim service for the boy."

"We are?"

"Yes, a Muslim service."

"God help us."

Chapter Forty-Nine

Amazing Grace

Fort Bragg, Army Intelligence
December 15, 2001 10:21 AM

"Colonel Bongers, the White House is on the phone for you."
"The White House? For me?"
"Yes, sir. The Chief of Staff, the Honorable Mr. Stafford.'
"For me?"
"Yes, sir, line three."
Bruce pushed button number three, wondering, 'What would they want from me?'
"Colonel Bongers here."
"Colonel, thus is Clancy Stafford at the White House. How are you this morning?"
"Fine, sir. What gives me such an honor on this cold winter day?"
"Well, our press secretary brought to the President's attention that you're organizing a mass funeral early next year and advised him of the potential motivational impact it may have on the..."
"Mass funeral?"
"Well, maybe that was not a good choice of words. Maybe I should have said, 'multiple'. Anyhow, we'd like you to send us the

details of what you have in mind, but tell me briefly, what's going on, Colonel."

"Briefly? Early this month, a number of Airmen, a woman pilot and an Army Intelligence Soldier were killed in action in Afghanistan. I attempted to arrange *one* funeral at Arlington, with the proper pomp and ceremony, emphasizing two things: the dedication and courage of our young men and women in the service and the glaring stupidity of the whole affair, people killing one another because of religious differences."

"Well, that's quite a mouthful, Colonel and I think that's well conceived, but…"

"But, sir, it won't work out that way, because I contacted all the families and the overwhelming majority wanted their loved ones buried nearby instead of in Arlington, with just three exceptions…"

"Well, that's understandable, so what are you going to do?"

Bongers said to himself, 'If you just quit interrupting me, I would tell you.' But to the phone he said. "We have arranged for simultaneous services all across the country, so we can have a lot of local media participation that will carry our message hither and yon. The national media can hone in on Arlington with worldwide coverage, because these young people should be recognized for…"

"Well, that does sound grandiose and you have all that set up, so far?"

"It's all set, except transportation and other logistics, but that'll be in place…"

"Well, so just three will be interred at Arlington?"

"Three??? No!!! Two!"

"Two? Didn't you just say three, Colonel?" Stafford started to sound annoyed.

"No, sir. I said three did not insist on being buried nearby, but one of them will be buried in Bushnell National Cemetery in Florida, along with…"

"Why? He won't be nearby? Where's home?" He sounded like he was talking to some dummy.

"His home is in Morroco, but his parents con…"

"Morocco? What's he doing in our National Cemetery? Is he a Muslim?"

"He sure is, Mr. Stafford, but he…"

"Well, that'll require some serious explaining, Colonel. We…"

"It'll all be in the report to the President and it'll all be crystal clear."

"Well, what you're saying is that two Airmen will be buried simultaneously at Arlington?"

"That's correct, sir. Eleven AM, Eastern Standard Time, nine Arizona time and eight AM California time. It will all be synchronized to a tee and…"

"Well, get your report to me immediately. E-mail me directly. Here's my e-mail…"

After Bongers jotted down the e-mail address, he slammed down the phone and walked out of his office into his secretary's cubbyhole, flames flaring from his ears and his nostrils.

"That pompous ass! They sit in their swank offices, making big bucks while our boys are crawling in mud and dying in flames. That belligerent pompous ass!"

His secretary looked at him in surprise. Her boss rarely lost his cool. Something must have really riled him up.

"Georgia, find the President's personal e-mail address. I'm gonna send it direct. Now Stafford might still get to read it first, but I'll chance it. If that SOB had said 'WELL" one more time I would have thrown the phone at him. Do you have the report to General O'Doull still in your computer? Okay! Forward that to the President. I'm not gonna spend one more minute with these asses up there…" and he walked back into his office.

Baffled, Georgia executed the Colonels orders.

Army Intelligence, Fort Bragg, N.C.
1:10 PM

"Colonel Bongers, the White House on three."

"Tell'em I'm in conference. Take a message." He bent over his paperwork and picked up an outside line.

Within ten minutes... "Colonel Bongers, the President's office on the line and they told me to get you out of whatever conference you were in."

"You kiddin'? What line?"

"Line five sir."

"Bongers here."

"Just a minute sir. Hold for the President." The line went dead while Bruce's eyes nearly popped in sheer amazement.

"Colonel Bongers, George Bush here. That was an interesting report we just received and I want to congratulate you on making all these tragic, but necessary arrangements, but I have some questions for you."

"Yes sir. Of course, sir." This was the first time in his life that he had talked directly to a sitting President.

"First, were these deaths in direct connection with the discovery of the nuclear waste?"

That put Bongers in a pickle. He had been sworn to secrecy. "Sir, they were the result of an attempt to pinpoint and destroy Bin Laden's hideout in a canyon, sir."

"Second question; Is the Muslim boy going to receive a military funeral and why?"

"Yes sir, because he was an undercover agent in the service of U.S. Army Intelligence. Yes SIR!" He emphasized the 'sir".

"Is he going to be buried at Arlington?"

"No, Mr. President, as my report states, he'll be interred in Bushnell National Cemetery in Florida." He felt like saying; 'Can't you dummies read?' But he wisely kept his mouth shut.

"Good work Colonel. I'm planning on being at Arlington. I agree with you, it's high time we let all the world know, not just Americans, what our men and women are going through and how much they're willing to sacrifice. Good work, Colonel." And he was gone.

Central Command, Tampa, Florida
General O'Doull's office. December 21, 2001

"No General, this is final. I have enjoyed working with you and Army Intelligence, but after twenty-five years, it's time for me to go home and grow along with my four boys. The oldest one just became a teenager and I need to be there as he develops. I've had an exciting career and I wouldn't have traded for any other job in the world, but my recent experience with these young boys that we're now burying makes me realize, more than ever, how important it is to be there with the kids as they mature. I have accepted a position with the F.B.I., that will keep me close to home and I'm looking forward to being home in time for supper on most nights of the week."

He lifted an empty coffee cup, put it back down and continued, "General O'Doull, it has been a tremendous honor and a great learning experience, working with you, but I guess, these last few months have really gotten under my emotional skin and it's time to bow out. You see that all my papers are in order and I will bow out on February one, 2002."

"Bongers, I hate to lose the most competent man on my team, but having kids myself, I will no longer argue or plead with you. I wish you all the best in your new endeavor. I just hope that the FBI appreciates what a prince of a fellow they have found in you." He stood up, came around his desk, grabbed the Colonels hand, pulled him close and gave him a bear hug.

"Godspeed, Bruce. Godspeed!" After releasing the colonel, a snappy salute ended it all and he returned to his desk, without looking up.

"Thank you General, and Merry Christmas!"

The End

EPILOGUE

Farewell!!!!!

January 8, 2002
Arlington National Cemetery

Four Pave Low helicopters interrupted the President's speech as they thundered over the assembled crowd. The formation was as tight as the wind-milling rotors would allow and the down draft of the mighty war machines blew up dust plus an occasional hat, military as well as civilian. Everyone stared in awe at the show of power and flight precision and Mr. Bush waited till the sound and the wind abated, before he continued.

"As we pay homage today to two Air Force heroes, who flew, fought and died together in a distant hostile land, we are reminded of the ultimate sacrifices that all of our young military men and women face on a day to day basis. Our armed forces, when they enlist, are aware of the dangers attached to their duties and are willing to give their lives, so we can continue to live in freedom. We need to say 'thanks' every day to the good Lord and to our troops for protecting us from an evil that is beyond our imagination. Why would anyone, in the name of the Lord, be willing to kill innocent women and children? Why do we have to sacrifice these young lives in order to stamp out that hatred that exists between peoples

of different races and religions? Why? Because these young men and women are the only earthly resources we have to eradicate this evil, no matter where in the world it may show its ugly head. These young airmen, that we are returning to the earth today, as well as all the others that are being interred in different parts of the country at this very hour, are a prime example of the American spirit of dedication and love for their county and for their fellow Americans. May God rest their souls. God bless America."

Fort Walton Beach, Florida
Saint Mary's Church

The overflowing gathering of former high school mates and a sprinkling of Airmen and Officers from Hurlburt and Patrick, listened intently to the eulogy that was being delivered by Sean Pagliari.

"*The gentlest soul I have ever known was my brother Juan Pedro, known as J.P.*

After a horrendous accident in his native Peru and a life that was doomed to be lived in a wheelchair, he never lost his sense of humor or his respect for God. His unbridled optimism helped him overcome his disabilities with the help of my Father, Emil, and the generosity of the Shriners. When the tragedy of the Twin Towers hit our Nation, all he wanted to do was fight the unseen enemies and help his fellow soldiers as a Para-Rescue Jumper in the Air Force. He switched immediately from Reserve to Active Duty and was assigned overseas in hunt of the murderers of Nine/Eleven. It was during that hunt that tragedy struck and he sacrificed his life in the process of saving others. Many of you, like myself, ask, 'Dear Lord, why did this have to happen? Why did a young, promising life have to be snuffed out, while he still had so many years of service and goodwill ahead of him? Why Lord? Why is there so much hatred and cruelty in the world? Why can't your love permeate the hearts of all peoples, so we can live in peace and harmony? Why, oh. why?' We have one consolation. J.P. and his brother are forever united in the Kingdom of God. Let us pray as Jesus taught us to pray; "Our Father..."

He broke down in tears.

Columbia, New Mexico
Iglesia de San Marco.

Four people, kneeling in front of the Altar, praying for a soul that had left them forever. *"Madre de Diós, please guide Juan Pedro's soul to your Son and..."* Margie broke out in sobs and both her mother and father embraced her and tried to sooth her.

"Pero, por qué? Mama, por qué? Papa, digame, por qué?"

National Memorial Cemetery of Arizona
Phoenix

Four A-10's from Davis-Monthan in a tight echelon formation, roared over the lines of uniformed airmen and civilians, where Captain Susie Overton was poised over an open grave in a flag covered casket. Right over the crowd, as the last notes of *TAPS* echoed in the distance, Hog Number Two pitched up sharply in a symbolic *'Missing Man'* maneuver, emphasizing the loss of the young female Jet Pilot.

After the casket was lowered, a 7 man squad lined up behind the open grave, raised their rifles and fired a three round salute to the fallen Captain.

With every shot, Mrs. Overton, held tightly by her husband, John, shuddered and sobbed, *"Why John? Why? Why our daughter? What had she done? Why John? Why?"*

As he accepted the folded flag that had draped the casket, he said, *"Honey, she died, doing what she wanted to do, **fly and fight for her Country**."*

Camp Butler National Cemetery
Springfield, Illinois

"This is just symbolic. Airman Specialist Eric Clifton Bowman is only here in spirit. His body has not been located, but his soul rests with God, for all eternity. He gave his life in the line of duty. A duty, as he saw it, was to assure us here, and in all other peace loving nations, that we will live free forever. May God rest his soul.

In due time, his remains will be interred here, so this will be his final resting place. Let us pray..."

Chaplain Lieutenant Colonel Harvey Johnson made the assembled friends and relatives hold hands as they said thanks and asked for guidance for Eric and the leaders of the Nation.

"May God bless America. Amen."

"Amen, Father, but why?"

"Come on, Elizabeth, come. Let's go." Mr. Bowman took his wife's arm and steered her away.

Fort Scott National Cemetery
Kansas

An Air Force company from Saint Louis had smartly marched behind the caisson, drawn by an armored HumVee from the chapel where the final ceremony had taken place. All the proper words had been spoken, many tears had been shed and now, it would finally be over. For more than a month, the family had lived in agony, not knowing what had happed to their son and then not being sure whether his remains would be buried in Afghanistan, half a world away, or whether he would be laid to rest at home, Fort Scott, Kansas.

Finally, they would feel some closure. Although they did not understand the specifics of his death, they did know that he died as a result of enemy fire. A rocket fired by a fanatic Muslim. The Presbyterian Minister had suggested that according to the scriptures, they now had *to forgive the enemy and pray for them.*

As the sound of the gun salute still rang in their ears, the distraught father whispered in his wife's ears,

"Forgive them sonsabitches? Like hell! I'm gonna spend the rest

of my life killing as many of them heathens as I can. Pray for them bastards? Is he kiddin'?"

San Francisco National Cemetery
San Francisco, California

"Lieutenant Grau was the finest example of American heroism. Time and time again, he would lead his team in harm's way in order to save the life of a fellow American.

Air Force Colonel Brightson spoke from experience. He had trained thousands of young Para Medics and George Grau had been just one of them. He knew the kind of mettle these men were made of.

"Every time an emergency occurred, every time a plane went down, every time a man was wounded in the field, George and his team would climb in their chopper, knowing that it could very well be their last flight. Unfortunately, one morning, a month ago, it was. The rescue of a downed A-10 pilot in the rugged treacherous mountains of Afghanistan was their mission for that day. It ended up costing the lives of seven men and a woman, the A-10 pilot. They went out and died a terrible death at the hands of the Taliban and we can only say now, that their sacrifices have not been in vain. We will continue to fight evil in this world and with God's blessing, we will prevail.

Thank you George Grau and all the men and women in our services for protecting us and keeping us free."

Iglesia San Cristobal
Huaycan, Peru

"Pater Noster, Omnipotento," Father Dominico Cabrera turned toward his congregation, consisting of all the Nuns, Juan Pedro's mother, siblings, plus a hundred friends and relatives. He changed from Latin to Spanish for the benefit of his audience and closed his eyes.

"Our Father, who art in Heaven, we thank You for all the blessings You have bestowed upon Juan Pedro, who grew from an invalid to a fighting man, willing to give his life so we can live in peace and harmony. We, who are left behind don't always understand Your will and Your ways, and we sometimes wonder, why a young hero like Juan Pedro is called to Your side before he even had a chance to live his life as a man. We don't understand, Lord, but we accept Your judgment and pray that his sacrifice was not in vain, but that it will lead to better understanding between peoples of different races and beliefs. Please be with his Mother in this, her darkest hour, and strengthen her resolve to carry out Your will here on earth until all of us are reunited with Juan in Your Kingdom forever. Amen."

"Amen." The tears kept flowing.

Dade City, Florida.
United Methodist Church.

"Let us celebrate the life of Joe, Yousef Mohammed and J.P., Juan Pedro Pagliari. Let us be thankful for the many years of joy and love they have brought into our lives. Let us never forget that these foreign born boys, who adopted the United States as their homeland, volunteered their lives in the service of our armed forces, in order to help us live free and void from danger. Let us stand and sing along with the choir, one of Joe's favorite songs, 'MEMORIES.'"

Chet Dixon, the oldest of the siblings had delivered a heart rendering eulogy about his adopted brother, whom he had learned to love like one of his own. There wasn't a dry eye in the house. George and Tracy Dixon had decided that they would participate in a graveside ceremony, but they couldn't get themselves to join in the Muslim service in the Mosque in Tampa.

"Any religion that endorses killing of innocents and even makes them believe that they'll go to Heaven by doing so, is not a religion that I can endorse..."

"But George, by going there we're only paying respect for Joe and his family..."

"I ain't going and that's it. I have never been a hypocrite and I'm not about to become one now. That's it. I'll gladly invite his folks in our house as people, but not as Muslims. That's it!"

As a result, Colonel Bongers attended the service in Tampa, not knowing what to expect, and they all agreed to be present at Bushnell National Cemetery.

Joe's body was in Tampa, while John's was laid in state in front of the Altar in the Methodist Church in Dade City. Emil had insisted on a Catholic Service, but Bongers settled it all by suggesting a service in Saint Mary's up north and one in the Methodist Church in Dade City. Then the final ceremony would take place at Bushnell, where both of the boys would be eulogized and interred with full military honors from MacDill, Fort Bragg, Hurlburt and Patrick.

"Chet," Tracy sobbed as she clung to her son. *"I'm so glad that you never joined a service. I could not bear to lose another son."*

"Mother, Dad served in the Army in Korea. If it weren't for people like Dad and Joe and John, we'd all be communist by now or we'd all be speaking German. Who knows Mom? One thing is for sure, we need guys to stand up for our rights and be willing to fight for them, even die for them. You know that Mom. Stop crying. Like the Preacher said, let's be thankful for the years we had him as our son and brother."

Shiners Hospital
Tampa, Florida

In the little chapel, some of the older nurses and volunteers that remembered the boys, gathered for a brief prayer.

The oldest volunteer, 79, with 22 years of service to the Hospital remembered them well and said it all.

"God delivers and God taketh away. Why He would take these fine young men from us, is beyond our comprehension. Finer people are rarely born and the fact that both of them volunteered to serve and were willing to die for our country tells us that we have done a good job in this hospital. Not only to repair them physically, but

also to instill in them some sound values of honesty, pride and love for this nation."

The Islamic Society Of The Tampa Bay Area Mosque
Tampa, Florida

Bongers wore his smartest black suit and conveniently had on black loafers, because he was asked to take those off before he could enter the inner Sanctum. He realized that *Sanctum* was not the proper term, but for a lack of Arabic, he settled for it in his own mind. He was handed a small carpet, more like a little runner, which was beautifully embroidered and he realized this was to be his prayer mat. There were no pews or benches in the wide open space, so he followed the example of the other *believers* and knelt down behind the Mohammed family, who were donned in full length outfits. Miriam's white and gold-trimmed pants, shoes and dress were absolutely stunning. Bongers wondered if he had made a mistake, wearing black until the Moroccan Ambassador and his entourage entered, all in black.

The Mullah, complete with a full beard and white turban, lead the small congregation in prayer, of which Bruce didn't understand the first word. He rose and kneeled, bowed and lowered his head to the floor in unison with the rest and did his best to follow the sequence of events.

The casket was open, on the left side of the crowd, the lid draped with an American flag. It dawned on the Colonel that he had forgotten to ask if there should be a Moroccan flag as well, or maybe only a Moroccan flag. After all, Yousef had not yet been sworn in as an American Citizen.

The body, however, was laid out on an altar of sorts in front of the congregation. It had been washed and wrapped according to Muslim tradition.

After twenty minutes, the Mullah stopped praying and singing and turned around indicating to the crowd that the service was over and four men in long white caftans lifted the remains and carried it to the open casket, closed the lid, started to roll the covered casket out of the inner room, where the job was taken over by Air Force personnel in full uniform. The flag was positioned properly over the gold and white box, the blue and the stars over the head.

Bongers stood and saluted as the procession passed him and he stepped up to the religious leader, shook his hand and thanked him for his help and prayers.

Ibrahim Mohammed and his brother were helping Miriam along, who was wailing again, which seemed absolutely acceptable inside that Holy Place.

"*LAYSH ALLA? LAYSH?*"

WHY, ALLAH? WHY?

Florida National Military Cemetery
Bushnell, Florida
January 8, 2002

Detachments from MacDill Air Force Base, Hurlburt Field, Patrick AFB, Army Intelligence from Fort Bragg, ROTC units from the University of Florida and Florida State stood at attention as the rifle platoon fired their rifles in honor of the fallen comrades.

Many civilians ringed the casket, but most of the TV cameras centered on the white clad foursome, where two men in long coats supported a veiled woman in a dashing white and gold outfit. She cried continuously and sometimes wailed out loud, *"Laysh Allah?"* The whole world was witness to her grief.

At precisely 11:30, a bugler played a sad and solemn rendition of TAPS and one hundred and fifty soldiers of many different ranks snapped a salute.

Thirty seconds into the mournful tune, four airplanes roared over at 200 feet and Emil, in the number two airplane, pitched up in a "Missing Man" tribute, exactly over the open grave. There was

hardly a dry eye in the crowd.
It was a fitting farewell.

Two rows from the ceremony, a young widow wrapped fresh flowers into a tight knot and inserted them in a copper vase. While situating them in front of the simple headstone, her seven year old son asked, "Mommy, why are there so many people at that funeral over there? When Daddy was buried, there weren't that many. Why Mommy?"
"Because they were brothers."

The End

The following are some excerpts from Frits Forrer's other books

Excerpt from:

Five Years Under The Swastika

Pappa has preceded him down and is warming milk on the electric stove. Mama and Jopie file into the kitchen too and Mama begins again: "You should…"

"HUSH!" Pappa interrupts softly, but sternly. Mamma gets cups down from the cupboard and puts cocoa mix in them, waiting for the milk to get warm.

"Why Pappa? Why? What have they done? And that little girl, what's her name? The granddaughter? They hurt her Pappa! Why Pappy, why? What did SHE do?"

Pappa stirs the chocolate milk. "Come sit at the table."

Frits turns, Joop and Mama are deadly quiet.

"Drink your cocoa! Watch it, it's hot. Hold it…. let me add some cold… here you go. Stir it! Okay, okay."

"Why Pappa, why? I know what you're gonna say: They're JEWISH right? But what did they do? They're not rich Jews that ruin the world and all that garbage. They're poor working people. He's been working for the County-Water-Department for as long as we've known him. He goes to work on his bike at four in the morning, every morning, I know Pappa, he's not rich, I know! Why then Pappa, why? They'll never come back, I know it. They're gonna kill'em!"

Tears are running down his cheeks, Mama is not doing much better and Jopie is staring in his chocolate milk as if there's something fascinating in it.

Mama hands Frits a handkerchief: "Here, dry your tears. Drink your cocoa."

"There's nothing I can say, Frits... nothing! Goddamnit!"

Pappa's last word shoots out with such vengeance that all three of them look up at him, startled.

"Sit down, Herman, drink your cocoa too!"

She's worried that his ulcer will flare up. "Why don't we all drink up-up-up and go to bed. It's too cold in here. Take your cocoa if it's too hot and let's go. Come boys."

Frits is still crying uncontrollably.

"Come in bed with us."

For the first time in years, he's in bed between his father and his mother, his skinny body shaking with the sobs that won't stop.

Finally, with his head against his father's chest, he falls asleep, blissfully.

The WOHLSTEINS were the first.

Excerpt from:

Smack Between The Eyes

"Now comes the hard part!" Frank walked away from Joey, who looked like a businessman on his way home. Nice suit, white shirt and a very conservative tie. His brown briefcase and a laptop bag swung over his shoulder completed his disguise.

Several detectives, including a cleaning lady, were posted near the arrival spot and two were at the end of the ramp, in case anyone wanted to escape from the rear door.

The large bus slowly rolled to a stop. The door opened and Frank stepped up to give the folks a hand, exiting the bus. Some refused his hand, some gratefully grabbed it.

Frank looked at each face as they unloaded and tried to match it with the pictures he had received on the fax and the e-mail.

The only one who bore the least bit of resemblance was an elegant gentleman in a light suit, blue shirt and white tie. His white fedora and his goatee gave him the look of a Caribbean planter.

After the last passenger descended, Frank boarded the bus, scanned it quickly and jumped off.

"Joey! That's the one! The guy with the black hat!" He mouthed it, rather than holler it, but Joey got the message. He ran after the disappearing figure in the crowd. Frank followed. Luck was with them. The elegant planter stopped to look around.

"Probably looking for Nita." Frank thought.

The man reached into his coat pocket and Frank as well as Joey pulled out there guns. The man's hand came out with a cell phone that he flipped open in order to dial, so he never saw the two officers rushing toward him until he heard: "Hands up! You're under arrest!"

His reaction was swift. With his left hand, he threw the cell phone at Frank and with his right hand he reached in his pocket and fired a shot at Joey, hitting him in the hip.

Frank ducked and the phone hit him in his bus driver's hat. In that very second, Hotta Hotta fired off one more shot, turned and disappeared in the crowd.

PANDEMONIUM!

People falling to the floor, officers shouting orders, women screaming and Frank jumping over bodies, trying to get to the fleeing man. An off-duty policeman tackled Frank, thinking he was the culprit and the gunman escaped.

All the police ended up with was a white hat and a cell phone.

Frank was sooooooo mad, he could have spit bullets.

ISBN 0-9714490-6-6

Excerpt from:

The Fun Of Flying

Pieter drove around, looking for a quiet spot and settled for a corner lot, surrounded by trees. From the debris on the lot, they built a campfire and concentrated on the task of opening up their beer bottles without the benefit of a bottle opener. That was an interesting challenge!

Two guys would take a bottle each, hook the 'crown-caps' together and pulled till one of them came off, while the they other guy got sprayed with beer. Harm was soaked in no time flat and took off his beautiful jacket and threw it someplace. Soon, his shirt was soaked as well and inasmuch as he couldn't handle the buttons in his inebriate state, he tore the shirt to threads.

Meanwhile, some 'serious' singing was being done by the campfire and everybody was in 'excellent' voice that night.

Somewhere during the evening, it was decided that throwing beer bottles all over the place was not very civilized, so they improved the situation by organizing a 'trapshoot'! One guy would throw his bottle in the air, while others threw theirs after it, trying to hit it in mid-air.

Their 'hit' averages stunk, but it felt like a refined kinda way to discard the empties.

Just as the averages were improving by the light of a bigger and improved campfire, sirens started screaming in their direction and soon two police cars ran unto the sidewalk, spitting out four bulky policemen.

"Hands up over your heads!" They meant business!

The boys didn't.

"So nice of you to come! Find a seat and we'll see if we can find you a beer."

"Shut up and raise those hands!"

"In our country, we are more polite than that!"

"We don't give a shit about your country! UP! Up! Now! Put your hands on top of the cars! Now!"

"That won't be necessary, Mr. Policeman. We believe that they're your cars."

"Shut up, I said. Put those hands on the cars!" They were getting mad and rough and started pushing.

"After you, sir!"

"Like hell! Up! Up!"

"Officer, all we were doing was singing a few songs. Is that so bad?"

"You're all under arrest for 'Disturbance of the peace'"

"Officers, if you ever came to visit in our country, we would treat you a lot nicer, I'm sure."

Meanwhile the cops felt them down, but other than 'hiccups' they had nothing on them.

"Get in the cars!"

"After you, sir. After you!"

"Negative. Get the hell in!"

On the way to the station they asked the cops if they had any special requests and they would gladly perform them for'em.

The total ride only took only five minutes and they were put in a big cage with just one more occupant; a dead down drunk who stared at them with wide eyes and a dumb look on his face. He had probably never seen a spectacle like that before in his entire life.

Seven guys, profusely thanking the cops for the ride and offering to pay the cab fare.

Once left alone, the songs started up again and at the stroke of midnight, they stood at attention and sang the American and Dutch National Anthems.

The policeman on duty thought it was very funny and kept supplying them with ice water. Nice touch.

ISBN 0-9714490-3-1

Excerpt from:

Tampa Justice
No Money, No Justice.

Your Honor, I was not informed of all the things that are involved in probation and I want to change my plea to Not Guilty, so I can have a trial and that will clear me for sure."

Well 'Fisheyes' objected vehemently. He had his 'conviction' and he was not about to take a chance on losing it.

"Mr. Fernon?"

"Your Honor, I do not want to represent Mr. Forrer in a trial, because I told Mr. Forrer that I don't do criminal work."

"Then why the hell did you take my case?"

"Mr. Forrer, you will maintain order!"

"Yeah, but Judge, I hired him to...."

"Mr. Fernon, raise your right hand. Is the testimony you're about to give, the truth, the whole truth and nothing but the truth, so help you God?"

"I do."

"Go ahead Mr. Fernon, state your case."

"Your Honor, I told Mr. Forrer, I don't do criminal work and I can not represent him in a trial."

THAT LYING BASTARD! I presented him with two CRIMINAL summonses and he took my thousand dollars to represent me.

"Very well, the motion to change plea is denied and we'll schedule a restitution hearing. Case dismissed."

The bastards! Just like that, in a matter of seconds I'm stuck with a verdict and there's not a damn thing I can do about it. I'm on a five year probation and I'm stuck with it.

To make matters worse, I received a notice from the Department of Professional Regulation that because of my "Nolo Contendere" plea, my Contractors License was revoked.

Apparently, when someone pleads "No Contest" in a construction case, it is assumed by the Department that the person is Guilty and it calls for an automatic revocation.

In other words: I was put out of business.

ISBN 0-9714490-5-8

Excerpt from:

To Judge Or Not To Judge

Pandemonium

J.F.K.
1:30 PM

Three people down! Two shot and one knocked unconscious. Two on the outside of the x-Ray check-in, one on the inside. For a minute or two there was so much confusion, that undercover security police nearly tangled with undercover FBI agents. The problem was everyone was incognito. Nobody was in uniform, not even a jacket with FBI on it or an I.D. card around their necks or pinned to their chests. Bongers' loud voice finally restored order and had the law enforcement officers holster their pistols again without any more friendly casualties.

Peter was the only one so far and Bruce wanted to make sure it stayed that way. It took a little while to convince the locals that Peter was NOT with the FBI and NOT a suspect, but he DID work with them and shouldn't have been shot in the first place. Ambulances roared up to the entrance, EMS personnel raced in with stretchers, I.V. bottles and medicine bags. City police officers tried to take control, than backed off and offered help and cooperation and ten minutes later, all there was left to do was clean the blood off the floors and get the passenger lines moving again.

The Feds had cuffed the captives and moved them into the Rembrandt room temporarily, much to the frustration of the KLM personnel, who had to transfer their cherished first class customers to other, less luxurious quarters. Bruce had everything under control again except; *what to do with the two terrorists?* If the CIA snatched them from his possession, which was certainly within their rights, he might be limited in his access to them. If the New York City police took over, defense lawyers would immediately be informed according to the law and of course, they would tell their clients to zip their mouths.

He called his New York counterpart and got some good advice. The City police would just hold them in *protective* custody in their maximum security prison at Rikers Island and that way, the FBI and CIA could interrogate them while awaiting transportation to Guantanamo Bay where al the Taliban and al-Qaida prisoners were being held. Federal laws provided them with that loophole and Bongers would have at least a few days to put their noses to the grindstone and find out what that whole plot was all about.

A police paddy wagon was provided and while the city cops transported the culprits, Bruce had a chance to track his shooting victims, Peter and Sahira, to the Queens Hospital where emergency surgery was scheduled to take place any minute.

In Washington, Travis washed his hands of the transactions, 'cause he would have to inform the CIA immediately and Bongers had begged him for patience.

"I gotta have some time with them, Lester. If the CIA big shots get involved, the Arabs may clam up altogether and I need to find out what this is all about. I'll get it out of them. I know these clowns, I've worked in the Middle East long enough to know how to deal with them. I'll play one against the other. Just buy me some time

Lester. Stall them by saying ; *'There is an operation in progress, details will be released as soon as they become available.'"*

"Okay, Bruce. I have to trust you on that, but keep me posted immediately, okay?"

"Will do. Thanks."

The New Jersey Bureau Chief knew he was walking a thin line, but he had seen it too often, that when too many different agencies or individuals get involved, the suspects tend to draw into a shell and that wouldn't really help anybody.

"Bruno," he asked his sidekick, "get me a ride to Queens Hospital and hold it for a trip to Rikers Island. Preferably a local cop who knows the territory. Thanks."

He reached for the coffee pot that was ready to serve some first class customers and filled a tall mug. "Good God, I'm hungry. Forgot to eat. Well, it'll have to wait a little longer." He finished the hot tasty liquid. "Good stuff. Must be Dutch."

Rikers Island was originally purchased by the Rykers family in 1683. It's located in the East River between the Bronx and Queens and had many different uses over the years. Most memorable was the training of African-American soldiers during the civil war and the conversion to a prison in the 1930's. The facility houses over 15,000 inmates and is now connected to Queens by a bridge. With the cooperation of the Warden, Bongers should be able to keep his culprits secluded and hidden from the press and over ambitious lawyers.

"So far, so good!" He said to himself as he climbed into a patrol car for the trip to Queens Hospitals and his innocent victims. "Let's hope they're alright."

ISBN 0-9714490-7-4

Excerpt from:

The Golden Pig
(El Cochino de Oro)

The sharpshooters unpacked their rifles, mounted their scopes and loaded the magazines. One shot with a Remington 30 odd o6 and the other had an H&H 222. Bongers admired the weapons and after putting on the safety, the shooter handed him the H&H and Bruce balanced the weapon in his hand as if he were guessing the weight, He shouldered it, pointing out the window and said: "Nice weapon, very light."

"Love it. Very flat trajectory. I bag groundhogs at three hundred yards.'

"Really? That's great." He handed back the rifle. Ten more minutes and they should be there. The silver snake in the distance grew larger by the minute and soon became a brownish band of muddy water.

"Target to our right at one o'clock." the pilot announced on the intercom, turning about ten degrees. He was looking directly at the mansion, but his passengers couldn't see it from the passenger compartment. Bongers undid his safety belt and got up in order to look over the pilot's shoulder. The captain in the left seat pointed straight ahead with his left hand while keeping his right on the joystick.

"Got it" He stared at the beautiful layout of an antebellum plantation with a massive lawn in front of the two-story colonial. "The plane's moving!" he shouted suddenly and indeed, although it was barely as big as a flea from this far out, they could detect movement. The yellow and black flea was drifting away from the dock.

"Get'em," Bongers ordered.

"Sir, please sit down and buckle in." The pilot spoke without looking up, both hands busy on his throttle and his control stick.

"Right." But he didn't budge. "They're gonna take off down river." He turned around and hollered: "Get ready. Secure that window. Hand me the hailer." That last order was directed to the co-pilot who handed him a mike that was connected to a bullhorn. The chopper nosed down and the throttle had the engine screaming. Their speed went up by forty knots.

Below and ahead, the yellow and black bug had turned with the bend of the river and after it passed two tugs with multiple barges in front of them, its wake became longer and wider, leaving two silver streaks in the water behind it.

"Get next to them." Bongers remained upright, holding on for dear life.

At that point the chopper was doing at least one hundred and thirty knots, while the little seaplane was struggling to pick up a take-off speed of sixty, so they closed fast. The helicopter pilot had to bank steeply to the left in order to end up in the same direction of the seaplane and Bongers was thrown into the side of the craft.

"Told you to buckle." The pilot said calmly as the G-man struggled to get back up. It didn't take long. "Fly alongside him, same speed."

The copter lurched back, its nose pitching up fast, but this time Bongers held on. Their speed bled off from 140 to 70 in no time, but Bruce lost sight of the plane. Thank God, the pilot didn't because all of a sudden, the little seaplane and the helicopter were flying formation, just fifty feet apart.

The man in the little bug wasn't aware of anything except his rate of climb and his speed. He was doing a good job. The plane was climbing at 400 feet a minute and his speed was slowly creeping up to ninety. Then, all of a sudden, he had the shock of his life. Over the noise of his engine, he could hear the drone of another motor, much bigger and louder than his. He looked to his left and there was a copter, fifty feet back and a loudspeaker bellowed: "Throttle back and land. This is the FBI."

His reaction was instinctive. In a second, he turned the plane on its right wing, dove to the ground and gave it full throttle. It was a case of desperation of the worst kind. There was no way he could outrun a helicopter that size, but his nerves were shot by the events of the last twenty four hours. He realized that his maneuver didn't work very well. Within minutes the helicopter was back in position off his left wing. By now, he was skimming the sea grass and flying between the cypress trees. He figured if he could stay on this heading and at this altitude, he'd be over the swamps of Texas and before long he'd be over the Gulf of Mexico, where he would have an advantage. He'd have more fuel than the chopper and they would have to land somewhere and he could possibly make Mexico without refueling. He concentrated on staying as low as he dared and he even throttled back a little in order to conserve gas. He was cruising at 110 and that was not bad. The annoying load speaker came on again: "Throttle back and land or we'll shoot you down."

Henry was gaining more confidence. He said to his wife, who was crying: "Shoot me down with what? They don't have rockets or a Gatlin gun. Who are they kidding? Mow me down with a peashooter?"

At that same moment, his side window shattered. "What the hell was that?"

Inside the copter, the window of the passenger compartment was lowered and two rifles were sticking out in the slipstream.

"Can you hit the gas tank or the engine?" Bongers was still very much in control, but also buckled in. Flying formation on the left of the plane gave him a front row view. Both guns fired. Both gunners aimed again. "Go.!"

This time, fuel streamed from the left wing and the cockpit disappeared in a fog of vapor. Henry banked sharp right, but he didn't have a chance of losing the chopper. It was nearly too easy. When the plane leveled without any attempt to slow down or land, the Jersey director ordered: "Take him out."

The shooters aimed for his head, but the buffeting of the chopper as well as the aircraft made them miss, still the 30-06 hit Robinson in the left shoulder and he inadvertently pulled on the stick with his right hand and the plane went straight up.

"Watch it!" Bruce hollered, because for a moment it seemed that the seaplane would land on top of the helicopter. The captain banked sharply and threw the coal to the engine and in seconds they were at three hundred feet, making a steep right turn and looking down on a spectacular sight. The seaplane had been yanked up so steeply, that it stalled and slid back momentarily, then it nosed over and glided down toward the swamp below it as if it were going to dive into the murky waters. The plane behaved as if someone was still at the controls, but Henry's body was slumped backwards and against the door, so the plane handled itself and just before hitting the water and sea grass, it nosed up again while the floats hit the surface and the plane glided along.

Up in the helicopter, they wondered if Mrs. Robinson was an accomplished pilot, but Bongers wasn't taking any chances. "Hit the pontoons. Shatter them if you can." Below them the throttle was still wide open and it looked as if it could take off again. Four shots apiece rang out and the floats started to settle a little deeper in the water, while the gas from the left wing still made for an impressive spray. From up above they watched a scene, reminiscent of a movie. With the motor running full blast, the plane sank deeper into the water until the propeller hit and at first just churned, but then seemed to be grabbed by a magic hand that pulled it under water and the plane dove, rolled on it's back, went under momentarily and floated back to the surface, upside down, the floats sticking up out of the water.

ISBN 0-9714490-8-2

About the Author

Born in Belgium of Dutch parentage, Frits grew up along the German Border in Eastern Holland, enduring five years of German occupation and relentless bombing by the Allies.

This led to his first book, *Five Years Under The Swastika.*

At age twenty, the Royal Netherlands Air Force shipped him to the U.S. for training with the U.S.A.F., earning his wings in October of '53. After completing 'gunnery' in Arizona, the young pilots returned to their home country flying the F-84 Thunderjet. Result; *The Fun Of Flying*.

Upon completion of his military duty, Frits came back to America, this time as an Immigrant. After twenty years in the New York Metropolitan Area, Frits and his young family, (one girl, one boy,) moved to Tampa, Florida, where he became a General Contractor, which was the basis for; *Tampa Justice, No Money, No Justice*.

He stayed active in the flying business, maintaining a Commercial and Instructors' rating, flying with many Flying Clubs and the Civil Air Patrol.

On a trip to Arizona, he met his present wife Katy whom he married in 2000.

During Hurricane Ivan, they lost their home and most of their possessions and decided to spend the rest of their lives on a boat. They now live on a 51 foot Cruiser, where Frits hammers out his novels and they sing their hearts out with several choirs and entertainment groups. He visits his old Squadron and his many relatives in Holland on a yearly basis and lives a happy and active life, speaking, singing, boating and writing.

Printed in the United States
107634LV00004B/430-477/P